Library of
Davidson College

MODERN TURKISH SHORT STORIES

STUDIES IN MIDDLE EASTERN LITERATURES—NUMBER NINE

AN ANTHOLOGY OF MODERN TURKISH SHORT STORIES

Edited by Fahir İz

Minneapolis • BIBLIOTHECA ISLAMICA • Chicago
1978

COPYRIGHT

An Anthology of Modern Turkish Short Stories is copyrighted under International and Pan American copyright conventions. Copyright © 1978 by Bibliotheca Islamica, Inc., Box 14474 University Station, Minneapolis, MN 55414, U.S.A. Manufactured in the United States of America. All rights reserved. International Standard Book Number: 0-88297-021-6 (cloth), 0-88297-022-4 (paper). Library of Congress Catalog Card Number 77-89828.

This work is fully protected under the revised copyright law and unauthorized copying is strictly forbidden. Address any questions or requests relating to copying or reprinting to:

Permissions Office
BIBLIOTHECA ISLAMICA, INC.
Box 1536
Chicago, IL 60690 / U.S.A.

PREFACE

Until recently, translations from Turkish literature into English have been infrequent and generally limited to specimens of poetry. A few Turkish novels and short stories have been available in English only during the last thirty years or so. A number of contemporary short stories have been translated and published in various American and English literary reviews, and an anthology was published in Istanbul in 1973 in a limited private edition.

The present volume covers the period 1900 to 1975. It is based on an original corpus of eighty-eight stories which I proposed after my friend Bruce Craig suggested including a volume of Turkish short stories in the series *Studies in Middle Eastern Literatures* published by his press. The titles selected were distributed to colleagues for translation.

Although I tried to make the selection as representative as possible, this could only be partially achieved for various reasons. Some stories proved in the working unsuitable for translation because they were either too idiomatic or too local in character. Some were inadequately rendered while others, alas, were submitted too late. But even so, I hope that the present anthology will give a general idea of the development and present state of the Turkish short story.

I am happy to thank all individual translators and especially Ms. Janet Heineck for her conscientious and never-failing assistance in the editing of this work which so greatly contributed to its final completion.

Fahir İz
Istanbul, July 1977

CONTENTS • AN ANTHOLOGY OF

Introduction by Fahir İz   9
Ferhundeh the Maid by Halit Ziya Uşaklıgil (*Taylor-Saçlıoğlu*)   27
My Nephew by Müftüoğlu Ahmet Hikmet (*Zilfi*)   36
Life Is Sweet by Memduh Şevket Esendal (*Zilfi*)   41
The Secret Shrine by Ömer Seyfettin (*Zilfi*)   45
The Frog Prayer by Ömer Seyfettin (*Taylor-Saçlıoğlu*)   52
Zeynep, My Zeynep by Halide Edip Adıvar (*Taylor-Saçlıoğlu*)   58
The Aegean Floor by Halıkarnas Balıkçısı (*Dankoff*)   67
The Karabulut Family by Halıkarnas Balıkçısı (*Heineck*)   75
The Peach Orchards by Refik Halit Karay (*Gamm*)   79
The Girl Who Heard Voices by Yakup Kadri Karaosmanoğlu (*Taylor*)   87
The Pigeon Shoot by Yakup Kadri Karaosmanğlu (*Dankoff*)   91
One Drink of Water by Reşat Nuri Güntekin (*Taylor*)   96
Wasting Government Time by Fahri Celâlettin (*Dankoff*)   101
Summer Night by Ahmet Hamdi Tanpınar (*Dankoff*)   107
Toy Carts Five Kurush by Sabahattin Ali (*Taylor-Saçlıoğlu*)   115
The Voice by Sabahattin Ali (*Taylor*)   119
The Valley of Violets by Sait Faik (*Taylor-Saçlıoğlu*)   129
Love Letter by Sait Fait (*Hickman*)   135

MODERN TURKISH SHORT STORIES

The Marriage of Shepherd Ali by Kemal Tahir (*Taylor*)	138
Jelal the Bricklayer by Orhan Kemal (*Taylor-Saçlıoğlu*)	165
Two Girls by Orhan Kemal (*Taylor*)	169
Rain Was Falling at Shish-hane by Haldun Taner (*Taylor-Saçlıoğlu*)	171
Sebati Bey's Expedition to Istanbul by Haldun Taner (*Zilfi*)	189
Civilization's Spare Part by Aziz Nesin (*Heineck*)	193
People Are Waking Up by Aziz Nesin (*Heineck*)	200
The Great Wrestling Camel by Samim Kocagöz (*Taylor*)	205
In God's Plains by Necati Cumalı (*Halman*)	212
Üsküdar and Hayri Bey by Oktay Akbal (*Heineck*)	216
Kır İzzet's Garden by Talip Apaydın (*Heineck*)	223
The Loan by Talip Apaydın (*Heineck*)	231
I'll Give Birth in the Mountains! by Fakir Baykurt (*Brosnahan*)	236
Yaran Dede's Stones by Fakir Baykurt (*Broshahan*)	244
Ruined Mansions by Sevim Burak (*Brosnahan*)	248
The Last Bird by Bekir Yıldız (*Taylor*)	262
Resho Agha by Bekir Yıldız (*Brosnahan*)	266
The River by Füruzan (*Mitler*)	273
The Homecoming by Vüs'at O. Bener (*Hickman*)	281

INTRODUCTION
by Fahir İz

There is a very old tradition of the narrative genre, both in verse and in prose, in Turkish literature. If we leave out verse as not directly relevant to our subject, prose narrative has been a continuous feature throughout the pre-Islamic, Islamic and modern/Western periods of the Turkish literary development. We can find the earliest examples in the eighth century Turkish inscriptions in Siberia and Outer Mongolia near Lake Baikal, which give account of the history of the second Eastern Turkish Empire (680-740 A.D.). The following is a passage from the inscription of Kül Tigin ("Prince Kül").

I did not become ruler over a wealthy and prosperous people at all; I became ruler over a poor and miserable people who were foodless on the inside and clothless on the outside. I and Prince Kül, my younger brother, consulted together. In order that the name and fame of the people, which our father and uncle had won, would not perish, and for the sake of the Turkish people, I did not sleep by night and I did not relax by day. Together with my younger brother, Prince Kül, and together with the two šads, I worked to death and I won. Having won, I did not let the people split into two opposite parts like fire and water. When I succeeded to the throne, the people who had gone in almost all directions came back utterly exhausted, without horses and without clothes. In order to nourish the people, I, with great armies, went on campaigns twelve times, northwards against the Oguz people, eastwards against the Qitan and Tatabi peoples, southwards against the Chinese. ...   Since I had fortune and since I had good luck, I brought the people to life who were going to perish and nourished them. I furnished the naked people with clothes and I made the poor people rich and the few people numerous. I made them superior to the peoples who have great states and esteemed rulers. ... When Prince Kül was twenty-six years old, we went on a campaign against the Kirgiz. Having opened our way through the lance-deep snow, we marched up over the Kögmän mountains and fell upon the Kirgiz people while they were asleep. We fought with their kagan at the Sona mountains. Prince Kül mounted Bayirqu's white stallion and attacked; he hit one man with an arrow and stabbed two men through the thighs. ... If Prince Kül had never existed, you all would have been killed. My younger brother Prince Kül passed away. I mourned. My eyes which have always seen became as if they were blind, and my mind which has always been conscious became as if it were unconscious. ... I mourned deeply. ...[1]

In about 745 A.D., the Eastern Turkish Empire was replaced by Uighur Turks who ruled in the same area until 840 when they moved southwest to present-day Eastern Turkestan (the Sinkiang region of China). Buddhism, Manicheism and Nestorianism flourished among the Uighur Turks who, inspired by the neighboring Chinese, Indian and Middle-Iranian literatures, produced prose tales of mostly religious character.

By this time Islam had reached Central Asia and, in the early eleventh century, the Turks joined the Arabo-Persian cultural world and gradually assimilated its literary system and aesthetic values. This resulted in the formation of the so-called court or *divan* literature both among Central Asian or Eastern Turks and later among their Oghuz cousins, the Western or Ottoman Turks. This was an upper-class literature *par excellence*, cultivated later in Turkey exclusively among the *medrese* — or Palace School — trained intellectual elite. It never penetrated to the mass of ordinary people who, from the very start, developed a parallel folk literature of their own with which the popular mystic literature of the dervishes must be included.

The prose narrative of the classical Eastern (Chaghatai) and Western (Ottoman and Azeri) Turkish of the Islamic period followed the tradition of the Arabo-Persian school and adapted and elaborated the common themes of Islamic literatures.

---

1. Talât Tekin, *A Grammar of Orkhon Turkic*, Indiana University Publications, Uralic and Altaic Series, v. 69 (Bloomington: Indiana University, 1968), pp. 267-271.

Folk literature during this period is extremely rich. There exists immense narrative prose material in the fields of religious, epic, romantic and didactic literature, many episodes of which can be considered early examples of the short story. There are also straightforward short stories such as the Dede Korkut stories. Presumably echoing the surviving fragments of the lost Turkish epic, the *Oghuzname*, these are a collection of epic tales with pre-Islamic and Islamic elements preserved in a sixteenth century manuscript. They were probably compiled in the fourteenth century in Eastern Anatolia, reflecting however the nomadic life of the Oghuz tribes in Central Asia in the eighth to eleventh centuries. Here is a typical episode from the first story.

At break of day Dirse Khan rose up from his place. He took his own dear son with him, he called his warriors to his side and went out hunting. They hunted game, they hawked after fowl. One of those forty treacherous scoundrels approached the boy and said, 'These are your father's words: "Let him chase the stags and drive them and kill them before me; I would see how my son rides and handles a sword and shoots, than I shall be glad and proud and confident." ' How was the boy to know? He was chasing and driving the stags and hamstringing them before his father, saying, 'Let my father watch my riding and be proud; let him watch me shoot, and be confident; let him watch me handle my sword, and be glad.' Those forty treacherous scoundrels said, 'Do you see the boy, Dirse Khan? He is chasing the stags over field and plain and driving them before you. Be on your guard! He will pretend to shoot the stag, but it is you he will kill. Before he can kill you, see that you kill him!' As the boy chased the stag, he kept passing in front of his father. Dirse Khan took up his strong bow, strung with wolf-sinew. He rose up in his stirrups and drew mightily and shot far; the arrow struck the boy between the shoulderblades and felled him. Deep went the arrow, the red blood welled forth and his bosom was filled with it. Clasping the neck of his Arab horse, he slid to the ground. Dirse Khan wanted to fall sobbing on his own dear son, but those forty treacherous scoundrels would not let him. He turned his horse's head and started back to his camp.

Dirse Khan's lady, because this was her son's first hunt, had them slaughter of horses the stallions, of camels the males, of sheep the rams, to feast the nobles of the teeming Oghuz. She gathered herself and rose up, she called her forty slender maidens to her side and went to meet Dirse Khan. She raised her head and looked at Dirse Khan's face. She turned her gaze to right and left, but did not see her own dear son. Her inward parts quaked, her whole heart pounded, her black almond eyes filled with bloody tears. She called out to Dirse Khan, declaiming; let us see, my khan, what she declaimed. ...

So saying she lamented and wept. Dirse Khan did not answer his lady, but those forty treacherous scoundrels came to her and said, 'Your son is alive and well; he is hunting. He'll come soon, today or tomorrow. Don't be frightened, don't be worried; your lord is drunk, that is why he cannot answer.'

Dirse Khan's lady turned away. She could not bear it; she called her forty slender maidens to her side, she mounted her Arab horse and went in quest of her dear son. She reached Kazilik Mountain, whose ice and snow do not melt in winter or summer, and she climbed it. Up she galloped, from the lowlands to the high places. She looked and saw that crows and ravens were alighting in a valley and rising, settling and flying up. She spurred her Arab horse and rode in that direction.

Now, my Sultan, that was the place where the boy had been laid low. The crows and ravens, seeing blood, wanted to settle on him, but he had two small dogs, who kept chasing them away and would not permit them to settle. As the boy lay there, Khizr on his grey horse appeared to him. Thrice he patted his wound with his hand saying, 'Fear not, boy, you will not die of this wound. The flowers of the mountain with your mother's milk will be salve for it.' Then he disappeared. Suddenly the boy's mother galloped up. She looked and saw her own dear son lying, bedaubed with red blood. Crying out to her son she declaimed. ...

As she said this, her voice penetrated to the boy's hearing. He raised his head, he suddenly opened his eyes and looked at his mother's face. Then he declaimed; let us see, my Khan, what he declaimed. ...[2]

---

2. *The Book of Dede Korkut*, tr. Geoffrey Lewis (Baltimore: Penguin Books, 1974), pp. 33-36.

The most varied and original examples of narrative prose of the classical Islamic period are to be found not in the storybooks proper but in the chronicles and histories and in accounts of travellers and ambassadors. These contain episodes which are perfect short stories. Along with powerful descriptions of everyday life in the cities and in the country, army life during the campaigns in Europe and in the East or in fortresses, palace intrigues, revolutions and other important events, they offer interesting studies of characters and human relationships, all of which fully compensate for the lack of drama and the novel. Among the great masters of narrative prose of this type we must mention the outstanding historian Selaniki (d. 1600), Mustafa Ali (d. 1600), Peçevi (d. 1649), Naima (d. 1716), Fındıklılı Silahdar Mehmet (d. 1724) and the famous traveller Evliya Çelebi (d. 1682), whose ten volume *Seyahatname* ("Travel Book") contains a great number of stories of all types.

The following examples may illustrate this point.

[Dervish Bik] is quite a talented young man. Because of his sickly constitution he devoted himself to the occupation of a physician and acquired expertise in diagnosing from pulse and urine. At one time he became a portrait painter and also tried himself in miniature painting. In this, too, he was able to show his art. The best men at wedding feasts and those presiding and prominent at funeral repasts would turn to him. He is a pleasant gentleman, accurate in his guesses and experience and firm in his grasp and understanding when it comes to writing down the affairs of the *begs* or, in the case of a decision concerning a public matter, in using fine devices, in cutting out the robe of imagination so as to make it fit exactly the body of appropriateness. Sometimes his excessive generosity pushed him to boundless prodigality, and then he becomes a famous example for a gentleman who because of his temporary lack of cash does not show himself to others for several days, hides in the harem so as not to detract from his honor, perhaps not appearing under the pretext of being sick, announcing that he has taken a laxative.[3]

● ● ●

On 23rd Rejeb [the Indian ambassador] came to the divan and

---

3. Âlî, *Mustafa Ali's Description of Cairo of 1599*, ed. Andreas Tietze (Wien: Verl. d. Österr. Akad. d. Wiss.), 1975, p. 60.

presented his gifts. They included three valuable presents, of an estimated combined value of 3,000,000 piastres — a turban-crest with a diamond bigger than the Sultan's, a sword, and a dagger. Since the ambassador was one of the ulema, the vizier, the Mufti, the Kadiaskers and other high dignitaries all gave receptions in his honor, at which learned and worthy men, masters of the arts of conversation, were present, and entertained the ambassador with scholarly discussion and witty repartee. These receptions were held in world-adorning palaces and in heart-delighting waterside pavilions, so as to show him the strange and wondrous sights of Istanbul. Indeed, it has never been heard that an ambassador has been received with so much attention and deference. After the ambassador had been treated with full honors, a letter of reply was written to the Emperor of India. An emerald-hilted dagger, twenty beautiful slave-girls and a finely caparisoned horse, whose trappings were estimated to be worth 90 purses, were given as gifts to the Emperor, while the ambassador was given 6,000 pieces of gold, a fur robe, and a caparisoned horse. A meeting was held to choose an ambassador to accompany him back to India. According to ancient custom it would have been proper to send a man of experience from among the ulema or scribes, or else a man of eloquence from among the scholars and literati. In fact however, these necessary qualifications were disregarded. Zulfıkar Aga, the brother of Salih Pasha, asked for this embassy, saying: "I need no expenses. I will pay for it out of my own pocket." ... The vizier and the mufti held counsel on whom to appoint. Certain learned men were put forward, whereupon someone said: "If you appoint a man of culture and discernment, then besides his travel expenses he will require a personal allowance, and will pester and burden us with claims and demands for attention."

With this in mind, they decided on Zulfıkar Aga, and said to him: "Call on the ambassador ... give him a fine reception, be friendly and sociable, but in company keep silent. Don't feel that you have to talk, and then commit some gross error." This is how they instructed him. This ass then set out with indescribable pomp to call on the ambassador, inform him of his own appointment, and invite him to a reception. The late Manoglu says that of the literary set he invited no one, of the poets only Jevri Chelebi, and of the wits of Kadizade's following, Ebu Ahmed-oglu. These two men were friends of his, confidants and intimates; they were to entertain the ambassador, and also to use their skill to cover up his own blunders, if he made any. ...

Since, as he was a wealthy man and an ambassador designate, it was not proper to put him to shame, and since equally he lacked the capacity to be taught or made to understand, they found no way but to remain silent. ...

Ebu Ahmed-oglu gave an account of the affair to Manoglu, who was a friend of his. "Looking at it impartially," he asked "at a time when ulema and scribes and men of letters are available, is it proper to send such common fellows on embassies, just because of their money? Are such scandals compatible with the preservation of the honor and reputation of the Empire?"[4]

• • •

When the pasha and his retinue approached the feast-tent, Assaf Bey and several hundred of his mail-clad Arabs separated themselves from the other Arabs, who stayed at the far end of the field. Assaf himself spurred his horse forward, dismounting when he came into the pasha's presence. He then walked forward so that he might take hold of the pasha's stirrup. The pasha also made to dismount, and while they were moving towards the feast-tent, the water-carriers and musketeers who had loaded their firearms with double-shot made ready.

When Assaf came to kiss the pasha's skirt, two muskets were suddenly discharged into his breast and a third, from behind, into his flank. Now this Arab was a devilishly tall man — like a minaret — and so he was not knocked down by the impact of these shots, since under his clothes he also had put on three of these shirts of mail. The shots had penetrated one shirt but had been caught in the others and so had had no effect within [i.e., had not wounded Assaf]. At once the Arab realized what he had to deal with. He drew his sword; the Arabs who were with him formed a circle around him and got him as far as his horse. He mounted and then, with his men, bore down upon the group of men beside the pasha. After these Arabs had killed more than twenty of the *iç-ağa*s and the pasha's men, they

---

4. Bernard Lewis, *Istanbul and the Civilization of the Ottoman Empire*, Centers of Civilization Series, no. 9 (Norman: University of Oklahoma Press, 1963), pp. 169-172.

made off towards the other Arabs who were lined up at the protected end of the plain.

To them Assaf cried, "Come on! These scoundrels have wronged me!" And at once these many thousands of Arab cavaliers shouted out "The bastard!" with a single voice and raised a frightful screech to the skies, brandishing their lances.

The pasha was in the middle of his troop. The Arabs fell upon the many thousands of horsemen who were round about. Every man whose horse was swift made off for the Aleppo road, escaped, and was saved. The Arabs also sped down the Aleppo road, but some of them headed for the pasha's troop. Its soldiers resisted them and there was a fight. After several men had perished on each side, the Arabs withdrew and the pasha also got to Aleppo.

Thus a great disaster did take place.

Thereafter Emir Assaf did not put his trust in non-Ottomans, but he did make it more and more plain that he was in revolt. Other Arabs also took courage and began to do more mischief and more wickedness than before.

When news of this was rumored in the capital, they deposed İbrahim Pasha and transferred Aleppo province to Derviş Mehmed Pasha who had been removed from the governorship of Baghdad and was now sent to Aleppo.

My late father, the *serdar* of Aleppo, Mehmed Agha, used to tell this story: "At the time of the Assaf affair, I was in the troop of İbrahim Pasha. Of the pasha's men only twenty or thirty were killed and some forty or fifty of those who were left behind were stripped. But most of the city men who had gone out for the show were stripped and many of them were wounded."

Later on, the government turned a gracious face to Assaf. This attitude was assumed as a measure of policy. Still later, Bektaş Agha, the *kethuda* bey, came forward as Assaf's protector and became his official representative in Istanbul. When Assaf's firman of confirmation was granted, Bektaş Agha sent my grandfather, Küçük Ali Agha, to communicate the order of confirmation to Assaf Bey, picking my grandfather because he was an able, outstanding citizen of Aleppo. Bektaş Agha ordered him to use such measures as would bring Assaf back again into the circle of obedience.

On that occasion my father accompanied my grandfather into the desert. When they reached Assaf, the emir — as was the custom —

drew up his troops having clothed his Arabs in armor, and formally received the imperial firman and the robe of honor.[5]

The eighteenth century witnessed the beginnings of the transformation of Turkey in the military and educational fields. During its last decade, a writer diplomat named Giritli Ali Aziz (d. 1798) wrote his *Muhayyelat* ("Imaginary Tales"), a collection of stories mainly based on traditional kinds of tales in which, for the first time in Turkish literature, appear sketches of characters and descriptions of life in contemporary Istanbul in colloquial language. This work is a forerunner of a new narrative literature which will develop in the course of the literary modernist "Tanzimat" movement pioneered by İbrahim Sinasi (1826-71). Şinasi, his associates and their disciples achieved a radical reform in Turkish literature. They introduced new concepts and ideas from the West, published the first Turkish newspaper, wrote the first Turkish play, and adopted from the French many new literary genres such as the essay, the novel, and the short story.

If we leave out Yusuf Kâmil Pasha's celebrated translation of Fénelon's *Télémaque* (1862) in an elaborate style reminiscent of the extreme examples of court literature, the path to the definite break with traditional narrative was paved by the publication of translations of several European novels. Turkish versions of Victor Hugo's *Les Misérables* (1862), Daniel Defoe's *Robinson Crusoe* (1864), Bernardin de Saint Pierre's *Paul et Virginie* (1870), Voltaire's *Micromégas* (1871), Jonathan Swift's *Gulliver's Travels* (1872), Alexandre Dumas pére's *Le Comte de Monte-Cristo* (1873), and many others inspired the first Turkish novels. The lexicographer and writer Şemsettin Sami (1850-1904), the popular writer and publicist Ahmet Mithat (1844-1912), and the poet and patriot Namık Kemal (1840-88) published their experiments in this new genre in the 1870s.

Ahmet Mithat, the most prolific and versatile writer of the early modernists, greatly influenced prose writers of the following generation, and was also the pioneer of the modern short story in Turkish. He published his first collection of short stories, *Kıssadan Hisse* ("From Tale to Moral"), in 1869 in Baghdad, where he was active under the patronage of the governor and famous liberal statesman Mithat Pasha

---

5. Lewis Victor Thomas, *A Study of Naima*, ed. Norman Itzkowitz. (New York: New York University Press, 1972), pp. 8-9.

(1822-83) as printer, publisher, and writer. They were primarily edifying stories original or adapted from the French. When Ahmet Mithat settled in Istanbul in 1871, he began to publish a series of short stories in pamphlets, *Letaif-i Rivayat* ("Pleasant Tales"), which made this genre very fashionable in Istanbul periodicals. Partly inspired by Ali Aziz but mainly as a result of his observations among the ordinary people for whom he was writing, Ahmet Mithat made extensive use of the style, themes, and technique of the Turkish popular arts and folk literature, i.e., shadow plays (Karagöz), public story tellers (meddah), improvised plays on set themes (ortaoyunu), and folk tales of various kinds, and blended these with elements from contemporary French writers.

Another pioneering work, the *Müsameretname* ("The Book of Evening Entertainments"), a collection of short stories in twelve parts, was also published during the early 1870s by Emin Nihat, about whom very little is known. Traditional elements predominate in these stories.

But it was Samipaşazade Sezai (1860-1936), the youngest writer of the Tanzimat school and better known as the author of the first "realist" Turkish novel, *Sergüzeşt* ("Adventure"), who wrote the first Turkish short stories completely stripped of traditional elements and folklore. He wrote very little. Some of his best short stories were collected in the volume *Küçük Şeyler* ("Little Things") in 1892.

A contemporary of Sezai and a free lance writer, Nabizade Nazım (1862-93) studied French realists and naturalists and produced from 1886 onwards long short stories with the same technique well adapted to the Turkish scene. One of his best stories, "Kara Bibik" (1890), was the only contemporary description of Anatolian peasant life, and became the forerunner of the "village literature" movement of the republican period after the 1930s.

The periodical *Servetifünun* lent its name to a group of younger literary modernists associated with it beginning in 1896, when the authoritarian regime of Abdülhamit II was at its zenith. Political and social topics were taboo. It is not surprising that the motto of the new literary school was "art for art's sake," for which they would be bitterly and perhaps unfairly criticized by the following generations.

The master of the short story and the novel of the *Servetifünun* period was Halit Ziya Uşaklıgil (1868-1944) who, inspired by the French realists and naturalists, perfected the technique of narrative art in Turkish and eliminated from his work the padding used by most

Tanzimat writers. A prolific writer, Uşaklıgil describes in his short stories the life of the middle and lower middle classes of the capital in a comparatively simple and natural style. His novels, however, written in the most elaborate and precious style, depict the "westernizing" upper and upper middle classes.

The *Servetifünun* school produced some minor short story writers like Mehmet Rauf (1875-1931), better remembered for his novel *Eylül* ("September," 1900), the first attempt at psychological analysis in Turkish literature, and Hüseyin Cahit Yalçın (1874-1957), better known after 1908 as a journalist, who usually described in his short stories the cosmopolitan life of the Levantines in Istanbul. Müftüoğlu Ahmet Hikmet (1870-1927), also a minor follower of the same school, later joined the "Turkist" movement in 1911. His monologue "Yeğenim" ("My Nephew") became popular for its vivid and humorous description of cultural tensions of the period.

The most prominent of the writers who remained outside this group was Hüseyin Rahmi Gürpınar (1864-1944), novelist and short story writer. As I have written elsewhere, Hüseyin Rahmi occupies a unique place in the history of pre-republican Turkish literature. Unlike most of his contemporaries, he did not follow any earlier Turkish or French model, but soon assimilated various influences and developed a powerful independent literary personality. His combination of the colorful Turkish popular tradition of storytelling, careful study of naturalist technique, accurate observation of the life and types of Istanbul, penetrating analysis of the social problems of his time, and an acute sense of humor and satire made Hüseyin Rahmi Gürpınar the most original of all Turkish novelists until the 1930s. Unfortunately, Gürpınar's writings do not lend themselves to translation, although attempts have been made, because of the peculiarly local character of his topics and his occasionally extremely colloquial style.

Following the restoration of the constitution in 1908 and the reestablishment of freedom of speech and of the press, most Turkish writers came under the influence of the emerging political and intellectual trends such as Ottomanism, Islamism, Westernism, and Turkism. Several daily newspapers and periodicals represented these currents. The average Turkish intellectual felt himself an "Ottoman citizen." But Ottomanism and Islamism gradually proved to be failures when, immediately after 1908, all non-Turkish elements of the empire began to set up nationalist associations with separatist tendencies. Italy's invasion of Tripolitania in 1911, the combined attack of the Balkan states in 1912, and the anti-Turkish attitude of the European powers served to strengthen Turkish national consciousness. During the years before World War I, and particularly during the traumatic years of modern Turkish history between 1911 and 1922, the majority of young writers sympathized with "Turkism" and joined the movement of *millî edebiyat*, "nationalist literature," inspired and guided by the sociologist Ziya Gökalp (1876-1924), the theoretician of Turkish nationalism.

Three freelance short story writers who started their careers during this period developed independently. Halikarnas Balıkçısı (1886-1973), who settled in Bodrum (ancient Halicarnassus) on the Mediterranean to which he had been banished in 1924, wrote there his romantic novels and short stories, often with an epic touch, about the sea, the life and struggles of seamen, fishermen, and sponge fishers of the area in an unpolished but attractive style.

Memduh Şevket Esendal (1883-1952), a politician and diplomat, wrote a few novels and many short stories in which he describes with idealistic optimism and unusual simplicity and naturalness episodes in the life of the "little man."

F. Celalettin, the pseudonym of Fahri Celâl Göktulga (1895-1975), was a follower of the H. R. Gürpınar tradition. In his very original short stories, mostly character studies, he deals with odd, peculiar, and even slightly unbalanced characters whom he places in nostalgic settings of bygone days.

Leaving out individual cases which we must regard as exceptions, the following are the main characteristics of this period of "nationalist literature":

1. Realism is no more an isolated case and gradually replaces romanticism in most works.

2. Istanbul ceases to be the center of everything. The characters in novels and short stories begin to explore Anatolia; in some cases they are Anatolians.

3. Colloquial Turkish is increasingly used instead of a formal or precious language.

Two prominent members of this movement were already well established names in 1911. Halide Edip Adıvar (1884-1964), novelist, patriot, and feminist, who began her career with romantic, often passionate novels, joined Mustafa Kemal Atatürk's Nationalists in 1920 and wrote novels and short stories which reflect her personal experiences in Anatolia during those turbulent years. The other, Yakup Kadri Karaosmanoğlu (1888-1974), a close friend of Adıvar, was a mystic in his youth and developed into a master of period novels. His best short stories are also products of the war years in Anatolia. However, the contribution of these two eminent writers to the short story is outweighed by their achievements as novelists.

During this period, the short story was particularly represented by three writers. The first, Ömer Seyfettin (1884-1920), who pioneered the language reform movement in 1911 and who systematically used colloquial Turkish with an element of humor, wrote unsophisticated short stories for ordinary people, inspired by his experiences as an officer in the Balkans, by the conflicting ideologies of his time, and by episodes of Turkish history.

Refik Halit Karay (1888-1965), the undisputed master of Turkish prose between 1908 and 1928, started his career as an essayist, humorist, and political satirist. His pungent satirical essays brought him into conflict with the Committee of Union and Progress, the party in power. As a consequence, he spent five years (1913-18) in exile in northern and central Anatolia, where he collected material for his best group of short stories, *Memleket Hikâyeleri* ("Stories from the Country"), which was published in 1919. These are powerful descriptions of provincial life told with a rare virtuousity of natural style.

Reşat Nuri Güntekin (1889-1956), known mainly for his bestselling sentimental novels in the 1920s and later for his "social" novels, wrote a number of short stories of the same type, of uneven value, most of them intended for popular magazines.

But the fundamental change, which is indeed a revolution in Turkish literature in general and in the novel and short story in particular, took place during the republican era (proclaimed in 1923), especially from the 1930s onwards.

This fact can best be illustrated by comparing the characteristics of the writers of both periods.

Pre-Republican Period (1860-1930)

1. Most writers belong to the upper or upper-middle classes of the capital, Istanbul. Provincials who join them have to adapt themselves to their way of life.

2. The writers live, as a rule, in Istanbul, except in cases of banishment, voluntary exile, or government service in the provinces or abroad.

3. Most of them are educated in the best schools of the capital or, as was customary, trained in government offices.

4. They usually follow a government career and may reach high offices: minister, senator, ambassador, governor, etc.

5. Almost all know one Western language and many follow French literary activities.

6. Their topics are limited. Only a few of them occasionally touch on social problems.

7. Many of them write in an awkward, rhetorical, bombastic, or precious style. Very few use natural straightforward Turkish.

Republican Period (1930-70s)

1. The majority of writers belong to provincial middle or lower-middle classes; many come from a working class or peasant background.

2. There is a new capital in the middle of Anatolia: Ankara. But Istanbul and Ankara cannot claim to monopolize young writers. Many live in other cities and towns.

3. Very few of them are able to complete their education. Many leave school to make a living; some do not attend school after the age of fifteen. Those of peasant origin are educated in village institutes, and quite a few "continue their studies" in prisons, taught by fellow prisoners.

4. They make a living as primary or secondary school teachers, minor government officials, or as workers or employees in newspapers or other establishments. Some survivors of the preceding generation of writers obtained high positions as diplomats or members of Parliament during the early stages of the republican period.

5. Very few of them, and those mostly among the first two generations after the 1930s, know a Western language. The majority are not in touch with any Western or Eastern literature.

6. They write on a large variety of topics and make extensive use of autobiographic materials and of personal experiences, but they concentrate on the life and conditions of people in provincial towns, villages, and shanty towns. They expose and discuss political, social, and economic problems.

7. They use a language based on spoken Turkish with an increasing number of provincialisms.

There is also an enormous difference in numbers. As against just over a dozen prominent names between 1860 and 1930, several dozens of outstanding writers can be enumerated during the period from 1930 to the 1970s. Therefore, only the names of the most representative short story writers can be mentioned here.

The foundation of the literary review *Varlık* ("Existence") in 1933 by the writer and publisher Yaşar Nabi Nayır (b. 1903) is a turning point in the development of contemporary Turkish literature. Since then dozens of reviews have appeared and disappeared, but it was *Varlık* which impartially encouraged all young talents and launched almost every outstanding name of the following three decades.

If we leave out minor authors and those of previous generations still writing, Sait Faik Abasiyanik (1906-54) is one of the two dominant names in the short story during the 1930s. The work which secured his reputation began to appear in *Varlık* in 1934. Considered both the pioneer and the great master of the contemporary Turkish short story, Sait Faik describes with nostalgic romanticism and poetry, linked with a strong autobiographical element and feeling for nature, the life of simple people, seamen, fishermen, vagabonds, and children in a spontaneous and straightforward though not always polished style.

The other outstanding name of the decade is Sabahattin Ali (1906-48), the pioneer of social realism, who wrote extensively for the first time on life in small towns and villages of Anatolia. The harsh conditions of Anatolian country life and the bitter struggles of the peasants and small town people against nature and their human environment are powerfully and mercilessly described in his short stories. Although there had been sporadic and individual earlier attempts, it is Sabahattin Ali's work which initiated "village literature," which was to become a strong literary movement from the 1950s onwards. The short story in this movement is particularly represented by writers of peasant origin, trained in the village institutes.

The movement was given a strong impetus by Mahmut Makal (b. 1930), a peasant boy from central Anatolia, whose direct realism in his notes, sketches and impressions of his own village, which appeared in *Varlık* in 1948 and were published in book form as *Bizim Köy* in 1950, created a great sensation. Outstanding "peasant writers" of this trend who were educated in the village institutes and contributed to the contemporary short story and novel are: Talip Apaydın (b. 1926), Ahmet Başaran (b. 1926), Fakir Baykurt (b. 1929), Dursun Akçam (b. 1930), Ümit Kaftancıoğlu (b. 1935), and Osman Şahin (b. 1938).

Other writers of peasant origin but trained in city schools, or writers of the middle class or lower middle class, born and partially educated in cities, also contributed, with their short stories and novels, to the "village literature." Among these are Kemal Tahir (1910-73), Kemal Bilbaşar (b. 1910), Orhan Kemal (1914-70), Samim Kocagöz (b. 1916), Yaşar Kemal (b. 1922), and Bekir Yildiz (b. 1933). Of these, Kemal Tahir and Yaşar Kemal concentrated on the novel and each produced only one volume of short stories.

Writers of "village literature" concentrate on the problems of the peasantry little known by city intellectuals, and reveal and discuss the evils which have cursed the Anatolian villager for centuries and prevented his breaking out of his isolation: ignorance, blood feuds, illiteracy, the engulfing power of superstition and ancient custom, and above all the dearth of land and water, all exacerbated by the stifling power of landowners and religious leaders and the indifference of government officials. Their subjects became, in time, the further problems of growing economic and political consciousness, industrialization, and the almost mass migration to the cities and abroad in the desperate search for work and betterment. Despite the fact that some writers gradually tended to become repetitive and to stereotype characters and situations, this type of "village literature" has been a healthy contribution, bringing to the forefront old abuses and long-ignored realities.

Some of the abovementioned writers such as Kemal Tahir, Orhan Kemal, Samim Kocagöz, İlhan Tarus (1907-67), Faik Baysal (b. 1918), and Muzaffer Buyrukçu (b. 1928) also describe life in provincial towns, the life of simple people in the grip of influential notables, or that of Balkan refugees or migrant peasants in large city suburbs and shanty towns.

The stories of Oktay Akbal (b. 1923), Nezihe Meriç (b. 1925), the poet Sabahattin Kudret Aksal (b. 1920) and to some extent Tahsin Yücel (b. 1933) are somewhat reminiscent of those of Sait Faik in that they use autobiographic elements to describe memories, moods, and impressions.

Another group of writers, parallel to a similar shortlived movement in poetry, tried the abstract and obscure and experimented with new forms, techniques, and styles: Feyyaz Kayacan (b. 1919), Bilge Karasu (b. 1930), and Leyla Erbil (b. 1931).

The prolific writer Mehmet Seyda (b. 1919) has examples in his many short stories of all types, techniques and styles with particular emphasis on psychological analysis.

The short stories of the poet and playwright Necati Cumalı (b. 1921), written in a polished and flowing style, have deep human warmth, poetry, and indomitable optimism.

Humor allied to social and political satire is brilliantly represented in the short story by Aziz Nesin (b. 1915) and the playwright Haldun Taner (b. 1915). An extremely prolific and popular writer, Aziz Nesin aims by merciless ridicule to do away with the social evils of intolerance, bigotry, superstition, and tyranny. Haldun Taner describes with subtle irony characters and situations of a society in transition.

Füruzan (b. 1935), one of the remarkable new names in the contemporary short story, became famous in the early 1970s for her original and attractive "stream-of-consciousness" style and by her choice of realistic types from among the helpless, the unhappy, and the doomed.

Among short story writers as well as novelists, there are many more new names than one can adequately deal with here, all of whom try to express and describe the many facets of a society in the grip of rapid and continuous transformation.

FERHUNDEH THE MAID
Halit Ziya Uşaklıgil
(Translated by Virginia Taylor-Saçlıoğlu)

Ferhundeh had grown up with the little lady. This privilege of having been raised with her had given Ferhundeh a special position among the servants and an exceptional worth. How many times had she heard the master say, "Ferhundeh is like one of the family"? For this reason, whatever they did for Hasna, the same was always done for Ferhundeh — a little more frugal, a little more flimsy — but always the same. At least, a similarity and resemblance in regard to color was always to be observed. If Hasna was bought, for example, a pink silk dress for the holidays, a woollen or cotton print, but probably pink, was got for Ferhundeh. This, for Ferhundeh, was a sufficient test of intention.

For this reason, when go-betweens began coming to Hasna in order to arrange a match for her, Ferhundeh felt a secret joy. These go-betweens were supposed to find a husband for her too, since she was never treated differently from the little lady. When the go-betweens came, she was if on wings, flying up and down the stairs. Leaving her responsibilities to others in order to bring the veils and dress cloaks, she ran about breathlessly, reporting news to the little lady, and carrying on long arguments over clothes to be worn. Then she would disappear for a while and return five minutes later in a completely different dress. The most important responsibility belonged to her: serving the coffee to the guests. For this occasion, Ferhundeh also would get dressed up.

She had made it a habit of trying to dress exactly like the little lady. If, on a given day, the little lady were going to receive the go-betweens in green silk, Ferhundeh would immediately make up her mind to wear her pale green cotton.

Then, the little lady in front and Ferhundeh following, they would enter the presence of the go-betweens. After serving the coffee, Ferhundeh would withdraw and, lowering her eyes to a point even with the little lady's chair and blushing with a genuine shyness, would wait with a heartfelt tremor, the coffee tray in her hand, and thus live for five or ten minutes together with the little lady the life of a young girl receiving go-betweens.

When taking leave of the go-betweens, she would run excitedly together with the little lady, close herself up in a room with her, throw her arms around the little lady's neck and, with an overflow of joy which she couldn't contain, would kiss the little lady, despite their warnings of "Have you gone out of your mind? What's happening to you? Pull yourself together, Ferhundeh!"

The first few times, she said, "Oh, my little lady! If you only knew how nervous I was!" And later, "I've become used to it now. I don't feel sorry anymore. Just you be a bride and —"

She had a deep conviction that the go-between would definitely bring something for her and that a share would be appointed for her in the engagement matters which had the house in a whirl. There was no need for either her or anyone else to mention this directly. It was such a natural thing that speaking of it would actually spoil it since, that is, she was treated just the same as the little lady.

She was sure of her own beauty. In fact, after the go-betweens began to come, she had made comparisons between herself and the little lady, had noted their respective points and, in the final account, had not come up with any characteristic of which she herself couldn't be justly proud. Sometimes she was ashamed of her short, black eyebrows and small, puffy, dark eyes. Still, she had a pretty figure with a body gradually tapering from her broad shoulders and a color like pink cashmere undulating under a frozen surface. Ferhundeh the maid had determined this by examining herself carefully and at great length with an old fragment of broken mirror that hung in her room and hadn't discovered anything insignificant. There was only one thing for which she envied the little lady. Yes, she admitted it. She was envious without trying to conceal it: her blond hair. She paid no attention to her brows, her eyes, or her complexion. She found virtues and values worthy of herself in these. But the hair. Oh, if only it were possible to change it, to make these black things blond, golden blond like gold thread.

● ● ●

After the wedding had been decided, she was still far from being joyful because of a nagging fear. In fact, one night, sensing that she had yielded to that fear more than was necessary without even noticing it, she shrugged her shoulders and brought herself back to reality with a sharp reproach. Crazy girl! They're not going to have a double wedding. There's a time for everything.

She wasn't jealous. On the contrary, she was more eager than anyone else for that awaited event to come quickly. Every morning she reminded the little lady of the necessity of going shopping. On these shopping expeditions, she fraternized with all the ladies. Gathering the decorated boxes of slippers, the countless packets of cloth, the gold-embroidered bundles, and the towels in her arms, she ran home behind the little lady with the parcels overflowing from her arms, not permitting anyone else to carry them. As she held and squeezed these things under her arms and on her bosom, a feeling of closeness to marriage took root in her soul, and from it a scent of dream and a presentiment of joy flowed into her heart.

What things she carried home in this mood! What things she brought from a thousand corners of Istanbul, breathless from exhaustion, her veil clinging to her cheeks wet with perspiration! And all the while she enjoyed carrying these things, she thought of herself and her own wedding. Although she appointed her own position with a natural sense of justice and modified her daydreams accordingly, countless hopes were raised in the depths of her heart as she planned a smaller, cheaper, and plainer trousseau for herself on a lesser scale than all these things. The fabrics, the embroidered cloth, the silver sets. "I'll buy one of these too, not quite so fancy," or "I can certainly find a cheaper version of this. What's the difference if it is smaller?"

When she brought these things home and everyone rushed up to her, she turned into a ball of fire. As far as possible, she showed them to no one and wouldn't tolerate anyone touching them. The right to look and touch was reserved, after the little lady, only to herself. She jealously guarded them from everyone.

Just as she guarded her privileged position on the shopping trips, so she also forbade anyone to interfere in the sewing and things to be done at home. When they told her one night that she was tired and should go to bed, she sobbed bitterly and moped for hours.

One day, after the master and mistress had a short whispered conversation at the table, they looked at Ferhundeh and smiled. Her heart leapt and she involuntarily lowered her eyes.

That night Ferhundeh kept inventing pretexts for entering their presence because she wanted to get some whiff of the meaning of that smile. "I wonder what's going on?" she thought to herself. She was sure of the outcome. "I wonder who wants to marry me?" she mused.

The next morning, she heard the mistress's voice. "Ferhundeh! The master wants to speak with you."

She almost fainted and for a moment she couldn't answer or move. Her knees were shaking. When she entered the master's presence, she was unable to raise her eyes and look at him. Finally that blissful moment of annunciation had arrived.

At first the master spoke in clipped sentences. "Ferhundeh, you have grown up together with Hasna. Up to now I've always treated you both the same. You have won the admiration of all of us."

Ferhundeh could hardly breathe. The master continued. "Now Hasna is going to a strange household. If she has no one close to her, she will be extremely unhappy. We've decided to send you there with her. Do you hear, Ferhundeh? You are going to go with Hasna. We trust you and know well how faithfully you will serve her. Then, in a year or two, at the proper time, you will certainly get your reward. Do you understand, Ferhundeh?"

Ferhundeh understood. She went forward, kissed the hem of the master's gown, and left the room with a great joy in her heart. Yes, she was happy. Such a direct promise was better than remaining in a dubious position. In one or two years? What difference did a year or two make? It would pass in the twinkling of an eye. She had understood the significance of "the proper time": after the little lady had had a baby.

After this incident, Ferhundeh had a new buoyancy. Until that day she had always felt the nagging of a small fear, but now a hope with a clear and explicit date had definitely been planted on the horizon of her longing.

Ferhundeh was everywhere at the wedding. Instead of one Ferhundeh there were a hundred. She was encountered at every turn and seemed to be in charge of everything.

This wedding was a sort of rehearsal for her own. As she scurried about in the crowd in a flurry of happiness, she viewed herself partly as a bride.

They called her "Girl! Girl!" addressing her as a bride's maidservant. That day Ferhundeh, surrounded by a rising spirit of respect and getting a taste of her own wedding which was to take place in a year or two, at the proper time, filled the house with joy and excitement.

After that day the period of waiting began. She hadn't the courage to ask directly. Rather than give cause for adversely influencing her secret hopes by the intervention of a slight word of curiosity, she would wait quietly and reticently. But days and months passed without any news of the expected developments. One day, angry, ashamed, and, for once, annoyed by the little lady with whom she always discussed everything without ceremony, she got up the nerve to ask, "My little lady, I'm all alone. When am I going to have some pleasure?"

But the answer she received was not at all pleasant. "My God, Ferhundeh! You too? Don't I have enough difficulties being a new bride?"

That day Ferhundeh got a bad headache. After cutting several slices of lemon and squeezing them into her coffee, she bound up her head and went around the house like that all day until nightfall. Her poor heart was finally beginning to rebel. In other words, the little lady was first going to wait until she was older, then have a baby, and after that Ferhundeh would be considered.

She was finally beginning to become irritated. She invented pretexts for quarrels. If the new husband raised his voice a little, she would go upstairs and weep for hours.

When she awoke in the morning, she would sit up in bed and try hard to calculate how much time had passed since the wedding. "It was after Mevlut. That summer we went to Kadıköy. Then we stayed in Chamlıja for a year. Now summer is coming again." She tried to add up the years one by one and arrive at the sum. Suddenly her heart clenched with a cry of astonishment. "It's been three years! One year we spent the summer here. That means four years. Four years. And the little lady still considers herself a bride."

From then on she turned against the little lady. That morning when she came downstairs, she did all her work with a sour face and a frown.

One day there was news in the house. "The bride is pregnant!" they said. At last Ferhundeh was relieved. She wanted to be sure of the reliability of the news. She ran to the little lady and asked her directly without hesitation. "I think so," she answered with a smile.

Oh, how this uncertain answer saddened Ferhundeh! For days and weeks she was unable to sleep. When the news was finally confirmed, she had a great feeling of relief and security. Now it was no longer a question of a doubtful period of waiting but a definite delay.

She regained all her former joy and activity and no longer left the little lady's side. She looked deep into her eyes and wanted to hold her arm whenever they descended the stairs.

She asked incessantly, "How much longer? Has it been eight months yet? Then there's just one more month, say thirty days?"

The strain of waiting was making her pale, and she was losing her strength. Her whole life was passing in fevers of pathological nervousness.

She loved the child madly. She immediately took over all responsibilities, even guarding the duty of washing his diapers from everyone else. As she scrubbed his jackets and shirts, her voice could be heard all the way from the laundry room. "How nice! How sweet! He even has his own little underpants just to fit."

But, despite all this affection, the child failed to bring her any good tidings. As Ferhundeh sang lullabies and rocked his cradle, the months began to pass one by one and fade into the past.

Finally, she lost the strength to wait. A heavy feeling like a taste of disgust permeated her longing. As her footsteps gradually became heavier and heavier and her body began to sag, she wandered sluggishly about the house.

She was no longer called Ferhundeh the bride's woman but Master Sabit's nurse. As this title gradually passed from mouth to mouth, Ferhundeh became known as nurse. This seemed to age her by twenty years.

Once, on a holiday, they sent the boy together with his nurse to his grandfather's house. On the way back, the master said, "Wait a minute, Ferhundeh. The time for recompense for your services has finally come."

Then the master opened a drawer, cracked his pen against his thumbnail, took out a piece of paper and, with a great deal of thought, dipping his pen four or five times into the inkwell, wrote for a long time. He read over what he had written, inked the seal which he took from his pocket and, after pressing it carefully on the paper, handed it to the boy who had carefully watched the operation. "Here, Sabit. Give this to your nurse and put her finally at ease."

Up to that moment Ferhundeh had not understood. This speech of the master's revealed the truth. She almost collapsed out of joy and happiness. Taking the paper from the boy's hand, she threw herself at the master's feet.

The moment of happiness which she had awaited for such a long time had come! At last she could become a bride and that black hair, in which a few strands of white were becoming visible, could be made blond, golden blond like gold thread.

When Ferhundeh returned home that evening with the document of emancipation, the little lady's husband wanted to add something of his own to her measure of recompense.

"Nurse Ferhundeh, I will provide your wedding. Just let Sabit grow up a bit and go to school."

It was as if a vital wind had blown over Ferhundeh's fire of hope which had been slowly smoldering and dying out for some time. This piece of paper had revived and rekindled all the strength of her dreams. She pulled it out of the box from amid the bundles of linens, kissed it and, as if pondering thoughts filled with deep mysteries, looked at the writing happily. Then she went up to a mirror and examined her hair. One, two, three. Oh! There were several of them now, but since it would be dyed—

• • •

The problem of Sabit's going to school involved two other big disappointments. The master and mistress, who for years had been an obstacle to her chances for marriage, left the family in mourning one after the other. These two blows crushed the last power of Ferhundeh's hopes. She was angry with the whole world, particularly with that piece of paper. At night in bed she tried not to think or dream of the future. There was a bitterness in her poor heart which made everything look gloomy. In this sulky mood, as Sabit grew bigger, as Ferhundeh's shoulders slumped more, and as her steps became slower, the white hairs at her temples steadily increased.

One night Hasna Hanım flew out of her room with a shrill laugh and excitedly called to Ferhundeh, "Nurse! Nurse!"

She too called Ferhundeh "nurse" now. As Ferhundeh approached, both Hasna Hanım and her husband were still laughing. Hasna Hanım said, "Ferhundeh! Have you heard? There's a man who wants to marry you."

Ferhundeh stared in astonishment. She didn't believe it.

"Don't you believe it, nurse? The master is saying that the manservant charged with Sabit's care wants to marry you."

Ferhundeh didn't reply. She turned around and left the room. As she walked away they heard her muttering, "All right. Wait and wait and wait and then get a tutor."

When they realized that Ferhundeh didn't want the tutor, the news was passed to all the neighbors, to the women who came to the house, and to agents for servants that there was a marriageable male in the household. From that day onward, a new period of feverishness began for Ferhundeh.

The marriage question had been revived again, and go-betweens even came to the house. But as time passed, the white hairs increased with unflagging persistence, and Ferhundeh was still waiting.

"Nurse! Do you know where we are taking you today? To look for a girl for Sabit," Hasna said one day.

Ferhundeh was dumbfounded. How could it be? Had Sabit reached the age of marriage already?

Then she made a calculation in her mind. They said Sabit was twenty-two, and he had been born four years after the wedding. When Hasna became a bride she was twenty, and they said that Ferhundeh herself was two years older than Hasna. In that case— She couldn't add and couldn't calculate such a large sum by adding up the years one by one. But a big knot twisted in the depths of her heart.

Ferhundeh found enough strength to do all the running at this wedding. As she dashed about the crowd this time she could hear them whispering, "The groom's nurse! The groom's nurse!" That night she locked herself in her room and got out that piece of paper which she had ignored for years. The paper was yellow and brittle and the writing faded. She threw herself on it and wept and wept.

The wedding passed, and as the months dragged along again in an unbroken chain, another layer of snow was added to Ferhundeh's hair. One night the newlyweds called their nurse and started to plead.

"The manservant is still begging us. He's constantly nagging. He's expecting the peace of his last years to be secured through our kindness."

The two of them embraced Ferhundeh and kissed her sagging cheeks. They caressed her snow white hair.

How nice it was going to be! They weren't planning to release the two of them. Again they would all sit here and look after the baby who was on the way.

The bride and groom started to talk about the new baby.

"Isn't that right, Sister Ferhundeh?" she was saying. Yes, even the new title would last just a short time. In a few months the baby would be born and Ferhundeh, who was still denied the chance of becoming a bride, would be the nurse of the new baby.

Ferhundeh was unable to oppose the wedding day planned at the insistence of the entire household. She was dressed up and seated like a bride. Finally she had become a bride, but she hadn't dyed her hair blond, golden blond like gold thread. She hadn't wanted to because it was no longer black but white, snow white like silk thread.

MY NEPHEW
Müftüoğlu Ahmet Hikmet
(*Translated by Madeline Zilfi*)

Greying, with a wreath-like beard, he had fastened his frock coat from top to bottom. His cylinder of a fez was tilted back to reveal his broad, creased forehead. His shoulders drooping, his body bent forward, the lines of his face almost suggest mocking: an expressive elderly man between fifty and fifty-five years old.

I have a nephew. He finished his education in Paris. Do you know what it means, "He finished his education in Paris"? He devoured me, finished me off, that's what it means. When I was exhausted, expense money from me gave out as well. As soon as the expense money was at an end — quite natural, isn't it — the education also ended. His expense money was money he extracted from me. But what is this education of his? I can't figure it out at all.

"Uncle, you don't understand anything. I am a master scholar of all of the sciences of the university!" he says. He says, but if he's a master scholar of all the sciences of the university, I'm the master madman of all the manias of the insane asylum! Look here, let me explain it to you. A while ago my nephew made me a lot of ornamented porticos and gilded domes in his zeal to learn architecture. As he failed to lay a firm foundation, he ventured to study melting technique in metallurgy. When liquefaction got heated up, our gold began to melt away. My nephew tired of this, too. When he took up farming, in his desire to be showered with the bounty of the earth, he fell in love with a florist, and in the process exhausted my fields. Finally one morning I came face to face with my nephew. His collar, like a white marble ring, was throttling him. His long curly hair under his unblocked fez had reversed itself like turkey feathers against the wind. On his chest he had attached a plasterboard cravat big enough to serve as a mattress for a newborn babe. Facing me, he inclined his head. From force of habit I stretched out my hand for it to be kissed, while he, without moving, extended his lips toward me. Neither of us knew just what to do. My hand remained suspended. Finally, wrapping himself around my neck, he kissed my lips familiarly again and again. I was embarrassed about my poor unkissed hand. Helplessly I withdrew it. At that point, as he pulled a white handkerchief from the back pocket of his knee-length frock coat, I made note of the crude artificial rings of vermilion, green, and blue that seemed almost to be making sport of me from his fingers. I don't know whether it was because he had kissed me on the mouth or what, but in an awkward gesture he wiped his lips and nose with his handkerchief. With an innovative folding, quite at odds with the folding practice of our old nurse, lo these many years, he puckered the handkerchief at the center, twisted it, and rolled it up. [*He mimics*] He threw himself down onto a cushion. He swayed back and forth, back and forth, and then stood up ramrod straight. Our nephew had departed "our nephew"-hood and assumed the guise of a remarkable machine. He could not stay seated on the cushion. He could not be at ease on the couch. He didn't like my attitude. He didn't like the way I walk. He didn't like the way I look. He didn't like my drawing a breath. Huh! He just plain didn't like anything about me. He had the temerity to throw the house into disorder, to change everything. He asked, he shrieked, he insisted that the servants wear white gloves when serving coffee, that İbish, the cook, put a white linen skullcap on his head, and that the house steward Köse Kahya shave every morning. One night when I entered his room to offer a bit of advice, I was confronted with a hideous sight: our nephew's face is brilliant yellow from a piece of cloth tied from beneath his nose to the edge of his ears. He's lying there in a trance, his feet propped up on the headboard, his hands swaddled in cotton, his eyes closed. "Disaster!" I said. "Disaster!" I flew out of the room. "Doctor, oh mercy, doctor!" We were all astir in the house, running into each other. As we carefully entered the room with the doctor, my nephew got up from the bed, surprised. Cries of "he's killed himself" from the women in the hall filled the house; my nephew started with fear at this, wanting to flee. We beg him to lie down again; we tuck in his hands and feet. Confusion, noise, pandemonium reign.

[*After a short pause*] Finally the matter was ironed out. On the following day my nephew had intended to go on an outing to Kağıthane. In order to force his feet into new boots, he elevated his legs, fancying to bring the blood down. He spread cream on his hands and face to soften them and make them shine. He wrapped his mustache in a press in order to make it stand stiff. And in this pain and torment he dozed off for a restful sleep. What could be simpler, more natural than that? These are the fruits of five years of the day-in and day-out [*laughing and shrugging*], day-in and day-out, uninterrupted education in those lands of culture. Do you understand? After five years, a stance like a Napoleon, hair like a Humbert, a mustache like a Wilhelm. That's it. That's enough to acquire a new mind. Ah!

[*He takes a deep breath*] And one morning I noticed that there was reveling, laughter, rowdiness going on in the large salon. I opened the door a bit: my nephew had seated his sister atop the piano, and though the nurse, the housekeeper, and the womanservant were also there, he had them all immodestly bedaub their arms and expose their bosoms — and wasn't he making them do the can-can? "My God!" I said. "Long-suffering God!" I said, but to no avail. I sprang at once into the room; I seized him by his powdered hair, and took him into the men's quarters. This was our nephew's "civilizing" mission: to explain Boccaccio's tales to his old nurse, and to regale the serving-women with Moulin Rouge adventures. This was "spreading civilization." But this was no time for levity. "My boy, don't you know that East and West can never meet? Won't you ever understand that they are totally opposed to each other? Then listen to me," I said to him.

I became very serious. I buttoned up my frock coat. I put on my glasses. I wiped my nose [*he mimics*], and cleared my throat [*he coughs*]. "Listen," I said. "For one thing, among us it is respectable to keep our heads covered but to show our feet. Among the French, on the contrary, it is good manners not to show the feet and to bare the head. Here's a second thing: for us for a long time the first floor of the house has been for the servants and the upper story for the masters; among the French, on the other hand, the first floor is for the masters, and the upper floor is for the servants. Three: the carpets we spread out under our feet they hang on end. There's more. Four: for us it has been men on the right, women on the left for a long time, but among the French the men are on the left and the women on the right. Five: we eat pilaf and macaroni last. They eat it first. Six: for us it is considered good breeding to say very little while eating and to eat quickly. But for them it is customary to speak often, to tell stories, to drink coffee during the meal, and even to wash their hands at the table.

Seven: for us it is considered very bad manners for children to meddle with adult speech. For them, on the other hand, it is a sign of a quick mind. Eight: twelve o'clock for us is either morning or evening, but for them it is either noon or midnight. Listen!" I looked and saw that my nephew had dozed off at the word "midnight" and had started to snore. I shook him. "I'm not done yet," I said. "Listen! Nine: for them it is absolutely necessary to sing a song standing up, but for us we have to be sitting. Ten: the French celebrate New Year's, and they get a little drunk. For us, Muharrem, New Year's, is a day of mourning, and for ten days we can't even drink water. Eleven: for us blue eyes are a sign of discord and the evil eye and are unlucky, but for them blue eyes are blessed, so blessed that even the angels favor them. Twelve: we begin writing from the right, the French from the left. Thirteen: in the Western languages lots of letters are written but they aren't read. With us, they are not written but they are read. Pay attention! Fourteen: we put the date in letters at the bottom. They put it at the top. Fifteen: for us contentment is a virtue, for them indolence. Sixteen: for us, shaving the mustache, at least..." While I was speaking I raised my head, and when I looked at my nephew whom I seemed to have left behind I saw .... he had become bored long since, and had slipped away. He had "laid tracks."

I was furious. Before I had calmed down, tumult erupted from the kitchen below. Our nephew had attempted to extract pistachios from the custard pudding with the tips of his long fingernails. Just as İbish, the cook, flew out to demand that I forbid my nephew to enter the kitchen without trimming his filthy nails, didn't my nephew, with the help of Pavli the coachman and Hajador the footman, grab the poor cook's hands and feet and, assuring him that he would be more chic, more European, try to shave the poor fellow's mustache? İbish's head turned crimson. He took a rolling pin in one hand and seized a piece of firewood with the other. Brandishing them, he roared until his voice gave out, "My honor has been disgraced. Don't stand at this door again. I'll make you disappear!" I looked on. It was most unseemly. I rescued my nephew, thrusting him into the harem.

The time had come to teach him a lesson. I considered the matter carefully. From that day forth, I endeavored to find a solution to the situation. I determined to execute a "trial by travel" in some little corner of Anatolia. Zonguldak sprang to my mind. "Zonguldak! Oh! Zonguldak! Now you'll see about the can-can act at the Moulin Rouge! Zonguldak, may your life be blessed!" So saying, I got rid of my nephew with a mining engineer's career in Zonguldak.

Exactly five years later to the day, when my nephew, who used to fit into his bottle like champagne, returned from Zonguldak, he was as calm and placid as milk. He had given up.

LIFE IS SWEET
Memduh Şevket Esendal
(Translated by Madeline Zilfi)

July. Afternoon. A woman's voice from nearby, yelling about one thing or another. Perhaps she's scolding her child. A cat leaps from the muezzin's walls to the porch. A few houses away a chicken cackles, and a rooster helps it along like a practiced accompanist.

His mother, sitting below with two neighbor ladies, is talking rapidly, animatedly, for some reason. It's plain that they're gossiping. The tabby cat, its legs extended, is stretched out on a cushion, sleeping. On top of an old, dilapidated bureau rests his mother's Dresden bridal lamps, their glass shades broken, and a pair of gilded *conche* glasses under beaded lids. In the corner, below a black drape, the Prophet's description. Everything in its place, life as it always is.

Hafiz Nuri Efendi took his umbrella from behind the door and went out onto the street. Whatever for? Does he have something to do? Is he going to see someone? He has no job at all. It's possible that he might never have occasion to go out. But he's outside. His feet brought him straightaway to the junction of two crossroads. On one side a grocery store, on the other the wall of a dervish cemetery. Across the way can be seen a railroad track in an empty field between two houses. In the empty patch of field, a holiday swing stands leaning to one side. The bulging middle of one of the houses is propped up by three long poles. A yellow tin-plated streetcar passes by, joggling and rattling its way toward Yedikule. The streets are empty. A paralytic man in dervish garb passes by, waving one arm in front of him and dragging one leg behind. The street becomes empty again. Suddenly he hears a noise. The train is on its way. A freight train from Edirne speeds by, shaking the ground and houses as it goes. A head-spinning passage. Its cars can be seen passing through the narrow gap between the two houses. Nuri Efendi is discomfited. You've come all the way from Edirne to Istanbul. How many paces are there left to Sirkeji? Couldn't you have traveled just as well slowly and peacefully? Instead you come through like a madman, all fuss and bother. Hafiz Nuri Efendi stops to rest in a corner. Suddenly he sees someone beside him. Kavafın Shükrü. Did he come out from the back street?

"Are you waiting for someone?" he asked Nuri Efendi.

"No!"

"Are you planning to stay here?" he asked.

"I don't know. I'm just standing."

"Do you have anything else in mind then?"

"No. What else would I have in mind?"

"It's possible — someone —"

Nuri didn't answer. After a while Shükrü asked again, "So, you're going to stand here?"

"I'm just standing. I don't know," he said.

"If you want to come along, come on. I'll take you to Kumkapı."

Nuri assented with a bow. "Let's go, if you say so. Let's go," he said.

"We'll walk and have a look around, if you like."

They walked on. They crossed to the sidewalk opposite, turned into the street on the right and went out to the railroad track. "You go on. I'll catch up," Shükrü said, and he went into a lumber warehouse there.

Hafiz Nuri Efendi walked on, leaning on his umbrella as he went, looking at the gardens on either side, at the lettuce and the cucumbers. When he heard the whistle of a train, he turned around to wait. Then he turned back to the road and walked on with umbrella waving. It was hot, his long jacket clung to his shoulders, and his fez was sticky with perspiration, but he didn't mind. He continued to walk. Although it was early, the beach at Kumkapı was crowded. Two scarf printers had spread scarves out to dry on the rocks along the shote. Nuri Efendi di walked on. He entered a passageway and wandered out behind the local train station. In the area leading to the tracks he met Halil, a local coal dealer.

"All's well, I hope, Nuri Efendi. Where are you off to?"

"To tell the truth, I don't know. I'm just going along. Shükrü was supposed to come, but he hasn't come yet," he said, taking a look behind him.

"Which Shükrü?" Halil asked.

"Shükrü the cobbler."

"Are you going somewhere in particular?"

"No. He just said 'Let's go,' but he hasn't come."

"You can't rely on that fellow," Halil said. "I wonder whether he got stuck somewhere. I'm going to the quarter. Come on, let's go back."

"All right, let's go back."

They started back. Halil began to explain that he had come to buy coal but had not been able to strike a bargain. They had not taken five steps when they heard someone behind them calling out to Halil. Halil gathered from the shouting that the sale was going to be put right. He turned to Nuri Efendi. "You go ahead," he said. "I'll catch up."

Nuri Efendi walked on. Taking the road that he had come by, once again alone, he came to the door of the local coffeehouse. In the center of the room two men playing backgammon sat facing each other on low wicker chairs. Nuri Efendi went in and sat on a third empty chair. He rested his elbows on his knees, brought the handle of his umbrella to his mouth, and began to watch the game.

One of the players lost a game. The same man lost the second game as well and, having lost a match, was angry. He attributed his losses to Hafiz's having brought bad luck. "He came in and ruined my dice throw," he thought, but wouldn't say so aloud. "Hafiz," he said, "when this game is over, I'll play you a match."

"But I don't know how to play backgammon," he said.

"You don't know how to play backgammon?"

"I don't know!"

"What? If you don't know, why have you been hanging around to watch?"

Hafiz shrugged his shoulders. "No reason. I was just watching."

The man who had won arranged the pieces for the second match and took the dice in hand. "It's strange," he said. "You've been coming to the coffeehouse for fifteen years and you haven't learned backgammon?"

The players began again. When the man who had lost before lost yet another game, his patience gave out. "Hafiz," he said. "In truth, you came in and ruined my throw. Move away a bit and sit over there."

Hafiz Nuri Efendi grew a little angry at this. "What harm am I doing to you?" he wanted to say, but he didn't. He rose, went to the door of the coffeehouse, and stood there. "Perhaps I'll go home," he thought.

It was now about time for afternoon prayers. Evening was approaching. Rounding the corner, he bought a loaf of bread from the grocery store and went home. His mother unlatched the door. The smell of food cooking on the brazier filled the whole house. He went up to his room, put on his houserobe and Damascene shawl and sat at the window. Evening vendors passed by. The color of evening enveloped the quarter. From the streetcorner, a child called out to his brother, "Come, Hayri, your mother's calling you!" A little girl, a bunch of parsley in her hand, her clogs clattering, went by. The son of Gaffar, the neighbor, struggled to put two empty baskets through the garden gate. Two women, apparently having gone somewhere and overstayed, were hurrying home. His mother's clogs could be heard moving about in the kitchen. "How sweet life is," he thought. "One's life is as one lives it."

THE SECRET SHRINE
Ömer Seyfettin
(*Translated by Madeline Zilfi*)

A few days ago in Tokatlıyan, Sermet introduced me to a young Frenchman, a friend from the Sorbonne, a handsome, slender and well-mannered young man with sandy hair and porcelain-blue eyes, but a fanatical Orient-lover.

His first words were these: "My dear friend, you don't know yourselves. By supposing Europe to be something special, you don't see your own good points, nor do you know how to experience your own mysteries."

I smiled at the reprimand, not being able to figure out at once whether he was right or not. "What can you know about what we don't experience or can't see?"

"I've seen it with my own eyes," he said exuberantly. "For three years I've lived in Sermet's house. Everything is Western; dining room, bedroom, his wife's clothes, his brothers' and sisters' clothes, their manners, even their minds, their very way of thinking, are all Europeanized! Ah, where is Loti's Turkey?"

"Loti's Turkey is over yonder," I said.

"Yes, that's what they say. But it's a world you don't enter. What a shame that you don't cherish that picturesque world!"

"There are those among us who love it," I said.

"And are you one of them?"

Saying "yes," I nodded my head with exaggerated zeal. These Westerners who don't venture beyond the limits of their "fixed ideas" — what innocents they make of themselves! And this young Frenchman is one of them. We began to talk about Turkey. He asserted that we aren't acquainted with ourselves. We call our most beautiful, richest and most esthetically pleasing streets foul. For enormous avenues, for European buildings devoid of beauty, we value geometrical lines that kill nature. His anger at Turkey's Greeks went beyond the bounds of resentment. He had such hatred for Beyoğlu. "What a disgusting Western caricature! My God!" he'd say, usually going pale with loathing. His head was filled with Loti's fancies. To the signs of our wretchedness, what we call our poverty, our brutality, our ignorance, he says, "Marvelous!" And he was bewildered at how we could feel no esthetic stirring in the face of those endless dunghills and owl-topped ruins. Finally, he asked me to take him to an un-Westernized Turkish home. At once, I thought of my old foster mother who lives in the outlying neighborhood of Karagümrük, that extremely devout, extremely stoical, and extremely conservative woman who lives with an old black serving woman older than herself, and subsists comfortably enough on a small income left by her husband.

"All right then, let me take you to the home of an absolutely un-Westernized old widow," I said. He thanked me. He was pleased.

"When?"

"Today. In fact, now if you wish."

"Is it possible?"

"It's possible. Only we'll buy a fez for your head," I said. To go this way, on the instant, would give no opportunity for ceremony, for guest formalities, in the Turkish-style house. Its true character and quaintness would show through as it was to this Orient-loving Frenchman. Sermet choked from laughter at the poor fellow's joy. We bade him goodbye, engaged a car and went down to Beyazıt. At a shop we bought the little Frenchman a fez as red as a fresh liver. We had it cleaned up and blocked. He didn't want to ride the streetcar.

"There below. Is that a completely Turkish quarter?" he asked.

"Yes, a completely Turkish quarter."

"In that case, may I ask that we go on foot?"

"Fine," I said. We walked past burned-out areas. The weather was foggy, cloudy, and overcast. An almost painful melancholy mingled with the calm of houses in ruins, of lonely remains. On the way I gave him instructions. I would tell my foster mother that he was a Circassian.

She was not a woman who would overdo the seclusion of women. But perhaps she wouldn't want to welcome a Christian to her house. This simple bit of intrigue would kindle the young Frenchman's imagination all the more. He stood facing wooden houses black, decayed, leaning to one side, and with tumbled walls and burst roofs. "What a view! What a view!" he said, as though he couldn't be dislodged from it. We were able to reach the house in two hours. It was a three-story, wooden, somewhat dilapidated building. We knocked on the door. The old black woman opened it.

"Is my foster mother not here?" I asked.

"She's at a neighbor's. Please come in."

"Very well, Karanfil Dadı, run over and tell her that I'm here and that I have a guest with me. We'll be staying the night with you," I said. We went in. We climbed a great staircase, passing by clean but gloomy woodwork. The young Frenchman swooned at the guest salon. A beautiful Persian carpet was spread on the floor. The walls were decorated with framed inscriptions that my late calligrapher foster father had left as remembrances. Sofas with cushions in dark red drapings were blanketed by crimson throws. We sat down facing each other. He was filled with admiration for the latticework.

"I feel almost as though I'm in a dream," he said. When my foster mother arrived, he, like me, kissed her hand. By turns he would forget the fez on his head and involuntarily would bow. My foster mother didn't notice much of this, but —

"Your manner of speaking doesn't resemble Circassian," she said.

"Dear mother, this isn't the sort of Circassian that you're familiar with. After the migration, a new Circassian language developed. It got mixed up with Russian and Caucasian!" I said persuasively. I pretended: "This guest, a Circassian, so to speak, came to Istanbul in order to make the pilgrimage." When my foster mother reminded me that it was not the pilgrimage season, I thought of an explanation. "He came early to learn a little Turkish in Istanbul."

"Ah, to be a pilgrim at that age! What good fortune, what good fortune! May your turn come next!" she said.

"Amin, amin!"

The European suddenly recognized this word that had popped out of my mouth and, intent upon showing his expertise, repeated in his own language, "Amen, amen!"

My foster mother insisted on my making the pilgrimage with this Circassian. In short, we talked nothing but pilgrimage, preachers and the like right up to mealtime. In spurts I rattled off translations into "Circassian" of all my foster mother's advice. As we sat down at the dinner table, the European gave himself up completely to esthetic raptures. The silver tray that issued forth only for foreign guests made the poor man delirious. He abandoned his fork and tried to eat with his hand as my foster mother was doing. I didn't bother. I said that eating with one's hand was peculiar only to old women. We rose from the table as he was beginning to assert that sitting cross-legged on the floor was the most comfortable position in the world. We had our coffee. I showed my guest the Ottoman books, left like souvenirs in my foster father's library. He was filled with admiration for the books' decoration, the bindings, and the miniatures. When it became time to retire, I directed him on up to the top floor with Karanfil. They had made up his bed in the room above the garden. On the way I pointed out this and that. "Good night," I said, and left off at a room on the second floor. At night a storm came up. A violent rain poured down. In the morning the weather had turned quite lovely. I found the Frenchman awake and dressed. He was sitting on the bed writing something.

"Bonjour."

"Bonjour, mon ami!"

"What are you writing?"

"Oh, my feelings."

"Are you that much moved, then?"

"I can't describe it. I can't describe it to you."

We went downstairs and breakfasted. We kissed my foster mother's hands. I brought the Frenchman on foot to Fatih in order to submerge him all the more in the quaintness of the Orient. We sat down at a coffeehouse across from the mosque. I ordered a water pipe for each of us. Telling him not to puff out, I taught him the process of smoking efficiently. We began to enjoy ourselves. In order to get a rise out of the poor fellow again and to work up his excitement, I said "My dear fellow, take a look at that shrine across the way. What elegance, what majesty, no?"

The Frenchman smiled. He didn't seem all that excited. It seemed odd to me, the indifference of this man who had been more aflutter yesterday, like a madman, in the presence of fallen-down fountains and twisted walls.

"Don't you like this monument, or what?" I asked him.

"This temple is nothing," he said, and his blue eyes narrowed as he smiled again.

"What do you mean 'nothing'? This is one of Istanbul's greatest monuments."

"This is nothing. This temple is nothing."

"What do you mean?"

"I've seen a more impressive one than that."

"It's not possible," I said. "When did you see it?"

"Last night."

"In your dreams?"

"No."

"Then where?"

"In the house."

"In what house?"

"In the house that we slept in."

I was confused. "What did you see, dear fellow?"

"Something that Pierre Loti could not have seen! A mystery unknown to any other European." I smiled. "Yes, I have seen your secret shrine."

"What secret shrine, dear fellow?"

"It's useless to keep on pretending. I have seen it! Last night I saw your private shrine, your secret shrine that you've been hiding from Europeans for centuries. But you can be sure I'll guard this secret. When I go to Paris I won't write about it for the newspapers. The memory of it will stay hidden in my notebook like some sacred thing."

"I don't understand a word of what you're saying," I said.

"Don't keep on. I saw it, I saw it."

"What, dear fellow?"

"Your secret shrine!"

"Secret shrine or whatever, we don't have it."

"Your denials are for nothing. I have seen it."

"Strange, very strange," I said, shaking my head.

The little Frenchman could not resist. He pulled a Morocco-bound notebook from his pocket. "Just listen. Did I see it or didn't I?" he asked. He began to read the last pages:

"Morning. I'm writing these lines with great emotion, with delight. Yesterday on Sermet's recommendation I went with a Turk to this Istanbul's most unexplored spot. Perhaps Casanova, Pierre Loti and the like thought they had seen the Orient by drinking a coffee apiece in the men's quarters of mansions and summer homes. The real Orient exists among people not often seen. So I have seen something that no other European can have seen. The place is the home of an old widow. An extremely pious woman. The interior of the house, the table service, customs, manners, all of it completely unspoiled. Everything is *à la turque*. At night they had me sleep in a room on the topmost floor. I woke up very early in the morning. I got out of bed. A strange inquisitiveness gnawed at me. I left the room on tiptoe. There was a room opposite. The door was ajar. I pushed it slowly. And suddenly what do I see? A secret family shrine!

"White blinds were drawn down. Between them a pale bit of light shines through. Large framed inscriptions hanging on the walls. In the corners stand iron-bound caskets made of heavy walnut wood. Doubtless in these caskets are the mummies of the beloved dead. I tried to open one of them. It was impossible. It was locked. Elsewhere on the floor stand a number of jugs, large and small. Some are of copper, some of porcelain. There are valuable things in them. For example, the one in front of the first casket, on a line with the door, is an extremely valuable vessel, its sides embellished with gold. The one in the corner is a green vase. Who knows what sort of clay it's made of? Angles are stretched out with some segments of cord in a proportional relationship whose meaning within the context of the shrine I'm unable to grasp. Above these sacred angles are hung what are undoubtedly some relics of the deceased. Holy water stands in the jugs. Some of them are full to overflowing. I tasted of those mysterious holy waters that come from Mecca, Medina, or who knows what holy sanctuary. Somewhat acrid. At the bottom of the jugs is a slight, very slight, earthen sediment. I drank from every vessel. All have a taste. My heart began to pound. I departed with the excitement of a blasphemer, a deceiver, an infidel who has penetrated a forbidden shrine. I thought those caskets would suddenly open up and, from within, aged Turks who had died hundreds of years before would rise up with their turbans and scimitars and walk over me. It was as though the inscriptions on the walls were about to fall. The contents of the holy vessels became agitated, as though at that moment they would turn into a sea and drown me there. I sense inside me now the fury, the silence, and the sublimity of those sacred waters.

"A mysterious, vague torpor, a fever, courses through my veins. My mind is a blank. I hear the resonant echoes of an unknown vault. I feel such an incomprehensible exhilaration that—"

I couldn't restrain myself. I let out such a roar of laughter that the Frenchman dropped the tube of his water pipe from his hand. A bit more and the water pipe would have overturned. I had startled the customers who had come to take their morning pleasure. They stared at me fixedly.

The Frenchman asked, "What are you laughing at?"

"Just that you did not enter a secret shrine," I said.

"Oh, then what did I enter?"

"My foster mother's storeroom."

"Storeroom?"

"We don't have chests of drawers, mirrored bureaus and so on in our houses. Our belongings are all in boxes, and the boxes are all kept in one room. Those iron-bound walnut boxes that you thought were caskets are our clothing chests."

"And the inscriptions on the walls?"

"My foster father's work. My foster mother doesn't sell them inasmuch as they're mementoes." The Frenchman didn't believe me. I was still laughing.

"And the geometric shapes made of cord? Those relics?"

"It's cord for hanging laundry when it rains. The angles, the triangles, were formed accidentally. What you thought were relics are castoff clothing."

The Frenchman still didn't believe me. His blue eyes clouded over. He shook his head as though he had caught me in a lie.

"And that holy water. What do you say to it, dear fellow?" he said.

"It rained last night. My foster mother's storeroom has leaked for as long as I can remember. Realizing that if the rainwater dripped from the roof it would soak the floor, Karanfil the night before must have lined up those vessels," I said.

Like his famous compatriot who thought the *mashallah* inscriptions over our houses were the billboards of a national insurance company, and that the amulet slippers that swing on our eaves were shoes left stuck there by thieves fleeing from roof to roof, the Frenchman stopped a moment and thought. He drew deeply on his water pipe. His notebook that had rested open in his hand he thrust into his pocket. "Don't laugh, friend. Even in your storerooms there's such a mysterious, such an incomprehensible, such an impalapable, such a religious quality that—"

"Like what?"

"It's such a thing that— You're blind. You don't see it, so that's that," he said.

But in no way did he say what this thing was that only he saw and we could not see. Indeed, it is known that Turks are very courteous in their judgments. The response came right to the tip of my tongue: "If we're blind, then it's you who are mute!" But I remained silent. I didn't utter a sound.

THE FROG PRAYER
Ömer Seyfettin
(*Translated by Virginia Taylor-Saçlıoğlu*)

The world of the provinces. In other words, the life outside Istanbul. How pleasant it is. Only the ones who live it know this. On one hand the notables and the hojas, on the other the civil servants, officers, and teachers, and lastly the local farmers. Every class, every circle has its own separate coffeehouse, separate entertainment, and separate taste. The one man who could be said to be "interclass" is the town doctor. He talks and fraternizes with everybody. He goes to the coffeehouse of the civil servants, officers, and teachers. As for the pharmacy, it's the private club of the notables, and the lawyers' offices resemble the pharmacy to some extent.

In short, the provinces are an extremely pleasant world of their own. For seven, eight, or perhaps nine years I was a secondary school teacher in a town not far from Istanbul. In the self-sufficient world of the province, the school, too, is another world. In fact, a world within a world. Twenty different men — old, young, intelligent, stupid, talkative, quiet — formed by four or five schools whose programs and aims are all contrary to each other: the principal, the assistant principal, the teachers, the supervisors, the administrative officials, and boarding students who had come from the most distant corners of that vast empire of ours. A flock of children of every race and every type, not Turkicized in anything other than their language. Yet, among such manifest contrasts, what a convivial harmony it was. Religious fanatics, reactionaries, liberals, and finally those with no profession or special character lived together as brothers. There was a mathematics teacher who was open-minded to an extreme degree. The biology teacher was an earnest youth who viewed all of us as complete ignoramuses. I was the literature teacher. The French teacher was a Jew. When he was monitor at the evening study hall, he would write the words the boys asked him in his pocket notebook in Latin letters and the next day would get their meanings from me. Once they asked the poor man what "divine rapture" meant. He misunderstood and wrote down "divine coffeepot."

He accosted me in the teachers' room and asked, "What does 'divine coffeepot' mean?"

"It doesn't mean anything," I said, smiling. But he insisted.

We found the student who had asked the question and opened his book. When it became clear that the poor man had misunderstood, it became a private joke between us. The poor man's nickname became "the divine coffeepot."

Then there was the principal. I've never seen such a fanatic about law and order in this world. To begin with, he never socialized with those beneath him. He lived outside the school society like a Greek god. His nickname among us was "With a view to." When we gathered in his office on assembly days, to which he attached the utmost importance, he wouldn't let any of us say a word. Instead, he would make each of us write separate memos saying "With a view to," and, whatever the difficulty was, he would think he had solved it as soon as he had something written down and had added the notorious "With a view to" to the same words and sentences.

Among our group of friends my favorite was the religion teacher, Bahir Efendi. After the religious school, he had also completed the university. He was nearing fifty, a man persistent in his convictions, persuasive, good-natured, and eccentric. He was friendly with me because we shared the same ideas on education. I am firmly convinced that education should always be conservative. The duty of teachers is to insist on a good old-fashioned training for the children. Life, not the school, is the place for social revolution. Since he thought the same way I did, the two of us along with our followers formed a lobby in the general meetings and didn't give the liberals, those partisans of modern education, a chance. What I liked best about Bahir Hoja were his expressions such as "those against, those indifferent, those for," always very lively. He spoke argumentatively and waved his right arm with the agility of a Karagöz puppet, as if he wanted to embody his words in the form of a fist. His only shortcoming was his water pipe. He was so addicted to it that he couldn't do without smoking it ten times a day, at the coffeehouse and at school.

Now the water pipe. It's not small like cigarettes but awkwardly large. One has to hide it from the principal and the inspectors. While sitting in the coffeehouse one day, we were speculating about the possibility of a portable water pipe. For example, its top could be removed after smoking, and it could be made to resemble a water bottle and to fit into one's pipe pocket.

"What about the tube?" asked Bahir Hoja.

"You could put it under your robe and wrap it around your waist."

"It would break."

"You could coil it up inside your fez."

"It wouldn't fit."

As we were talking, we saw the town doctor come in. He came up to us, said hello and sat down. On Friday they were all going to the Bektashi dervish lodge. There was going to be roast lamb, music, and wine. He invited us to come, too.

"We can't," I said. We were teachers. We couldn't participate in such parties.

But the doctor insisted. "You won't drink. You'll stop up your ears and cover your eyes."

"If you'll take my water pipe I'll come," said Bahir Hoja.

"We'll take it," replied the doctor. "In fact, I'll take it myself." He gave his word.

What an easygoing, unpretentious young man he was. It was almost as if he were the life of the town. The sick were cured more through his words than his medicines.

● ● ●

On Friday we went all together to the Bektashi lodge. It was like the vision of a paradise still fresh from some blissful bygone days, as if the winds of the storm called history had never passed through the century-old plane-trees nor over the quiet roof of the secluded building. The pool, large enough to look like a natural lake except for the fence around it, was sleeping in emerald shadows and dreaming of water lilies. We relaxed on the mats that the dervishes had spread. The telegraph operator took his *ud* and the real estate official started to play the *kanun*. The fiddler Aleko had come too, and the music began. The doctor said, "I'm the cup bearer," and offered some wine to everyone. He stopped in front of Bahir Hoja.

"But I have my water pipe."

"Just a sip?"

"I've never touched a drop in my life."

"Take a mouthful, gargle it and spit it out."
"What for?"
"It's an antiseptic."

Bahir Hoja didn't like to appear like an extreme fanatic in these gatherings. He put the pitcher of *raki* to his lips, but the doctor tickled him and made him swallow a few drops. Although he denied that he had swallowed any, those few drops made him as happy as if he had drunk a large jugful.

We were laughing and having a good time. But our ears were buzzing. There was an incessant, hellish uproar in this green paradise. In the pond there were perhaps a million frogs. And they were screaming at the top of their voices, so much so that we almost couldn't hear ourselves talk.

"Damn!" said the doctor. "How can we make them shut up? Our eardrums are going to burst."

"No matter what you do, you won't be able to silence them," replied the dervishes.

With the exception of Bahir Hoja, we all got up because the uproar was unbearable. Stones, dirt, whatever we could get our hands on, we started to throw into the pond. The frogs, as if infuriated by our attack, began to bellow even more loudly. The doctor lit newspapers and threw them at the frogs, thinking they would be frightened and run away. But no. No matter what we did, they didn't quiet down but became even more excited. It was impossible to hear the music.

"There's nothing to do but get out of here," someone said.
"Where shall we go?"
"To some place far away from the pond."

While we were discussing such a migration, Bahir Hoja, whom we had forgotten over his water pipe, said, "If I want, I'll silence them in a second."

We heard him say it.
"How?"
"I'll cast a spell."
"Well?"
"They'll be quiet instantly."

Although our pleasure had vanished due to the noise, we all smiled again.

"These frogs aren't a simple migraine that can be turned off by a spell," the doctor was saying. "They're a real brain concussion!"

But Bahir Hoja was swinging his fists again with the zeal of an enraged Karagöz and swearing at our scepticism. On one hand, his yelling, and on the other, the uproar of a million frogs. In short, it was like a drunken brawl. No gaiety remained in the gathering.

"Everybody sit down," said Bahir Hoja. "I'll go to the edge of the pond and cast a spell. If they don't quiet down, you can spit in my face."

"Okay, in that case, Hoja."

We didn't believe it, but we all sat down thinking that at least some fun would come out of it. The hoja stood up, took his water pipe in hand and went to the edge of the pond. He turned his back to us. We saw him blow on the water. Before a minute had passed the frogs suddenly became quiet. Not even a peep came from the pond. We were amazed.

Making a triumphant fist, he came back.

"For the love of God, what did you do?"

"Didn't you see? Don't you even believe your own eyes? I cast a spell," he answered.

After half an hour the frogs started to croak again, but we were no longer worried. Bahir Hoja would get up, go to the edge of the pond and quiet all of them again with a spell. When he got up, he never left his beloved water pipe behind with us. "You're drunk, you'll break it," he would say. We stayed there enjoying ourselves until nightfall. Even Aleko the fiddler believed in Bahir Hoja's spell. The doctor didn't believe it, but he didn't have the nerve to deny the result that he saw with his own eyes. The local officials couldn't even continue drinking their *raki* they were so astonished. The Bektashi dervishes stared absent-mindedly at the spellbinder, but who knows what was going through their minds?

The next evening Bahir Hoja and I were sitting next to each other in the coffeehouse reading the Istanbul papers. I was thinking so hard about how he had silenced the frogs at the lodge as if by giving a command that I couldn't understand what I was reading. If I were to come right out and ask him, I was sure he would say, "Don't you trust your own eyes? I cast a spell. Are you blind?" and silence me just like the frogs. But I was no fool. I prepared a clever, scientific trap for him. First, I distracted him from the papers. Then I started a pleasant conversation on a spiritual matter. He was very interested in such things. I explained that animals have no souls but live outside the spiritual dimension of creation, just as plants do.

"I am also of that opinion," he said.

"No, you aren't. You're lying."

"I swear it."

"No, you're lying."

"How do you know?"

"Because you cast a spell on the frogs. That means that you didn't know that animals don't have souls."

He removed his arms from the table and leaned back. He looked intently into my eyes. He was caught in a dilemma. I had pushed him into a corner. He knitted his bushy brows.

"I didn't cast a spell on the frogs!"

"Then how did you silence them?"

He wouldn't open his mouth. He was in deep trouble. He had no alternative. He was either going to admit his ignorance or tell the truth.

"Tell me, then, what you did that quieted the frogs."

"Well, are you an imbecile? Are there really such things as spells?"

"What did you do?"

"I dangled the tube of my water pipe."

"Well?"

"The frogs took it for a snake. They immediately fled to the bottom of the pond."

But one of the features of provincial life is not to give away secrets.

"One shouldn't destroy the beliefs of simple people. They have no need for scientific truths. Don't tell anybody that I showed the water pipe to the frogs. Let them think I cast a spell," said Bahir Hoja.

I never let the secret escape my lips. The whole town heard about the hoja's miracle. The Bektashis themselves had witnessed it, and even the doctor's doubts gradually melted away. Whenever the subject of the miracle arose, the poor doctor would always shrug his shoulders humbly and say, "How many unknown things there are in this world, and our knowledge isn't equal to one-billionth of them!" And he no longer laughed his usual jolly laugh.

ZEYNEP, MY ZEYNEP
Halide Edip Adıvar
(*Translated by Virginia Taylor-Saçlıoğlu*)

Tall Osman had come from the Black Goat tribe and settled in the village of E. He had set up a farm there which won the admiration of the whole area. He had such imperturbable, straightforward, and unfailing common sense, such as is found only among the ordinary people, that he dominated his surroundings and was soon known as one of the richest landowners in the area.

The butter, cheese, livestock, and fields — in fact, the entire management of the farm — which depended on his intelligence and skill became a model for others. There was no farm in the province of İzmir with which he hadn't acquainted himself, walked over, and examined closely. The farm's agricultural matters were managed by a young Anatolian Greek from İzmir, named Yorgi, who had studied in Athens. His diligence had so impressed Tall Osman that the old Turk, who at first looked down upon Yorgi with all the toughness of a bully and a chieftain and who considered Greeks second-class humans, by and by began to offer tobacco to Yorgi and to have long conversations with him. The shrewd, crafty, and quick-witted Yorgi began to get a little closer to the owner of the farm every year.

When Tall Osman settled in İzmir, he married the daughter of a retired Istanbul pasha and brought his beautiful and fragile wife to the farm. To their daughter Zeynep, who arrived a year later, Yorgi's wife Kalyopi was nurse at first and then acceded to the position of having a say in all the affairs of the house. Whenever the lady of the house went to İzmir or Istanbul to buy things for Zeynep or necessities for her own wardrobe, she always took along Kalyopi who, with her small eyes, plump body, and cheerful, clever, and handy way, took all matters concerning Zeynep and her mother into her own hands.

Although Tall Osman never abandoned his nomadic dress and traditions, he was completely unopposed to the fancy and beautiful dresses which his Istanbul wife bought from the richest Istanbul dressmakers. The deep affection which bound him to his fair-skinned, dark-haired wife was part admiration and part primitive worship.

After Tall Osman lost his wife, which was before Zeynep could say "Mommy" or had learned to walk, he never remarried. Zeynep proudly concealed her matchless beauty, which stemmed from her mother's fragility and her father's strength, as her most prized possession. The amusements to which the landowners of the province were addicted entered Tall Osman's life very rarely, and he lived on his farm confirmed in strict and severe abstinence.

The fame of the eighteen-year-old Zeynep, with her tall litheness like a young cypress, her silky black hair flowing in waves around her clear complexion, her contemptuous dark eyes, her mischievous dark brows, and her soft, fiery lips like a pomegranate flower, had set İzmir afire and had even spread to Istanbul. The year that she stayed with her maternal aunt in Erenköy she had learned everything that Istanbul girls know.

She could read and write, speak French, and play the piano and the lute, and she dressed with a faultlessness many Shishli ladies might envy and with a special taste all her own. She talked, sang, and thought, and was a girl of effervescent strength like the most charming waterfall of a carefree life. But her spirit had a Black Goat tribal element which the Istanbul girls lacked. Taking tea with her aunt at Tokatlıyan, she was a head taller than the tiny, dainty, painted, coquettish, and languorous Istanbul girls, and her spirit too towered over the oppressive air of Istanbul like the rarefied atmosphere of peaks, rocks, winds, and plains. She would always return, like a young cypress unable to live amid hothouse flowers, to her father who, with his knee-length peasant breeches and kerchiefed head, was yet tall and dark like an ancient cypress. To play and sing for him and teach him the ways of city life in the evenings, and then to ride with him for hours on horseback and hunt birds and deer with a skilled master like him — these were the things she loved best.

Zeynep, whose spirit and womanhood were developing with such a rich life and beauty, had become a new and endless world of joy for her father. After her Istanbul trips, which were gradually becoming less and less frequent and from which she returned more quickly every time, she would bring such new life, new ideas, and new scenes, gathered and improvised from the spoiled ways of the Istanbul women whom she mimicked and mocked with an astonishing proficiency, that her father sometimes awaited her, whom he feared to let out of his sight, with the thought that perhaps she would be better off in Istanbul.

The great burden on Zeynep's father gradually began to make itself felt on the farm. He went round the fields, folds, pens, and stables with a strange attention and anxiety, but he took no interest in them. A tense and nervous grin appeared on Yorgi's face, who welcomed this development with an outburst of buffoonery, and Kalyopi's small eyes shrank and constricted with worry.

After the First World War when his military service came due, Yorgi disappeared. For a long time this was a great loss for Osman, because Yorgi had been such a help to him in many ways. Furthermore, Yorgi's dodging the military, after having been practically adopted and nourished for so many years on Turkish bread, had offended Osman. But another event soon displaced this loss and concern. Zeynep's aunt had a son who was a reserve officer. As soon as the war had broken out, while he was studying agriculture in America, he returned to his country. Since he lost his left foot in the first offensive at the Dardanelles, he was released from service, and when Yorgi disappeared he had come to his uncle's farm as a foreman. In this way, Süleyman's coming to the farm brought it new life.

Zeynep was much more interested in the life of the farm now. With flat-heeled, ankle-high shoes on her feet, a full, short cloak on her back, and a white kerchief on her head, she went all over the farm together with Süleyman.

These three people, bound as partners to earth and nature, were living such a sincere, wholesome, and self-contained life around the fire in the evenings that Tall Osman had not tasted such perfect joy even in his short-lived married life. The old man had everything he could wish for around him. During the last dark days of the country before the armistice of 1918, Zeynep and Süleyman kept telling each other with smiles that it wasn't natural to be so happy.

When Tall Osman said he was going to give them to each other in marriage, they weren't surprised because they had come to feel that they were born for each other and were destined to be mates.

Finally, one month after the armistice, Tall Osman went to İzmir to see a lawyer about some farm matters and to make preparations for the very simple wedding of Zeynep and Süleyman, as if he were going to establish a strong, solid front against disaster by marrying the two young people in this day of national catastrophe. Zeynep had everything she needed. He wasn't going to go to Istanbul. What was the point of a bridal outfit? A party for the neighbors would be enough. As Tall Osman was leaving, he kissed his daughter's forehead and cheeks with more emotion than usual. He embraced Süleyman and whispered in his ear, "Watch out! The Greeks may be getting dangerous."

Süleyman found his father-in-law's concern excessive, and after a hearty laugh he accompanied him on horseback as far as the boundary of the farm.

When he was returning in the evening, the moon rose and cast its light from behind the pink and white blossoms of the almond and plum trees onto the roof of the women's quarters. From a distance the agitated and drawn-out bleating of lambs and sheep entering the fold punctuated the silence, and the strange howling of a dog could be heard in the district otherwise enveloped in the colors, sounds, and lights of joy and beauty. The dog's dismal howling continued all night.

In the dining room which opened onto the almond grove, Zeynep was sitting next to the window. She hadn't yet lit the lamp. Süleyman greeted her with a flick of the horsewhip. There was an enchanting transparence and luminosity on Zeynep's face just like that in the moonlight. She had flung her freshly washed black hair down her back in two long, thick braids in order that it might dry, and with her long white gown, white slippers and white face, the long shadows of her silky black hair and the soft light of her eyes darkening in the moonlight made Süleyman's heart strangely uneasy.

They immediately asked Kalyopi for food and light. Both felt a heaviness in their hearts and a ferment of excitement whose cause they were unable to understand. After supper they sat side by side and looked out the window at the farm washed in moonlight and at the empty horizon. The dog's dismal howling continued. In order to subdue the strange agitation coming from the foreboding which had distracted both of them, Süleyman began to sing in a boisterous voice. The folk song known as "Zeynep" which he had begun as a joke was cascading over his lips like a holy devotion straight from his heart. Zeynep reached for Süleyman's long *saz* which hung on the wall next to her own lute and handed it to him with a smile.

Süleyman took the *saz* without interrupting his song. His lips wore a roguish smile but his heart was caught up in Zeynep's black and white beauty. As he sang with more and more abandon, his voice took on a more crazed and bitter fervor with every repetition of the word "Zeynep." Zeynep, even at their engagement, had not been overcome by such a strange feeling. Every "Zeynep" seized and plucked her heart in Süleyman's two hands. It was as if it were being torn out and fastened to Süleyman's heart in his broad breast which swelled with the waves of his voice. These two pure and forceful creatures seemed outwardly stunned by the atmosphere of this spell and fascination whose origin they didn't know. Suddenly Zeynep extinguished the lamp and was dancing in the light which filtered through the window, clapping her hands and swaying from side to side like a peasant girl. While her slim, young white body was undulating with laughter that would shatter crystal, her long black braids were swaying with such soft, sweeping swoops and her tiny pomegranate mouth was smiling at Süleyman with such distant joy and playfulness that this mock minstrel singing the "Zeynep" song tasted the romantic miracles of the legendary Turkish troubadours with a deep belief.

Suddenly a dark figure passed by the window and the dog again howled dismally. Zeynep froze. Süleyman looked out the window. Kalyopi was coming through the almond trees, and a dark figure, who seemed to Süleyman to be wearing a hat,* receded. He raised the window suddenly and called out, "Kalyopi! Who were you talking to?"

"No stranger."

"Who was it?"

"My lord, man! Why all this curiosity?"

Kalyopi was trying to smile but suddenly she could find nothing to say. "Let me come in. I'll explain." She tried to put them off.

Sunday she had gone to Anastasya's house. Anastasya's nephew had come from İzmir. Yorgi was apparently in İzmir. The man had brought news from him and had come here to bring her the message.

Although he didn't want to show it, Süleyman was extremely suspicious. Zeynep still hadn't lost her joy and, patting Kalyopi's fat cheeks as in her childhood, asked, "Is there news of Uncle Yorgi, Nanny?"

As they were parting that night, Süleyman gave Zeynep's hand a long kiss. He had fear and despair in his heart as though this beautiful woman moving out of his sight would never be his. That night he lit the lamp in the dining room window under Zeynep's bedroom and cleaned his rifles until three in the morning.

*Not worn at the time by Turks, implying that the shadow was of a Greek.

The next morning Zeynep woke up with a headache and a slight fever. Only by breakfast time was she able to get up and dressed. She found Süleyman in the dining room with such a disappointed and frightened look on his face that she suddenly burst into tears.

"What's happened, Süleyman?"

But Süleyman, casting a meaningful glance at Kalyopi, merely said, "It's nothing, Zeynep."

Kalyopi was behaving strangely. She stood in front of the door for a long time and scrutinized the movements of the two young people, especially Süleyman, with an endless curiosity. Doubling up with laughter, she repeated with a triumphant taunt, "You sure were curious last night, weren't you?"

After breakfast Zeynep and Süleyman went outside for awhile. They walked. Her fever had increased and her temples were burning. But when she saw that Süleyman had gone up to the door with his rifle, she sensed that something extraordinary had occurred.

"What is it, for God's sake?"

"It's nothing important. This morning the enemy entered İzmir."

"What's happened to my father?"

"What could happen? He certainly knows how to protect himself. Are you afraid, Zeynep?"

"No. Where did you get the news? Have they done anything yet?"

Süleyman was looking straight ahead with worried, clouded eyes, but he couldn't bring himself to say anything.

That evening he couldn't sleep for worry. He gave guns to the shepherds, Osman and Ali, and had them sleep in the room under the women's quarters. He himself slept on a couch in the living room under Zeynep's room.

For the first two days, a mood of dark confusion and deep, endless grief plunged the people into such a state that they were unable even to talk about the details of the İzmir tragedy.

On the third night, velvet roses of fever bloomed on Zeynep's cheeks. She was unable to hold her head up from fever and worry, but she said nothing.

While she was saying good night to Süleyman, she rested her aching head for a moment on her fiancé's shoulder and with eyes full of tears said, "If only you had some news of my father, Süleyman."

Süleyman, stroking her head like a child's, tried to smile. "What can happen? Don't worry. There's nothing to be worried about."

Falling back onto the bed, Zeynep fell into a deep sleep full of nightmares. In her dreams Kalyopi was always strangling her and dragging her by the hair. Yorgi had his face pressed against the glass and was sticking out his tongue, and a hundred dogs were attacking her skirts and howling in unison.

Zeynep awoke to a hellish sound. In the room below a hundred rifles were being fired at once, hundreds of lights were bobbing up and down outside the curtains, and amid the explosions, shouts, and curses, foreign songs could be heard. She threw herself from the bed. They were murdering Süleyman. She was going to run, she was going to do something, but the second volley of shots, the sound of footsteps entering the room, the crude, blood-curdling curses, the moan of a wounded man— Zeynep covered her ears tightly with her hands on the bed. As soon as she realized they were torturing her wounded Süleyman, she fainted.

Then, a sudden awakening from a long darkness, a sleep of death.

She didn't know who had dragged her into the dining room. Her nightgown was in shreds, her feet were bare, and somehow her red shawl had been tossed across her shoulders. In the room eight or ten crazed and drunken enemy soldiers with wild faces were drinking. Standing amid seven or eight local Greek peasants, with his lieutenant's cap and his sword, was Yorgi. He was introducing her to his friends in Greek as "the mademoiselle of the house," and the mad and vulgar scene went on.

With his drunken, bloodshot eyes and disgusting guffaws Yorgi said to Zeynep, "Your father was good to me in the past, so I'm going to spare you. But you must dance for us. The captain here is a big man, and if you want he'll take you, little girl!"

But Zeynep, in the smoky, bloody room with its five lighted lamps, seemed a little larger than everyone else, and her eyes appeared so cool and terrifying that no one dared approach her openly.

Then, with the look of one who has drunk much but not become drunk, she pulled her shawl around her shoulders with the sang-froid of an animal trainer whose heart doesn't pound in the cage of a wild animal and went straight towards them.

Looking deep into Yorgi's eyes, she shouted in a fearless voice, "Where is Süleyman's body?"

Yorgi blinked his drunken eyes stupidly. In Zeynep's black pupils he saw Tall Osman's imperious, dark look.

"I didn't kill him, I swear!"

The one-eyed, swarthy, skinny, hideous captain started to laugh. He spoke in Greek.

"I killed him. I chopped up his head and carved out his eyes."

Then Zeynep did something which surprised everyone.

"You are the *kapitanos*?" she asked. "In that case I shall dance only for the *kapitanos*."

Perhaps Zeynep had lost her mind. The drunkards seemed to sober up for a moment and were looking at the captain strangely. Yorgi covered the corpse on the floor behind the table with military cloaks.

Zeynep cast off her shawl.

"Cover him with this, Yorgi!"

She spoke and moved so coldly and stonily that suddenly she resembled a commander who had recently received his command. She emptied the wine and *arak* bottles which Kalyopi had lined up on the table one by one into the soldiers' glasses, and amid their vulgarity she seemed calm and majestic. By encouraging the captain she had at least saved herself from some of the soldiers' indecencies. The captain was trying to incite the others to loot the farm. While they stuffed their pockets, he would amuse himself with the beautiful Turkish girl.

"Drink to me," the captain was saying.

While the soldiers were stripping the room, Yorgi said, "Dance like you danced last night for Süleyman."

An hour later the group looting the farm had grown frightfully with the addition of the Greek peasants. While they were drinking in front of the almond grove, someone stood up behind the closed curtains of the room where Zeynep and the captain were sitting. A strange creature appeared. In her white dress and disheveled hair, Zeynep threw herself out of the window wildly singing "Zeynep, My Zeynep" at the top of her voice. Off to the side the women's quarters were in flames.

Then she let out a blood-curdling scream. "*Kapitanos! Kapitanos!*"

Those who rushed into the room found the captain next to Süleyman with a sword plunged into his heart up to the hilt.

They were unable to save the captain's corpse from the smoke and flames.

Outside, in the light of the flames, Zeynep was singing "Zeynep, My Zeynep" and dancing, clapping her hands in the air and swaying like a peasant girl.

The wild men, as if sobered from their drunkenness in fear and astonishment at this sight, no longer wanted to continue the attack. But the village priest, Angelos, performed his duty.

THE AEGEAN FLOOR
Halıkarnas Balıkçısı
(*Translated by Robert Dankoff*)

The tangerine and orange trees sparkled from their tips to the ends of their branches in the moonlight, their flowers seeming like snowflakes that had landed on the trees, but a musk-scented snow, cool and warm at the same time, and their petals raining to the ground like very snow, covering the earth with specks of light. Each breath of the wind carried their scent for miles out to the open sea. The moonlit city, its whitewashed houses stretched along the shore, was sunk in a deep sleep. Only two people were not sleeping. Sitting on chairs at the shore, they were discussing the steamer *İnebolu* which had sunk a day or two before.

"My money, my money!" One of the men, a sailor to tell from his clothes, was addressing the other. "Exactly twenty thousand *liras*. It's in Ahmet's little safe. He was bringing it to me. How many fathoms did the steamer sink in, I wonder?"

"That I don't know," the other replied. "Alish is coming tomorrow. He's a sea wolf. He'll know what to do. He strolls about in fifty fathoms as though he's walking on the street. It's a good thing we learned his boat *Skafandar* was in Ayvalık, and sent him a telegram. Otherwise who could know what strange ports a boat might be in that left its harbor two months ago? You're cursing your luck, but in fact you're lucky! Look, we snapped our fingers and we found the man."

The other one groaned. "My money!"

• • •

They had had no news from their wives for two months. They had not stopped at a harbor with a post office, and after they finally landed at Ayvalık to get their mail, they put out to sea on the same day. This two-month absence from home had the effect of a great distance which causes a native song to captivate a person when he is far from his native land. In the divers' eyes their wives appeared cleansed of all their faults, and in their hearts and memories the everyday life they had spent in their homes became an exotic song.

That night they veered into a desolate bay. The stars, shining so far away, seemed surprisingly near, nearer than they seemed from the land. Was this because of the sea air or the night hour? The sailors, stretched out on the deck, felt close to one another, just like the stars. Their hearts overflowed from within and into the hearts of the others. This was an unusual state because on the sea, no matter how softhearted a man is, he has to appear thick-skinned, and even if his head is split open as the result of a practical joke he has to laugh it off as though nothing happened. That same day, when the mail was being distributed, and every man's banging heart was in his throat from worry verging on torture, even then they grit their teeth and put a tough look on their brows. Those who wander in exile do not admit that the everyday life of their homes can flow on its unruffled course. They think great disturbances must take place there to accord with the violence of their own feelings.

And what things turned up in their letters! Some of the wives had enclosed a cigarette which they had rolled with their own hands with the idea that, after all, it was a cigarette from home. Some had snipped off a piece of their wedding gowns and sent it along, as a token of the first day they gave themselves to their husbands. Those who received such letters stared at the moon and wove fantasies in a vapor of happiness. Those who received no letters — they were in a bad way. One such was Lostromo Süleyman. He was a grizzled man. One month before setting out to sea he got married. He only wanted to talk about his wife, but the words stuck in his throat. The sixty-year-old Captain Hüseyin was trying to comfort his friend's grief.

"You're a fool, Süleyman, old man. You haven't had a thing to eat tonight. Does one give up a beautiful lentil soup like that for the sake of a woman? I've hinted politely to you for how long now. Don't expect a letter from the strumpet. Forget her, old man. There's more than one fish in the sea."

"Stop it, for God's sake, Captain Hüseyin. You don't understand."

"What is there to understand? Come on, I'll tell you frankly. The strumpet has turned her back on you, and that's that! Cut the cord with a stroke of the knife, and end it once and for all. That's better than letting it drag out, like a slow puncture in a tire."

Playboy Davut and Kara Ahmet were talking in the stern. Kara Ahmet also had not received a letter that day. Though he did his best to hide it, his tear-filled eyes gleamed brightly, even in the moonlight. With a broken voice he said to Davut, "It's a damned nuisance smoking a cigarette without a mouthpiece. The smoke keeps getting in your eyes and makes them tear."

Davut kept twisting his greyed, curling mustache as if trying to lengthen it. "Ah, my son," he replied. "I understand. It's clear you're suffering. A long and sad time. And because it's long and sad, it's unbearable. Don't take it so hard, my boy. It's not worth it. Let's see, how old are you anyway? With men of your age luck is like a woman. Sometimes she loves you and lets you embrace her. Sometimes she doesn't love you and turns away. When my first wife died I too wept, in streams. Then my second wife ran off with another man, and again I wept." But a sudden squall on the land made the trees rustle and drowned out his voice. Way up on the mountain a solitary jackal howled sadly.

Diver Alish also had not received a letter from his home in Marmaris for the past two months. With his grizzled sailor's head bent forward, he was narrating in a loud, cold voice, "Her body was a white fire. When she put on clothes, it was as though the fire went out." His voice took on a moaning quality that nearly made the words unintelligible. "She was as sweet as my own soul. Our hut in the village was way up on the summit, overlooking the sea. Together, from above, we would watch the waves come in and go out. Once when I was away at sea a gentleman with fine clothes came to the village. I did not see him, but when I returned I heard the gossip. I did not want the smile she smiled at me to shine on another man. I asked her. I had bent over her. The wind was blowing. Her hair was flying. Sometimes it touched my face. 'You love the fellow, don't you?' I said. She started straight up in front of me. 'Yes,' she said. She was not ashamed. Do you see these two hands? With these hands I grasped her throat. I forced her on her knees in front of me, on the ground. I pressed, I pressed. I kept on pressing. I was looking at her eyes. They opened wide. Then they froze like stones. Her face went awry. Her half-open lips slid to one side. Saliva dripped from the corner of her mouth. She was about to suffocate. I was afraid of myself. I was going to be a murderer. I opened my hands. She fell down, pale. She had not died, thank God. I kissed her for the last time. Then I ran away. I ran without stopping. I ran. I was burning up."

It was very late. Most of the divers and sailors were nodding in sleep, as if to say "Yes, yes." Some of the crew had fallen asleep, and some were just lying and looking at the moon with open eyes. The sailors on deck, in the moonlight, resembled dead and wounded soldiers lined up on the battlefield after a battle is over. Now and then the pulleys on the mast or the bolts on the deck made a "je-e-ek, je-e-ek" sound, and this chimed in with the gnashing of someone's teeth or the sudden raving of someone in his sleep. Muhsin the Waddler at one moment cried out in his sleep, "I'm a son of a bitch if I'm lying. I don't have ten cents!" Those who had not fallen to sleep laughed. Just then, from the land, they heard the hooves of a horse coming at full gallop. A loud voice cried out, "Hey, boatmen! Is Diver Alish of Marmaris with you? He has a telegram, also a money order. And I brought a spare horse for him."

• • •

After he arrived in Ayvalık, Alish went by car like lightning through İzmir, Aydın, and Milas. To Alish in his excitement the car advanced at a snail's pace. Finally from the top of the hill he saw Bodrum castle, the shining white city, and the islands of the Sporad Archipelago. That was near Marmaris. He would quickly finish the job of diving to the steamer *Inebolu*. Then he would go over to Marmaris and see Chakır Hatije, who had not sent him a letter for the past two months.

In Bodrum he met Mr. Hashmet in the Yalı Café. After the usual pleasantries, Alish asked Mr. Hashmet how many fathoms the boat was under.

"I honestly don't know. But it can't be very deep. Ahmet was in one of the luxury cabins. One of the cabins ranged along the dining room on the inside. Two days before embarking at Marmaris he sent a letter. He wrote that he would be traveling with a Marmaris woman, and that he would put the money in a little safe."

"Alright, how much will you give me to retrieve this money?"

"Two hundred and fifty in advance, five hundred more after you've brought it up."

Captain Ateshoğlu Murat, who was boozing it up in a corner of the café with some '49 Yeni *raki*, spoke up. "Hey, brother, that's too little! Who knows what kind of water the steamer is in? That amount isn't even enough pay for the job of finding the steamer."

"I think the steamer will be found easily," said Mr. Hashmet.

"As long as it's left to thinking, the job is easy. If I think my aunt has a beard, then she's my uncle. I myself know of four steamer carcasses on that shoal you talked about. You have to find out which is which, first of all. On the sea floor it's like looking for a needle in a haystack," replied Ateshoğlu. While talking, he downed a glass.

The old diver called Grandpa Crab got to his feet on the other side of the room and came over walking sideways with his paralyzed legs. He raised his arm, which was also paralyzed, and put his huge hand on Alish's shoulder.

"Time was when I too was young and vigorous, straight and strong, just like you. Now look at me. 'Hey, Crab,' they said, 'come on and dive. Hey, Crab, bring up sponges, bring up money.' They said we'd bring up money, and they ruined me. At your age, when I was on the sea floor I never paid attention to an arm or leg going numb and itching. 'Oh well,' I would say, 'it's the cold, or it's a cramp. It's this, or it's that.' And that was at forty-five fathoms! One day I dove to twenty fathoms. When I came to the surface and got out of the diver's suit— But why tell you? You can see for yourself. From that time to this my legs won't hold.

"But I'll tell you this," he added. "My paralysis is only on land. Just let me down fifteen or twenty fathoms, put the pressure of that water over my body, and give me a four- or five-mile-an-hour floor current— By God, on the sea floor I'm like a bird, like a balloon."

Mr. Hashmet paid no attention to these words. He was thinking about the money he was going to pay. "Seven hundred and fifty *liras*," he said, adding, "and for an easy job, not worth seven hundred and fifty *liras*."

Grandpa Crab spoke up again. "That's not very much. Because you just now said— First he'll come from the deck to the head of the stairway. He'll go down the stairs. He'll turn left and right four or five times. Every time he turns there's a danger the air hose will form an elbow, the air supply will be cut off, and the diver will suffocate. For you this job is a matter of twenty thousand *liras*. For Alish it's a matter of life or death."

Mr. Hashmet and Alish arrived shortly afterwards at the mouth of the İzmir Gulf, where the *İnebolu* had sunk. A diving boat was hired. The boat passed out of the muddy water of İzmir harbor into the emerald water outside, and then beyond into the dungeonlike dark violet of the deep. It advanced for hours. Then the two sailors standing at the bow shouted, "There's the shoal!" A green spot appeared above the deep blue sea valley. They came over it and weighed anchor. The shoal was very wide. It was as if the soil of the deep sea floor had rebelled against the ocean resting on it and, starting fitfully from within the green darkness, had struggled to emerge from the water and into the sun. The divers surveyed the depths with sea windows. A huge black stain appeared over a shelf-like projection of the shoal. That blackness was the steamer *İnebolu*. The scene underwater was gloomy. Schools of bream and groupers swam lazily around the mast and the chimney.

Alish immediately put on his oilcloth diving suit. They put the helmet over his head and screwed it tight to the metal ring at the throat. As they turned the wheel of the oxygenator, the suit began to swell up with the flow of air. Alish hesitated a moment. In this job the possibility of death was ever present. But he was used to it and finally shrugged off the danger. He opened the air valve with his hand and dived into the water. As air escaped through the helmet, his body became heavier and descended easily toward the bottom. Clouds of air bubbles flew up from Alish. The *İnebolu* seemed to be rising toward the diver. He alighted on the ship. Varicolored fish with calf eyes, seeing the whiteness of his hands, butted against them. Alish hit them back with his fists. Schools of small fish passed before the glass of his helmet. Some looked at Alish, resting against the glass and opening and closing their mouths and gills regularly. Had Alish been a novice he would have become dizzy at this sea world, striking and revolving before his eyes.

From the pitch-black cave of the dining room door a huge leer-fish emerged, whiter and whiter, into the sun, and glimmered silvery blue. Alish heard something go "clack, clack" in the distance. This sound, like two people slapping each other on the back, was a shark opening and closing its gills and approaching at top speed. The shark reached the diver and stopped in front of his glass. Its eyes were like automobile headlights. It eyed Alish with its leaden, frozen look. Alish felt a wave of nausea. He bent his head toward the shark and opened the valve. A jet of brightly shining air bubbles poured over the shark. It took off at once, as though struck by lightning. Considering the way the shark had approached the steamer, it must have fed on the human corpses there and, having tasted the bait, had been frequenting the ship.

Alish entered the dining room together with thousands of small fish and began descending the stairs. As he advanced, the green gloom turned into a purple darkness, then into a deep velvet blackness. The diver lit his torch. The small fish entering the electric light wheeled around like multicolored Roman candles. Crawling on the floor and ceiling of the dining room were a colorful assortment of sea worms and insects. Alish walked on tiptoe in the dark silence.

The cadavers of two ship's stewards and three passengers were floating in the dining room along with the fish and the jellyfish. Alish opened the door of one of the cabins. Two rather large fish escaped like lightning through the portholes. With the current and eddy caused by the door opening and the fish escaping, a woman's body came from inside the gloomy cabin and, turning about in the water, landed on Alish. The corpse's face struck Alish's face. Alish screamed in horror. His hair stood on end. Stepping back, he let his torch survey the room. Swaying on the ceiling like two balloons were the bodies of two blond-haired children. They had been floating freely inside the room and, bumping the ceiling, remained there. "A mother and two children!" Alish thought. "That means this isn't the right room." He did not know why. On his way out he closed the door slowly and carefully so that the fish would not eat the children. In the cabin next door, he found a woman holding her child in her arms. Probably she had tried to hide the child from the water and save it from drowning. The steel fingers of horror twisted Alish's heart like a laundered garment. "This filthy business isn't worth a million *liras*," he said to himself. "Now that I've become mixed up in it, God let me finish it quickly! I'm going to Marmarıs."

Never in his life had he longed to see his Hatije so much as at that moment.

He opened the door of the third cabin. A man who exactly fit Mr. Hashmet's description floated into his torch light, half bald, with a black moustache. The sea worms, having climbed up to the ceiling, had passed onto the man and had completely eaten away the softest parts of his body — his eyes. "By now," thought Alish, "they must have gone from the eyesockets into the brain and, eating that, have made their nest there."

The sea worms hung from the man's nostrils and mouth in clusters, like leeches. Alish looked around the room with his torch. The light struck a woman. Some strands of her hair had caught on the couch leg and her body floated, suspended by the hairs. Her back was turned toward Alish. Hanging free as she was from the head down, the woman was dancing with the current as though alive. Alish had heard that the woman was from Marmaris and had boarded at Marmaris with that fellow. "Who is it? Do I know her?" he wondered, and added, "Whoever you are, forgive me."

He took the woman by the throat. Her flesh had become as soft as butter, and his fingers sank in. He turned the woman's face around. Because the sea worms could not crawl on four or five strands of hair, they had not touched her eyes. Through the round glass in front of Alish's face, the woman's deep green eyes looked mournfully into his own.

It was then that Alish nearly went mad. He could not believe what he saw. Suspiciously, he looked more carefully. Again he could not believe it. An uproar, as if the sky had fallen, a mortal blow, a cry, whistle, scream tore through his brain. The eyes were Chakır Hatije's. He understood why she had not written for two months. Had he seen her in that situation alive he might have done something criminal in his first angry attack. But now the woman's green eyes were looking into his, as though pleading with their glance, "Forgive me! Look! I've received my punishment! I'm so repentant. I suffered so much while I was drowning," she seemed to be saying.

Alish, no longer angry, instead felt that mysterious compassion of the human heart. He pitied the woman. It was he who felt like saying to her, "Forgive me." He decided to reverse his steps and go outside. But it was as though no more air remained in the helmet, as though the ocean had gathered together and leaned on him with all its weight. He suffocated. He was crushed.

● ● ●

The pilot holding the rope in the boat above was a master at this job and understood the slightest twinge of the rope. Something was happening. He pulled the rope. It was caught. He ordered more air given. The air did not go through. For three hours they struggled, and finally drew up the air hose and rope with their ends empty. The living heart, which did not buckle under the terrible Aegean depths, burst in the depths of that mysterious compassion.

Mr. Hashmet was hopping up and down on the motor deck and tearing his hair. He bellowed like a calf. "My money, my money is gone!"

THE KARABULUT FAMILY
Halıkarnas Balıkçısı
(Translated by Janet Heineck)

Once upon a time, the family Karabulut thronged like the stones on the Milas road. One ran into them in Küllük, Bodrum, and Marmarıs. They were all hardworking sons of the sea. But storms drowned and extinguished them one by one. Finally, the seventy-year-old Karabulut Selim Dede, his son Direk Mahmut, his two grandsons, eleven or twelve years old, and his four small granddaughters were all who remained in Bodrum. In order to illustrate this wonder, Selim Dede used to point to his fist, which resembled a huge walnut log, and say, "In order to move the oars at sea, the five fingers must help each other. We stay together and live." Nevertheless their boat, the *Kısmet*, sank. Selim said, "Whatever we do, such is our fate. If the boat sinks, we'll be saved, thank God."

No one used to tease Kerpeten Agha Halil or laugh at him, because they were anxious that perhaps one day they would need him. Kerpeten Agha used to stand on foot, in sun and rain, from morning to evening, leaning against the eaved wall of the coffee shop next to the mosque. His clothes had frayed from his back, ragged and tattered. When people saw him, they considered him less than human, but according to what the villagers said, he counted his money not piece by piece, but by the shovelful. He used to make a loan to whomever wished, on equivalent security. He had come up with a thousand and one ways to help his fellow man.

Although he was not a seaman, he had four or five boats. He used to rent them to whomever wanted one. He would also give them money if they wished. When a boat returned from a trip, someone else would get the money he lent, a third of the profit from the boat rental, and a share of the boat, too. Because of this, his boats were called "the devil's boats." When Kerpeten Agha was asked why he didn't go to sea, he used to reply, "If I should drown, who would look after the Muslims on land?" The Karabuluts, who had no boat, used to get both money and one of his boats from Kerpeten Halil in order to bring coal from Finike. The journey to Finike took place in fine weather. When they started back, Direk Mahmut sent a telegram to his wife Kara Ayshe from Marmara saying, "We're coming tomorrow night." The following morning, because she knew Mahmut loved baked gumbo with lamb meat, Kara Ayshe bought what she needed from the market and cooked the meal, singing all the while. Two small daughters, the third was at the breast, were asking, "What will father bring us?"

• • •

The season was that treacherous September. The seamen were stricken as though hit by a bullet between the head and the back of the neck. When the boat passed between Rhodes and Sümbeki, the color of the sea and the sky began to resemble the Finike coal in the hold. Suddenly a southeast whirlwind which struck and trampled down the earth, breaking hundred-year-old trees on land like chaff and bringing ruin to the sea, started to blow. The boat was running right before the wind as though pursued by a thousand demons and devils. The black phosphorescent water was burning like white flame, and it was as though sparks were flying in the wake. Oh, my God! This was pandemonium! When the boat was transferring goods at Tekirburnu, lightning was pouring out of the dark sky. When it burst out from the first promontory, those on the boat saw, by the lightning flash, a tornado beside the second cape. This pitch-black monster which began from the sea and reached toward the sky, spiraling and spinning at great speed, was roaring as though it would overcome the thunder, drinking the sea and ascending to the clouds, and from there blowing violently on all sides. The ship's rigging was leaning to the southeast, on the port side. The ship couldn't pass between the twisted headlands because it would certainly be spread like soft butter on their rocks. If the boat were headed to the open sea, the squalls that were now bending the masts like whips and making the deck creak would rock the rigging from port to starboard, and the boat itself would turn ninety somersaults as though it were a tossed nutshell. Sometimes the craziest course of action is the wisest. The boat made for the space straight ahead of the tornado. The probability of death was ninety-nine in a hundred. While the ship was rushing toward the gaping mouth of death, Selim Dede took his two grandchildren in his arms. The two boys had secretly come onto the boat at Bodrum and had hidden in the hold. Their mother, Kara Ayshe, who couldn't resist the boys' entreaties, had said, " Alright, go and hide in the hold." Selim Dede, so that the boys would not be aware of approaching death and not endure torment, said, "Sing a song! Give passage, sea! The Karabuluts are coming! Call on God!" He raised his voice. The thin voices of the two small children of the last Karabuluts were mixed with those of the adults. But they could not overcome the sea's roaring, the tornado's whistling, and the tear-choked weeping of the wind. Selim Dede turned and looked at his son Direk Mahmut for a moment. It was as though fire were sparking from his eyes watching the tornado. He was standing bolt upright at the rudder; the two rows of his clenched teeth shone when the lightning flashed. The ship entered one side of the tornado at top speed but didn't emerge from the other. The tornado tossed the last Karabuluts into the air together with their songs, their last prayers, and the flying sails like pieces of paper burning in a roaring fire and mixed the lightning with the clouds. The keeper of the Tekirburnu lighthouse, the late Veli of Bodrum, saw the event and telephoned Bodrum.

• • •

The night the Karabuluts were to come, the sea at Bodrum's Değirmen cape was snoring and now and then would let out a deep sigh like uneasy sleepers who turn from one side to the other in their sleep. The sailors had made fast to the boats four or five anchors from stem to stern. Those in the coffee shop were saying to each other, "It's not the day to go to sea. The boats' bottoms should be drawn up onto the dry beach. A man should take his children on his knees in front of his fireplace and should feel that behind him his wife is looking after the house."

The countryside learned that the Karabuluts had died. But Kara Ayshe didn't know. The following evening she was watching the sea, taking her three children and going up to Göktepe on the other side of Yenimahalle. The child at the breast was crying. The baby's weeping was breaking the woman's heart. It was like a bad omen. She sang the child a lullaby in a voice that made one feel the trembling of her tears.

Then two neighbor women came toward her. They asked after her health, as if there were nothing out of the ordinary. Then came two sailors, friends of her husband's. They talked about this and that with her and, after looking at her with pitying eyes, departed. They were speaking between themselves in a low, nearly inaudible voice. The miserable woman was suspicious and afraid of this unusual kindness. She held her baby close as though they would take it from her hands. Others came and took her by the arm. They led her toward her house. The other two children were hanging on to her coat. The woman was looking with frightened eyes into every face she saw. When she passed before the coffee shop, everyone inside came out and looked at her. The wretch, unaware that she was a widow, was saying only, "My God, my God." When she saw every one of her neighbors gathered before her house, she understood everything. Not one man by the name of Karabulut was to return to land. The woman let out a long scream, plunged her fingernails into her thick hair and tore it out, and collapsed into her house.

THE PEACH ORCHARDS
Refik Halit Karay
(Translated by Niki Gamm)

The road which went to the river, once free of the small town, passed through innumerable peach orchards which extended as far as the eye could see. Even in the shady places which the overflowing tributaries left muddy and damp in June, the plants would continue to sprout the whole summer. While the hot sun matured the fruit on the hills of trees, clover sprang up in the damp earth and the meadows fluffed up. In the coolness of the waters, the fresh grass smell, and the shade and abundance, spring in these gardens stretched all the way to winter.

On still, hot days filled and permeated with the scent of the peach overflowing everywhere, those who were free came down from the town in groups and, after bathing in the river, lay in the shady meadows. The ripe peaches on the high branches released their odor from the stalks and it trickled slowly, continually, to the ground with rich fragrance and into the meadows among those reclining. Nor did it end with the crop gathering, for half the crop remained on the trees maturing and eventually falling to the earth to mix with it and be lost.

These sheltered, dim, fragrant places came pleasantly to those freed from the dust-scented, hot streets filled with the screaming of the town's children. Toward evening, the government officials put *raki* in their saddle bags, mounted their donkeys, and came to these gardens. They set up their drinking trays, indulged in conversation, and read poetry. The pleasure of the peach orchards sent their reputation to far shores and everyone's tongue. Many officials devoted to pleasure and fond of amusement longed for this place and gathered here, so that the town became a free and easy stopping place for libertine judges and roguish civil servants. Its people became so addicted to pleasure and amusement that no sin remained which was not tolerated.

Here was Anatolia's Saadabad. As in the original Saadabad, musical instruments played continually, professional dancers performed, and poetry was read and written. Most of the liquor-prone administrators and officials were poets. They wrote poems in the style of Nedim, discussed meter and mysticism, and talked about the whirling dervishes and other mystic orders. Their lives passed sweetly in talk and music. These pleasure-loving officials refrained from meddling in things which would bring them trouble. They virtually made the town their own, put up houses, opened pools, and built arbors. Naturally, most of these were men whom the previous ruler had not regarded favorably and had sent here as punishment. Without hope of promotion, they attached no importance to official matters and looked to their own amusement.

It was a hot, oppressive summer day. The newly arrived secretary-general was astonished that no one else remained in the office at the time of afternoon prayer. All had set out for the peach orchards, mounting one of the soft-saddled, sturdy, steady donkeys in the inner courtyard of the government building. Everyone down to the secretaries, scattering hellos to each other, joking, buried in the midst of overflowing saddlebags, was going off into the distance contentedly and hurriedly. Outside the city, a dust cloud which touched the sun between the meadow and the orchards, growing and broadening more and more, pointed out the road they took.

Agah Bey, although uninformed about world affairs, was a man who had grown up with theories, obstinate and with no taste for pleasure. After leaving the school of political science, he fled to Europe, but through the intervention of an influential man he was able to return to Istanbul. After he had been detained for four whole months in the Ministry of Public Security detention ward, he was finally sent here with the position of secretary-general.

In Anatolia, staying in inns and sleeping in villages on his way to his assignment, sorrow filled his heart, and he decided to serve his country earnestly. Weighty thoughts of reforms, reorganization, and reconstruction filled his head. He thought that in this very small community he would see to great affairs and accomplish works which would astound everyone. He would work without stopping or resting. "Boldness is necessary," he thought, and he was sure that he could bring to reason every one of the supervisors and administrative officials. He did not comprehend the laziness and inertia which was gripping the country. "What is this somnolence, this indifference?" he asked himself, and could find no answer.

No, he would be an entirely different sort of official: a European civil servant. And this small country was such a good testing ground.

But the first day he fell into despair. The civil administrator talked to him about how little business there was in this town and about taking life easy and resting from his exertions. The town judge, reading verses from Yahya, spoke of the pleasure of love and the necessity of libertinism. The accountant, between *salaams* and ringing laughter, found an opportunity to praise the doubly distilled twenty-two-proof *raki*. The trust property administrator also came in and, upon Agah Bey's mentioning that he was single, advised him that here he would not suffer. The first district gendarmerie chief, a powerfully built, senile man of about sixty-five, disrespectfully used vulgar language to his face in welcoming him and, for no reason, described the prophyry marble clock tower in the square and the broad stone platform of the high domed public bath built by one of the sultans. To whomever he met, he also spoke of the peach orchards and talked about the life of pleasure and amusement.

Agah Bey was bewildered. At once he grimly rejected the accountant's proposal of "If you wish, let's go to the orchards. Our mounts are ready. We'll have fun!" He remained alone in the government building.

In the glaring, blinding brightness of the midafternoon sun, he was compelled to walk like a stranger these streets unknown to him. The inner quarters of the town were silent and still with the emptiness of festival days. He met no one, apart from a few old grandmothers and now and then the men who carry water from the fountains. Those too looked at him strangely as though surprised at his walking there when everyone else was in the orchards. Later it became an angry, hazy sunset; amid the voices calling one to prayer the dim, sleepy lights lit up one after another and dreary night wrapped the town. He went to bed early.

Only a few hours had passed when he was awakened from sleep by gay voices and ran to the window. Red-flaming torches illuminated the narrow streets, and the officials on their soft-saddled donkeys which he had seen daily in the government building courtyard came by rather tipsily, joking and laughing. The noise of those late-stayers could be heard in the distance. Agah Bey became angry. These men who were up to their necks in a sea of pleasure and amusement passed their lives in an unworried, calm, fish-like manner, and were never concerned about the world. Starting the next day, he decided to appear more zealous, more resolute, and more harsh to these vulgar, ordinary men and to treat them more roughly. He fell alseep again, his fists clenched, his heart rancorous.

Every day in this city which rocked with wedding-house gaiety the new secretary-general suffocated with boredom. At first he was busy with his work and thought that he would have no spare time, but his duties were few. Yawning, he relaxed in his room and slept. At first, he zealously gave detailed memoranda to the civil administrator concerning the improvement of the community, and of plows and scythes, and the necessity of changing the oxcarts.

No response came. Whenever he opened a conversation about progress and civilization, they would listen to his long, nervous, frustrated points with such meaningless, vacant looks not even etiquette and politeness could hide that he would feel like crying. No, it would not be possible to do any work. Lack of funds and the laziness of colleagues were obstacles to every enterprise. The enthusiasm which was bubbling in his heart, his wish to serve, slowly faded and cooled. This was an unendurable life.

Anyway, his friends who were also in government were weary of him and had turned away from this fellow who wouldn't see reason, who didn't understand amusement. The former secretary-general was remembered with longing. He was a roguish man from İzmir. The night he first came to town they took him for a free meal. He drank and drank and became so exuberant that he attached wooden spoons to his fingers and, amid the men whom he had so recently met, clattered out folk dances for hours. And he was a poet. In the morning he would immediately write a poem to describe the gathering of the night before. He attained the approval of the civil administrator and even the judge kissed his eyes and said, "Worthy man, you are the Fuzuli of the age!"

The present director understood nothing of poetry and *raki*. So why had he come? Why had he become a problem for the group? Although two months had already passed, they could not even bring him to the nightly drinking in the peach orchards. They could not induce the thought of pleasure and amusement in his head. The accountant extolled twenty-two-proof peach vodka in vain. In vain did the trust property administrator praise the daughters of Eve whom he smuggled into his house.

One day the accountant insisted that he would be offended if he refused. They wouldn't stay late, they wouldn't make him uncomfortable; it would be just an outing in the country. The judge, the trust property administrator, the postal official, four or five people, no crowd. He feared that it would be rude this time to refuse. "Okay," he said. In the town he was suffocating from loneliness and idleness. Once he came, perhaps he too would enjoy it, seeing this gathering as naturally appropriate; it was nonsense to remain shy of the beauty of nature.

In the afternoon they mounted the donkeys who were ambling, soft-saddled, comfortable animals; it was a strange gait which these tiny-footed creatures had, a quick, rhythmic swaying. Agah Bey was pleased, especially when they entered the peach orchards and were saved from the dust and sun. The moss-like, dark green, half-damp clover and the sound of water enhanced one's pleasure. They went a long way, winding between two high hedges covered with oleaster and blackberries. The smell of the peaches relaxed his nerves. He watched with a strange, desirous eye the girls who, now bending, now rising, were gathering fruit. At intervals they would come across women in groups, their faces damp, their hands filled with bundles. These were returning from the river. It was the custom of the area in summer that both sexes enter the water in the open and bathe for a long time, joking together and shouting to one another. How big-hipped and large-bodied these women were. They had amorous looks too which, like intense heat, brought palpitations to his heart.

The accountant was fond of a kind of opaquely colored, almost pink peach *raki*. "Let us see what you will think of my water of eternal youth." He extended the bottle inquiringly. Agah Bey drank it; it was a pleasant drink, a little astringent, but heavily scented and odd-tasting. On the far side the secretaries were busy setting out the *raki* table and preparing snacks and salads; the janitors, nearer, were making a fire and roasting *kebabs*. This roasting and its smell mixed with the peach scent gave a man a pleasant appetite in the evening's coolness. They were drinking continually and eating spoonful after spoonful of hot roasted eggplant covered with yogurt and salads with sauce.

Toward nightfall they returned. From the branches, a reddish half-moon rose up sadly, splitting the darkness, while someone at the back of the group was singing out loud a line from a famous song: "I cannot stand your cruelty any more." At intervals a large drum rumbled, like a propeller striking the Bosporus waters on still nights.

Agah Bey was slightly tipsy, and they took him to his home. At once he undressed and went to bed. Unfamiliar, heavy, leaden sleep — vulgar sleep — which rested his stomach's weariness and his existence but not his brain, was so pleasant.

The next day was Friday. Early, his friends sent word that they were going to the river to bathe. On the way back they would eat lunch at the water mill and would drink their evening *raki* at the top of the pool which the civil administrator had recently made.

He didn't want to go. But in this dung-soiled dusty town how did one pass a long day alone? Moreover, he had never seen the river. Even if he didn't bathe, wasn't it necessary to see it once? They mounted the donkeys and, after passing the peach orchards, plunged into an uncared-for, dense, luxuriant quince grove.

On both sides of the water a number of small pools were enclosed with entwined branches and sheltered by their shade. The water which fell from above deepened the river there and made it easier for bathers. Agah Bey was not of a mind to swim. He just watched for a while, thinking it looked pleasant. This hot, sweaty body of his, poisoned with the evening's alcohol, naturally would be refreshed and benefit from the cool water. For him, they found a finely sanded, enclosed deep pool, and he bathed freely.

Upon returning, this perfumed air easily entered his body whose appetite was growing as though the aroma was flowing into his blood, and peachy, cool, delicious breath filled his lungs.

At the water mill, they found cooked to a complete turn a fat kid goat roasted on a spit which had been sent out there and prepared earlier in the morning. In addition, five or ten different kinds of dishes were ready. They ate so much that they had no strength to start walking. At the side of the stream beneath the huge willows whose branches were hanging down, they spread out and fell asleep one after another.

At the house of the civil administrator, the evening passed in a more cultured manner and more elegantly. *Raki* was offered from cut glass and crystal decanters, and hors d'oeuvres like fish roe and caviar, which were rare in Anatolia, were eaten. A director of the district tax collection office who had come to the area on vacation played a beautiful violin, and a title deeds registrar made a perfect imitation of the noises of the Istanbul open market. They were very amused.

Agah now joined every party at once. Finally they said that he would need to purchase a donkey for himself. Men were sent to the villages and markets. A large, firm-gaited, comfortable donkey was found for him and a new velvet saddle with purple tassels, ribbons, and fringes was built. Now in the evenings, the secretary-general joined the others in the inner courtyard of the government building.

Most of the memoranda and the decisions were neglected. Of course, he no longer had time for working and resting. In August, the hunt began. They rose early and spread into the vineyards, and shot all kinds of partridge. The entire town was under obligation to serve the amusement of the officials. For days the gendarmes from distant villages brought famous hounds; in winter, the greyhounds were reserved for the rabbit hunt. This was a perfect, carefree life.

At one party, he was taken aside and the criminal court judge, who was surreptitiously guzzling *raki* from his coffee cup, said to Agah, "Let's get you married, son. In this country you shouldn't remain single!" It was a real problem. He too felt he was suffering inwardly, melting away.

One dark night, the trust property official invited him through the back door of his house into a low-ceilinged room on the ground floor. Inside were two women. Both of them were pretty, plump, and well-known. They were smoking cigarettes in an experienced manner, accustomed to men, and they conversed happily in fine language, their accents refined from thus half-secretly serving a long line of officials.

One was dark, tall and shapely; her breasts under the narrow vest remained young and firm. She stared deeply with dreamy, pleasant eyes. The other was blonde, large and striking. She braided her long hair in fifty-six strands and let it go down her back like a rare shawl. On their heads they had tied identical, crocheted kerchiefs. They wore shirts edged with the same embroidery stitch, and on their feet were a kind of rose-colored stocking. Their boots were of soft, yellow leather.

The brunette sang folk songs in a full, self-possessed voice, and the blonde danced coquettishly. Agah Bey found this party much better than he had expected. "Truly a nice, pleasant thing!" he said, thanking his friend. The other told him all about the town, how sometimes the roughnecks gathered in front of the homes of women of this kind and at midnight would frighten the quarter by firing clumsy muzzle-loading gunpowder pistols. The following day the policemen would seize the guilty and thrash them soundly in a jail cell; then the incident would be closed.

When winter came, evening gatherings began again. They gave

helva parties, reserved that famous, magnificent bath for private use, and ate food garnished with pickles. Here there was a toleration for parties and amusements which were forbidden in the capital and in the provincial government centers. No one saw much beyond the pleasure of being able to enjoy himself easily at little expense, and no one was intolerant of it.

Agah Bey very slowly changed his habits. Now he could not do without *raki*. He had his *raki* distilled before his eyes from the pure pulp in an earthen still. Nor could he remain without a woman; visitors frequently entered his house by the back door. He became accustomed to walking about coolly and in breezy comfort in his house robe. He would undress as soon as he came home, set up his *nargile* in the room off the garden and seat himself in the corner. Let the party begin. He relaxed among his comfortable corner pillows on a puffed-up mattress and side cushions; he gained more and more weight.

He had no further desire for work. Even amusements such as chess with the chief judge and backgammon with the accountant at the coffeehouse with the fountain kept him inside, preventing his going to the office. Besides, winter passed lightly, like autumn, in this mild country on a slope overlooking the Mediterranean. If a little breeze blew cold, they threw dry olive logs on hearths which reached to the ceiling and, while stuffing turkeys and roasting geese, they fully enjoyed the winter. This carefree, insouciant life had extinguished the fire in his heart. Now, when he recalled his ideas on duty, improvement and reforms in days gone by, he would smile, gurgling his *nargile*. To excuse himself he would say to his friends, "I was green. What could you expect?"

Eventually, the second summer came. A ripe, relaxing fruit smell from the window would fill the room. Intermingled with warm wind, it would call everyone to the numberless peach orchards which stretched as far as the eye could see. Agah Bey, who used to give speeches against somnolence in his tight frock coat the previous year, now, after deeply inhaling this fragrant air, would stretch comfortably in his full house robe with its sleeves pushed up, recline on a newly fluffed-up pillow and say,

"Delightful!"

THE GIRL WHO HEARD VOICES
Yakup Kadri Karaosmanoğlu
(Translated by John Taylor)

As we descended the rocky footpath, the horses' legs began to shake, and when we saw the willow trees and the cool spring, we felt a need to rest. At the foot of the slope was a small, old village. We saw the black roofs from above.

"This is Garipler?" I asked my travelling companion.

Garipler was melancholy and desolate, sqeezed into the bottom of a naked, rock fissure. Soon we would pass through it and come up the other face. My companion left his tired horse to itself. He fell on his knees and put his hands and face in the water. I had at least to lead my horse to the trunk of one of the willow trees and pulled him towards the grove. My companion stood up where he was squatting.

"My God, sir, don't tie him there. It's a saint's tomb," he called out.

I looked around. There was nothing that resembled a tomb, but under the tree I was approaching were some pieces of green painted rock, and above the stones, hanging from a branch, a broken lamp. My companion, standing some distance away with his sleeves rolled up and wiping his arms with a handkerchief, pointed to the branch and its hundreds of bits of colored cloth.

"Yes, exactly there," he said.

My companion was a man from that region and knew every inch of the whole area. I asked him what sort of tomb it was, whose it was, and what danger could come from tying an animal to it. I laughed and walked over to his side. But his attitude was serious, as though he were about to explain something very important. "Let me tell you, sir," he said, after he had taken his tobacco box from between the folds of his sash and passed it to me.

This is his story.

"This tomb is the tomb of the girl who heard voices. She has no love at all for strangers, and that's why I told you not to go near. I saw the girl who heard voices myself, sir, because it has been only three or three and a half years since she died. She was a girl from this village, but she was more beautiful than the girls of any city, more learned and more wise. She memorized the Koran from the village hoja and knew a lot of hymns. Her voice was wonderful; once a week she would read religious poems to the women of the village. She was sixteen or seventeen. She had hair so long it hung to her ankles, and everyone who looked into her eyes trembled like a leaf. Her real name was Emine.

"Four or five years ago Emine was betrothed to the richest and most reputable young man in the village. The gossips had it that these two young people had loved each other from childhood and that's how they came to be engaged. But the week they were engaged war broke out, the cursed war in the Balkans, and the young man left and joined the army. In fact, he was wealthy. He could have bought an exemption, but he didn't want to, and also his father wanted him to go. He left and never came back. First, we heard that he had been taken prisoner by the enemy. Then news came that while fighting the Serbs — maybe in Monastir or somewhere — he was killed. This terrible news left the whole village in mourning; from seven-year-old children to seventy-year-old adults, men and women cried and cried. There was no one in this or in the surrounding villages who hadn't loved him. The strange thing was that this news didn't give Emine any extraordinary grief. It didn't make her wail or cry. She merely didn't eat or drink or speak to anyone for a few days. She didn't do any work, but just wandered about sadly. That much was natural."

My companion stopped talking. When he had finished his cigarette and blown it from his heavy lips to the ground, he took on a more devout attitude and continued his story.

"But one day something changed. Her face turned as yellow as a lemon and her eyes began to burn like fire. Often she would stretch her head out and say to those around, 'Quiet! Quiet!' She would listen to a voice that no one else could hear. 'What are you listening to, Emine?' they would ask, but she didn't answer. Days passed like that. Emine was quiet. She listened. But not too much time passed before she began to recite the words she was hearing. 'Go, Emine! The enemy is coming. Go, Emine! The enemy is surrounding the homeland!' she would say. 'The first time,' she said, 'I heard it in my sleep. I opened my eyes and listened, and I heard it again. Now I hear it more and more often. It comes as though from afar, like from the beyond!' Sometimes the voice said to her, 'Emine, why are you doing nothing?' Sometimes, 'Go! Go, Emine! The enemy is coming! Why are you doing nothing? The enemy is surrounding the country!' Before long we knew what these words meant. The news spread that the Balkans were lost. But Emine didn't hear the news, or if she heard she didn't understand. She didn't hear or understand anything but that voice. 'Emine, the enemy is coming! Emine, they're surrounding the country!'

"Then suddenly one night she flew out into the street. She ran, screaming from one end of the village to the other, 'We're going! We're going! Get ready! Now! We're going!' 'Where? Who's going?' they asked her. 'Women, girls, no matter how young! To the enemy! To war! To war! To war!' The village was alarmed. They thought she had gone crazy and shut her in her house and locked the door. 'Let me free. I'll go alone. Didn't Black Fatma go? I'll go too. It's a duty. A duty!' said this girl who heard voices. Then she would suddenly go silent. Her eyes would bulge, and she would stretch out her neck and listen to that voice from the deep, from far off. While she listened to the voice, she was quiet and peaceful, but when she started to repeat the words herself, no one could restrain her. 'Don't interfere with her. She is wiser than all of us. She has attained a place we will never reach,' said the village hoja. So everyone left Emine to herself. Five or six days later, the girl who heard voices disappeared. 'In the middle of the night, we were all sleeping comfortably. Emine got up, tore her father's scimitar from the wall, and left,' her mother said. She left, but for where? They searched the mountains, the valleys, and the hills for days, but she was not to be found. Emine had mysteriously disappeared."

At this point my companion left his story again for a while. He rolled another cigarette and drew on it sadly.

"Then one morning before sunrise, one of the villagers, a shepherd named Mehmet, found her at the head of this stream lying on her face. He poked her. He tried to lift her and saw that she was dead. Her clothes were torn and her body was covered with wounds and bruises, but her eyes were looking somewhere and her mouth seemed to be smiling. Mehmet ran to the village and told them. They came and looked, unable to understand how it had happened. Justice officials and doctors came from the town. They said that there was a large knife wound under her left breast. That's what they said, but no one, not her mother, her father, those who washed the corpse nor any one from the village, said they saw the wound. But that's not important. Finally, they brought her here and buried her, and for three nights there was a holy light over her grave. Now all the villagers call her 'the girl who heard voices.' They've forgotten her real name.

"People come to visit not just from Garipler, but from all around. But the most faithful visitors are the young women and girls. Young men leaving for the army don't go without stopping to make vows to her for their safe return. It has been two years since the present war started. It's a custom now. The young women and girls whose men are at war come in the evening, climb the cliff on the other side, turn their faces toward the tomb of the girl who heard voices, and call out, 'Is he killed or returning safely?' The girl who heard voices answers them from the deep. Sometimes she cries, 'Killed,' and sometimes 'Coming home.' "

"Why don't they come up close and ask? Why do they only shout from afar?" I asked my travelling companion.

"Because she doesn't answer when they are close."

"In that case, let's call when we climb the other side."

"Only if you have someone fighting in the war. Otherwise it's useless."

However, we mounted our horses, passed through the village, and climbed the other slope. I felt an evil curiosity and inquisitiveness that might destroy the innocent faith of the village women, and I couldn't keep myself from crying to the girl just once. "Girl who heard voices, girl who heard voices!" I called. The rocks returned my words.

THE PIGEON SHOOT
Yakup Kadri Karaosmanoğlu
(Translated by Robert Dankoff)

"No-o-o, don't touch my pigeons."

One of the things in life the elderly farm owner loved most, perhaps *the* thing he loved most, was his pigeons. Ever since he was a young man, not his fields or his sheepfolds, his stables or his chicken coops, occupied him so much as the pigeons he kept in the courtyard of his barn. That was why, even though his family name was widely respected, he was known both in the town and the village simply as "Birder" Hüseyin Bey.

Bird-raising is like drink, women, and gambling. Hüseyin Bey knew nothing of these three addictions, which can destroy homes, disperse families, and end in death or a life of crime. But his bird-raising took their place. There were times in his life when, for the sake of this occupation, this hobby, he simply sacrificed his wife, his daughters, and his business. He forgot them. He lost hold of himself, in the distracted state of an ecstatic.

By now he possessed the most beautiful, the most rare, and the most pureblooded pigeons in those regions, perhaps in the world. For thirty years, and with a thousand cares and a thousand attentions, he had raised who knows how many generations of these delicate creatures and had expended who knows how much sweat in this science, so that today he could finally spend the happiest hours of his life amid these poor, noble birds, honored with the purest natural selection. He would call each of them by its own name. To an untutored eye, these creatures appeared the same color, the same height and shape. But they had secret marks, apparent only to him, which distinguished them from one another. Some had thin, coral-colored rings on their necks. Some had golden spurs on their ankles. Others had green specks under their wings, or red stars on the inside of their eyes. He saw. He knew.

In the courtyard they had their separate suites, each according to its rank. Every evening Birder Hüseyin Bey would see to it that each one of these beautiful birds with human spirits withdrew to its own chamber, with its own sweetheart. Until then he was unable to sit back and eat his dinner. "I wonder why Dilfiraz didn't couple with Yashar this evening," he would say. "I wonder why Ak-kadın had a falling out with Süleyman Usta. I'm afraid Serfiraz has her eye on Mesud, but I don't want *those* two to breed. I wonder what to do, what to do." With these worries sleep would not come the entire night. He would keep tossing in his bed, and his wife, lying next to him, would become irritated and say, "Hey, what if you concerned yourself a little with me too?" But Birder Hüseyin Bey thought about matters of love and sex only in terms of his pigeons.

When they would all rise up and fly at once, his happiness was boundless. He would walk in his courtyard for hours with his cane in his hand, his head turned up, his mouth open in amazement.

He was in just this posture in the middle of his courtyard late one afternoon in the spring of 1919 when a troop of enemy soldiers entered his farm on the same day that they entered all the surrounding villages. Suddenly he sensed his men running in all directions about him and heard his wife and daughters inside talking in alarmed tones. He turned around and looked. The enemy troop was making its way on horse and on foot through the open courtyard gate like a group of tired travelers quietly alighting at an inn. It was probably the first time in Birder Hüseyin Bey's life that his head was lowered while his birds were in the air. He walked toward the strangers, his face pale, and demanded with the authority of one who was still lord of his estate, "What is this? What do you want?"

At this, one of the strangers approached him, smiling. "Hello, Bey," he said with a familiar air. "We're not strangers."

Hüseyin Bey felt that he recognized the young enemy sergeant who spoke these words with his hands stretched towards him, but he could not remember very well. The sergeant grinned impertinently. "Don't you recognize me? Don't you remember Ispiro? Ispiro?"

"Ah, yes," Hüseyin Bey said at once.

Five years before, this man had spent six months as Hüseyin Bey's servant. He was a clever lad and a bit of a thief. Becoming more and more familiar, he put his hand on the old man's shoulder and bent down to his ear. "We're going to stay here a few nights," he said quietly. "The officers can't be comfortable in the village houses. You'll have to show us your hospitality."

Hüseyin Bey was bewildered. "Of course. Let them come in."

It was at this point that some of the enemy came over to the old man, smiling and talking, and asked if they might use the pigeons flying about in the air as targets. Hüseyin Bey shook his cane nervously. His voice was half angry, half threatening. "No-o-o, don't touch my pigeons!" But he hardly finished these words when next to him a gun cracked. With the alarm of a man whose skirt has caught fire, Hüseyin Bey took the one who shot the first bullet by the arm and shouted, "What are you doing? Be careful!"

But while he was busy with this man, another raised his gun to the sky, and a second shot whizzed in his ear. One of the birds turned and turned in the air and very slowly began to drop down. A great distress rippled through the flying caravan. Hüseyin Bey dropped his cane. His whole body shook. His face and beard were the same color. Ispiro came up to him. "What is it, old fellow? Forget it!"

"Forget it? Have you gone mad? Tell these people to stop or, by God, there'll be trouble afterwards."

"Trouble? Oh yeah? Hey, wake up, boss. Those days are over."

He did not hear, he did not even sense, the boundless contempt in these words spat in his face by his former servant. Now all his senses were occupied with the guns rising one after another to the sky, the bullets whizzing, and the pigeons turning, turning, and then very slowly dropping to the ground like huge snowflakes. Helpless, he began to plead, "That's enough. I beg you, enough! I'll give you anything you want. You can't eat those, you can't drink them. It's a sin, a sin."

And their answer: "A sin? Maybe in your religion." Ispiro laughed insolently.

One of the target-shooting officers turned around and shouted something in his own language. Immediately, several of the privates who were busy with their animals hurried over to gather up the falling birds. Some had landed in the courtyard, some on the roofs of the barn, others in the pond outside or in the vegetable garden, or still further away in the fields. The enemy soldiers, seized with the joy of mischievous children under this rain of white pigeons, clapped their hands, shouted, or danced up and down.

Poor Hüseyin Bey lost hold of himself and knelt down where he was. He could no longer say anything, but watched this wild shoot, while huge teardrops trickled from the corners of his eyes. Again Ispiro came up. "Why are you so upset?" he asked. "Forget it. Let them enjoy themselves a little. Let them have a good time. We've been fighting for so many days now. Can we have any tidbits this evening better than these birds? We're all together now."

Hüseyin Bey tried to say something, but the words stuck in his throat. Now his tears had stopped, and he stared straight ahead with a frightening, expressionless gaze.

They were piling up the white birds in bunches, on top of one another, in the middle of the courtyard. The ones that escaped the slaughter had scattered and flown off. The men finally wearied of their sport. One of them came up to Hüseyin Bey with a smile and in extremely bad Turkish said something like, "What do you think? We're good marksmen, aren't we?"

The old man did not answer, but raised his head and stared at a point in the air. After a while he lowered his eyes. He approached the white pile in the middle of the courtyard and bent over. Before him were sixty or seventy pigeons. One by one he picked them up by the wings and head. Holding them in his palm, he kissed some of them on the beak and stroked others on the feathers with a lover's caress.

Ispiro was talking with the officers at a distance. He turned to the old man and shouted with that insolent sneer, "Send those things inside and have them grilled!"

Birder Hüseyin Bey did not move. He heard nothing, but continued to caress the dead birds, bathed in blood, and to pass them over his face and eyes.

One of the officers pointed out the old man to Ispiro and made a gesture with his hand to his head as if to say, "Is he crazy?" Ispiro shouted again from the other end of the courtyard, "Hey, that's enough. It's you I'm talking to. Are you deaf? Send the pigeons inside."

Birder Hüseyin Bey still did not move and did not turn his head. Then the former servant, together with the officers, approached the man, who was bent down by the side of his dovecote. One of them shook him by the shoulder, another pulled him by the beard. A few crouched down near him, but they stood up just as quickly. They all drew back at once and repeated to each other the gesture that the officer had just made to Ispiro. Indeed, a strange and dreadful look had come into the man's face. There was a metallic glitter in his eyes, and his gaze was as fixed and steady, as hard and aggressive, as a spearhead. His spotless white beard was now dyed with the crimson blood of the birds he had passed over his face. It seemed as though a piece of the Turkish flag were wrapped around his chin.

ONE DRINK OF WATER
Reşat Nuri Güntekin
(*Translated by John Taylor*)

"It's a beautiful day today, Daddy. Will you take me for a walk?"

"Okay, Nevin. Tell them to find a carriage."

"No, Daddy, I want to walk. This time last year we went down the path on the other side of the woods to the sea. Let's do it again."

"That was nice, but —"

"You're afraid I'll get tired, aren't you, Daddy? Do you think that because Nevin was a little ill, she's no good for anything? I can walk like I used to. You must have seen me in the house just now. I played the piano and watered the carnations. I even washed the dog in the pool. I'm well now, Daddy. You'll see. In a month I'll be even stronger and more cheerful and a more misbehaved girl than I used to be."

The afternoon sun played in the curls of her sandy hair like gilt and silk and gave a light pinkness to her transparent skin.

"Next spring we're going for a real trip together, aren't we, Daddy?"

"We surely are, Nevin."

Hamit Bey took his daughter's thin wrists in his hands and for the first time in months had the courage to look into her eyes. He knew that her visit on earth would end in a few months. Each time he looked into his daughter's eyes, which were like yellow, spotted, wild violets, he could not escape the thought: "Nevin is dying, and in a short while I will have to close these beautiful, sweet eyes with kisses."

• • •

Hamit Bey was a doctor. However, he had more the spirit of a politician than a doctor. He had spent the first years of his youth in prison and in exile, but didn't have the stamina for that life. He was honest and firm in his morals and had a passion for reading and reflection.

Under the influence of this reflection, he began to see political life as mean and all that struggle and gossip as petty and unnecessary. In the second phase of his life, Hamit Bey became an apostle of free thought. Now and then he would debate with his old colleagues. "What's the good of changing regimes? Before anything else, one should change people's minds. Men cannot be good and happy while they are living under the influence of superstitions. I would like to be an extraordinary doctor, to carry out a great operation on humanity. I want to excise the root of desire and pain called 'heart' and dry up the source of contagion called 'imagination.' Only when that is done can man be happy. Think about the happiness of the man who is born, lives, and dies under these conditions. Every child is born like a world of darkness, and the torch of ideas is lit gradually. Life among these lights looks like a festival. Then one day he would close his eyes to this bright world without ever knowing the meaning of greed, suffering, or eternity."

Dr. Hamit's dry, harsh, and material theories had always somewhat frightened those around him. But his precise habits of mind and his sensitivity and affection which flowed from a secret source, the heart which he denied, gave him a strange attraction.

• • •

When his wife died, he was forty years old. His daughter, Nevin, was left without a mother at the age of twelve. He could have begun a new family, but though he was still young, he had grown strangely tired of life. He decided to devote his life to Nevin. He was going to apply his views to his own child and raise a skeptical, open-minded, happy, and materialistic young girl.

His first step was to separate her from the Circassian nurse who told her fairy tales and from the lady hoja who covered the heads of the children with green scarves and made them chant hymns.

In order to penetrate the child's mind better, he played with Nevin by the hour. Later, he took the young girl on his knees and slowly began to instruct her in his ideas.

Nevin had reached her eighteenth year and idolized her father. She had grown up to become an unprejudiced, informed, and moral young woman. In her manners and appearance, she still resembled a young girl, but in mind and spirit she was completely different from the other children of the family. Hamit Bey took pride in her, calling her his "beautiful creation." But this "beautiful creation" lacked one thing: joy and desire.

• • •

Nevin had been ill since the end of winter. She had tuberculosis, and despite all her father's care, it worsened every day. Hamit Bey's world crumbled over his head. But he had one remaining fatherly duty: to make his child happy until her death. He often thought of the night he would return home after leaving her in the earth. He thought that if he had fulfilled all of Nevin's wishes, he would be able to endure the pain of that night more calmly. But there was nothing Nevin wanted. No matter what he suggested, she would only lower eyes. "You know best, father," she would say.

• • •

They descended along the path through the trees to the sea. Nevin let her headscarf drop to her shoulders. She walked ahead of her father with her child's head yellow in the evening sun, her eyes happy and sweet.

At the moss-covered remains of an old fountain, they came across two poor little girls. The elder seemed twelve and the younger one seven. The small one filled the tin mug in her hand from the fountain and approached Nevin hesitantly. Hamit Bey smiled. He took a coin from the pocket of his waistcoat and held it out to the child.

"Take this, my girl. We don't want water."

The girl wouldn't take the money, and with a strange insistence she held out the water to Nevin. Hamit Bey spoke to her older sister.

"Why is your sister so insistent on having us drink?"

She answered with a bashful smile. "Our mother died. She's buried in that little grave over there. The hoja said that at night the dead people burn in their graves from thirst. If the children who are alive give water to the thirsty, they cool the dead too. When we give water to people who come by at night, Ayshe sees our mother in her dreams in a green veil. Don't you, Ayshe?"

The little girl still hadn't let go of Nevin's skirt. She nodded her head and smiled.

Her older sister continued. "Today no one came by. 'Let's go now,' I said. But Ayshe cried, 'What would our mother do without water?'"

Nevin fell to her knees as though to see the young girl's face better. Hamit Bey saw her take the mug and put it to her lips as though she were kissing a sacred object. He seized her wrist.

"What are you doing, Nevin? Are you going to drink that filthy water? Do you want to be sick?"

Nevin cried quietly. "Let me, Daddy. Don't let Ayshe's mother burn without water like mine."

"What are you saying, Nevin? Do I hear this from your mouth? And you, a free-thinking young lady!"

The girl kept crying, "What does it matter? Anyway, Ayshe believes it."

The tears flowing from Nevin's faded cheeks mixed with the muddy water in the mug, oozed from the corners of her thin lips and dropped onto her trembling throat and breast.

Hamit Bey let her drink. It occurred to him that she was drinking from a river of dreams and consolation, and that all his care and affection did not make her as happy as this muddy water. After drinking it, Nevin would die happy.

• • •

Nevin took water from the fountain in her hands and washed her face, but she couldn't stop crying. Hamit took her hands with a shamed, hesitant grief.

"Let me drink some water from your hands, so our deaths won't be left without water!" he said.

When Hamit Bey drank the water from those hands that in a few months would be earth, he felt a new life. Crying silently, the young girl wrapped her arms around her father's neck and kissed him again and again with wet, trembling lips.

• • •

"Daddy, now we can open our hearts to each other. I want to tell you my deepest feelings. You know how much I used to cry at night. Now I understand it. How I used to enjoy those bitter tears! Whenever a piece of incense is burned, I smell the day of my mother's death with its delicious poison. Oh, that day! Old and young, grown-up men and tiny children all threw their arms around each other and cried. The whole house was a single moaning, crying spirit. Even the one who had died. She was with us, father. And I believed that all these people bound together by blood and spirit and love would be together in the next world as they were in this. In my nurse's tales and the hoja's words, I saw my mother and myself walking, like Ayshe's mother, in green veils in the gardens of paradise. The other girls were with the hoja singing sweet hymns in their green headscarfs, and you took me away from them. You told me that the eyes that are closed in this world never open again and that all these people who love each other and are separated by death rot by themselves, each in his own grave. At first I believed you, Daddy. But your skepticism began to gnaw at my heart.

"One night we were returning from Chamlıja. You showed me the heavens, the stars, and the Milky Way. You said that those heavens were completely empty, that even the lights we saw there were illusions. For a child who believes that as soon as she closes her eyes in this world she will open them in another and find all those she has loved, to think that we all rot alone in our graves —

"For years I couldn't accept that hopelessness. For years I felt the pain of that final and hopeless death. I would lose you and all my loved ones just like I lost my mother. We would never look into each other's eyes again. We would never love each other again.

"Finally, I was the girl you wanted, father. An honest, straightforward girl who lived with her mind. I didn't believe anything anymore. I was superior to those around me. But what a sad pride.

"You weren't content with that, father. You doubted love, fidelity, and everything I had become accustomed to on the earth. Men who didn't love and understand each other, who were content simply to follow a humanitarian duty, and a world filled simply with the light of ideas were not enough for me. I am going to die, father. You don't have to hide that. What kind of consolation are you going to give me when you send me to the grave? Don't be so unhappy because of my death, Daddy. Why be unhappy at the untimely death of someone who lost the joy of believing and loving?"

• • •

Nevin died before she said these things to her father. Now Hamit Bey hears these complaints from the memory of her dead lips.

The old man had the fountain on that lonely, wooded road repaired. Every day, toward evening, he goes and sits there and prays that the village children or the traveling dervishes will turn from their roads and take a drink of water.

WASTING GOVERNMENT TIME
Fahri Celâlettin
(*Translated by Robert Dankoff*)

"How much is that handkerchief? I like it. I was looking for one myself to use as an ablution towel. I couldn't find one like that."

The man across from me received the question coldly and put off this fellow he did not know with a noncommittal answer. Then, with undue haste, he called over an acquaintance of his who had boarded the steamer just before it put off.

"Don't ask where I've just been. The Ministry of Pious Foundations again. Those fellows are shameless. They refused to apportion the prebend on the revenue of ninety-eight of the one hundred twenty-eight shares of my building. I submitted a requisition. They said they didn't know how to read the siyakat script. It seems there was only one person left after that famous reorganization that took place when the late Hakkı Pasha was grand vizier, a certain Nuri Efendi, and he wasn't on the regular staff. The old fellow was qualified in the matter and for the love of God, and five hundred fifty *kurush*, would read registrations in the *siyakat* script. After he was left out in the cold, what should he do but write up an advertisement and open a little shop near the registry office. God knows he doesn't earn less than thirty *liras*.

"What could I do? I searched up and down and found the old fellow. I just wanted to take him over there and have him read the ledger. Well, I encountered him up in his old barn lying on his back, and it turned out we were acquainted. My aunt on my mother's side, Abdulhalim Efendi's wife — but not the Abdulhalim Efendi on the customs board, I mean Chengelzadeh's wife — it seems he is her foster-aunt's second husband. What do you think? He recognized me. He got up, kissed my hand, offered me this and that, and paid his respects.

"'I beg you, Nuri Efendi,' says I. 'My situation is terrible.' I told him the story from start to finish. The poor fellow took off in front of me, panting and wheezing. And for nothing — he would not accept compensation. The world persists for the sake of such people, and that's all there is to it. We went over there. They said it was their noon break. Two hours we waited. Nuri Efendi choked and wheezed, one coughing fit after another.

"There's a remedy famous since the time of the physician Galen. You take what's known as wormwood. It's something like asafetida, found on the common male fern. They have it at Tunuslu in the spice market. You boil a hundred fifty *dirhems* of it in water and add twelve *dirhems* of peppermint oil. Then take two seeds of *Croton tiglium* (no more than two! they're dreadfully purgative) and crush them in a marble mortar for half an hour. Add them to the other ingredients and drink it down, toward dawn. It is most efficacious for emptying the system, both below and above. It's been tested, too. Well, I recommended it to the old fellow and just recently ran into him at Yenijami. He had done as I said and now he's hale and hearty, frisky as a lamb. Anyway, my friend, one topic leads to another.

"After we waited on our feet for two hours, we went to the Bureau of Old Registrations. There was a whippersnapper of a chief secretary and he says, with his nose in the air, 'The chief clerk hasn't come in yet. Please wait outside.' So we put our trust in God and paced up and down for another hour. Finally the gentleman did come, but it seems this time he left the key to the state archives inside his prayer rug. 'What kind of troubles are you causing us petitioners, my good man?' I ranted up and down, and poor little Nuri kept mumbling to himself. 'Good efforts are never wasted, my friend,' says I. He certainly was a stout old geezer. 'I want my money,' he says and gets up to leave. 'Don't do this to me,' says I. So we decided to apply again the next day.

"I hired a two-horse carriage early in the morning. He lives in the Sanakor quarter, in a house without a number on Toprak Street. 'Hop on,' says I. Well — the old upbringing — he would not sit on my right in the carriage. He kept on pleading, 'Come what may, I have a debt of honor to your worthy person. I won't forget your late father's kindness even when I stand at Judgment.' Anyway — I won't drag it out — we arrived at the registry office. However, that day — it was just my luck! — I had another case in the lower court at 2:00 P.M. We found the chief clerk. 'Without permission of the general director, I cannot show you the registration,' says he, and quite adamant about it, too. Well, I took matters into my own hands and plunged into the man's room.

'Goodness, Haji Bey,' he said when he saw me. 'Is it you again? But don't you know this is wasting government time?'

" 'I'm fed up with this term. Everywhere it's "wasting government time." I go to the police. It's "wasting government time." I have business with the gendarmes. It's "wasting government time." What kind of business is this, my good man? For two days now I have been bringing your former official here, Nuri Efendi, who has a bad liver. "The chief clerk hasn't arrived," they tell us. The chief clerk arrives. "He's forgotten the keys inside his prayer rug." I ask you, is this fair? The man is signing documents with one hand and plumbing his drawer for almond candy with the other. What a glutton!'

"Well, to make a long story short, he finally gave the open sesame. Then it turned out that the chief clerk had entrusted the keys to the office boy, and that the office boy had gone over to the Sublime Porte. Eventually we found the fellow, and with a catch in our breaths we went into the damp storeroom. If Nuri Efendi had gone and choked to death right there, God protect us, they would have accused me of strangling him and held me responsible. Well, what do you expect after trudging from court to court? Don't think it didn't give me a fright! The poor old fellow was in a wretched state with his dropsy. He searched the '57 registers for two hours and simply could not turn up the record. Well, sir, they used to write among the ancients that even the *elif* of the siyakat script is an ocean, a star in the sky. Finally, in '72, he found a marginal note containing the basic register of the *wakf* stipulation concerning the expenses on behalf of the one stipulated in the *wakf*. He found it all right, but meantime my rheumatism was acting up. We had it recorded. The sum of deferred rent paid on the *wakf* deed up to '92 amounted to four thousand three hundred thirty *kurush* and seventy *para*. They couldn't find ten *paras*. 'For heaven's sake,' I said, 'keep the ten *paras*. 'Impossible,' they said. 'It would be unlawful gain.' 'I have the receipts in my hand,' I said. 'Are they stamped?' they asked. There was a little secretary with a curly beard at the table on the left. 'Haji Bey,' he says, 'don't be concerned about it. We'll get the record out in one day.' So where is it?

"Back and forth, back and forth with the documents. Finally, on the thirteenth day, we were able to have an order drawn on the Bureau of Trust Funds. I immediately presented the petition to the Court of Pious Foundations. The trustee of the Bayram Pasha *wakf* interfered. 'Is the agent, Hasan Efendi, still alive? If so, have both parties been notified?' They transferred the investigation to the police.

"Well, I wasn't about to wait on the side lines. Wasn't the copy of the judgment in my hand? I referred to the court bailiff. Since the other party's residence was unknown, instead of being sent, the judgment was hung in the hall of the court. Afterward, however, Corporal Hüseyin informed me that they had paid off the imam and the *muhtar*. God curse the one who bribes and the one who accepts bribes! Why do you think his residence was unknown? To gain time!

"Meanwhile, the next day — let me see, what day was that? The second Tuesday of August. Tuesday is an ill-omened day, and that's all there is to it! Tuesday to Tuesday makes eight, Saturday makes eleven — on the twelfth, Sunday. What should I see? Well, I knew it all along! He hires Shevket as attorney. He's an imposter anyway. The former prayer rug keeper's second cousin, he lives in Shehremini and wears smoked spectacles. What do you think? They appoint him proxy. I was just about to get up and plead my case when I gave the judge a look out of the corner of my eye. He was looking at the defendant and smiling slyly. As God is my witness, I saw it with my own eyes. Well, my friend, I am not one to be taken in by such tricks. God knows, I can smell a rat a mile away. He was laughing over his beard and under his mustache. Then he points me out to several of the members and says — I swear, I heard it with my own ears! — 'This man's vocation is wasting government time.'

"Now I ask you, is it proper for a judge to show preference? Just as I expected, he said he had decided to reexamine the case in default. 'No, sir,' says I. 'That is unacceptable. I have spent exactly thirty-four years merely to execute the notification in default. How can the decision of the mighty State Council be swept under the carpet? Some favoritism is being shown in this matter.' 'Go and make a formal complaint against the court,' says he. 'That is exactly what I'll do,' says I. 'Do your worst,' says he. 'And that too,' says I, 'with God's permission.'

"You must know the story about the late hoja, how he was coming home one rainy evening with some packages in his hands. The night watchman stopped him and said, 'Hoja, where is your lantern?' The hoja replied, 'God's moon is the *molla*'s lantern,' and kept going. There was an iron hoop on the ground, and when he stepped on it it came up and struck his knee. The poor hoja dropped his package, he was so startled. He seized the hoop and threw it on the ground, and it bounced up in the air and this time landed on his head. The hoja burst out crying. He lay down in the middle of the road, stretched out in the mud, put the hoop on his chest, and shouted, 'Go ahead. Squash me to death!'

"That is just how I felt. I was ready to burst. Well, I had the decision appealed on the one hand, and on the other I submitted my petition of formal complaint against the court. The judge flew off the handle. And that rascal Hayri, the court errand boy, poured water all over me — deliberately, too — with the excuse that he was going to water the potted plants. Meanwhile, who should I run into but the deputy prosecutor? I really lost my temper. He was very respectful, even a bit embarrased. 'Rıfkı Bey,' says I. 'Is this just? I was winning my case even during the time of the former minister, Halil Hamada Pasha. In Section 1124 of the Code of Justice — look it up if you like, it's on page 674 of the Amire Printing Office edition — the statute relating to *wakf* rent is quite clear, and I have the official decision in my hands.' 'You're right,' says he, 'but who reads a letter about love and loyalty?' 'No, sir,' says I. 'That isn't the point at all. What is false cannot be the basis for analogy. Private injury is preferable to public injury. The rights of tiny orphans are at stake in this matter, if I should die.' He tried to pass the whole thing off with a joke. 'What't that, haji? Do you mean you've got another one on the way?' He's a queer lad.

"Anyway, there I am going down the stairs, and everyone's eyes are on me. What is it about me, my friend? I've got a bad reputation. Even the shoe attendant laughs behind my back. They say I'm touchy. Well, wouldn't you be?

"The *sher'î* court appointed a two-year period of delay according to the opinion of counsel. Haji Pasha's heirs failed to place their claim within the statute of limitation. Was this my fault too? Every ten years I reopen the case. As long as the matter reaches the stage of written correspondence, it means that it is still moot. Isn't that so, for God's sake? Don't agree just to please me. It seems that Haji Pasha's mother was a freed slave and consequently was not the pasha's lawfully wedded wife but his concubine. If anyone raises an objection, I can prove it with the family tree. She sprung from the loins of Suyoljuzadeh. Her mother died when she was seventy-four. Even during her fatal illness, the daughter showed no sign of senility. Her will was not written down, but there were witnesses, reliable ones, too. At that time, I was of age. The proof of majority does not fall to me. It is clear from my identity card. Even assuming they exaggerated my age on that, the date of my birth is written inside the cover of the calligrapher Hafiz Osman's

Koran in my father's own handwriting. Even my father's collected poems is in his own hand. Let the experts verify it and give their judgment. 'The finger cut by the *sheriat* does not hurt.'

"In the relevant section of the Imperial Land Code, it is quite clear. Even the provisory decree issued during the vizierate of Sait Halim Pasha in volume seven of the law code did not nullify it, though to be sure this is not wholly clear, but I've spent heaps of money in this matter. From the portion of the plot measuring seventy-two cubits and one-quarter *dönüm*, twenty-one out of thirty-two shares belong to me. My brother died without issue. His shares fall to me beyond the shadow of a doubt, according to the book on inheritance. On one side is a soup kitchen, on the other side a public thoroughfare.

"Why don't they use their brains? Would I trespass on holy ground at my age? They say there is some swindle in all this. They say my brother at that time had a wife and children, but can a man have children before he is fifteen? It doesn't matter whether I am married or not. My property will lapse by escheat. What concern is it of theirs? This is what is called sticking your nose into other people's business. Ah, my friend, they sent Jevriyeh Kalfa's daughter to be my nemesis. I took her in, thinking I would find her a suitable husband and marry her off, and now look at the aspersions that have been cast! Once in the middle of the night she said she was frightened and came to my room. I had the devil's own time getting her out the door again. What do you think? An affair of honor. No, God knows, I have no qualms in such matters, but what about those gossips Elmas Hanım and Asiyeh Hanım? They'll get what's coming to them."

He stroked his beard.

"The long and short of it is that I fretted over the case for fifty-two years. Eventually I won it, you know, on appeal. Justice prevailed, for what it's worth. But now I'm like a fish out of water. I have no vocation left. What is there for me to do anymore?"

SUMMER NIGHT
Ahmet Hamdi Tanpınar
(Translated by Robert Dankoff)

"The sick man used to lie in this room. For eight years he lay here. For eight years we listened to his screaming."

He looked at the walls with foreboding and fear, as though the sediment of ancient suffering were still there. "Why did they invite me here, after all?" he wondered. But what really angered him was that he had accepted this invitation. "To spend the whole night in this room—" He covered his face and looked through his fingers at the bed which the two sisters were cheerfully making. The younger one, who was a closer friend, chatted continually as she rearranged everything her sister set down. How attractive her suntanned body was in its lilac-colored dressing gown! She had to say something.

"How did you manage to get into this position?"

The young woman looked at the bed once again and then examined the area around it, looking for a place to sit. Finally she shrugged, as if to say "the most comfortable place is right here," and sat down on the edge of the bed, tucking her knees under her. Then she drew her sister to her side. The guest answered above the cigarette butts and ashes of the large ashtray in front of him.

"Atavism."

Zeynep, the elder, laughed, her voice choked. "Oh, we just made the bed. Isn't it a shame to mess it?"

"Don't worry, Zeynep, don't worry (drawing her sister by the shoulders into her own arms). We have to transfer a little of our own warmth, too. Here's a bachelor, going to sleep in this room alone all night!"

"The nights are short now. The roosters will be crowing soon."

She blushed at taking part in her younger sister's game. As if to hide this, she leaned her head on her sister's chest. Outside the room the old clock, left by the former owners of the house, snored as it struck the quarter hour. Then time resumed its usual dry ticktock, as though our life were a very dry thing, to be cut up in pieces by a little cleaver. The guest shook himself. "A thing like a well. Once you fall in you go deeper and deeper. Still, I'll listen to it. Now it will come out on top, now I — until I drown."

There was a breeze. On the windows facing each other, the curtains ruffled. From behind the house came the smell of the grass which the neighbor children had burned that evening.

"She has a lovely tan. Her body has become a glowing evening sun. There was a flock of pigeons in the café on the shore. The peacock was walking with his chest stretched out. His chest was like the sun, too, a bright deep green. Even though it was dark out. The little girl's eyes were like foggy mornings."

How strange! Everything always remained itself, yet always resembled something else as well. He sighed, and again thought, "How am I going to sleep in this room tonight?" He suddenly remembered the sick man. The sick man and the two women at his bedside. He calculated to himself. It was just thirty-five years ago.

"I wonder if they know they have invited me as a guest back to the strangest side of my childhood."

The younger woman, unaware of what was going on inside him, continued the story she had begun a while earlier at the dinner table.

"Fortunately, they're cross with each other. If they ever made up, we'd be ruined. They don't say two words to each other all day. They only talk when one of their acquaintances dies. As soon as my mother-in-law picks up the morning paper, she looks at the obituaries. Then she dashes into her husband's room."

She straightened her hair with both hands and imitated the conversation between husband and wife almost with their own voices.

" 'Did you see? Ahmet Bey died. It's in the paper this morning.'

" 'Who sees the paper? Once you get your hands on it in the morning, do you ever let it go?'

" 'It's in the paper this morning.'

" 'I haven't read it. Which Ahmet Bey?'

" 'My dear, it's Nuri Bey's son, the Nuri Bey who's a member of the state council.'

" 'Oh, him? Poor fellow. Isn't he the one whose daughter was always at the Suadiye beach? If it's he, we must go, we really must.

What time will it start?'

" 'Here, read it yourself.' "

For hours they would rehash memories of the deceased. When they returned, they gossiped about the people at the funeral! She sighed and again straightened her hair.

"It's just incredible."

Zehra shook and laughed with the dangerous, mature beauty of women approaching forty. Her face tightened as she laughed so that it seemed smaller. Her small, thin teeth, set neatly in her gums, sparkled pure white.

"Yes, it's just incredible. This is their only relationship. Every time my father-in-law returns from a funeral, he spends hours in front of the mirror. He looks and looks at himself, and talks about his acquaintances' ages."

"It sounds like your life is amusing."

"No, not so much. As one describes it, of course, because you only see one side of it. But it is hard to put up with when you're inside it. Every day in the house we plan someone's funeral ceremony. And every day we go back, back into some dead or sick person's life. With each new memory my mother-in-law is born again, grows up, marries, has children."

A deafening screech shook the room overhead.

"The last train has gone, too. I could go by tram, of course. But how can I leave without explaining everything?" A butterfly stopped just in front of his fingers. In a curious way it resembled a goby fish. "Everything resembles something else."

In this room thirty-five years ago he had known two other women. They were not sisters like these. And they did not love each other. Rather, they were enemies, but they came together at the sick man's bedside. His wife and adopted daughter. The one was round as could be, her feet all bandaged, aged and helpless. The other young, beautiful, and probably half-crazy.

There was a silence. The clock outside began to run as fast as possible. Can something divided into such small pieces belong to everyone?

The young woman toyed with her elder sister's hair. She was thinking.

"It's been twenty years now. Twenty years since we first met. He was a close friend when I was a girl, and so he is now. It's something like a benign neutrality. Strange! I still can't give him up. Why did I bring him here after all?"

The sisters too, under the star of the moment in which they were living, slowly began to have probing thoughts, like their guest. These probing thoughts, like roots underground, resembled one another, and mingled with one another in this resemblance.

Zehra was asking herself, for perhaps the hundredth time, "Do they love each other, I wonder? Have they ever loved each other? At first I thought she loved him. I was afraid that Zeynep's tranquillity would be disturbed. The day he came to visit us in Eskishehir, I began to fear for my own tranquillity."

"How I wished to get to know men when I was young! I was curious about nearly all of them. And I did come to know quite a few. But always through my husband. A husband is always a measure. He has too much of this, too little of that. Then this little and much become effaced. He seems just like him. But what is he thinking? Why is he so sick? I wonder whether something is wrong with his stomach."

She remembered the clean towels she herself had hung up in the bathroom and the bayberry soap she had put on the sink. "The only thing lacking is a toothbrush."

"Why did they invite me? Why here especially? This was the sick man's room. The whole neighborhood knew that. The screams all used to come from here."

"The whole neighborhood would wake up with these screams in the middle of the night. We would all wake up in our own beds and look around us in fear. Even the dogs were quiet when he screamed."

"Göztepe wasn't like this in those days. The villas were far from one another. We were living in the house across the way. Why didn't I tell them that I lived in that house, that I won't be able to sleep in this room. I should have told them everything right then."

"Was it you who cut down the walnut tree?"

Perhaps he asked this question in order to emerge, to come up on land, up into the common world. The whole evening had been like this. He had talked all the time as though he were emerging, coming up from under water.

"What walnut tree?" the younger woman asked. Suddenly she remembered and turned to her elder sister with an exaggerated look of amazement.

"Didn't I tell you he was a sorcerer? By God, he's a sorcerer."

Then, turning to him, "How did you know there was a walnut tree here?"

He did not know how to answer. The best thing would be to be silent, to let them forget this inappropriate question.

"It withered before we came. The year the owner of the house died."

"All the neighbors used to say that what kept him alive was this walnut tree. He planted it. He would live until it withered. And they used to say that beneath it was buried the child he had by his adopted daughter!"

This daughter looked after him until the end, together with his wife. He could see her at the sick man's side, with her long, thin legs, her slanting eyes, and her dark, somewhat coarse-featured face. When he met her she was already past thirty.

Zehra was trying to piece together what she had learned.

"Apparently, the sick man used to lie in this room. Did you know that the clock and the small chest of drawers outside are both left from him?"

"A bachelor. There's another strange word whose meaning I haven't been able to unravel. Life comes to an end in him. All at once a man, a thing that will go on, that must go on, comes to an end in himself. He said he was fifty. I wonder how he sees his life now? Because he has to see his life, he has to watch it."

She smiled at her guest from the midst of her thoughts.

"We should go and let you sleep."

"No, I'm not sleepy."

They were quiet again.

"Here we are watching over a sick man of thirty-five years ago. That is why the lamp is burning so palely. The clock is striking very far away."

"Life goes on in us. Zeynep has four children. I have three."

In her thoughts she traveled to her own house on the Bosporus. She entered her children's room and covered up the little one.

A moth struck the lamp. Then it fell on top of the table. Right there it spread its wings. It waited, as though content to die.

"Perhaps I think this way because I am married and a woman. A bachelor is left outside of life!"

They were all hidden within their separate thoughts, their separate loves. It had been like this all evening. She sighed again.

"We are watching at the side of a sick man of thirty-five years ago. That's why we are absorbed in our own lives."

"That woman's eyes were black, like coal. One day in the courtyard of our house— After that, I began to be more afraid of the sick man. I thought of myself as something belonging to him, like her."

"It was the muezzin, the one who recited the morning call to prayer at the little mosque next door to the house, who had watched them dig up the ground at the foot of the walnut tree. The neighbors said so. If the woman had not lain ill for weeks, no one would have suspected. Afterward, when she recovered, they rented a house in Aksaray and took her there. Some time later the man fell sick and she came home. And the wife accepted her, as though nothing had happened."

His whole body felt the shivers of that delight he had tasted thirty-five years ago in the courtyard, next to the well, without having understood what it was.

He stood up, went to the window, and then lit a cigarette and offered one to the women.

"It's too bad I am in this intimate position with both of you at once. I could have handled you one at a time," he joked. But neither of them laughed at the joke. This told him that they were truly at the sick man's bedside.

"What was his sickness supposed to have been, Zeynep?"

"Paralysis. The neighbors used to say he was paying for his sin."

"Yes, the neighbors used to say that. At first I hadn't understood what it was. But I didn't tell anyone, because she said to take care and not tell anyone. I kept it to myself."

He remembered the woman's words with strange delight. " 'Take care not to tell anyone. I'll come to you when I have the chance. And you stop at the house whenever you like.' "

They actually did as she said. When they had the chance, they met.

A freight train shook the room like an announcement of doomsday. It passed up the slope. The man followed the summer night landscape as it piled up in the wake of the train and then, gathering to a point, suddenly turned over. He longed for the tiny stations, the small official houses with flowerpots in their screened windows and their gardens watered in the evenings, and the cafés staying open until late at night. "Not to make a journey. But to avoid sleeping here."

"It actually happened like that. For six months we met nearly every day."

"They used to say she was half-crazy. But it wasn't this that frightened me. It was the sick man. And the child beneath the walnut tree. Still, every day."

He searched for the child's place in the dark with his eyes.

Zeynep kept looking at her guest from the place where she was lounging.

"Has he loved anyone, I wonder? I'm sure he has known many women. But has he actually loved? I had given him the flowers in my hand. When we parted, he gave them back to me. 'Perhaps you'd like to keep them,' I asked. He said he did not want to deprive me of them."

"No doubt it's better this way. I'm content with my life."

She breathed easily, and again thought of her own house on the Bosporus and her children. She would leave early in the morning.

"Come on, Zeynep. Get up! This man is sleepy. He keeps yawning (covering her own mouth with her hands)."

"The man was very handsome, wasn't he?"

"Which man?"

"The sick man. The owner of this house."

The woman again turned to her elder sister with the same, somewhat artificial look of amazement.

"Didn't I say he was a sorcerer? By God, he's a sorcerer. Where do you know these things from?"

Why did he not tell them everything straight out?

"I was born in the house across the way. I grew up in this neighborhood. I know the people in these houses. At night I would wake up frightened because of that man's screams. When I heard his voice I thought he was calling me to his side. As soon as he started screaming, my mother would come and talk with me so that I would not be frightened. That was when I was little. When I was older, it was completely different. This house played an uncanny role in my life. Yes, if I tell them everything I'll put them at ease. But then I'll have to tell them other things as well."

His life's secret would come out. That awful emptiness, and the curious chance meeting before that. Once again he looked through the window. He thought he would feel easier if he could see the place of the walnut tree totally empty.

"Then I'll have to mention the last day as well." He looked about himself, bewildered.

"She had crouched down at the foot of the walnut tree. As soon as I came through the gate, I saw her. With a stone in her hand, she was cracking the fresh walnuts and eating them. Her face was toward the sun. She was picking the walnuts with her fingers and then eating them. When she saw me her face lit up. In her eyes appeared the gleam I had seen that day in the courtyard for the first time. Suddenly her voice was low, as on that day. But I was not listening to her. I was looking at the walnuts in her hand. After a while she understood. She threw the walnuts out of her hand and ran away, into the house. We never saw her again in the neighborhood. And I — never again — never again with a woman —"

He stood up once more. He wiped his brow. Then he begged the women, "Why don't you stay a while longer? I'm not at all sleepy."

TOY CARTS FIVE KURUSH
Sabahattin Ali
(Translated by Virginia Taylor-Saçlıoğlu)

In the evening when the streets were crowded, a woman and child would come to the corner. The woman, wrapped in a full, black veil, would pull it over her face, leaving only her black eyes to stare lifelessly straight ahead in the half-light of the street. While the child stood next to her, she would crouch down and take a few toys out of a small sack. These consisted of a pair of wooden wheels attached to the ends of a stick. On top of the wheels was something like a little man made of four sticks nailed between the round pieces of wood, and as the wheels moved over the pavement the little man would spin around.

After the woman arranged the toys in front of her, the boy would pick one up and begin to walk up and down the sidewalk calling out in a thin voice, "Carts five *kurush*. Five *kurush* each. Carts five *kurush* each." For three or four hours until the streets were deserted he would continue like this.

The boy was eight years old, but at first glance he didn't look more than six. He was very small and skinny and his continually-calling voice was thin and trembling like a little girl's. When saying "five *kurush*," he would linger over the "sh" as if pressing it out between his lips. Like his mother, he always stared straight ahead and never raised his eyes.

A short distance from the corner where they stood was a large clothing store with a bright display window. Behind the huge panes of glass, neckties of various eye-catching colors, belts with chic buckles, wool sweaters, gloves, and a dozen other items, both necessities and luxuries, smiled at the faces of the passersby. While going by these things and setting themselves up on the corner, the mother and child tried not to turn their heads. If it hadn't been for the lights reflected on the wet pavement, causing it to shine here and there, they might never even have noticed that such a store existed.

But the majority of the passersby, especially the children, stopped in front of the dazzling window and fixed their eyes on the cleverly disordered heap of toys that stood in one corner. Then, turning back to the street with sad expressions, they would curl their lips in a pout at the wooden-wheeled carts which appeared before them and look annoyed, as if the remembered shapes of the beautiful toys in the window were being destroyed. But the little hawker wouldn't notice their lack of interest and, staring straight ahead, would call at short intervals, "Five *kurush*, toy carts five *kurush* each."

A large car stopped in front of the store. A plump, elegantly dressed woman and a boy of eight or nine wearing a white beret, gaiters, and a soft navy blue coat got out. Together they entered the store.

A little later, the boy came back to look in the display window and noticed the corner where the toys were. Just then the little hawker's voice was heard: "Toy carts five *kurush*."

The boy turned his head to look and went running to the corner. Grasping the hand of the boy standing next to the black-veiled woman, he said, "Hey! Are you selling carts here?"

The hawker raised his head and looked. He smiled immediately and after an "ah" of recognition said, "My mother can't come alone and she can't do the hawking, so I come along."

The boy wearing white gaiters thrust his wool-gloved hand into his coat pocket and pulled out a small sack. He took out a piece of marzipan, put it in his mouth and gave some to his friend. His mouth full of candy, he asked,

"When do you do your lessons?"

"When I come home from school. I study for about two hours and do my homework. Then we come here. I can't study at night, anyway. Gas is very expensive."

"Did you see our teacher? He just went by."

"He knows that I sell carts."

Seeing a woman and some children coming, the hawker stopped talking and called, "Toy carts five *kurush*."

The two boys were hand in hand. The veiled woman was scrutinizing them with sad eyes. The boy with the white gaiters asked his friend whether he was responsible for keeping the accounts.

"I just tried it at home but I couldn't do it. Tonight I'm going to ask my father."

"Why ask? It's very easy," said the other, and explained how.

Though they were deeply engrossed in their conversation, the little hawker never forgot to call "Toy carts five *kurush*."

The older boy nudged his friend. "Hey! The boy next to me has bad breath. I'll say something about it and come sit next to you. We'll work even better together!"

"The one next to me won't move, and I can't tell him to. He's one of our neighbors and poor like me."

He didn't go on. He was going to say, "They would say that I got rid of him and put a rich kid in his place," but he changed his mind.

They started to talk about other things, but just then the mother of the boy with the white beret, soft navy blue coat, and white gaiters came out of the store and looked around. She had packages in her hands. The chauffeur came running to take them and arranged them beside him on the seat. Looking toward the corner, the woman saw her son. Her face, smiling with the pleasure of new purchases, suddenly turned hard. She marched to the corner with swift steps. The boy, seeing his mother approaching with such fury, immediately became quiet and fixed his eyes on her with a surprised but smiling expression. For a moment no one budged.

The little hawker's mother had raised her head and was looking at the woman who came rolling up to them like a ball in her fur coat and snakeskin pumps.

When the woman reached them, she seized the bewildered, smiling boy by the wrist.

"What's going on? Who are you talking to?"

With the umbrella in her other hand she struck the little hawker, whose hand was still absentmindedly in the other boy's, across the shoulders. Then she screamed,

"What trash! Look here! Is this anyone for you to talk to?"

The boys let go of each other's hands, which then swung at their sides. The black-veiled woman had crouched down at the base of the wall, and the little hawker's eyes were filled with tears from the pain in his arm.

Seeing the tears in his friend's eyes, the other boy, because there were still many things he hadn't learned, said with a protest erupting from his heart, "Mommy! He's my schoolmate!"

The woman, her face turning bright red, interrupted her son. "Tomorrow I'm going to telephone your school. I'll teach them to put you with those who aren't of your class!"

She pulled her son by the arm. As she walked away, she cast humiliating and crushing looks at the little hawker and his mother as if she wanted to stamp them to the bottom of the earth. Her son was still turning around and looking back, and when he saw his friend turn his tearful eyes away, his own eyes too began to fill.

The little hawker went on calling in his thin and trembling voice, "Five *kurush*. Toy carts five *kurush*."

THE VOICE
Sabahattin Ali
(Translated by John Taylor)

1

The truck taking us from Beyshehir to Konya broke down at a pass called Barsakderesi. The driver and his helper raised the hood. They took a pile of tools and instruments out from under the seat and spread them on the ground. A repair job began that lasted for hours. Sometimes both of them were under the machine, lying on their backs, tinkering with the bottom of the engine, and sometimes one was in the cab pumping the gas and turning the engine over while the other worked with the set of porcelain-topped plugs.

In the afternoon sun, the heat under the tarpaulin was unbearable. One by one the travelers jumped down and scattered. Some of them watched the driver with curiosity.

"Is it finished?" they asked excitedly, when he paused and raised his head from the engine to rest.

My friend and I and a few of the less curious travelers walked to the west side of the pass. We sat in the shade on some rocks to wait and survey our surroundings.

A little ahead of where the truck had stopped were two tents and near them some spades and a handcart beside the road. Further on, there was a team of road workers busy moving sand and breaking rocks.

Behind us, the sun buried itself in the ridge, while across from us the pine trees scattered on the hill tops turned red. The valley was abandoned to the spreading dark. It was a cool, spring evening, and we began to hear the murmuring sound of the creek flowing nearby.

On the road a few cars and trucks passed. Their drivers stopped beside our truck and asked our driver whether he needed anything. Two of the women travelers had become more and more anxious as it got late and were constantly pestering the driver. Finally, they found space in a truck and went on toward Konya.

The other travelers sat in groups and related things to each other. One was an old man with a wooden leg who said he was a grocer from a village nearby. He walked to the truck, put his sack on his back, tossed a few curses at the driver, and set out on foot.

It was fully evening. The road workers began to return to their tents and light their fires. Our truck sat motionless at the side of the road like the body of a giant animal. The driver and his helper were covered with oil and dirt, and black sweat beaded their foreheads. They sat at the side of the road having a long rest.

Most of the travelers were used to events like this. They merely shook their heads, opened the lids of their baskets, and had something to eat.

When some time had passed and it was completely dark, the driver got a lamp from the road workers and set to work again. A sudden silence had fallen among us, and we lay motionless.

The trees on the hills had lost the sun and were buried in a faded, bluish light. I looked at my friend's face. His eyes were fixed on the horizon. The dark pines sparsely scattered on the hillsides were silhouetted against the still-light sky.

"We're about to see the moon," my friend said, after watching them for a while.

At just this moment the air, filled with the smell of thyme and the fine crackling of the fire, was shaken by the light sound of a *saz*. My friend was a musician, and he sat up. He frowned with concentration and listened.

The sound of the *saz* was coming from the road workers' tents. After a well-executed introduction, the *saz* grew quiet and a man began to sing. We had never heard the song before, but it seemed familiar.

> A leaf, I withered, dried and fell.
> Night wind, scatter and crush me,
> Carry me far — home to my love,
> Press my dust to her naked feet.

Now I sat up too. Although the *saz* had begun a transition melody, I still heard the singing in my ear.

My friend looked at me as though to say, "What is this?"

"Fantastic!" I mumbled.

The voice began again and set the whole valley ringing.

> I took my *saz* and wandered in the world
> And now return repentent to my love.
> Why ask these women what to make of me?
> See me and what I am apart from you.

I had never in my life listened to a man's voice so full and sweet. I was amazed that such a meaningful and enrapturing sound could come from a human throat. My friend got to his feet and pulled me up, and we started to walk toward the workers' tents.

Four or five people were sitting in the field in front of the tent. Picks and shovels were scattered around them. While a lamp swung in the door of the tent, shadows moved uncertainly and stretched away into the valley, their heads lost in the darkness.

A young man who didn't seem more than twenty was sitting in front of the tent on a handcart turned on its side. He was playing the *saz*. His face was against his shoulder and his eyes on the ground, so that we couldn't see his features clearly. His lamp-lit forehead was covered with sweat. Under his quick fingers, the long neck of the *saz* trembled like an animal. His right hand was beating the strings with small, sure movements, and every time it approached the body of the *saz*, one would think that between that piece of wood and the flesh there was some secret but important and meaningful conversation.

A light spread over the tent and the place where we were and crossed the valley. We looked up and saw the moon passing the hill tops and rising into the sky. The young man playing the *saz* raised his head too, and, narrowing his eyes, looked at the bright face listening from the sky. Then his hand slowed, his eyes closed, and he tightened his throat. We watched him with fascination, while he sang his song to the moon.

> The moonbeams play on my lute.
> (Who can express these feelings better than I?)
> Come, crescent-eyebrowed love, and sit on my knees.
> With you on one side and the moon on the other —
>   come embrace me.

The other travelers had gathered. Everyone watched this red-faced youth with amazement. His moving hands spoke a mysterious language. He fixed his eyes on the ground or on his instrument, which jumped as though it wanted to fly from his arms. After a short pause, without raising his head, he sang a faster song but in the same deep, sweet voice.

I've lost eight years away from home,
No companion for my sorrow.
Don't ask some mortal, ask your heart
If one day you will follow.

After two strong chords, he lay the *saz* aside and looked up. Some of the people cheered. He tried to smile, his gaze falling on no one in particular.

My friend went up to him and asked, "What is your name, son?"

"Ali."

"Where are you from?"

"Sivas."

"Where did you learn to play the *saz*?"

"I don't know. I've been playing since I was a child."

"And the singing?"

"The same with that. Later I wandered with a couple of minstrels."

My friend looked at me. "Look, if we searched for years we wouldn't find such an extraordinary voice. I can't let this one escape."

He turned and asked the young man's age. Twenty-two. He took his notebook out of his pocket and wrote in it, asking the youth's address. The boy was confused. He didn't have an address. Here today, there tomorrow — he worked on the roads. "How about Ali from Sivas on the Beyshehir road?" Finally, he gave the name of an inn in Konya where he stayed now and then. My friend took all this down.

"Gentlemen, the vehicle is ready!" said the driver now, who had been listening with us to the *saz* for some time.

My friend would have had the youth sing a few more songs. When he saw the other travelers arise, take their bags, and start for the truck, he sighed and turned to Ali, who was standing up.

"If I send for you, come right away. I'll find you a good place. You can work with some real musicians, and the *saz* would get even better. How's that?"

Ali agreed without understanding anything.

We slapped him on the shoulder and said good-by.

All the workers together said good-by. When we left they gathered around Ali, laughed, and began to talk. They were probably explaining my friend's words to each other and trying to make out to just what a good end Ali had come.

2

Once we got to Ankara, my friend was ceaselessly occupied with the business of that young man. He was committed to getting him a place in a conservatory. That's how it stood when we talked about it.

"You just don't know, brother," he said. "That boy's voice is still in my ears. I'm not inexperienced in this. I know the human voice very well, but I haven't often heard a voice like this."

I felt the same as he did, but in order to seem a little wiser, I said,

"You're right. But couldn't the effect of that night have had something to do with the impression the voice made on us? The moonlight. The sound of the stream we heard and then lost. The narrow, winding valley between the mountains, and finally the voice, completely unexpected, spreading out of the workers' tent into the open sky. Isn't it possible that all these things, in that strange silence, put us in an unusually romantic mood, and that an ordinary or better than average voice could seem so fantastic?"

Despite all this, there could be no objection to the idea of bringing Ali to Ankara, listening to his voice, and getting him some training and development. No matter how far wrong we were, there was no denying that we were faced with a first-class talent.

My friend was living in daydreams. He saw Ali from Sivas as a renowned, world-famous opera tenor giving concerts in the cities of Europe.

"To see him in a tail coat and his red face sticking out of a white collar. What a great thing that would be!"

Finally he got what he wanted. He applied to a number of offices and arranged to have Ali from Sivas brought to Ankara. In fact, the people he contacted on the matter were searching for new talent. They were giving auditions frequently and selecting students to train for the opera. Word was sent to Konya, and, after a short search, the young tenor was found. The city of Konya paid for his trip, and he was sent to Ankara.

As soon as I entered the office of the school holding the audition, I recognized Ali from Sivas waiting at the edge of the room, his *saz* in his hand. His face was a little more red, and he looked frightened. His heels hung over the flattened backs of his shoes, revealing socks full of holes. He moved his feet as though the rug were burning them. With two fingers he held the neck of his *saz*, which rested on his arm like a gun. He didn't look at the talking and laughing faces in the crowd, but gazed along the walls and the floor.

After greeting the people in the room, I talked to Ali. I asked how his trip was.

"Not bad."

The *saz* on his arm was new. I smiled and looked into his face, and he understood at once.

"I found it at the inn where I stopped. I bought it for eight *liras*. It wouldn't be right to play for these gentlemen with a cracked *saz*!"

In that brightness, his black, beautiful eyes gave me the same somber feeling they had on that evening. When I looked closely, I saw that those large, dark eyes were living in a world of dreams. I wanted to see with them for a moment.

Who knows what he made of his trip here? Certainly he had no idea of my friend's plans for a career with the opera and the concerts in Europe. Maybe he thought that some of the important people in Ankara would listen to him and give him tips. Maybe he thought a more secure future awaited him, that someone might like him, give him a place as a servant or a doorman, and support him so that now and then he could play for gatherings and earn a little money. He might have heard that sometimes even governors took care of minstrels that way.

While musicians of various nationalities, speaking Turkish, French, and German, were filling the room, there was a knock at the door. Two people entered. One was an education inspector. He was bringing a boy who had applied to the ministry a little earlier for an audition. He was a brave-looking and slightly fat young man with light, curly hair, who said that he had graduated from middle school and that his teacher had liked his voice. The men and women in the room greeted him. It was an audition for tenors, and they would listen to the two of them together.

We all went out. My friend opened the door of the audition room with a pleased and self-assured air. It was a large room with a parquet floor and a new stage at one end. On the stage in one of the front corners was a grand piano. The room was suddenly full. Groups of people began to talk in French and Turkish. Some of them were arguing with each other, and their unnecessary noise made my head begin to ache. A young German woman went to the piano and tried the keys. Ali from Sivas had never seen such an instrument before. He looked at it in amazement, and then, probably so as not to betray his inexperience, tried to put on an air of indifference. At this point, one of the young musicians put a metal chair painted white on the stage and said to Ali,

"Sit down."

Another musician spoke up.

"My dear, how can anyone sing sitting on a chair? Have him stand."

"He's done it, though. Have you ever seen one of our country poets playing the *saz* or singing on his feet?"

During this debate, Ali looked at the bare white walls and the large curtainless windows. The place looked like the operating room of a hospital. He glanced at the crowd of men with the fearful eyes of a patient looking at the doctors about to lay him on the operating table.

"It's not right to sit him on a chair and make him sing like this. He's used to sitting cross-legged, and might be anxious," I said to one of the young musicians at my side.

He nodded in agreement. But then he said, "No, really, that wouldn't be proper. How can he sit cross-legged in front of these Europeans? We'd have them laughing at us!"

Perched on the white metal chair, Ali looked as though he were sitting over a fire. The hand holding the *saz* was shaking, and the sweat from his anxious forehead dripped through his eyelashes and the peachfuzz on his cheeks.

The people who were talking gradually lowered their voices. Everyone either found a chair or leaned somewhere against a wall and fixed his eyes on Ali, who was suddenly alone in the center of the stage.

The young man pressed his knees together and clenched his teeth. He put his *saz* in his lap. But he couldn't get it in place, and looked around in bewilderment. When he saw the people staring at him, the sweat began to fall onto his yellow shirt in huge drops. He took the cherry-bark pick into his fingers and plucked the strings a few times.

The sounds cleared his mind for a moment. An expression of quiet came to his face. After playing a little more, he stretched his neck and prepared to sing. It seemed that he wanted to cough, but he was too bashful. Finally he looked away from us and into a corner of the ceiling, and began to sing a folk song.

His voice was still beautiful, but there was a rasping noise mixed with it. These strange noises were not very noticeable when he sang loudly, but they showed themselves clearly when he lowered his voice. Ali noticed it, too. He tried to control it, but the effort only tightened his throat muscles and reddened his face the more.

One could easily see the two round, ribbed, motionless muscles stretching down both sides of his throat. Ali sweated to force his strong voice through this vise. Finally, he finished his song and, taking his *saz* in his hand, stood up.

One of the German musicians spoke up immediately.

"Not bad, not bad. Let's hear the other one," he said, motioning to the light-haired youth with his head.

The young man went up the four steps to the stage with a self-assured smile on his face and, without even waiting for the people in the room to become quiet, began to sing a folk song from a popular record. His voice was light and sweet at first, and then it gradually swelled until it filled the room in waves. He sang really beautifully. Despite his imitation, in a few places, of a singer with quite ordinary talents, it was clear that he had the makings of an excellent voice. As soon as he finished the song, the same German shouted,

"Bravo! This boy we can teach something!"

At this point my eyes were fixed on Ali. He was gazing into empty space as though he had no connection with anyone in the room and looked bored. A young woman at the piano motioned him to her side with her hand. She was going to test the candidates' pitch. Playing a simple melody with her right hand, she said in German.

"Sing this."

One of the Turkish musicians explained.

"Come on, sing the same as the piano."

Ali looked at me, and then searched out my friend's face. "Oh God," I said. This poor young man had been brought face to face with an instrument he had never seen in his life. He had never heard its sound and didn't know its name. He didn't even understand what was being said to him. I had to explain.

"My son, you make the same sounds that this lady plays."

The woman at the piano repeated the melody, and Ali, tightening his throat again with a great effort, began to sing.

        I sent word to my lover's home —

A few people laughed, and Ali stopped at once.

"No, my dear fellow," I said. "You're not to sing a song. You're to imitate these sounds."

A few notes flew out of his anxious throat, and one of the Germans, waiting impatiently, pointed with his hand to the light-haired tenor and said,

"Let this one do it."

One after another, the melodies that the piano played poured from the young man's mouth like clear rivers of sound. Those who wanted to finish the business quickly perfunctorily directed Ali to sing one more song. Ali tried even harder than the first time. He sensed that everything depended on this one song, and he sang the most beautiful one he knew. It was not bad at all. Some of those present nodded their heads as though to say, "Excellent!" But as soon as Ali had finished and was off to the side, they forgot him. The light-haired youth sang a tango he had learned from a record. There was no doubt that he had a beautiful voice. The audition had gone far enough, and they passed to an intricate dispute about how the boy had to be trained. The problem of the budget was discussed. He was to have begun his studies before June, but it was said that he couldn't. No one was aware that Ali from Sivas was standing to one side in the same room. My friend, who had brought him to this place, was standing next to the disputants without listening. Neither he nor I had the courage to go up to him, or even to look him in the face.

When I slowly raised my eyes, I was amazed. There was nothing of the tragic to be found in him. As shortly before, he was staring emptily at the walls. It was as though the people in the room were less to him than atoms. There was not the slightest trace of grief or anger on his face. In fact, he had the relieved and peaceful manner of someone who had been rescued from a long annoyance or torture. When his eyes happened on the light-haired tenor and paused for a moment, perhaps he looked at him with a slight amazement or curiosity. I searched for some jealousy or envy but couldn't find it.

His *saz* was like a weapon again, resting on the floor next to his foot, and this foot, with a slight movement, was rising and falling on the parquet. Then I felt something hurt inside me. The young man was revealing himself, his despair, his disappointment, and his broken hopes in this small motion of his foot. He was the ruler of every part of his body. Not even a stirring of the skin allowed expression of his inner feelings. The soft light of his eyes burned in a deep, eternal peace. But without noticing, this man emptied himself with this tiny, nervous agitation of his right foot. Never in my life had any crying or any human face seemed so meaningful or so painful.

I pulled myself together and walked to his side. I had to say something to him, to talk with him. How would he return to Konya? Had he given the last of his money for his *saz*? What was he going to do now?

As soon as I went to his side, his foot stopped moving. My friend came too. He began with a hastily prepared lie.

"Ali, my son! They were pleased with your voice, but you're a little old. Here they don't take students over twenty. We're going to do something special for you. But it might take a while. You go back to Konya, and when the business is ready we'll find you and send word."

Ali listened to all this with raised eyebrows, as though it were of extraordinary importance. He even tried to memorize it. But when his eyes fixed on me, I was taken aback. Somehow these huge black eyes revealed to me that their owner didn't believe a word of this nonsense.

We had to do something, so I said,

"Come on. Let's go to a restaurant and eat!"

The discussions in the room were continuing, and no one noticed our departure.

We ate our fill at a *kebab* house, and while we ate we didn't speak at all. There was no possibility of deceiving him. We couldn't even say,

"Forgive us for all the trouble we caused bringing you here!"

I was thinking of all this when we left the *kebab* house. Ali swallowed a few times and lowered his head, as though he wanted to say something.

"I brought shame on your head, sir. Forgive me!"

Then, as though he were explaining some amazing event, he opened his eyes and added,

"In that room I couldn't find my voice at all!"

He left us and went off.

The next morning my friend got together a few *liras* for him and went to his inn to put him on the bus and say goodbye. The innkeeper told him that Ali from Sivas had sold his *saz* for two *liras* for the fare and had left for Konya on a truck at dawn.

THE VALLEY OF VIOLETS
Sait Faik
(Translated by Virginia Taylor-Saçlıoğlu)

My friend sat brooding, with his head between his two huge hands. In front of him stood a quart bottle of wine, its contents half consumed. The unappetizing bean salad and lone mackerel on his plate looked apologetic, as if they were alive, and gave the impression of having been abandoned by someone who, having starved for days, was attacked by a sudden stomachache upon sitting down eagerly at the table. The food left uneaten by people who frequent such third-class taverns always reminds me of the unconcealed regret in the faces of unwanted old maids and reluctant bachelors.

My friend's name was Bayram. He was a big-boned man who spoke with an Albanian accent. At one time he had sold almonds which he freshened up by a process involving ashes and vitriol. Then he sold lottery tickets. After that, he worked as a chauffeur earning thirty *liras* a day and became rich, in a manner of speaking. He dropped his former habits, dressed as a hooligan again and knew the prettiest girls in disreputable taverns. Among these girls was one named Seher. She was truly a girl like the dawn, in keeping with the Arabic sense of her name. Bayram started to live with Seher and I used to see her in his carriage.

"Hey man!" he would shout. "This is real class, wouldn't you say?"

He would strike the horses on the back with the whip and the wiry mares would tear down the street like lightning. While he was living with Seher, Bayram got into many scraps on her account. There were even knives pulled. One day while escaping from one of these rows, he was caught. He had to spend seven or eight months in the clink, and during this time the inevitable occurred. Seher took up with an officer she had been keen on before, and she stopped coming to the bar in their district of Istanbul.

After that, Bayram couldn't work. The bones in his back stuck out like carriage poles come loose from a horse's harness, and he started drinking from morning to night. He spent all his time looking for Seher, and when he finally found her he whipped out a giant knife and stabbed her in the throat. But Seher didn't die, and she didn't even tell anybody who had done it.

Although Seher came to the bar again when she got out of the hospital, she refused to speak to Bayram. This wounded him to the quick, and Seher's comradely discretion bound his hands and arms like horse tethers. After a while, they made up. Bayram sold his mares and carriage, and Seher consumed the money. There was nothing she didn't do to destroy Bayram, who was working someone else's carriage for ten *liras* a day. She gallivanted about with all the people who got on his nerves, until finally he could no longer drive the carriage and started selling almonds again.

It was during this period, when Bayram was drinking away all his earnings in the tavern every evening, that I ran into him again. His face, no longer alight, had taken on the appearance of a European city blacked out in wartime. The lustre of the fiery eyes in that lean, pale face had fled, and he had a hacking cough. His dull eyes sparkled only with the glaze of alcohol, the one thing that enabled him to face the shame of those days when he had tried to defend his honor by killing Seher.

Seeing him despondent that evening, I said, "What's eating you, Bayram? Don't be such a fool."

"Have a seat," he replied and called out to the Greek waiter, "Barba! Another bottle of wine."

Sweet white wine was brought and we got very drunk. For a while Bayram looked at me in a strange way, as if he were going to say something and then changed his mind. I just ignored it, but finally he said, "I love you like a brother. Do you love me too?"

"Can you doubt it, Bayram?" I returned.

"In that case, will you take me home?"

"Okay, if you're drunk."

"No, not to my room," he protested. "To my home, my real home. I haven't been there for seven years."

"Seven years?"

He was smiling.

"Seven years ago I left home one morning. I was exactly twenty years old. It was February, but our valley was warm like a spring morning. It smelled of violets. I sold some flowers at the flower market and made nineteen *liras*. I had never had a drink, so I had one. I had married three years before, but I had never had a perfumed, made-up woman, so I went to one. After that I didn't go home. I don't know whether the folks back there are alive or dead. I've never run into any of them anywhere. I had an old father, a mother, a wife and two kids, one a year and a half, the other nine months. I started selling almonds. You know the rest."

He summoned the waiter again. "Barba! Another bottle of wine, but make it red this time."

"Bayram! You've had too much already," I cautioned, and I asked the elderly waiter how many bottles there had been.

"I'm amazed," he replied, in a Greek accent. "I can't believe it. Seven, if I haven't lost track."

But Bayram insisted sheepishly, "Bring it. I'm not going to drink."

But again he drank, and I ordered still another bottle. When we emerged into the street, neither of us was in a condition to stand up straight. We stopped at the bar and asked Bekir about Seher. She had gone to Tepe, a district known as "the hill," so we jumped into a taxi and headed for Tepe.

On the way Bayram kept saying, "I'm going to give her a crowning she won't forget when we get up there."

Fortunately, she wasn't there. From Tepe we proceeded on foot. The wind was cold and damp and icy clouds were floating across the sky. From time to time a strange, distorted moon, bearing little resemblance to the familiar one of more sober evenings, glided into view. At first the wind was in our faces, but later it switched to our backs and pushed us along.

Suddenly we stopped in a still place. Before us in the darkness a huge summerhouse appeared. Beside its garden wall, we came upon a cabbage patch. Bayram in front and I behind, we headed across the spongy earth straight toward a dark hollow in the distance. As we descended, the wind stopped. A little later we were in a very warm place, and I heard the sound of water. Charming lights beamed from three or four tiny houses in front of us, and dogs were barking. When we knocked on the door, a small girl's voice could be heard from the stairs.

"Mommy, somebody's at the door."

"If there's someone there, open it. Your grandfather must have come back from the coffeehouse."

"I'm afraid."

"What's there to be afraid of?"

"Two men are at the door."

"You silly girl! Who could it be but your grandfather and Uncle Hasan?"

The door was opened. A small, blond girl's shiny blue eyes fastened dumbly on Bayram's face. Then the same sparkling eyes turned to me and scrutinized me. The door was closed in our faces.

"It's a thief, Mommy! A thief, a thief!"

A fair-skinned, dark-eyed woman with her head covering held between her teeth appeared before us, her eyes growing wide with surprise. At first, she stared like that for a while. Then she pulled the head covering from between her teeth and stepped back.

"Please come in," she said.

We went inside. Immediately in front of us rose a staircase. When we had gone up ten steps, we were at another door. We went inside and found ourselves in a room with an iron stove. Inside, the room was full of the acrid odor of children and the scent of linden flowers. We sat on the sofa. A wooden table was brought to the center of the room and a copper tray, its redness twinkling here and there, was placed on top of it. On the tray were pickles, cheese, jam, and six hard-boiled eggs. We sat down and ate everything in complete silence. While we were eating, a small boy opened the door, looked at us and ran away. The little girl served. The young woman, her hair pulled tightly back now and not even her forehead showing, silently entered and left a few times and gathered up everything after we had finished. Then she lifted the lid of a large wooden linen chest and spread two beds. We all avoided each other's eyes and frowned, as if we were cross with each other.

When I work up in the morning, I saw Bayram in front of the window smoking a cigarette. I sat down next to him on the sofa and looked outside. Before me in the mist stretched a garden. At the side, covered half with straw and half with glass, was a shed evidently used as a greenhouse. I opened the window, and a lovely scent of violets filled my nostrils. The air was balmy and pleasant. As the mist lifted sluggishly, a vegetable garden was spread out before my eyes. Cabbages, flowers, parsley, and lettuce reared up like horses. On the farther side, among the flowers, other gardens and dilapidated houses were visible. The whole valley was filled with the same plants, the same animals, and the same scattered, tumbledown cottages. Everywhere there was the smell of violets, and right in the middle of the road a rippling stream was flowing. We must have passed through this stream the evening before when we came to the house, but my feet hadn't even become wet.

An old man approached us and Bayram said simply, "My father."

For the first time since evening, we began to talk. The old man looked at me. "Welcome, my boy," he said.

Then an old woman brought milk and asked the man, "Are you going to go to the market? Shall I get the cart ready?"

The man looked questioningly at Bayram, who answered, "I'm going to go to the market, mother."

Only the old woman wiped away a tear that kept trying to slide down her wrinkled cheek. No one else seemed to show any emotion at the homecoming.

The little girl brought a huge bunch of violets and gave them to me. A woman, who had turned white as a sheet, ran up grasping a load of celery which she threw into the cart. Without lifting her face, she looked at Bayram, and I looked at him too, but he paid no attention. The woman watched for a long time from behind the cart until it disappeared from view. Before it turned the corner, Bayram stood up, turned back and cracked the whip in the air over the white horse straight in the direction of the woman who was watching. Without waiting to see the woman run into the house to escape, he turned the corner. The house disappeared from our view.

But the scent of violets persisted, and how pungent, how beautiful was the smell of the celery! I didn't know where we were going, but it didn't seem appropriate to ask.

We jumped down from the cart at a marketplace, and traders surrounded Bayram.

"Have you finally returned from military service? We thought you had died, Bayram!" They were all talking at once.

"I'll be off now, Bayram," I said.

"Drop by sometime," he replied.

I passed over a few roads, descended a slope, ascended another, descended again and found myself in a familiar village.

I haven't gone to the valley of violets for almost a year now. I'll look for it, I said to myself one day, but I couldn't find it. Then last year on a cold February day with a few friends, I came upon a cabbage patch near the village of Mejidiyeh. In front of us a valley opened, whose view, depth and strangeness attracted us. As soon as I stepped on the spongy earth, I knew immediately where I was. We ran down the soft slope into the valley, which was unbelievably warm. The scent of violets filled the air as we walked along the stream. His wife was bent over, probably gathering herbs. They straightened up and looked at us, but Bayram didn't recognize me, and I didn't say anything.

Passing alongside the garden while walking up the hill to the Albanian village, the scent of violets still reached our nostrils, and, leaving a day in May behind, we found February waiting for us like a whiplash.

LOVE LETTER
Sait Faik
(Translated by William C. Hickman)

We were talking about the world situation. You didn't want me to go into my feelings about you then. Still I don't see anything wrong in that. Isn't it just what people do when they console one another in hard times?

During the War of Independence both the Greeks and the Abkhazians occupied our town. We friends and neighbors would gather in one place, turn out the lights and sit together, giving each other comfort and strength. I remember one terrible, stormy night: it was our own house. The lightning flashes chased after each other with dreadful noises. The trees in the garden spoke with an old, otherworldly language. From a distance we could feel the sea butting against the rocks and hear the rocks muttering at the sea and the sea at the rocks. We had come together, all the people of the house, in one large room. In the blue gleam of the lighting we could see each other's faces. Our house was in a forest, some distance from the village. Lightning was flashing all around. With a feeling less of fright than of being together, with a pleasure, even, which came from never before having been brought together like this after midnight, I saw those pale dear faces — my mother and father, my sister, my aunt's oldest daughter — blue and very close in the cold brightness of the lightning. If we'd had close neighbors I'm sure we would have invited them too.

But don't suppose that I only want you on stormy nights like that. If I could, one calm day in a seaside town of whitewashed houses dozing at noon I would put you in a boat and take you out in it a little way from the shore, as though crawling along the bottom, the boat only a hand span above it, with shadows reflecting off the surface of the water from gardens and hammocks, people sleeping and pine trees bent down over the shoreline. I would row you about showing how the tiny fish scatter in the water, how the pebbles on the bottom lose and regain their shapes and how the mosses play in the currents — green, yellow, reddish brown and even white. I would be happy when the scent of you reached my nose with a momentary breeze. I would show you my face, healthy and without pain, at that moment growing radiant and convalescing in love, and explain only with my eyes how much I love you. I would tell you everything simply through the little wrinkles of pleasure in the middle of my face.

But we don't live in such a tranquil, cloudless world. At moments like this I always imagine myself a hero. Come close to me. Never mind the lightning; let me see the color of your eyes, copper tinged in its light. In this world of war and violence where people destroy one another, if only they knew, even if they don't see it — not just two people but thousands of people — that far removed from religion and ideology, far from everything, yet in spite of everything, that they love one another. Without making grand pronouncements, without saying "This is the truth," let's do the one thing which man has been doing ever since he was man, where we have a sense of ourselves in another, where we understand our weaknesses and our strengths: come, let us have love.

Perhaps everything is the truth. It may be that in every fight or quarrel there is a right and a wrong, a just party and an unjust. But in love there is no right, no just or unjust; there isn't even any "truth." In love there is only a single thing which "becomes" out of the absence of those other things: beauty.

I don't believe in anything, my dear. I don't believe in the existence of you or of beauty — not "your beauty," that's something else — but beauty with a capital *B*. It would be better though not to say, "I don't believe," because all the newspapers and magazines, the whole world, is smirking at us. They call us "the ones who don't believe."

But they are the ones who make war and we are the ones to end it. If I say so it's not that I don't consider I've put on the airs of a great writer. Still, you expect from me some sort of involvement in the world. If, like the great thinkers of the day, I can't resist carrying on at great length to justify myself, I apologize, excuse me. I repeat:

If they are the ones who make war, we are the ones to end it. If you're content with our not being able to see each other for the whole winter, then there's no problem. I'll see you again in the summer. Perhaps then the war will be over. We'll make the outing I promised you.

There aren't any white houses along the shore of our island, but there are plenty of jagged rock cliffs with pine trees clinging to them and the shadows of rocks and birds and hilltops and flowers. . . Since my voice isn't very good I thought of taking along a record player in the boat.

Don't worry. The record won't be a voice solo. I'll find one with a chorus singing, the childlike voices of women and the girlish voices of children all singing together, a happy song.

You don't like vocal solos do you? What an unpleasant thing. What a conceit. What a miserable thing, the shouting of a single person on a phonograph record! . . .

THE MARRIAGE OF SHEPHERD ALI
Kemal Tahir
(Translated by John Taylor)

1

Ali took his coarse shepherd's cloak onto his back and drew easily on his cigarette.

Sitting cross-legged, he was as wide and as tall as a short, fat man standing up.

Blind Ahmet, the herd's follower, spoke to him. "The animals are getting up to the highway, master."

Ali lowered his cigarette from his mouth and called, "Dadaaa! Dadaaa!"

The master shepherd's thick voice rolled down the hill like some huge living creature, and Blind Ahmet thought to himself, "This time they won't come back. They're going onto the road for sure."

The night was bright from the moonlight on the sea, and though the road was some way off, the row of telegraph poles and the railroad tracks on the far side were clear.

The flock could be seen dimly, like some slipping piece of the earth itself. When it heard the shepherd's voice, it stopped and turned back.

Grazing across the field, the animals enveloped the slope of the hill. Blind Ahmet knew how the flock was trained to Ali's voice, but still he was surprised that they listened to human words.

They set out from İskilip in March with five hundred yearling lambs, and after grazing them a month in the mountain pastures of Yapraklı and two months in the pastures of Ilgaz, Forty Springs, Birdrock, Belan, Yaabasan and Little Ilgaz, they drove them to Istanbul.

So that the animals wouldn't lose weight, they slept them during the heat of the day and in the cool night would graze or walk them. Since they were on the road only two hours out of twenty-four, it had taken fifty-five days from Little Ilgaz.

There was a train whistle in the distance.

Blind Ahmet first saw the sparks spraying from the smokestack. They were thrown into the moonlight, lit red the rock sides of the cuts, and went out.

It was a long freight train, and it passed in darkness, shaking the foundations of the earth. The small red point at the back of the last car reached a curve and the sea was lost.

The train came from Istanbul and was going toward Ankara.

Blind Ahmet looked straight ahead and asked, "Master?"

"What?"

"Where are we now?"

"Above Gebze. There are four stops left on our road. Wolf Village, Samandere, Long Meadow, Üsküdar. From there the car ferry to Okmeydanı." Ali drew out the last syllable of the last word as though to say,

"And this business is finished."

Osman had been the most famous shepherd from the soil of İskilip. But since he married and went to work as a sharecropper for Rıza Bey, it was said that Ali was the only brave shepherd left. There were none who knew as well as Ali how to train the flock to the voice, how to tell the good weeds from the poisonous ones, or how to diagnose and cure sheep's diseases.

According to Ali, a good shepherd doesn't make the sheep jump ditches, doesn't frighten them, and drives them slowly. If he doesn't know the times for sleeping, grazing, and watering, the sheep lose weight, and if the fat tails crack, the sheep are ruined.

For Ali, there were three important rules for the shepherd, and he repeated them at every opportunity: a brave shepherd keeps the wolf from his sheep; mountain, water, wind — everything living and dead is an enemy to the shepherd; the lonely shepherd curses everyone — his master, even his own sister — and he must."

At the head of a flock, Ali was accustomed to bravely depriving the wolf of its share of the sheep, to vigilance against everything living and dead, and, when he was alone and angry, to cursing loudly. This fact was known to everyone. In the eleven years he had been a master shepherd, he had brought each flock to Istanbul in perfect condition.

Because his age was understated on his identity card, he had gone into the army when he was twenty-nine, and in the two and a half years that he was in the Second Artillery Regiment there was no other soldier as strong or as striking.

He was close to seven feet tall. In the market of Chankırı, he couldn't find a cloak that would cover his back. He was fearfully strong. He ruled those five hundred animal lives from the time he took them as twenty-five-pound lambs, pasturing and watering them where he wished, until they were eighty-five or ninety-pound sheep. He tried to keep a very serious countenance, but he had a round, red face, his fat cheeks seemed always ready to smile, and his eyes like amber beads looked soft no matter what he did. From time to time he considered that he did not look as awesome as he wished, and it made him sad.

When the flock reached the top of the hill, Ali called out, *"Kis! Kis!"* without moving his body, and the animals turned again. Ali rolled a cigarette, lit it, and, moving the match end around his teeth, turned to Blind Ahmet. It was the custom of the master shepherd to quiz the follower when there was nothing to do.

"Look here, Ahmet," he said. "How many stops are there from Ilgaz to Istanbul?"

Blind Ahmet was lying face down. He got up on his knees and began to count: "Ilgaz, Osmangölü, Anbardere, Hamamlı, Wolf Lake, Gerede, Hunchback's Mill, Bolu—"

"Is that right? Did you get from Hunchback's Mill to Bolu by horse?"

"Ah, just a minute, sir. Hunchback's Mill, Hunchback's Mill— "

Ali took his cigarette slowly to his mouth. He couldn't remember the next stop himself, and he became irritable.

"When you're thinking about something else, you lose the way," he said, and to himself he counted, "Hamamlı, Wolf Lake, Gerede, Hunchback's Mill—" He remembered and announced in a loud voice, "Koroğlu Devreti."

Blind Ali didn't notice his master's hesitation. "Yes, that's right. That's it. Koroğlu Devreti, then Springberry, Yumlutepe, Deve Bairtan, Narrows, Duzje, Blackwater, White Mosque, Hendek."

"Good work!"

"Hendek, Kargalı, Haabasan, Fork Bridge, Tersyeri, Adapazarı, Serveren, Infant Lake, Longfield, Kırazolu—"

"Good work. You know it. That's enough. Now tell me. Where does a brave shepherd have to be the most careful?"

"A brave shepherd keeps his eyes open near Bandır, Chumcholu, and Bath. There's lots of thieves there. They dig a pit and cover the top with sticks and grass, and a sheep falls in and gets left behind."

"Good work. How do you know when the sheep have the staggers?"

"From their eyes. The vessels in their eyes turn yellow."

"OK. You know that too. Good work. Now what about splenitis?"

"If there's splenitis, you drive the flock into a stream. Make them cross through the water a few times; walk them into the current. It cures the disease. If you have a gun, fire it to scare them, and run them back and forth. If normally fifty of the animals would die, only twenty or thirty will die."

"How does a brave shepherd know where an animal was born?"

"They scream like a train."

The two men laughed.

"And how do you train the flock to your voice?"

"As soon as I take the lambs, I work for one or two months. I spread a rug or sack on the ground. I scatter some wheat on top. I cry to the flock, 'Dadaaa!' They learn to come and eat the grain. Then they don't need the grain. They come to the voice."

"You really learned that. That's good. If you don't train the sheep but try to chase them with your feet, you spend every cent you earn on shoes. Good work. Now you're a shepherd. You can get a follower and bring them Istanbul yourself now."

"Not me, master." Blind Ahmet looked straight ahead and smiled. "I still have to spend a lot of time with you."

Ali sighed.

"Don't bother about me. This is our last trip together. Didn't you hear I'm getting married? I'll be a sharecropper for Rıza Bey, just like Osman."

Blind Ahmet was happy. He was nineteen years old. He had been a follower for five years and made twelve *liras* a month. He wondered whether Rıza Bey would take him on as master shepherd. As master shepherd he would make twenty *liras*. He would wander with the herd seven months. Hiding his fingers from the master, he added them up. In seven months he would earn a hundred forty *liras*. Every ten days he'd get three pounds of fat, fifteen pounds of cracked wheat, and if he was addicted to tobacco, Rıza Bey would pay for that too. And with four other children to feed his father would be happy.

To conceal his pleasure, Blind Ahmet asked, "Is it worse being a shepherd than a sharecropper, master?"

"It's good being a shepherd. But it's for the young. I'm too old for it now." Like all young men speaking of old age, Ali thickened his voice.

"No, master. You're still a young man."

"I'm too old. I became a follower for Osman when I was twelve. I wandered as a follower for twelve whole years. Then I was a master shepherd. Since then, I've been wandering over mountains and slopes. It's a hard job. A difficult art. Now and then in the villages they say, 'Is there anything more beautiful than being a shepherd? Wandering in the mountain pastures. Drinking from the cold springs. Milk, yogurt, meat, and cream for free!' I laugh. Don't listen to them. It's pure nonsense. If it rains, a shepherd looks ridiculous. Toward evening, you count the sheep. There's two or three missing, and you have to find them. You sink in mud up to your chest. Your clothes are torn to pieces. You have to find the sheep, dead or alive. It's shameful to lose a sheep, and your master will doubt you. He'll be thinking, 'Did he slaughter the thing and eat it, or did he sell it?' "

Ahmet believed his master. He began to worry. "You're right, master. It's bad, being a shepherd."

"Look at Rıza Bey. I said, 'I want to be a sharecropper,' and he didn't even say, 'We'll think about it.' He's going to give me a field, an ox, a donkey, and seed. Just because I'm an honest worker. If you want, you can curse the flock. Don't give a damn. Leave them to the wolves. Or butcher one for the meat, let the dogs play with the skin, and tell the master the wolves did it. If you do these things, you'll lose your honor, and you'll stay a shepherd until the day you die. When you're young it's nothing, but when you're old it's a real shame. If you don't have strong legs, or lose your voice, you can't manage the flock."

Ahmet had to console himself. "A farmer's work is hard, too, master. The earth wears a man down. I know from my father."

"Certainly, that's hard, too. Is there anything that isn't hard? There's no easy way to get your bread. What's good is to have a place — a home, a household, a stove. It's fine for people with a father and mother, but for people like me, without anyone, it's difficult. Once I sell the flock, I've got nowhere to go. This is what Rıza Bey said to me. 'Farming is a hard job. You can't plow, sow, weed, winnow, and manage the farm by yourself. Let me find you a sturdy wife!"

"He's right."

"We were thinking of Kamil's daughter. You know Kamil? The Kamil from Hanging Village."

"I know him. Fatma's father."

"Yeah. That's the bastard."

For some time, he had been looking at the sheep. The animals were nearing the railroad tracks, and he called them back.

"That's the bastard. He's a relative of mine on my mother's side. Up until March, he had agreed to sell me the girl. The bride price was sixty *liras* and eight hundred pounds of grain. Rıza Bey sent twenty *liras* and a hundred pounds of grain. He was going to give the rest at the wedding."

"That should've been good."

"And it would have been good if Kamil hadn't backed out. But he backed out, the bastard. Now what will I do when I go back?"

"Don't get into trouble because of a woman."

"We'll see. Fate."

Ali was tired of talking. He lay on his back. The sky was bright, and a cloud was blowing quickly across the face of the moon like smoke.

"Once you're out of the army, you've got to get married."

If only his birth had been registered differently. If he had gone into the army just one year earlier, he would have spent this summer in the village. Who knows? With the will of God, he could have been lying and sleeping tonight with Fatma on the earthen roof of the village house. Ali was thinking, and he was listening to the night.

The flock was slowly grazing its way toward him. When it suddenly quickened, Ali straightened up.

Hoofs were pounding the earth, and the sheep nearest the thicket were bleating.

Blind Ahmet jumped up after his master. "What's going on?"

"Run, God damn it!"

Ali threw the cloak off his back and grabbed his stick. He charged off, shouting to Ahmet,

"A wolf! Get the sheep!"

Ahmet couldn't keep up with Ali and decided instead to go after a few that had turned off to the side.

Ali ran between the flock and the thicket to stop the wolf, and to chase the flock toward Ahmet he shouted and bayed like a dog.

The animals were away from the thicket, but one was left behind. It bleated once and began to run straight into the underbrush after the wolf. Because Ali knew that sheep bitten by the wolf didn't know what to do and often would follow the wolf, without being surprised he began to follow it. Five or ten steps from the thicket, he caught up with the sheep and seized it by the wool of its tail. The animal bleated sharply and threw itself forward, struggling toward the wolf.

The wolf stood six or seven paces off, its eyes glowing red in the moonlight.

Ali held the sheep tighter and waved his stick, and when the stick whistled in the air the wolf backed off a few steps. The stick was all he had, so he couldn't throw it. He swung it whistling in a circle over his head and howled like a dog.

"Get away! Wolf, get away!" he shouted.

The sheep was trembling so hard it shook Ali's arms as it tried to get free. Ali was angry that the sheep could be so stupid. He took it by the horns and, without taking his eyes off the wolf, dragged it back a step at a time.

Each time he took a step, the wolf moved the same distance. Because its food had been taken from it, it was angry, and the gray hair on its neck stood on end. Each time the stick swung, the wolf growled so that the whole flock could have been driven wild with fear. Ali was frightened, and to keep his hands free he pinned the sheep between his legs.

For a while they stood face to face.

The wolf sat on its hind legs. It looked like a puny dog. Now that it understood that the shepherd was unarmed, it couldn't be frightened. Again and again, it bared its teeth and snarled. With that viciousness, if it had the intelligence to attack the flock, it would tear the sheep apart. Although Ali felt the danger, because he couldn't swallow the pride of several years' experience as a shepherd, he couldn't bring himself to sacrifice the one sheep before him, even if it meant losing ten or fifteen. He barked at the wolf and swung his stick. If his dog Alash hadn't suddenly become sick on the road and died, he would have grabbed the wolf by the neck and killed it. Trying to hide the sheep between his legs, he started to back away again.

When the space between them widened a little, the wolf stood on all fours and howled and bared its teeth.

Ali thought about what he could do with the flock, and he cursed Rıza Bey and his ancestors. There was no way to protect five hundred animals from a wolf as greedy as this, in this country, without any dogs. If he couldn't save the sheep by bravery, the wolf would definitely steal one sheep before morning.

He shouted to Blind Ahmet.

"Follower!"

"Yes, master."

"Get the flock together and take them down to the tracks, and don't let this damned thing know what you're doing."

"With pleasure."

"And watch out for the donkey, man! If we lose that, it won't be funny."

Ali slowly pulled the sheep back. He tried to stay close to the flock. As the wolf came near, he swung his stick and cried, "Get away! Wolf, get away!" Though it did no good at all, he bayed at it again. Then he felt a wet warmth between his knees. He bent down and felt with his fingers. A hot thickness stuck to his hand. In one blow, the wolf had torn open the sheep's tail. Blood was flowing, and the sheep struggling toward the wolf was in torment.

"You son of a bitch. You son of a bitch. To hell with my honor. I'll give you this one. I'll give you this one."

The wolf followed them as far as the tracks. Then it put its tail between its legs and, dragging its clawed feet, went into the thicket.

But Ali was shepherd enough not to be fooled by this trick. He took the sheep down to the edge of the sea. One side of the flock was along the sea and the other side was drawn up against the railroad cutting. Ahmet was walking in front, and he was behind.

When they got this far, the wounded sheep lost all its strength. It fell, and before it died they killed it.

Until morning, he watched for the wolf and was troubled by one question: a sheep could tell when storms, earthquakes, and floods were coming, so why did it run after a wolf that had ripped open its tail? Didn't it know that it would be killed?

There was much of God's doing that couldn't be understood.

2

Riza Bey wet his fingers with spittle and started to count the money. His fingers ticked off the bills as easily as prayer beads, his mouth moving as though he were reciting a prayer. His lips were bright red, and his round beard glowed black in the light of the gas lamp on the shelf. He sat cross-legged on the wooden couch. He was wearing a brown broadcloth suit, the jacket of which was amply cut and hung to his knees. The bottoms of his trouser legs were short and tight to display the tops of his fine house boots. A tasseled fez was stuck to the back of his head. He only used his black fedora when he went to town or when important officials came to visit.

Ali considered it shameful to watch someone counting money and kept his eyes on the ground. He was to the right of the door, kneeling, next to the stove. He was pleased that Rıza Bey had pointed for him to sit, but because he was too embarrassed to move he stayed on the cold Kurdish rug. His thick calves began to ache.

To the left of the door was waiting Hüseyin Bey, the youngest of Rıza Bey's four sons, at his father's service. His hands were together in front of him, and he kept his eyes on his feet. His legs were as thin as sticks, but Ali was astonished at how big they seemed wrapped in his tight pants and his red and blue wool socks. According to his identity card, Hüseyin was twelve, but Ali knew when he was born. In fact, in the spring he would be sixteen. He was the same age as Fatma, the daughter of Kamil, whom he was going to marry.

With black eyebrows that grew together across his forehead and a Roman nose, Hüseyin bore a close resemblance to his father. The lips under his Roman nose were pinched, thin and blue, and he was always biting them. His hunting jacket with diagonally cut pockets and his knee-length pants were made of good black corduroy. His waist was wound with a sash from Tosya. Although he was very young, he knew how to break a horse and how to shoot a rifle.

Ali remembered this and smiled at him as though to say, "Good work!"

At the corner of the couch, Haji Imam was sitting cross-legged, as comfortably as only he in the world knew how to be. When he had finished scratching his ear, he asked Ali, "Is Istanbul the same as it used to be, master shepherd?" Rıza Bey slowly continued to count the money.

Ali hesitated and looked at Haji Imam's mottled grey beard and round face. He was bewildered. He couldn't leave his patron's guest unanswered, and he couldn't startle Rıza Bey, who was counting.

Haji Imam slapped his hands on his knees.

"It's been forty years since I went the last time. Sultan Hamit was on the throne. We were in the Friday procession to the mosque. Are you listening, Rıza Bey?"

Rıza Bey nodded.

Haji Imam fingered his prayer beads loudly and asked Ali, "Is the Beyazıt Tower still where it was, master shepherd?"

"We go to the foot of Okmeydanı, Haji. It's still there, I believe."

"It will stand forever. That fantastic building was built during the reign of Sultan Mahmut. It's a tower of a tower. I've seen America, Romania, Egypt, Syria, Mecca, Medina, India, and Bukhara. I've visited them all. I never saw a tower like this. No, I made a mistake. There's one in the capital of France. But forget that. It's nothing like our blessed tower. How could it be?"

Haji Imam's lightly blackened eyelids and the thick silver watch chain on his chest shone in the lamp light.

Haji Imam was concerned about his appearance, and he was dressed to catch the eye. His baggy trousers and Albanian jacket were made of genuine English broadcloth and covered with silver embroidery and silk braid. He stroked his red and white cashmere sash and asked,

"Did you get the whole flock there, master shepherd?"

"Every one, Haji Imam."

"For the love— You're not a shepherd, you're the commander of an army."

There were beads of sweat on Haji Imam's lined forehead. It strained his heart to talk too much, and he stopped. He had a white skullcap with an embroidered edge, which he wore under his cap and never took off. He pushed it to the back of his head. He beat himself on the chest and said loudly to himself, "There's nothing wrong with you! If your windpipe weren't stopped up—"

Rıza Bey collected the bánk notes which he had spread on the couch in piles of a hundred each, and stuck them in the folds of his belt. He said to Ali, "That's it, son. Good work. You've turned out to be a better shepherd than our Osman. You said a wolf got one of the sheep. It doesn't matter. We aren't going to make a fuss over one sheep. Good work."

Ali was sorry he had lied to Haji Imam.

"Once the dog died, we couldn't avoid it," he said. "The wolf attacked us. It tore up the sheep's tail. It was near Gebze. We killed it. Are there supposed to be wolves near Gebze? But there were. I told Osman this morning. He was surprised too."

"No matter. No matter."

"Thank you, master, sir."

Rıza took a wallet out of his inside pocket. "First, let's take a look at the follower's account. From his twelve-*lira* monthly pay, he gets eighty-four *liras*. He has a debt of five *liras*. That leaves seventy-nine, doesn't it? We gave his father three hundred pounds of grain. That leaves sixty-nine *liras*? Here. Here's sixty-nine *liras*."

Blind Ahmet got up quickly. He took the money Rıza Bey held out to him and put it modestly into his pocket.

"Thank you, master, sir."

"Now let's see to your account. According to what I hear, you don't have a pistol. You must have been pretty nervous, unarmed against the wolf. A man has to have a gun. I've got one, with thirty-five bullets. You can have it for twenty *liras*. If it suits you, get it from Hüseyin. If you need it, we'll postpone the ten you owe me from when you were in the army."

With the bundle of money in his hand, Rıza Bey waited for an answer.

Ali stared at the lines in the rug. He couldn't get out a sound, and Haji Imam tried to encourage him.

"Speak up, master shepherd. You certainly need a pistol. It turns out that you owed ten *liras*. Don't worry. These things happen. But if you don't want this ten-*lira* debt to be accounted now, say so. Rıza Bey is a just man. It's better to ask than to refuse."

Hesitantly, Hüseyin Bey joined the conversation.

"There's one problem, father. Weren't you going to get Ali a wife?"

Rıza Bey pulled back the money. "You're right. I forgot. Is that what you want, then, Ali?"

Ali lowered his head all the way to his chest and mumbled something.

A smile spread across Haji Imam's face, and his white false teeth moved. "Silence means assent, Rıza Bey. Silence means assent. Of course he'll accept. Listen to what our prophet taught us: 'Womankind is neither Muslim nor Christian, and only one in forty is fit to marry a Muslim.' "

Rıza explained slowly. "After you left with the sheep, I sent for Kamil. Supposedly, he was sick and couldn't come. He sent word that he wasn't going through with it. He sent his greetings and his respect and said that with God's will he'd repay the money and the grain at harvest. I guess you already heard he went back on his word. The son of some immigrant is supposedly taking Fatma. He's paying a hundred *liras*. What do you say to this?"

Haji Imam didn't like the news at all. He turned his fat body to the wall and made a spitting sound. "Tuh!" He made a sour face. "He went back on his word. If he changed his mind, we can change our minds too. Isn't that right, master shepherd?"

Ali frowned. He was anxious and very ashamed. He thought it must have been that whore of a mother of hers telling that lout what to do. Otherwise he would have had to come when Rıza Bey sent for him.

Rıza Bey raised his voice. "Speak up, Ali! Look, Haji Imam is right. Are we going to forget this business?"

"You know best, master, sir."

When he heard these words, Haji Imam became doubtful. He leaned his head forward and tried to see into Ali's eyes. Then he winked at Rıza Bey.

Without looking at him, Rıza Bey demanded of his son, "What do you say, man?"

"With your permission, I'll kidnap the girl, father."

Haji Imam's good spirits returned as quickly as they had fled. "May you be blessed. You're a prince. May you be blessed," he smiled. "But look here. Be a little temperate. You've got twenty-five pounds of gunpowder in your heart. For sure, now. You're right, master shepherd. Force neutralizes cunning. In short, Kamil's girl has to be kidnapped. That's it. But Hüseyin Bey, can you do it alone?"

Rıza Bey's lips showed a little smile.

"Did you hear, man? Can you kidnap her by yourself?"

"If you order it, I'll do it."

"And if you end up in prison?"

"I'll sleep on the straw."

Haji Imam threw his coconut wood prayer beads on the rug-covered couch. "All right, you have my permission. Good luck. Take to the road. You're not Hüseyin Bey, you're a musketeer! That's how it is with young men. There's no holding them back. What do you say, master shepherd?"

"Thank you, Haji, sir."

Haji Imam turned proudly to Rıza Bey. "Are you listening, Rıza Bey? When fickle Kamil says he'll sell his daughter for a hundred *liras*, now he'll have nothing. The twenty is all he'll get."

Rıza Bey smiled for the first time all evening. "You have a gift for getting things done, Haji Imam. That's what I like about you."

3

When they reached Lime Hill, it was morning.

They stopped at the foot of a giant boulder. Below, Bayat Stream shone in the rising sun like the newly ground blade of a huge knife. To the north, high forest-covered mountains looked like grey clouds. There were five men. Except for Shepherd Ali, they were on horses and had rifles on their backs. The place where they had stopped was back off the road, and they could see only four houses of the village.

Ali held the horse's head while Hüseyin Bey jumped down. The others dismounted too and handed their reins to Ali.

Hüseyin Bey pointed with his whip. "Is that the girl's mother?"

Ali had been on foot. "The one on our side. There, sir. That one. That's her worthless mother. Her father's the one in the yard," he panted.

"You wait here with the animals. If there's shooting, don't be frightened. The bullets won't carry this far."

"With pleasure!"

Hüseyin Bey took his weapon off his shoulder and pushed a cartridge into the chamber. "Rifat, you'll go into the yard with me. You two will guard the road to the village. If anyone comes, fire into the air. But be careful. I don't want any mistakes or anyone getting shot."

When he said this, his voice was sharp and hard and didn't suit his stunted body. It was clear that he was used to giving orders and to losing his temper.

The four friends went down the sloping plain, crouched behind the low thicket, and descended straight to the house.

Ali collected the reins in his left hand and watched from behind like a soldier in charge of the pack horses. He had worn his old clothes, thinking of the four hours he would be on the road on foot. His tight blue cotton pants, yellow striped shirt, and black vest were patched. On his feet were flowered woolen socks and sandals made from pieces of an old tire. In this costume, Ali looked like the trunk of a thick tree wrapped in old cheesecloth. Protruding from the folds of his belt were a German silver tobacco box and the tip of a cigarette holder he had bought in Istanbul. His cap had slipped sideways, and his face was ruddy with a week-old growth of beard. His chest was heaving like the sides of some strange, frightened animal. He thought of all kinds of things, like singing and smoking a cigarette.

Hüseyin Bey was a brave young man. Ali coughed and smiled. Hüseyin Bey had said, "If there's shooting, don't be frightened." My God! In the army he'd seen a fifteen-gun battery fire at once.

When he thought of Fatma, he was amazed. That daughter of a whore was always laughing! He had never seen her sulky. A farmer had to have a courageous wife, and there was no woman stronger or more courageous than Fatma. She was short, but she had great endurance. Ali smiled like a wolf, showing the black roots of his teeth. "The pig's whore!"

He wiped the sweat from his forehead with his first finger and blew his nose violently.

Hüseyin Bey and his friends had reached the wall surrounding Kamil's yard. Ali took a step forward, as though to catch up with them.

The morning mist had cleared, and everything could be seen more easily now. He could see his future father-in-law's white beard. Kamil was squatting on the ground, chipping wood with a short-handled ax. Ali was amazed that he heard the sound of the ax only after it had fallen and risen again.

As soon as Hüseyin Bey and Rifat entered the yard, the dog ran out barking. Kamil didn't move. The girl's mother jumped up from the ground and put herself in front of the men. They talked for a moment. Then the woman shouted, "They've got us!"

She tried to grab Hüseyin Bey's rifle. Rifat hit her in the side with his rifle butt. She fell to the ground, and he leaned his gun against her chest.

At this moment, Fatma came out of the house and started to run to the hay rick. Hüseyin Bey went after her, caught up with her at the side of the storehouse, and grabbed her by the hair. The girl wrapped her arms around a post and screamed her heart out.

From where Ali was, Hüseyin Bey was very small, but one could see that with his rifle in one hand he couldn't easily pull her away. Ali muttered to himself, "Drag the dog's daughter! Drag the bitch!"

Unconsciously, Ali took the horses four or five steps forward. If it had been him, he would have had her on his back long ago. At that point, he felt such a fearful strength that he could have pulled out the post and put it and the girl on his shoulders.

Hüseyin Bey let go of Fatma's hair. He took his whip out of his bootleg and beat her on the side of the face. Fatma let out a long scream but didn't let go of the post. He hit her on the back of the head with his rifle butt. The girl held her head with her hands and threw herself to the ground. She struggled against him. Hüseyin Bey slung his rifle over his shoulder and wound her hair around his wrist. He was dragging her and hitting her on the back and the thighs with his whip.

Now the dog attacked him from behind. Rifat fired. The dog rolled over and fell to the ground. It struggled a little. When it was still, Ali said, "Too bad! It's sure dead!" He had brought the dog to Fatma's father himself when it was a pup, and he'd named it Killer.

Hüseyin Bey got the girl out of the yard. Rifat picked up Fatma's shawl, tied it to the barrel of his rifle and walked behind them. The two waiting at the village road took her arms. Ali ran his red tongue over his lips and said, "We took the woman."

The girl's mother was still screaming. Kamil hadn't moved or said a thing. When Hüseyin Bey got to the horses he winked to Ali.

Fatma struggled between the men and twisted herself back toward the house. She cried, "Mother, save me! Mother!"

Hüseyin Bey mounted his horse. "Ali, put her behind," he said.

Ali embraced the girl as though he were lifting a heavy ram. He squeezed her so tightly that her voice was cut off. Rifat held out the shawl with the end of his rifle. "Wrap this around her head!"

Ali leaned forward and began to run alongside Hüseyin Bey's horse. When he embraced her and put her on the horse, the buttons came off her blouse so that now and then her white throat flashed in the sunlight. Her naked foot shone against the horse's iron grey flank. Her shoes were probably in front of the storehouse. Who knows? Her hair was so long!

Ali was very pleased. He had never guessed how beautiful or brave Fatma was. When the horses slowed a bit, he leaned toward Hüseyin's mount. "Thank you, sir. Thank you, sir!" he said, and kissed Hüseyin's boot in its stirrup.

Fatma looked at Ali out of the corner of her eye. His sudden happiness was no stronger than her rage. If they would tie his arms behind him and set her free, she would bite his heaving chest, and that face, so sweaty it seemed to be crying — she would take her washing stick and pulverize it.

Her cheeks, where the whip had hit them, and the roots of her hair were aching more now. She leaned back so as not to rub against Hüseyin Bey but was afraid she would fall off the horse, and when she felt the soft, damp horse hair against her naked foot she almost cried.

As they descended again to the plain, Hüseyin Bey asked, "What was the idea of fighting us?"

Fatma didn't answer.

"Answer me, Fatma. You're engaged to Ali, aren't you?"

"I'm not."

"How's that, girl?"

"I'm not."

"But your father got twenty *liras* and a hundred twenty pounds of grain!"

Fatma was quiet.

"So what are you going to say to the police? You'll say you wanted to come."

The girl glanced at Ali.

His mouth was open. His eyes were pinched, and he was running with huge steps. The sweat coming out of his shirt stank. She wanted nothing to do with him and wouldn't even turn her head in his direction.

Huseyin Bey laughed nervously. "Did you hear, Fatma? You'll say you wanted to come."

"I won't."

"You will."

"If they kill me, I won't."

"Don't say it, then. You'll see what happens!"

The moment they entered the yard, Fatma slid off the back of the horse.

Hüseyin Bey called to the house. "Hey! Shadiye! Girl!"

"Yes, sir."

Shadiye was the daughter of Hüseyin Bey's uncle. She was a few years older than Fatma and came running, jingling the gold necklace on her breast.

"Look. We brought the one Ali will marry. You'll stay together. You'll forget your past foolishness, or you'll answer to me. Talk to her."

"Yes, sir."

• • •

Riza Bey's house was built on the top of a bare hill. It was a two-story house, the bottom made of stone and the top of wood. The only windows in the bottom were the four gun holes, one in each corner, for use against any attack.

After eating his noon meal alone in the kitchen, Ali was walking back and forth in the dark of the bottom of the house. He was ashamed and felt a need to tell his troubles to someone. When he heard footsteps from above, he went out in front of the house.

From there he could see the Red River, which cut around the hill like a wide, muddy boundary line, and the endless expanse of gently undulating, empty fields. The sky was perfectly blue and clear. The sun's heat made the air dance with a trembling vapor.

Ali dragged his feet around to the back of the building. He walked over to Blind Ahmet, who was sunning himself in front of a large rock at the edge of the vineyard.

"Hello, blind shepherd!"

"Welcome, master!"

Ali laughed guiltily and sat down.

Ahmet poked fun at him. "Men laugh when their business is wrapped up. When's the wedding?"

"The wedding? Look here. What do I know? Rıza Bey would know." Ali lowered his voice. "And I'm ashamed. Don't ask about it, Ahmet. I'm ashamed."

"Don't worry about it, master."

Ali lowered his voice some more. "Ahmet, what do they give you for kidnapping a girl?"

"I wouldn't know. Niyazi from the Karapıchak family kidnapped one. They gave him three years. The girl was under age."

"They gave him three years?"

"They gave him three years. If Niyazi could have passed himself off as younger, maybe it would've been less."

Ali thought a little. "They'll think Hüseyin Bey is younger than he is. Did you know his age is wrong in the register? And he certainly wouldn't betray us. Not Hüseyin Bey!"

"In that case, it's all right."

"Of course it's all right. How couldn't it be all right?"

"Has the girl agreed, master?"

"It takes time. Girls are coy."

"Never mind that. Hüseyin Bey said to her, 'You'll see what happens,' and if Hüseyin Bey says 'You'll see what happens,' he'll do something for sure. So! What do you say to that, Ahmet?"

"Anyway, it won't be left to Hüseyin Bey. Rıza Bey will straighten it out."

Ali had stopped listening to Ahmet. As far as he was concerned, anything about her coyness was nonsense. "The daughter of a pig!" he thought. She was so brave she hadn't shown any fear of Hüseyin Bey at all. His heart pounded when he remembered how strongly she struggled between his arms when he lifted her to the rump of the horse. She was something soft and violent, like honey. If he could only hold her like that for hours. That was all he needed, if she would agree. They would plow the fields together and together they would bring in the harvest. In a year, they'd have four and a half tons of grain. After they repaid the seed and divided the rest with Rıza Bey, they'd have two tons for themselves!

Ali wet his dry lips and closed his eyes.

At this point they heard one of the servants shouting, "Hey, Ali! Shepherd Ali! Hüseyin Bey wants you. The gendarmes are here. They're taking him to the police station."

Ali couldn't breathe from fear. Twice he tried to get up. Finally, putting his hands on the ground, he was able to stand.

4

Hüseyin Bey and the gendarme were walking a few steps in front.

It was mid-afternoon.

Ali walked behind, so frightened that he wondered where on the dirt road he could hide his lengthening shadow. For years, when he wasn't at the head of a flock, he had been very ill at ease. His body found its exact place with the sheep but wouldn't fit anywhere when he was idle. There was no comfortable corner for him to settle down in. However brave he was seven months of the year grazing the sheep, he was just that timid the five months he was without work. What he wanted most from sharecropping was to be delivered from this timidity. Whether at the head of the flock or tending the fields and the farm, what he needed was work.

He felt that if everyone were idle, the world would be very uncomfortable.

When the servant said, "The gendarmes have come," he started hiccupping. Now while he walked, this obstinate thing rolled up from his chest to his throat and shook his whole body every three or four steps.

He rolled a cigarette.

Each time he drew on the cigarette a hiccup followed.

His shadow was beating some of the time on the gendarme's back and some of the time on Hüseyin Bey's.

As a shepherd he was used to silence, but walking now like this without talking was frightening. He was afraid to death of the gendarme. Not because they beat you or took you to town with your arms tied.

That had never happened to him. It was just that he was afraid, even though the gendarme was a short, bow-legged youth. Ali heard him tell Hüseyin Bey that he was from Edirne and had four months left before his discharge. The barrel of the rifle on his shoulder shone in the descending sun as a thin blue line. He remembered the artillery regiment. "Front sight, rear sight. How many parts on the stock? How do you clean a rifle?" Guns, cartridge belts, uniforms — there was nothing to fear in these.

His fear grew worse because he couldn't understand what he was afraid of.

Hüseyin Bey beside the gendarme, without his rifle or his horse, was suddenly the size of a small child.

Ali thought, "Can you see that? If only we had told Rıza Bey. Shit!"

They turned a corner.

The Bayat township police station, standing alone at the edge of the road, seemed out of place and frightening. Not counting the cellar, it was one story. It had a gabled roof, unlike the village houses, and a flag waved on a pole at the peak.

Ali thought to himself, "They could throw me in the cellar. If they leave me all night — if Hüseyin Bey goes without me — shit."

He hiccupped, took off his cap, and wiped his head. He was sweating terribly.

Hüseyin Bey held back a bit and came near Ali. "When the police captain asks, you say you took the girl, Ali."

Ali staggered as though he would fall.

"My God, Hüseyin Bey!"

"Shut up!"

They went up the four steps.

Now Ali couldn't think at all.

Kamil was in the waiting room squatting on his heels at the foot of the wall, and he jumped onto his feet when he saw Hüseyin Bey come through the door. With his small face, white beard, and lashless, frightened eyes, he resembled a sick child with some cotton stuck to his chin. He wanted to walk over to Hüseyin Bey and say something to him. He took a step away from the wall, but when Hüseyin Bey turned his head, he stepped back again. He was wearing old sandals, white cotton homemade pajamas, a shirt that hung over his hips, and a short, tight-sleeved jacket. Tied to his head was a faded handkerchief. His costume went well with the fear and hopelessness in his eyes. His thin, dirty, blue-veined hands were clasped together on his chest.

The gendarme set his rifle on its butt and knocked on the door that said "Station Commander" over it.

There was a sharp, dry voice. "Come in!"

Ali's hiccups suddenly stopped. He made a decision. "Can I say I took her? How can I? By God, I've got to tell the truth. Can you imagine that? For sure, I've got to tell the truth."

Hüseyin Bey went and shut the door, and Ali listened closely. At every sentence, he looked at Kamil and nodded.

The commander started to shout. "You must not think that I don't understand, Hüseyin Bey. Just because you're young, your father's using you all over the place. You'll come to a bad end. You think about it. This isn't the mountains here."

"What happened, sir?"

"And then you ask what's happened, without any shame. My God! You landlords can't get away with that any more! The feudalistic age of the oppressors is finished! You attacked a home and kidnapped a girl. There were three armed men with you. Who were they? I want their names. One was Rejeb. Tell me. This time there's no escape. And I want the four rifles and the ammunition."

Ali was a little relieved. They weren't counting him. If they were, wouldn't the sergeant have said there were *four* others? How good it was he'd waited with the horses! How good.

He felt a great affection for Kamil, and was ashamed.

The commander was becoming more and more angry. "You beat the girl. You shot the dog. You threatened to kill the wife. Attacking a home — men hang for this, Hüseyin Bey! They hang, do you understand?"

"Wait, man, don't fly apart so fast. Why are you blaming me for all this? So a girl was kidnapped. That's how it happens."

"What do you mean, 'That's how it happens'?"

"I mean that's how it happens. Well, the fellow was engaged to her for a long time—"

"Engaged?"

"Yes, engaged. So he took her. That's how it happens. The girl is happy; the fellow is happy. It wasn't the way you heard it, corporal. Here, have a cigarette."

When they stopped shouting, Kamil became apprehensive. He got up and came over to Ali. From fear and shock, Ali was rooted to the spot. He was ruined. He felt nauseated. They give you three years! If he could manage, he would cry and beg for mercy. He turned to Kamil. "Tell them the truth, uncle. He's a lair. A liar! Let's go tell the truth."

While he was pleading with Kamil, the gendarme opened the door. "Which one of you is Ali?"

Ali grabbed his cap.

"Come in here."

Ali went inside, clicked his heels together, and stood at attention. He tried as hard as he could, but he couldn't make out the insignia on the commander's shoulder. He didn't know whether he was a sergeant or a corporal. The officer was a thin, swarthy man. The papers and the telephone on the desk increased Ali's fear. He wanted to plead with the commander, but he couldn't think of anything to say.

The commander asked, "What's your name?"

"Ali."

"You don't have a last name?"

"Ali Solumazoğlu, from Payapınar Village in İskilip, a son of Durmush, Ali Solumazoğlu, born 1914, İskilip—"

"What's your job?"

"I'm a shepherd for Rıza Bey."

Ali opened his eyes and looked at Hüseyin Bey.

Hüseyin Bey was sitting comfortably in a chair at the side of the desk.

"Look at me. What are you looking at over there? Tell the truth. Did you kidnap the girl?"

"I swear, commander."

"Tell the truth."

Hüseyin Bey broke in. "Tell him you're engaged to Fatma, Ali. Tell him the girl wanted to come. No one was armed, and the house wasn't attacked. Didn't you go and get her? Spit it out."

"Fatma and I were engaged, commander."

"Tell the truth."

"I swear, we were engaged!"

Hüseyin Bey explained. "Ali is our shepherd, so my father paid twenty *liras* and a hundred twenty pounds of grain for the girl. The bride price was set at sixty *liras*. In addition, we were going to give him eight hundred pounds of grain. Kamil was going to give the girl to Ali."

"Is that right, Ali?"

"That's right, commander."

The corporal gave an order to the gendarme standing by the door. "Get the one with the beard."

Kamil had his weak fist clenched on the string of his trousers. His beard was shaking.

"Look here, old man. Supposedly you were going to sell your daughter to Ali. Is that right?"

Kamil was about to collapse. When he entered this building, it never occurred to him that he would have to face Hüseyin Bey, but he realized his mistake as soon as he saw him. He had waited since morning on an empty stomach, and he was weak. He answered with clattering teeth. "We were going to sell the girl to Ali, master, sir."

The corporal was angry again. "You mean you were going to give the girl voluntarily!"

"Yes."

"You took the money!"

"Yes. Rıza Bey gave us twenty *liras*."

"You took some wheat."

"We took a hundred twenty pounds of grain."

"Then what happened?"

"We changed our minds. We were going to repay the money at harvest."

Hüseyin Bey got up and stood in front of Kamil. "Tell us, Kamil. Did you see me attack your house with your own eyes?"

Ali watched with amazement. Hüseyin Bey wasn't now the well-behaved young boy who had been walking beside the gendarme. His fists were on his hips, he frowned threateningly, and his eyes were cold. Now he was a man like his father, used to ruling men.

Kamil's whole beard was trembling. He looked from Ali to the corporal, and from the corporal to Hüseyin Bey. "I didn't see it, master, sir. I was getting firewood. The wife said it."

"You mean you didn't see me."

"I didn't see you, sir. I was getting wood."

The corporal squinted and leaned forward. "You say you didn't see him?"

"I didn't see him, sir. The wife said it."

"Well, if you didn't see them, you'll see now. I'll cut off your beard for you, you lying lout!"

The corporal took out a piece of paper and plunged his pen into the inkwell. After asking Kamil's name and date and place of birth, he yelled at the gendarme. "Take this one and throw him in the cellar. The good for nothing slanderer! Now we'll make out the indictment. We'll have him tried. Once he's in jail he'll come to his senses. It wasn't wisdom that turned this one's beard white! The lying scoundrel!"

When the door had closed behind Kamil, Hüseyin Bey explained. "The daughter is happy, the son is happy, and this Kamil will be happy too. Without a doubt, the trouble is that the woman was trying to grab too much money. How much money can you ask from a little shepherd like this?"

Ali's fear had lifted a little. Now he was surprised at Hüseyin Bey, standing in front of the commander of the police, lying to Kamil's face. What if the corporal hadn't believed him? What if Kamil had said, 'You were there. You attacked the house'? Shit! What if they had given him an oath? Would Hüseyin Bey lie under oath? What kind of man lies under oath? It's too much, too much!"

The corporal and Hüseyin Bey were talking about something and laughing at the ignorance, cunning, and thick-headedness of villagers.

When they stopped talking, the corporal became serious and looked at Ali. "You call us to the wedding. If you forget, you'll be in trouble."

He turned to Hüseyin Bey. "Tommorrow you send the girl, Hüseyin Bey. She has to tell us she went voluntarily." He lowered his voice. "And bring the old man around. The ignorant lout. It's a pity. But if the girl is under age, don't complicate things."

When Hüseyin Bey was leaving the room he stopped in the door and shouted jokingly, "With your permission, corporal, let me see this Kamil. Turn the bastard over to me."

"If you aren't going to sue him, there's no problem. But it's known he slandered you."

"There's no harm."

"Well, in that case, let's get him out."

The gendarme opened the cellar door, laughing.

"My God, sir — whatever you say — whatever you say. I was taken in by my wife. She said it. I was getting wood—"

Now he believed his own invention. Soon he would be crying.

Hüseyin Bey remained serious. "This time the corporal forgave you for my sake. Do you hear, Kamil? Did you give your daughter to Ali?"

"Yes."

"Then don't worry about the rest."

With Hüseyin Bey in front and Ali and Kamil behind, they went outside.

They walked without talking as far as the turnoff to Hanging Village.

When it was time for Kamil to leave them, he stopped. "Thank God, Hüseyin Bey, the business is settled. We've agreed to give the girl. You be just, too. Have Rıza Bey send half a ton of grain or so. Our storehouse is empty." He was squeezing and pulling his nose. "And send a little money, too. I'll be grateful, Hüseyin Bey. I was only listening to the villagers when I made the complaint against you. When they saw the rifles they didn't come, to save bloodshed. 'If we had, we'd all be dead,' they said. The cowards! And my wife forced me. Have mercy, sir. Let's keep the grain in the deal — and don't forget the money. You're a just man."

Hüseyin Bey frowned and thought a little. "You'll have to be patient about the money. My father's very angry you filed the complaint. As for the grain, we'll do something. Send the woman tomorrow, with the donkey. They'll give her some from the storehouse. If they don't, she can find me."

Kamil walked away praying. His beard was still trembling.

Ali suddenly burst out laughing.

• • •

When they reached the farm, it was long past sunset.

Shadiye opened the door, and Hüseyin Bey asked, "Has my father gone to bed?"

"No, sir. He's in the sitting room."

"What have you and Fatma come to? Did she agree?"

"No."

"What does she say?"

"She says, 'If Hüseyin Bey wants, let him kill me. I won't have Ali.' "

Ali was listening to his heart pound in the dark. He was ashamed of what Shadiye said and, pretending to wipe away the sweat, covered his face with his handkerchief.

"Why doesn't she want him? Does she want someone else?"

"There's no one else. The old woman filled her head with nonsense. She told her, 'What do you want with some shepherd from another village? He'll be a sharecropper, kill some enemy of the landlord, and spend ten or fifteen years in jail.' "

"So you couldn't persuade the little girl. That's too bad."

"I talked and talked. She wouldn't listen."

"Okay. Quick, take my mother and go sit with the family."

After the woman left, Hüseyin Bey and Ali entered the room where Fatma was sitting alone. It was the special room for Rıza Bey's guests. The floor and the couches were covered with rugs. There was a fire in the stove, and a small night light flickered on a shelf in the corner.

Fatma was cowering on the couch like a small woolen bag.

Hüseyin Bey asked angrily, "You didn't agree yet, girl?"

Fatma stood up without answering. Her black eyes shone with tears.

"Speak, girl. You haven't agreed?"

"Master, sir, kill me."

"I'm not listening to nonsense. If you don't say yes, you know what happens. Ali! Look here. Here's Fatma, and here's you. You will talk. If she doesn't agree, beat her. Out there are the brutal ones. Take her and give her to them. Let them have her and make her dance in the mountains. Let her be a whore. Let her pour whiskey for the rabble. I'll get you another girl from anywhere you want."

When Hüseyin Bey turned to go, Fatma ran to him and threw her arms around his knees. "Don't do it, sir! Kill me! I give you my life. Don't give me to Ali or to the others."

She began to cry. It was the terrible, muffled, silent crying of village women who don't dare to irritate men.

Hüseyin Bey pulled his boots away and went out.

When the door closed, Fatma jumped up from where she had collapsed on the floor and ran to the wall. She squeezed herself into the corner to hide from the light.

Ali didn't move. The light from the stove and the lamp moved on his body. He seemed larger, and his eyes and mouth seemed brighter and more alive. Then he walked slowly to the couch and sat down. He took out his tobacco box.

"Don't be mulish. Come here," he said. "Look, I've got some things to tell you." He coughed. "They wanted Hüseyin Bey at the police station. The corporal sent a gendarme." He carefully wet the cigarette paper and stuck it together. "I had to go with him. You know Hüseyin Bey isn't afraid. We went. Your father Kamil was there. He made a complaint. He said Hüseyin Bey attacked his house and kidnapped his daughter."

Ali got up. He squatted in front of the stove and lit his cigarette.

"But he couldn't deny the money or the grain he got. He was afraid of Hüseyin Bey, and he said, 'I wasn't home. I was cutting wood. The woman said it.' The police commander was really mad." Ali laughed thickly. "He called your father a lying lout and lots more besides. They threw him in the cellar. In the end, Hüseyin Bey had them set him free. Kamil agreed to this. You'll see. Tomorrow he's coming to get his grain. That's how it is."

Ali stood up in front of the stove. "Do you understand? Your father sold you to me."

Fatma didn't make a sound. She was sobbing to herself and believed what Ali said. Her father was a weak man. He was poor.

Ali came a step closer. "If you don't agree, you know what happens. I'll take you to those men."

Fatma was silent.

"By God, I'll give you to them. Look, I gave my word. They'll take you to the mountains and have what they want. You'll be a whore for seven villages. They'll sell you from one village to the other. You'll dance for the boys in their rooms. You'll pour whiskey."

He came to her side and raised his heavy hand like an ax. "All right. I'll beat you and give you to them. I swear I will."

When he couldn't think of anything more to say, he became bewildered and angry. With huge steps, he crossed in front of the stove and went outside. He came back with a long, heavy rope. He pulled Fatma's arms from in front of her breast and bound them tightly behind her back. Hatefully, he pushed her face down on the floor. The girl was screaming. He put his knees in the middle of her back and, kneeling on her with all his weight, tied her hands to her feet. He put her easily on his shoulder. He hesitated in the middle of the room and asked her once more.

"Don't be mulish. I've given my word."

She answered, "Don't take me. I'll agree."

"So there! I'm glad you've come around. Tomorrow you'll say to the police, 'I came with Ali of my own desire.' "

"I'll say it."

He put Fatma slowly onto the couch. Swearing, he undid the rope. "Quiet, now. Don't cry."

He waited for an answer. "Quiet, girl! Now look! There's a mattress in the cupboard. Spread it out."

Ali's voice was trembling.

Fatma opened the cupboard. She took out one of the thin mattresses on top and put it in front of the stove. She spread a sheet over it, put down a pillow, and piled a quilt at the foot.

Ali lit another cigarette. He stared straight into the stove, and watched Fatma from the corner of his eye. The girl was standing by the wall with her arms across her breast. She had henna on her fingers.

Ali lost his roughness. He asked with a soft voice, "Fatma, are the bath kettles full?"

The cupboard near the door had the bath things. Fatma carried two large copper kettles to the stove.

Ali had taken two puffs on his cigarette. He threw it into the fire.

When he took off his shirt, the smell of a man's sweat spread through the room. He sat on the edge of the bed and stretched out his legs.

Fatma came, as she had seen her mother do, and knelt in front of him. She put Ali's feet in her lap one at a time and pulled off his socks. Then, biting her cheeks, she pulled off his tight trousers.

She waited for the man to lie down and cover himself with the quilt, and she went to the corner and began to undress.

Outside there was the thick voice of a howling dog.

JELAL THE BRICKLAYER
Orhan Kemal
(Translated by Virginia Taylor-Saçlıoğlu)

Jelal was looking at his wife with big, green eyes ringed with dark circles.

"Don't do it, Shadiye," he pleaded. "For the love of God, put an end to this rotten business. I can't take any more."

Jelal's nineteen-year-old wife, Shadiye, was sitting in front of the only window in the dark room, which reeked of *arak*, watching the neighbor women who were doing their domestic chores in the muddy courtyard.

Jelal had an obvious hangover. His long, black lashes were moist. As he breathed, the hot, sickening odor of anisette filled the room, and his clothes were white with blotches of lime.

"You don't care about me, you don't love me, but it doesn't matter," he continued. "But just think of your son. Think of yourself."

Shadiye didn't budge. She continued to stare into the muddy courtyard and watch the women gathered there around the rusty pump in the center.

"They don't do you any good. They're hurting you. They're destroying you. You'll become a whore."

But he knew that his wife would continue to run after young dandies like a moth toward a flame, a vulture after a carcass, a honeybee flitting from flower to flower.

He sat down at his wife's knees and started to repeat the things he had just been saying. He described how she would end up and explained the folly of the path she was treading. He pleaded. He wept.

"If someone else were in my place, he would kill you," he said. "I can't kill you. It's not in my power. I can't kill you, Shadiye."

The woman turned angrily. "Kill me! Aren't you a man? Don't you have any self-respect? Pull your knife and kill me. I'm fed up with this life, anyway."

"I can't bring myself to kill you. I'm not able. Give up this disgusting business. It won't come to any good."

The woman sprang up and began to shout in a loud voice. "I say divorce me, but you won't divorce me. I say leave me alone, but you won't leave me alone. Damn your kind of manliness! A man with even a little blood in his veins would pull his knife, and that would be that."

She went down the stairs and into the courtyard.

Jelal stood up, too. He was reeling, and the room seemed to be spinning around his head. He looked out the window into the courtyard. His wife, with her plump white hand grasping the pump, was yelling and shouting angrily.

"What can I do if he's not a man? Even if he showered me up to my neck in diamonds, what would be the point?"

The neighbor women agreed. "You're absolutely right. You said it, honey. You call that being a man? So what if he's clothed her, fed her and taken her places! She's young and hot-blooded, but he's already forty-five. Past his prime! You shouldn't bite off more than you can chew! Everybody knows that. If you can't handle it, don't take it. Let him get a woman past the change to keep house for him!"

"A man with even a little red blood in his veins wouldn't swallow such words. I say 'Kill me,' but no, he says he doesn't have the heart."

Burning with shame, Jelal came down the stairs. As he passed through the yard, the women continued to snicker, and one of them called out, "Pansy!"

It was one of those late autumn mornings when the air is filled with the smell of crude oil from the huge, double-tired cotton trucks that snort as they pass. Jelal the bricklayer, his shiny steel knife in his pocket, mingled with the unemployed migrant workers from Anatolia and Syria. Then he stopped at the roadside tavern and drank three glasses of wine, one after the other, without eating anything. The wine upset his empty stomach. His dizziness increased, and the evening's drunkenness began again.

The tavernkeeper was lighting a cigarette.

"Give me one, Apostol," said Jelal.

"Apostol my eye! Talk right!"

"Aw. Why are you sore? If you are Apostol, do you deserve anything better?"

"Jelal, straighten up! You hear?"

"Then fill this glass."

The fourth glass was filled.

"Everybody has his problems," observed the tavernkeeper.

Jelal quickly drained the fourth glass. "Today an incident occurred in our courtyard, but it's too depressing to talk about."

The tavernkeeper, absentmindedly smoking his cigarette, paid no attention.

Jelal continued. "There's a fellow in our courtyard, forty-five, a friend of mine. And he's got a wife nineteen. He's no good as a man. He has an idea of what his wife is up to, but— Every day they fight. This morning the wife went into the courtyard and—"

The tavernkeeper became interested. "And then?"

"And then, a drama. 'Since you can't control me, divorce me. Even if you shower me with diamonds, I won't accept—' and more sweet words."

The tavernkeeper clicked his tongue in disapproval. "Can that imbecile still look into another person's face?"

"Who?"

"The husband."

Jelal the bricklayer pushed his empty glass forward. "Another one."

The tavernkeeper picked up the wine bottle. "He was right there?"

"He was there."

"Right there you mean?"

"Right there."

"What a fool!" The tavernkeeper shook his head as he filled the glass. "You mean he was right there and heard it with his own ears? Didn't he turn red?"

Jelal raised his glass with annoyance. "Cheers!" He smirked and downed the contents. "If it had been you, what would you have done?"

"What would I have done? I would have raised hell, man! Let her go into the courtyard and yell her head off! Let the bitch try to shame me— What would I have done? I would have thrown her down and slaughtered her like a sheep! Are you pulling my leg?"

"He caught her many times with other men and fought with them and beat them, but he cannot touch the woman because he knows it's his own fault."

"If it's like that, let him divorce her."

"He's in love with her and can't divorce her."

The tavernkeeper thought for a moment. "God forbid that anybody should be in a situation like that, brother," he said. "It's a tough question. Is there anything worse than being in love? The best thing would be for him to kill himself and be saved from it. Why is the woman to blame?"

Suddenly, Jelal pulled his long-legged chair into a corner and put his head between his hands. The tavernkeeper went up to him.

"What's the matter? Tell me. Why are you crying?"

Jelal, who had fixed his eyes on the ground, did not answer.

"Tell me. Why are you crying? Does a man cry?"

Jelal did not answer.

When he pulled out his shining iron knife, the tavernkeeper was frightened. He thought he understood what he was going to do. He did not want such a thing to happen in his shop and was sorry he had provoked him. He was alone in the shop. If he were to say he killed himself, they wouldn't believe him. There would be no end to it. He rushed out of the shop, alarmed, and called to the grocer next door. They stood by the tavern door.

"Do you see this man?" he asked. "I think he is going to commit suicide."

"Who?"

"This fellow. Jelal."

"Why?"

"I don't know, but I think because of his wife."

"Does a man kill himself over a woman? Why doesn't he just divorce her and be done with it?"

"But it isn't what you think." He told him the story briefly.

"I wouldn't wish that on anyone. It's a hard thing. Better call a policeman."

"No policeman would come without an incident."

"In that case, let's wait."

In a short time, a curious crowd gathered at the door of the tavern. As the crowd was growing larger, Jelal folded his switchblade and put it in his pocket, left the wine money on the counter, and left.

TWO GIRLS
Orhan Kemal
(Translated by John Taylor)

The man on the Ankara radio had wished us a good evening, and it was a good evening when I was walking home and turned the last corner to my house. Above, there were neither moon nor stars, and a sharp wind rustled the eucalyptus trees on both sides of the road. Suddenly I heard on my left in the darkness of the small, dilapidated houses the sound of someone's embarrassed, fleeing footsteps. I slowed down and searched in that direction. When my eyes were used to the dark, I made out a large shape moving away, pulling up its pants. I stopped. The sound of the footsteps faded away. Then I vaguely guessed something. Just where I was about to step two disheveled young girls came near me.

"What are you doing there?" I found myself asking.

"What's it to you?" they answered together.

Then they came up to me. "Hey, boy. It's just a question of money. The fellows who pay a little money are happy!" said the one on the right. She touched my hand.

Then I understood what was going on.

"If you're hot, you can come too!" the one on my left said.

"Yes, I am," I said. "OK, where do we go?"

"We've got a place back there. The watchman can't see it. Not even God can."

They walked ahead and I followed. When we passed a streetlight I looked at them carefully. They hardly looked as old as my nine-year-old daughter.

We turned a number of corners and passed through some narrow streets. Then we dived into a short, blind alley. We stopped by a pile of rocks in front of a high, barely visible white wall.

"Come on," they said. "Do it quick. Which one of us do you want?"

"You," I said at random. The other walked off a little.

"Come here!" said the one near me.

We sat side by side on one of the large rocks that had weeds growing out between them.

"First, the money," she said.

Then, afraid that her customer would leave, she said, "I'm sorry, but I've got burned a few times."

I put the fifty cents she wanted in her small hand. As she was about to start the business professionally, I said, "Wait! Not so fast."

I think she looked into my face, surprised.

"Why?"

"Don't you have a mother or father?" I asked. She shrugged her shoulders and said, "Sure."

"Do they know you're doing this?"

"Yes."

"They know?"

"So they know. What of it?"

"Is it they who tell you to go and do this?"

"They don't say that, but they say 'Go earn some money.' "

She explained slowly.

"We were working in a factory. At the cotton gins. Some officials came and said we were too young. We were fired."

There was a watchman's whistle near by. She was alarmed.

"Come on. Come on. Let's be quick about it."

I stood up. I wanted to get away from that rock pile. It smelled like an open toilet.

"Where are you going?" she asked.

"I'm going. You got your money," I said.

She ran off. She went up to her friend on the other side of the rock pile and explained something excitedly. When I passed them, her friend said,

" . . . which means he's just a fool!"

RAIN WAS FALLING AT SHISH-HANE
Haldun Taner
(*Translated by Virginia Taylor-Saçlıoğlu*)

An American photographer replaced the lens of his camera with the eye of a horse and took various photographs. We see from these photographs that on a horse's retina things and people are reflected twice as large as they actually are. I say "as they actually are," but it would be more correct to say twice as large as they appear to us, because whether or not we see things in their true size is another problem altogether.

In a subsequent German report based on the American photographer's findings, the writer concluded, "Now the fact that he sees everything as bigger than it actually is has produced a sense of inferiority in the animal and, since ancient times, has lowered him to the rank of service to mankind."

I don't know how the American photographer made the experiment with the horse's eye, but it seems to me that the German's hypothesis is probably valid for proletarian horses like the animals belonging to milkmen and garbage collectors. As for those aristocrat horses, brought up in special stables with a thousand varieties of attention lavished on them and boasting family trees just like the families of lords, it doesn't seem possible that they perceive human beings as bigger than they actually are. Not only have they transcended size, they don't even perceive things in proportion anymore. After being hand in glove with high society for so long, they have come to perceive human beings as small, in fact, Lilliputian, as if viewed through the wrong end of a telescope.

In any case, the horse who is the hero of our story is of the species that perceives everything half again as big because he was an ordinary garbage collector's horse. He had passed his twentieth birthday and was pushing twenty-one (twenty years for a horse being roughly equivalent to sixty for a human being), and since he had entered the ranks of the Municipal Sanitary Works during the administration of Muhittin Bey his retirement was approaching. Furthermore, his name was Kalender. With such qualifications, if he perceived things not only half again but even twice as big, no one had any right to object.

The event in question occurred at about three o'clock in the afternoon as Kalender was making his customary daily round in the district of Shish-hane.

A porter approached, balancing an enormous mirror on his back and, in an instant, without warning, Kalender saw his image in the mirror. Of course, he perceived this image as bigger than it actually was, that is, than we perceive it.

And he whinnied!

At this point two possibilities come to mind.

1. Kalender understood that the horse in the mirror was his own reflection, in which case the whinny was a result of a creature, accustomed to perceiving everything else as big and himself therefore as small, finally discovering his actual size and true worth.

But, in order to arrive at such a conclusion, it is a necessary condition that Kalender had previously never seen himself anywhere, whereas the possibility that Kalender, in the course of a life as long as twenty years and particularly in a big city like Istanbul, had not seen himself before was out of the question. Even if not in a mirror then certainly in a water trough, at the edge of a stream, or in a mud puddle he must have seen himself. In fact, while the garbage collector was emptying the garbage into the cart, he had often amused himself for long, lazy hours watching his reflection wrinkle and twitch as a light breeze stirred the surface of a puddle and admiring the pleasant picture formed by his inclined head against the background of blue sky and drifting white clouds. But seeing oneself in a mud puddle is quite different from seeing oneself in a mirror. Since mud puddles always lie flat on the ground, a persons always perceives his reflection foreshortened just like those newspaper photographs of preachers speaking from an elevated pulpit, and it cannot be denied that this type of photograph always shows a person, and therefore a horse, as somewhat more imposing than he really is. A mirror, on the other hand, because it stands up vertically, offers no such flattering optical illusion but ruthlessly shows a person as he really is.

For this reason, when a horse, accustomed to viewing himself from a favorable, romantic and artistic perspective, one day encounters the icy reality of a mirror, naturally it is going to produce a severe shock, and his whinnying must be considered an entirely normal reaction to such disillusionment.

Whether horse or human, we always find it difficult to accept old age. "I'm just the same," you say. "I'm still the same lithe stallion I was when I started at the sanitary works," you say. Days and years pass. The garbage of Shish-hane is never-ending, but that misty period of youth disappears into thin air like a wisp of smoke. One day fate holds a mirror up to your face and you almost lose your mind. "Is that me?" you ask in astonishment. "Is that shabby, decrepit, asthmatic horse Kalender?"

Yes, if Kalender recognized his reflection in the mirror, then it is possible that he thought in this way and for this reason whinnied.

2. Either that, or (and the police, shopkeepers and passersby tend to support this second hypothesis) the animal could have thought that the reflection in the mirror was another horse, a garbage collector's horse like himself, but a stranger and enemy who was going to run him down. In this case, his whinnying must be judged to be an entirely legitimate expression of self-defense.

Furthermore, due to the enlargement of the enemy horse according to the explanation above, one must not forget that he perceived the stranger as half again as big as he actually was. But no. If we remember that he was accustomed from birth to seeing other horses in these magnified proportions, then we realize that this played no significant part.

Nevertheless, whichever of the two hypotheses is correct doesn't make much difference, nor, in fact, does the optical irregularity which we discussed at length above. The truly important thing is what happened afterwards. He whinnied!

Whether from fear, astonishment, disappointment, or whatever kind of subconscious sense of inferiority, for whatever reason at all, he whinnied bitterly and peevishly and, like every startled horse, took the bit in his mouth and started to go backwards. But the street was on a slope and slippery with rain, and the cart began to slip backwards with such speed that it left the pavement and crashed into the window of an electrician's shop with a sudden burst of shattering glass.

Since no other ingenious American has yet constructed a microphone with a horse's eardrum and then used it to make recordings, we still don't know how much more intensely sounds are registered by horses' ears. But, again, they are no doubt registered more loudly because Kalender was thoroughly frightened out of his wits by the shattering glass and the explosion of a hundred-watt light bulb which flew out of the window, and he jerked the cart forward with a lunge.

It was at that moment that the real accident occurred.

• • •

Upon receiving the express telegram from the company in Sao Paulo, Artin Margusyan lost his composure. At the last minute, the company was lowering the price he had suggested by twenty percent. Hatless and coatless, Artin Margusyan dashed into the street and, seeing no need to summon the driver, slid behind the steering wheel. Now he was both driving the car and thinking. To be precise, one couldn't really call this thinking. A string of disconnected thoughts were passing through his mind. "God forbid that Antranik should get nervous and try to interfere," he was thinking. Antranik was both his partner and his brother-in-law. Although he himself was a Catholic and Antranik a Gregorian, they got along quite well together, so well that he had sent Antranik to bid in his place that day.

He glanced again at his gold-plated watch. Nothing could be considered yet. There were still fifteen minutes until the bidding would begin. Ah, dear Antranik, like a son to me. (He reached the intersection just as the traffic policeman gave the signal to stop. Each second that passed seemed like a year to Artin Margusyan. When the policeman finally gave the go signal, he stepped on the gas and took off with more pickup than he had expected.) Just what sort of jerk was this Lorenzo anyway to lower the price by twenty percent at the last minute? Who knows what kind of shenanigans were involved? (Drops of rain continuously showered the windshield.) Mumbling "Here's what's missing, here's the trouble," Artin Margusyan randomly pushed a button. But there was no change on the windshield because the button he had pressed turned on the taillights.

Of course, one wouldn't expect an amateur who still had a few weeks to go before getting his license to know as much about a car as a professional chauffeur. Artin Margusyan pressed a second button, and this one perversely set off the turn signal. But Artin Margusyan was a persistent man. In fact, he owed his success in business in large measure to just that quality of his. For this reason, he pressed a third button. Eureka! The two previously motionless wipers began to tick from right to left with the regularity of a metronome and clean the glass with the enthusiasm of a diligent housewife. Artin Margusyan took the curve at Tepebashı in the flush of this modest success, his taillights beaming in broad daylight.

"Okay, my boy, percentagewise you've lost. What commission would we have made from the first price? Trois fois quatre makes douze milles. Sept fois douze comes to huit cent quarante. Si le prix d'achat est abaissé de vingt pour cent, le bénéfice en diminuera d'autant." (When Artin Margusyan got excited, he would think in Turkish, Armenian and French all at once. Although he also knew a little English, by some stroke of wisdom it only came out when he smoked cigars.)

He smiled. "Do you have confidence in yourself, my boy? Does it seem that the bidding on the first price will be up to you? Still, the guarantee is on our side now. Just think how surprised Antranik is going to be when he sees me! And not just him, either. Ali Tomar, Kamil's boys, Anesti, Kevork Kavafyan, Naili— 'Gentlemen,' I'll say, 'I too can make a plaisanterie.' I'll wave the telegram in the air like a flag and I'll say, 'Gentlemen, don't waste your time. Coffee has never been offered anywhere at this price until now.'"

Just as he was thinking these thoughts, a huge number 515, white on green, appeared on the clearest and least foggy part of the windshield which the wipers were cleaning assiduously. It grew and grew like the trademark at the end of a Twentieth Century Fox film until finally, with a frightful crash, everything was instantly plunged into darkness.

• • •

"The animal flew into the road like an arrow," the streetcar driver was saying. "I immediately pulled the hand brake and prevented an accident. How could I have seen that there was someone behind me? Curse that creature of God! Why did he have to plow into the back of the car?"

The passengers were of the same opinion. The garbage cart horse had shot onto the track like a lunatic. Although the passengers were piled on top of one another like a deck of playing cards, they all took the driver's side. The one who was in trouble was the driver of the automobile behind them. If he had been an expert driver, he would not have been following so closely, and even if he had, when the streetcar began to brake, he would have noticed and would not have driven up the back of it like an ox.

The police would give the streetcar the right of way and would have to sort it out with the inexperienced driver.

All of the streetcars in back were lined up waiting. Of these lined up, waiting streetcars, the seventeenth one was just in front of the office of the head official of Beyoğlu. The force of the rain had increased still more, and a flock of crows which suddenly appeared from the direction of Kasımpasha flew, cackling and cawing, over the financial branch and out of sight.

Suheyl Erbil was badly irritated by the crows, the rain, the irregularity of the streetcars in the rainy weather, the drops rolling down the steamed-up windows, and especially by the smell of wet overcoats which permeated the streetcar. On account of this, he had taken refuge under the platform of the streetcar and was standing there. He lighted his pipe and tossed the match into the street.

In front of the head official's office six taxis were waiting with their flags lowered. Just at that moment a wedding procession appeared at the top of the steps. The groom was a middle-aged individual wearing a dark blue coat with a velvet collar. As for the bride, she was a dainty, young thing whose face was covered with a delicate veil. Why do girls always wear hats with veils for their weddings? The girl had a bouquet in her hand. She kept lifting her head and looking at the sky. Although the possibility that rain was considered a good omen for a marriage had crossed her mind, she didn't have the courage to say this to her husband in his velvet collar. That woman over there, shedding tears of joy with her handkerchief held to her nose, was probably the bride's mother. The bride and groom got into the front car, and basket after basket of flowers were placed in the car. The in-laws and relatives were distributed among the other cars. The last car was just opposite the platform under which Suheyl Erbil was standing. Three women and a white-haired man got into this car. The white-haired man must have just made a good joke because one of the women was still laughing and saying, "Bless you, uncle. You're a real card!" Why are such entertaining uncles always to be found at weddings?

When the automobiles had left, Suheyl Erbil sighed. He felt his bachelorhood and his loneliness even more deeply in such rainy weather.

"Now," he was thinking, "I should have a warm little house. A little woman, a sweet-blooded young thing, the easily excitable type like this one that just passed. The rest is just nonsense, by God. I would draw all the curtains in order not to see the rain. Not too big, just three rooms and a kitchen. A bird cage just our size. In the kitchen my wife's voice humming while she makes coffee. And in the furniture, in the air, and inside me the utmost joy of life."

Suheyl Erbil sighed again. Then he looked at his watch. The streetcar was still not ready to go. If he waited five minutes longer, he would certainly miss the ferry. He got off the streetcar and turned up his collar. Putting his hands in his pockets, he began to walk quickly.

Although Suheyl Erbil weighed eighty-three kilos, he was a young man of the highest degree of perceptivity. But, since an excess of sensitivity isn't becoming to a man, he always concealed himself behind an artificial hardness. He was thirty-two years old and still had not married. Although he had had several flirtations, he had never been able to make up his mind and show the courage to set up house with any one of them. Now he felt regretful when he saw that his hair was beginning to thin on top, and now and then he lamented, "I'm going to seed." He was a lawyer on the Ankara bar and earned an average income of three hundred to four hundred *liras* per month.

That's the sort of young man Suheyl Erbil was, and now, having turned up the collar of his camel's hair coat, he was descending the Shish-hane slope.

• • •

When Artin Margusyan smelled the sharp odor of ether in his nose, he thought to himself, "Since I'm smelling this smell, it means I'm alive." Of course, he thought this in Armenian. Maybe he was injured, but therefore he was alive. In any case, that was the essential thing. The rest could always be straightened out. Even if the injury were serious. Was the injury serious? he wondered. He didn't have the nerve to budge. He opened his eyes slowly. His surroundings were too hazy to be seen through the steamed-up windshield. There was a peculiar humming in his ears. Someone was bent over, bandaging his arm.

A woman was shouting, "He came to! He came to!"

These three words didn't seem at all strange to Artin Margusyan. He—came—to. Artin Margusyan would certainly know what they meant. He must have known. He—came—to. Certainly, my friend, he—came—to, he—came—to. Was it possible he didn't know? He knew but he just couldn't get his thoughts together and extract their meaning. This time another face emerged from the fog and said a few things. Margusyan couldn't understand anything that was being said. The man who was bandaging his arm repeated what was said to Margusyan word by word. Again he couldn't understand anything. Every now and then among these words there was a two-syllable word. License, ah—license. This word was not at all unfamiliar to Margusyan, but damn it—

The man who was bandaging his arm told the bystanders, "I'm going to give him some adrenalin."

When Artin Margusyan felt the prick of the needle in his arm, he thought to himself, "No, I'm not unconscious. I'm not unconscious, but I'm not completely conscious either."

• • •

People had gathered around the automobile and everyone was talking at once.

"Just look at the fenders. Boy, are they damaged!"

"He got what he deserved, the jerk."

A police commissioner and two policemen who had hurried up to the scene of the accident were taking down statements from Kalender's garbage collector and the witnesses one by one.

The electrician whose shop window had been broken burst out of his store and at once handed a bill of damages to the commissioner.

A girl in a white trench coat who had been looking at a lamp shade at the time the window was broken was now standing in front of the door of the shop waiting for the electrician to return. Suheyl Erbil saw her at that moment. Suheyl Erbil, however disgruntled he may have been by the rain and the smell of damp overcoats which permeates closed places in rainy weather, was equally disgruntled by everyday police incidents and random traffic accidents. Neither the crowd, the police, the wretched automobile, nor the injured and semi-conscious driver could keep him from where he was going. He slipped through the crowd congesting the pavement and walked in the direction of the bank district. Although the girl in the white trench coat would have preferred Suheyl Erbil to notice her first, when he passed without seeing her, she could no longer control herself and was forced to call out "Suheyl Bey!"

Then, as if embarrassed at what she had done, she bit her lip lightly and looked down.

"Serap. It's you!"

The young girl kept on biting her lip and as her face turned pink she smiled with a charming bashfulness.

"Yes. It's me," she said, raising her head and looking into his eyes.

Suheyl Erbil felt a warm lump in his throat. My God, how much more beautiful she had become! Why was his heart beating as if it would burst?

"Weren't you in Ankara?"

"I've come here on a case. I'm returning on Monday."

"Oh," answered Serap hesitantly. "That's nice."

With her neck springing forth like a tender stem from the collar of her white trench coat and her cheeks pink from the cold, she was the same Serap of five years ago. She hadn't changed at all. In fact, she was more beautiful.

"Are you happy in Ankara? With your life there?"

While saying this, in order to show her hand by some means or other, she made a pretense of straightening her rain hat. There was no ring on her finger. In other words, she was not engaged.

Stretching his lips to the left, Suheyl smiled an American smile.

"Ankara, Istanbul, İzmir," he mumbled. "Even New York, Paris, Barcelona. When a person is alone—and especially when it rains—"

"You would never have talked like that before," the girl said, smiling. When she smiled like that, two charming dimples appeared at either side of her mouth. Because Serap was aware of this, when she talked with men or with women who had sons of marriageable age, she would produce the dimples by smiling frequently. For this reason, even though she wasn't like that at all, everyone considered her a joker.

"It's true I wouldn't have talked this way before," thought Suheyl Erbil. "I was a greenhorn in those days. How carefree I was then! First youth, foolishness, the age of stupidity. The days we passed as rightists, leftists, racial purists, Turanists, anarchists, idealists, in order to be different from everyone else, to create a personality for ourselves. The times when we underwent torture with a perverse pride in order to show the girls around us that we didn't notice them even though our hearts were melting. Foolishness. And how lofty were our goals! In those days I thought becoming a representative was as easy as being elected to the steering committee of the student union. And now I've become an insignificant lawyer on the Ankara bar."

"Come under the eaves," the girl was saying. "You're getting wet there."

There was a feminine charm protective of men in the tone of her voice, and not just in the tone of her voice, either, but in her air and her personality, like those self-sacrificing wife and nurse types we often see in movies.

Serap was proud most of all of her good heart and her feminine compassion which permeated every cell of her body. She had even seen such a film two days before at the Melek Cinema. The subject was a woman who, in the end, softened a bad-tempered gangster with her love and compassion and won him both for herself and for society. How she would like to be that kind of woman in life! Even though Suheyl wasn't a gangster, still he was a hard youth. He always said that no one understood him. At the university he had paid no attention to girls, and at meetings with his male friends he would enter into endless discussions on the social order.

"That's just the way I am," he had said once. "Yes, I can't stand these self-centered people who never think of anything but their own profit. Even if I'm forced, I don't like them." They were in front of the university gate which opened into Merjan, the two of them alone. Serap raised an eyebrow and asked in a meaningful tone, "Not one of them? Without making any distinctions?" Suheyl hadn't answered this question. He couldn't have answered it. But Serap had understood everything from a light which burned in his eyes for a moment and then faded and from the blush which had suddenly covered his face. If Suheyl, that day, in that place, had not been carried away by a foolish pride, if he had said the three words that Serap had been waiting for, just three simple words, everything could have been different, everything. Serap could have gone to the most remote corner of Anatolia, and not just of Anatolia but of the whole world, with this hard youth whose forelock fell over his face. But Suheyl had not spoken those three words.

"What are you thinking?" asked the young man.

"Nothing," answered the girl.

"I'm curious. What were you thinking?"

"What was I thinking? I was thinking whatever I was thinking. Do my thoughts interest you?"

"And how! Please tell me."

"No, I can't."

"Do you remember when all our conversations ended in arguments?"

"When?"

"Then, my darling."

• • •

Artin Margusyan had finally regained consciousness completely. In addition to regaining consciousness, he was even euphoric now under the effect of the adrenalin.

"Let me go," he was shrieking in desperation. "Let me telephone my partner. After that I'll go wherever you want."

The policeman said, "You'll come to the station and telephone from there."

Artin pointed to his gold-plated watch whose crystal was broken and whose band was smeared with blood.

"I'll kiss the bottom of your foot, officer, sir," he was pleading. "In five minutes the bidding begins. If I don't send a message, I'm done for."

The police thought a moment. If it had been up to him, he would have permitted it. But the commissioner and the other policemen were busily taking down statements a little distance ahead. A crowd of people was gathered around. He said to himself, "Nothing is gained from being softhearted. Why should I worry about other people's problems?"

One of the passengers was taking Artin's side.

"Let him go, buddy. Maybe he'll lose money. Maybe he'll go bankrupt. He hasn't killed anybody."

Since the commissioner was coming toward him at that moment, the policeman frowned and barked in a voice at least as official as his uniform, "Don't interfere with my duty!" Then he turned to Margusyan. "Okay, friend, to the station."

But this time Artin Margusyan implored the commissioner more desperately.

• • •

It was as if Suheyl and Serap were not at Shish-hane. As if it weren't raining. As if no crowd of people were standing just three steps away. As if they weren't hearing Margusyan wrangling with the policeman or the continually ringing bells or the conversations or the street noises which became a chaotic blur from time to time.

"Maybe you are right," said Serap. "Maybe you're right but you must also think of the feelings of those around you. I wonder if I'm thinking incorrectly."

Margusyan was shouting at the top of his voice.

"Oh, yes, I understand. I caused a collision. I'm going to pay damages. And I don't have a license. I accept the penalty. Put me in jail. Do whatever you want. Just, please, I beg you, let me make a quick phone call."

"I admit to disloyalty," answered Suheyl Erbil. "But you tell me, how could I have written a letter? Especially after hearing about that affair with the military medical school student?"

The girl laughed.

"What a laugh! Whoever told you that was lying. For one thing he's my cousin. We're like brother and sister. And in addition—"

"Back your car up a bit, brother. Back, back, back. There. Fine. Would you mind giving me a hand? Let's push this car into a side street."

"I don't understand your concern at all. There was nothing improper about it."

"You mean you don't believe me?"

"No, I don't. And even if it were like that, it doesn't constitute any reason for—"

"I'm obliged to conform with the law. The rest doesn't interest me."

"Why do you keep on blowing your horn? If there weren't a road, would you just run over me?"

"Even if they give me the death penalty, they'll still grant a last request. Is humanity sold on the black market nowadays?"

"The black marketeer is your father! And showing disrespect to an officer on duty, eh?"

"182, my boy, 182. Are you asleep? They're giving the go signal."

"It never even crossed my mind. I only—"

"You only what? Tell me the rest. You don't know how to tell a lie, Suheyl Bey."

"Jemal Ağabey! Jemal Ağabey!"

"Which Ayten? The one that was in English philology?"

"Out of the way! Please. Let me pass."

"A sweet shop? What are you saying? I can't hear you."

"Here—"

"Jemal Ağabey! Jemal Ağabey!"

"It's awfully noisy here."

"Hey, what's the matter, Kazım?"

"I said it's awfully noisy here. Let's go to a sweetshop."

"There are only three minutes left, commissioner, sir. My entire family will be ruined."

"Let's go to a sweetshop and continue our conversation there. Or we could go to a cinema."

Lightning flashed in Serap's brain. Yes. She would take Suheyl to the movie about the reformed gangster. Then understanding would be very easy.

"I wonder how it would be?"

"It would be fine, of course!"

"My mother will worry."

"You can telephone her and tell her I'll bring you home myself after the movie."

This last sentence raised Serap's hopes to the skies.

As if on wings, the two of them rushed into a shop which had a huge telephone bell symbol on the door.

• • •

The passengers were dispersing slowly.

The road was cleared and the gathered vehicles had begun to flow like a flood.

Kalender was pissing at the base of a wall on the side street to which he had been driven together with the cart.

The commissioner, who had softened somewhat on the interval, was talking to Artin, who was still hanging onto his arm.

"What an uproar you've caused, you idiot. Okay, wherever you're going to telephone, just get it over with. And make it snappy."

"It won't take half a minute."

Artin in front, the commissioner and the two policemen behind, they entered the shop with the huge white telephone bell on the door. But Serap had the receiver at her ear and, standing on tiptoe in order to reach the mouthpiece better, was talking to her mother.

"Damn it," said Artin. If it had been left to him, he could have grabbed the phone from the girl's hand and quickly dialed the number of the bidding place. But Suheyl was planted in front of her like a wall and was scrutinizing the uninvited guests who had rudely entered their domain with the eyes of an angry bull.

Artin ran back out. His intention was to enter the first shop with a telephone that he came to. But the commissioner, who had previously softened somewhat, was not about to have his honor threatened by Artin's dashing from shop to shop.

"Hey, come on. Are we going to come to blows?" he peeved.

They wrangled loudly in front of the door. Again the commissioner softened. When he said "All right," Serap was still talking to her mother. Artin and the commissioner willy-nilly entered another shop two hundred meters further on. But Artin Margusyan could get no answer but the frustrated ring of the telephone at the other end of the line. He looked at his watch.

Now it was exactly thirteen minutes past three.

He opened his mouth in order to say "It's too late," but in place of words a whistling sound was released from his mouth like escaping steam.

For the second time in a half hour, he had fainted.

● ● ●

It was the month of November when this event occurred at Shish-hane, but in Sao Paulo, the same day of the same month, due to the difference in latitude, spring was reigning. Furthermore, although it was 6:30 P.M. according to the big clock on the front of the Central Bank at Shish-hane, the electric wall clock of the firm of Lorenzo and Filho, for the same reason, showed 1:30.

But, by a strange coincidence, the weather there that day was mild like the weather in Istanbul. As for this mild weather, it badly irritated the elderly Lorenzo. In fact, that morning he had arisen with a terrible pain in his shoulder. The pain started in the area of his right shoulder blade, went straight up, and from there, splitting into two, extended down the length of one arm and up as far as the elbow in the back of the other.

He put some mineral water into a glass, took a box of pills from his pocket and swallowed two capsules at once. The doctor had prescribed two of these analgesic capsules of B-complex for his pain. Although they numbed the pain a little, why did they have to make a person sweat buckets?

The tapping of a typewriter, reminiscent of machine gun fire, was coming from the next room.

Sevira Marono Lorenzo took out his handkerchief and, wiping away the huge beads of sweat on his nose, spoke in the direction of the glass partition next to him.

"Hey, Pedro. Ha novadades de Istanbul?"

His son, Pedro, his head in his hands, was thinking about the dark thighs of Conchita Montanegro, the Argentinian dancer at the bar from which he had returned toward morning. It was as if from amid these typewriter noises a hoarse trombone were still playing a solitary rumba. "Kumpan, kumpan, kumpan kumpanchero, chero—"

"I'm speaking to you, Pedro. Are you asleep?"

"Que mande?"

"Hasn't any telegram come from Margusyan yet?"

"No, father."

"He probably hasn't accepted the bid."

"At the last minute we lowered the price twenty percent. Those guys must be sleeping. Where the heil should I send my goods now?"

To talk like that wasn't unfair, either. The trucks coming from Fazenda were continually bringing coffee and emptying it into the lower depot.

The typewriter stopped. For a moment there was silence. Even the sound of the gas bubbles bursting in the glass of mineral water was inaudible. Lorenzo downed the remaining water in one gulp. Now he was both thinking and turning the empty glass upside down in his hand, as he always did when he was preoccupied.

Pedro got up and came to his father's side.

"We received an offer from someone named Alois Morgenrot in Hamburg," he said. "Do you remember? You weren't pleased that he wanted to do business on credit, but the guarantees were certain. If you like, let's send Mr. Margusyan's consignment to him just as it is."

The elderly Lorenzo looked at his son.

"Bravo," he said. "That's not a bad idea."

• • •

Little Helga was pleading, "Noch eins Papa, bitte noch eins."

Alois Morgenrot had made his daughter four sailboats from a three-month-old *Frankfurter Zeitung*. When she pleaded again, he tore out the financial page from another old newspaper. With a little effort he could get two more sailboats out of the faded page on which there was an out-of-date amnesty list.

Helga's buttercup-yellow hair was falling over her face. She was sailing the boats on a ragged rug that was supposed to be the sea.

"It's good that Helga isn't interested in dolls the way other little girls are," thought Alois Morgenrot.

Inside the room, the overture to Smetana's *The Bartered Bride* was coming from a tin-voiced Volks receiver.

Alois Morgenrot left his last boat on the rug and went to the window.

The snow that had fallen the previous night had considerably covered Hamburg's poverty. Morgenrot stared long at the new apartment buildings rising in the form of a cube amid the ruins. Whenever his eye caught these new buildings, a pleasant feeling like hope and courage warmed his heart. His own own life resembled those ruins. But, sooner or later, new structures were going to rise over these ruins and new shoots were going to sprout. When the time came, this torment was surely going to end. It had to end. What does Ecclesiastes say? "There is a time for everything under the sun. A time for birth and a time for dying. A time for sowing and a time for reaping that which has been sown. A time for killing and a time for healing. A time for destroying and a time for building. A time for weeping and a time for smiling. A time for dancing—"

Back in the room Helga was crying.

"Isn't Mommy ever going to come back?"

"She'll be here any minute now," said Morgenrot.

Frau Morgenrot had gone out shopping a little earlier. Alois Morgenrot's wife was a pure Hamburger, but Alois himself was the offspring of a Czechoslovakian Jewish father who had emigrated to Hamburg a half century earlier. Alois had still not been able to atone for this sin. First the Hitler monster. Then the disaster of the Second World War. Fleeing from one place to another. Even being forced to have a gold tooth extracted and sold for lack of money. Sickness, hunger, poverty. The situation he encountered when the war ended and he returned to Hamburg. Yes, although he hadn't rotted away in concentration camps like many of his friends and was alive and healthy, still this cursed unemployment problem was breaking his back. If he had a good income, say, twenty thousand marks, yes, an income of twenty thousand marks, he would be able to alter the course of his fate. But he didn't have such an income. Now, every day, he combed the financial pages of newspapers in every language he knew from beginning to end and then, with a rented typewriter, wrote impeccable letters to the foreign firms with which he had hopes of doing business.

At that moment the doorbell rang.

"Mommy's home! Mommy's home!" Little Helga was clapping her hands.

But Frau Morgenrot had a key and would not have rung the bell.

When Alois Morgenrot opened the door, he met the postman.

"Grüss Gott, Herr Morgenrot."

"Grüss Gott."

"There's a telegram for you from Brazil."

"What did you say?"

At first Morgenrot's face went white as a sheet. Then he suddenly flushed. He read the telegram, then read it again and again and again.

"Endlich!" he shouted at last.

In his joy he pressed a half mark into the postman's hand. The postman, who had never in his entire life received even a half-pfennig tip from Morgenrot, was afraid that the man had lost his mind. But Morgenrot, now hugging his daughter, had tears streaming from his eyes.

"I can finally buy dolls for you, Helga," he was saying. "Even the most expensive kind. Tell me, little one, do you want one? One of those dolls that closes its eyes when you lay it down and cries when you press its tummy?"

• • •

A silent November rain was falling softly on Shish-hane. In the air was the smell of moisture and soot. Every place was as slippery again as it had been two days before. Only today, instead of a mild west wind, an easterly wind was blowing.

Today Kalender had been tired since morning. He was pulling the garbage cart, full to the brim, slowly and gravely down the Shish-hane slope. Just at that moment he saw himself in a mirror. But today, he saw himself not in a wall mirror on a porter's back but in a newly hung, common traffic mirror. But, nevertheless, again he saw his image half again as big as he actually was, or rather as we see it.

But, in spite of this, he did not whinny.

Yes, he did not whinny.

In this case, two possibilities come to mind.

1. Kalender may have thought, "I once saw myself in a mirror for the first time in my life and the world collapsed. But that's over. Let's just not look. I no longer have a face that's attractive to look at anyway." For, in the event that he could have thought in this way, it is necessary to believe that horses are possessed of the ability to learn from experience and of the capacity to establish a logical link between the past and the future.

2. Either that, or (and this second possibility is far more reasonable) he was merely tired that day or had not slept well or was out of sorts due to boredom or, who knows, had some quarrel with the other stallions in the municipal stable and for that reason didn't have the energy

to whinny and rear and cause the commotion that he had caused two days earlier. In short, there are a few physiological causes for his not whinnying that are just as reasonable as the psychological ones.

Whatever the case may be, whether the first or the second possibility is valid, what is really important is not that but what happened afterwards.

Kalendar did not whinny.

He regarded his reflection in the mirror sourly and turned his head the other way. Then, with a gravity becoming one who has reached a mature age, he continued on his way with quiet dignity.

SEBATI BEY'S EXPEDITION TO ISTANBUL
Haldun Taner
(Translated by Madeline Zilfi)

Almost every human being has an addiction to something. If Sebati Bey, a retired Quarantine Office clerk, had one, it was flowers and more flowers. And with him, it wasn't just a passion, it was a sickness. If the topic of conversation happened to be the English queen, Queen Victoria would be his first association and, in consequence, Victoria roses. If a carved writing kit should catch his eye somewhere, he would immediately draw closer and examine the wood to see whether it was made of linden or of rosewood. In fact, he divided human beings into two categories: those who love flowers and those who don't comprehend them. The first were people of taste, sound, while the second, again by his own characterization, were deficient and unrefined.

He had neither home nor family. Is our poor fellow rash enough to venture on his own atop Maltepe's mountain? His passion has hurled itself against this as well. Maltepe's weather is well known. In the afternoon, a wild breeze stirs up, empties the whole area by its dryness, and disappears. But you will note that Sebati Bey's determination was such that he breeds flowers even in this inconvenient climate.

Recently the husband of his foster sister had obtained Japanese rose seeds from one of his friends. Knowing Sebati Bey's habits, they set aside a portion for him. For days the old man's insides churned with impatience. He would go to pick up the seeds. Still, he didn't dare to make the trip. Just think how far it is from Maltepe to Sarach-hanebashı! I'll go tomorrow. I'll go the day after tomorrow, he said, continuing to put it off. So it was that on this one morning he hit upon a propitious moment and determined to go. He won't wait for them to bring them, he'll go personally to collect the seeds.

Since the stationmaster knew very well that he seldom went into the city, he joked with him on every trip. "What's this, beyefendi, yet again off to prodigality?" And Sebati Bey, his bright red lips smiling from out of his snowy white beard says, "Get along with you! Would I be unfaithful to my roses?"

Since he was so pleased with his remark, he would repeat it everywhere and say, "The stationmaster said such-and-such to me, and I answered him so." That day the train arrived exactly on time, so they were unable to continue their bantering.

The noon train was almost empty. Sebati Bey leaned his head against the seat. Gazing out at the yellow fields slipping by below, and at the telegraph wires, now raised, now lowered, he began to doze off. As he left the train on its arrival at Haydarpasha, he was taken aback at the sight of flags hoisted all around. The day, which he thought to be an ordinary day, turned out to be Istanbul's liberation day. This is what you call out of the frying pan and into the fire. Who knows how crowded public transportation will be at dusk? I wonder whether I should turn back, he thought to himself. The ferry had left Kadıköy and was slicing its way through the sea. It's too late now. As the ferry drew alongside, he looked at the decks. Almost empty. He was delighted. Everyone had gone to Taksim, to the parade, and he was consoled by the thought that the crowds were gathering there. And wasn't it his good fortune to find an empty streetcar leaving from the bridge? So off he went to Sarach-hane.

They had a warm reunion. There was hugging and kissing, followed by a friendly chat. A bit of Nasrettin Hoja, Bekri Mustafa and Bektashi anecdotes. Suddenly he noticed that it was already evening. How short the days have become! Sebati Bey took the package of Japanese rose seeds in his arms, quickly said his farewells, and left his foster brother's house. He walked to Fatih in order to catch the bus conveniently at its last stop. He found room in front and rejoiced in his own cleverness as he sat down. Every now and then he plunged his hand into the paper sack and handled the seeds with his tapered pink fingers. What joy, what joy.

"Tomorrow I'll prepare a place for them next to the orange violets. And, let me see, I'll plant them one by one with a little prayer. I must get some fine valley sand from Rejeb Usta. And the imam's son should bring some pigeon droppings. When I lived at Langa I used to envy the very sight of the garden belonging to Nusret Bey, the harbor clerk. Now see the workings of fate. Years later fate has smiled on me, too."

He was surprised at how quickly they had arrived at the bridge. He had a feeling of disquiet, but he had forgotten the reason for it. Now he remembered. How will I get on the ferry? He had reached the dock, but, may God preserve us, the crowds! Walk along, if it's possible to walk in the throng. The ferry was crammed full. It had long since exceeded its capacity. If we don't watch out, we'll sink to a watery grave. An old man's life spark is a rather precious thing. "I'm not going. I'm turning back," he says, but the worst of it is, there's no turning back again. The crowd, in a fierce torrent, washes right down to the ferry. How can Sebati Bey's delicate frame resist this human tide? Thus faltering, he found himself on board the ferry. A policeman took pity on him. Taking him by the arm, he thrust him into the salon.

"Beybaba, walk over there a bit. You'll probably find some kind man who'll offer you his seat." And, in fact, a black-mustached young man, in an effort to curry favor with the made-up woman across from him, rose to give Sebati Bey his seat. God bless you. Sebati Bey placed his walking stick beside him and breathed a sigh of relief. Beside him sat a fat woman. Opposite was a gum-chewing Greek girl, her legs crossed. Undoubtedly a dressmaker. He felt irritation for such ruminating gum-chewers. The fat woman beside him broadcast a smell of sour perspiration mixed with rubber. It is asking too much for cleanliness in these people? Then Sebati Bey turned to have a look at the salon. Weary, sullen, frowning, irritable, bestial, a demonic array of faces. A pushing, shoving throng, piled one against the other.

Is this what the world is, what life is? Sebati Bey wondered. Is this how they live, in this blundering fashion? These men, what do they do? They leave in the morning and return at night. At noon they bolt down their food as they stand. Hurry up, you, hurry up. For what? To earn five or ten more pennies. And once they have earned it, what do they do? They pay it out at the movies, at gambling. Lord! Your minds astonish me. Is this what they call twentieth-century civilization? Oh Lord! Poor mankind! Oh Lord! The poor human race! Will you, too, fall upon such days?

Since Sebati Bey couldn't see past the crowds, he didn't realize that they had entered the harbor and were approaching Haydarpasha. But when the ferry bumped into the pier and he was nearly heaped on top of the tall man beside him, he gathered that they had touched land somewhere. He rose from his seat and, caught up in the crowd, began to make his way slowly. Again, pushers in back, pushers in front, and colliders on either side. To keep his package from getting crushed,

Sebati Bey tensed his limbs, bent over, crouched down and extended his elbow. He knew that they had reached the platform because of the cool breeze that caressed his forehead.

"Porter, porter here," youngsters cried out as they plunged into the crowd. They may have lice on them. One should take care not to rub against them.

Finally and with great difficulty they passed the ticket area and burst onto the stairways. Unfortunately, a military detachment had emerged from a freight car from Adapazarı and filled the train station. The soldiers, nonplussed, had no idea how to get away from the crowd. They stayed underfoot at the entrance to the road. Sebati Bey had to swerve to one side to avoid crashing into them. Thus it was that at that moment he collided with a young man who was running full speed to grab a seat on the train for his fiancée, and Sebati Bey fell to the ground. Immediately the package in his hand exploded with a pop and the seeds for whose sake he had risked a trip to Istanbul, those cherished seeds, scattered everywhere. Sebati Bey forgot his own pain and tried to gather the seeds together from where they had spilled on the ground. But the merciless tread of those running to make the train and the soldiers' iron-tipped boots ground them to dust.

Sebati Bey helplessly, mournfully looked about. After thanking the soldier who had helped him to his feet and set his walking stick back into his hands, he walked anxiously to the train. The cars were jammed, but unlike the ferry, no kind benefactor presented himself, so the old man was forced to remain standing. His left hand, upon which he had fallen, and his right kneecap ached terribly. Again, all around him those bold, mindless faces. A mass of panting humanity, grinning triumphantly because they had found seats.

Sebati Bey closed his eyes. These idiotic, insensitive, remorseless people who had scattered his beloved seeds and then ground them underfoot — he dropped his head forward a bit to avoid seeing them.

CIVILIZATION'S SPARE PART
Aziz Nesin
(Translated by Janet Heineck)

Everyone looked at the man who, although he had come into the coffee shop, did not greet the people there. One man, who raised his eyes from the fountain basin, said, "Hello, Hamit Agha!"

"Hello."

"What's wrong, Hamit Agha? You're panting like an old ox who is trying to climb a hill."

Hamit Agha turned to the old man who said this. "Thank God, Ali Chavush. I escaped from that awful thing. Praise be to God! How wonderful!"

"Congratulations, Hamit Agha. Is it that you have settled your debt with the bank?"

"No, man. Who was thinking of the bank debt? We just got rid of that burdensome tractor."

When they heard the word "tractor," the old men who had a moment ago been resting half-asleep sat up straight. A few of them raised themselves up from the chair wicker and dragged the chairs under them toward Hamit Agha.

"Really?"

"Did you get away safely, Hamit Agha?"

"Tell about it."

"I am free of it," he said. "God be thanked a thousand times that I should see these days."

Those who were listening became still more curious. They drew their wicker chairs a little closer to Hamit Agha.

Hamit Agha explained. "It's a long story. When my son returned from the army, he said, 'Father, I learned how to drive. Let us buy a tractor,' he insisted. Just then my daughter came to the village with her husband. My daughter and son-in-law are teachers, and when school is closed for the holidays, they come to the village. They too kept bothering me to buy a tractor. 'Children, what would be the good of it? Aren't two pair of oxen enough?' They say I am backward-minded. My daughter pointed to the calendar page on the wall. 'Look, father,' she said. 'We're in the year 1955. This is the twentieth century, did you know that?' My son-in-law gives an hour-long speech after every meal. 'We are in the machine age. To plow with a pair of oxen is a disgrace these days.'

"My son was making a calculation. 'How many day laborers do you hire to plow the field? Ten. For how many days do you plow? A month. Do you see,' he asked, 'that when you buy a tractor I can get through the plowing all by myself in a week? And after that I'll plow the fields of those who ask me, for money. In a year we'll make back what it cost us.' The son stopped talking and the daughter began. The daughter left off, and the son-in-law started in. 'And when the ox doesn't work, he eats while doing nothing. Is a tractor like that? When you want to make it go, you put in two cups of gasoline and drive away. If it isn't working, it doesn't eat. Oxen lie all winter in their stalls, eating and chewing their cud.'

"I was all alone. Whatever I said was useless. 'Oxen get sick,' they said, 'oxen grow old,' they said, 'oxen die,' they said, 'whereas the tractor is made of iron! It doesn't grow old, doesn't tire, doesn't die.' I was not likely to be convinced, but my wife began to say that Sergeant Musa and Kel Mahmut Agha had bought one. This tractor, evening and morning. My wife was the worst of them all. 'The village headman also bought a tractor. You're still waiting,' she says. 'Even Memish Hüseyin also bought one,' they said. To tell you the truth, friends, I was helpless."

The curious listeners were saying from time to time, "Well, Hamit Agha? Then what?"

"God knows I still wouldn't have bought one. The village teacher said, 'Hamit Agha, what are you saying? A tractor has the power of eighty workhorses.' By then I was completely convinced. Eighty horsepower! Giant's strength! What do you say? It would level mountains and rocks.

"I was exhausted by the nagging in the house. 'I'll buy it,' I said. Since even Memish Hüseyin had bought one, why should I be behind everybody? 'I'll buy one,' I said. How much did this hateful thing cost? They say the bank will give credit. They say there were three sizes:

small, medium, and large. 'Let's buy a small one,' I said. My son said, 'I don't want a small one.' My daughter said, 'When we buy one, let's get a large one.' My wife said, 'When the neighbors are all buying large ones, I don't want to be laughed at.'

"We made ready, went to the city, and arrived at the equipment office. A pleasant fellow was there. 'How large is your field?' he asked. 'Eighty *dönüms*,' I said. 'This small one,' he said, 'plows not just eighty but even eight hundred *dönüms*.' I was unable to make my people listen. 'The fellow is misleading you,' they said. 'We told you we want a large one.' 'Four thousand *liras* in advance,' he said, ' the rest on credit. No bargaining.' We returned. In the village I am Hamit Agha. If I said I don't have four thousand, who would believe it? We took the oxen to market. The poor creatures were born and raised in my hands. The gray steer kept looking into my eyes and weeping. The yellow steer was licking my face. Anyway, to make a long story short, we sold the oxen and put together three thousand. The rest we took as credit from the bank.

"We bought the large tractor from the equipment office. The cursed thing was lying there like a mountain. They had said two cups of gasoline. They gave it a gas can, fuel oil, and grease. My son climbed on top. We all got aboard. The tractor went into a trot. It was a wonder. On top we hung an old shoe, a bulb of garlic, a blue bead, and other things to ward off the evil eye, and said, 'Giddap!' In the evening when we reached the village, we drove around. It was wonderful.

"Those who saw us hurried to the equipment office. Do you know the muleteer Yusuf who has a ten-*dönüm* fallow field below the village? Even *he* went and bought a tractor.

"It wasn't evening before their tractors were leaving tracks on the village road. I can't say a bad word about my son's driving. He hits something and goes on by. He hit Memish Hüseyin's tractor with the back and, by God, in one stroke it became something to throw away. The huge thing to one side overturned like a tortoise.

"It was great fun. Every Saturday, we all climbed aboard and went to town. Tractors lined up like a railroad train in front of the movie theatre. My son drives the hateful thing with a swagger. While coming back from the village, the race starts. The one who strikes gets ahead. But just then didn't some scoundrel run into us? We came to a screeching halt. Oh my! We lit the street lamps; the cursed thing wouldn't move. We left that weight on the road, and we all began to walk. My son went the next day. Apparently the something-or-other broke. We looked everywhere. It was no use."

"Well, Hamit Agha? Then what?"

"I rented a pair of water buffalo from the village, and by hitching them to the huge thing I brought it back to town. They couldn't find the part that was broken. I went to the equipment office. 'This piece of equipment. Whatever it costs, I'll pay it,' I said. They said no. A huge tractor is brought to a standstill because of one tiny part? Oh, for my yellow ox! He had neither parts nor screws. His engine would never break down. My son said, 'Let me go to Istanbul and buy this part.' 'Son,' I said, 'it's plowing time. You hurry up.' My son goes to Istanbul and doesn't come back."

"So, Hamit Agha, then what?"

"Then, my friends, no news from my son. Plowing time comes and is going. We have no money to buy an ox. I hired another ox and plowed the field. Well, friends, there is news from my son. 'Father,' he says, 'I found a part, but I'm out of money. Hurry and send me a thousand *liras*!' I ran to the bank and wired the boy money. He arrived with a bolt in his hand the size of a coin. 'Hey boy, a thousand *liras* for this?' We sent for a mechanic. The fellow screwed in the bolt, and the tractor started to work. The winter had set in. We pushed the tractor into the stable and tied it to the post where the oxen used to be, while a tumultuous snowstorm was sounding on the roof. Meanwhile, friends, the bank loan and the installment at the equipment office came due. We had no money. The tractor brought us nothing but trouble. We borrowed money to pay the first installment at the office.

"We reached summer in the middle of all this. We made for the field. Just then it went bang, and crash, and stopped. What is the problem with this damned thing? No one knew. We brought out the expert from the office. Didn't he say its cogwheel was broken? 'Sell us another cogwheel,' we said, and he said no. 'Since this cursed thing has no cogwheel, why do you cheat us poor people?' 'Well,' he said, 'if you buy another tractor, then you can use its cogwheel.' 'Look around at our neighbors' fields. It's the same story. A tractor body lies in everyone's fields. Everywhere you look are chains, tractor treads, and piles of iron.' Oh, my yellow ox! Oh, my gray ox! You can treat them as roughly as you like. They're money whether dead or alive. This cursed thing is not an ox that you can slaughter when it grows old and crippled. You can't butcher it, cut it up, eat it, or drink it. The second installment was inevitably due. 'Take it back!' I said, and what did they reply but 'We aren't junk dealers.' I was ready to explode.

"A fellow in Adana makes parts for this miserable thing, they say. I said to my son, 'Go and clean up this mess.' The boy went to Adana. The man in question apparently said, 'Nothing doing without seeing the patient.' I said, 'Go and take it.' We hitched it behind the two oxen. My son reached Adana in fifteen days. The fellow was a doctor in this profession. He said that five hundred *liras* were stuck in this cogwheel.

"I sold ten *dönüms* of the field rather than be disgraced in the eyes of the world. I sent the five hundred, and my daughter and son-in-law arrived. I gave so much money to the scoundrel, let me have a little enjoyment from it at least. The whole family climbed aboard. I said to my son, 'Now keep back! Don't run it into anything! This miserable thing isn't a racehorse.' The boy didn't stop. Memish Hüseyin's tractor passed ours and my son urged ours on. The tractor was panting hard like a jackass that sees a jenny. But before I could say don't do it, didn't the carburetor break? 'Idiot!' I said to my boy. 'If it were an Arab horse, it would be dying of exhaustion. This monster structure, this infidel invention—did you think it was an Arab horse?' We push, but it doesn't move. Like a donkey that sees water, it doesn't stir from its spot. How I missed the black ox! When you told it, 'Come on, go!' it would uproot rock and mountain to go. I summoned my daughter and son-in-law and said to them, 'You fools! Tell me now in which year we are. Are we in 1955? I turned to my son-in-law. 'In which century are we? Is it the twentieth?' Oh, my gray ox! If you throw a handful of straw in front of him, you can kick him as much as you wish, hitch him to the cart, run to the field and harness him to the flail."

"Then what happened, Hamit Agha?"

"Then, gentlemen, wouldn't you know it? The installment was due. The second notice came. For the sake of our honor, sirs, we sold another ten-*dönüm* field. A screw fell out—five hundred *liras*. A thousand *liras* for a part the size of your finger. A bolt comes loose—a thousand *liras*. Its chain breaks. Spare parts couldn't be found. A patch here, a patch there. That blessed tractor started to look like my trousers. While it plowed the ground, it shook all over like someone who has malaria. Everywhere in our field one can find a screw, a bolt, an iron bar, a shaft, or a chain. It was as though the filthy thing had sprinkled its seeds in the field. They said that our assemblyman whom we elected from the Democrat party was coming to town. I went to him.

'What will happen to us?' I asked. 'Does a tractor the size of an elephant stop dead because of a part the size of a nut?'"

"Tell us what he said, Hamit Agha!"

"What could he say? He talked for a long time. I couldn't understand very much. 'How did people live in the past, in the Stone Age? Now it's the Iron Age, that is to say, the age of Democrat. Civilization and the country are turning into iron,' he said. I said, 'What you're saying is all very well. You brought this civilization, but where is its spare part? Come with me and look at the field. Our civilization is in pieces. It lies there like a corpse. Isn't there a smaller one than this? If this miserable thing hits something it doesn't move, if you say "giddap" it doesn't start up, and if you say "whoa" it doesn't slow down.' "

"Well, Hamit Agha? Then what? What did he say?"

"Then, gentlemen. 'We have ordered it from America. Until it comes, we are setting up a factory here, too. Wait a bit. We'll be turning out parts like rain,' said he. 'I can wait, but the bank can't wait. You tell the bank to wait,' said I. Just then another installment notice arrived. Let me tell you something. The sighs of the oxen have affected me. How tearfully that yellow ox wept when he was sold in the market! How sorry I was!

"To make a long story short, I sold every field and paid off the whole debt."

"Then what, Hamit Agha?"

"Then I called to my daughter and son-in-law. I took my wife and the boy out to the wreck. 'Either we repair this calamity of God's or I'll put the yoke on you, drive you like oxen, and plow the farm,' I said. They worked on the engine, kicked it once, twice, tore off and reattached a strap, tightened a screw, and put something else in place of the fragile cogwheel whose bolt was loose."

"Then, Hamit Agha?"

"Then, gentlemen, I could see that it wouldn't work. I gathered my son, daughter, son-in-law, and wife. 'Come on, folks,' said I, 'let me show you how to repair this thing.' I picked up a sledgehammer. I drove those people of mine before me like a flock of sheep. We came to the wreck. I struck the steering wheel and said, 'Take *that*, you twentieth century.' I struck the engine and said, 'Take *that*, civilization.' I struck the driving wheel with the sledgehammer and said, 'Take *that*. This is your spare part.' I swung the sledgehammer again and again.

Suddenly I saw that my wife was shouting, 'Help! My husband has gone crazy!' My daughter ran, my son-in-law ran, and my son ran the hardest. I threw away the sledgehammer and started down the road. I came straight here, gentlemen. I'm still sweating."

The listeners, wide-eyed with curiosity, asked, "Well, Hamit Agha? Then what?"

"Afterwards, what a relief! I escaped from the accursed, foul thing. A thousand thanks to God. It's as though I've been born again."

Then he called joyfully to the coffee shop owner, "Bring me a nice cup of coffee!"

PEOPLE ARE WAKING UP
Aziz Nesin
(*Translated by Janet Heineck*)

His last imprisonment was hard on him. After his release, his exile in a provincial district was particularly bad. When it was over and he returned, he found himself all alone in the confusing city crowd. His wife had divorced him while he was in prison.

A man in a spot like this becomes pessimistic through no choice of his own, especially if he has neither money nor means of livelihood. Should he withdraw from politics and look for a subsistence job?

First of all, he had to find a place to stay. Rents in the center of the city were very high, and not only there but in the suburbs as well. If he couldn't pay his rent, he would have to go to the bailiff's, and he was tired of having his battered typewriter and his one or two worn-out belongings confiscated. He was especially tired of his neighbors' interrogating stares, their frightening, curious eyes, and their hostile glances, as though he were the first strange thing they had ever seen. For those reasons, he was looking farther out beyond the suburbs and in isolated places for a small cheap house for rent.

Eventually he found such a place, a little one-and-a-half-room shack. It was in a tiny shantytown of about five or ten dwellings put up on a hill at about a two-hour walk to the city. In addition, he liked it that the shanties were a long way from each other. His held nothing but two old trunks full of books and one or two pieces of furniture antiquated long ago. Pages of old newspapers covered the windows of his shack in place of curtains. He was happy. Now he had to go out and find a job in order to get by.

There was a grocery store in a hut a bit beyond his house, just across from it. To the left of the grocer there was also a fruit seller in a jerry-built shed. He did his shopping at these two places. By constantly coming and going, he became acquainted with the grocer and the fruit seller. They both complained of their situation, because they earned very little. Business was slow. Hardly five or six customers a day came into the shops, and they were not free-spending customers, but left very little money. The men could not open up shop in a busier area because they did not have much capital.

A few days after he moved into the shack, a *simit* seller began to appear in front of the grocery. He came every afternoon and stayed out there until the sky grew dark. Later, a corn seller showed up next to him. In a corner of the fruit seller's, a man started to sell sweets, cake, and other things in the shop window. Just then, a shoeshine boy settled there, and a bit later an itinerant sherbet vendor and a candy seller, too. Even a shoe repairman turned up under an old umbrella.

In a short time, a small marketplace had come into being opposite the shack. A garbage collector would keep sweeping up thereabouts from morning to evening. A crowd of itinerant vendors had suddenly filled the place. Even an open-air coffee shop was set up between the grocer's and the fruit shop, and the comings and goings increased. In no time at all, the rooms of the neighboring shacks still vacant were rented.

He felt happy in this exciting, good-humored atmosphere, but he was still out of work. Although he looked hard for a job, he couldn't find anything. Those who were just about to hire him immediately changed their minds upon learning his identity from the police.

It was impossible for him to borrow much from his friends since they, like he, were penniless and out of work. At least he could share a friend's room in an apartment in town, sparing him the rent on the shanty he lived in. He had accepted this suggestion of his friend's, but it wouldn't be easy to leave this place. He still had some debts, small as they were, with the grocer, the fruit seller, and one or two of the peddlers, and he needed to pay his bills.

One evening while he was at home thinking about how he would sell his things to pay his debts and how he would move, there was a knock on the door. In walked three men: the grocer, the fruit seller, and the owner of the open-air coffee shop. He received these three guests, ashamed of his bare room. "Please forgive me. I have neither coffee nor anything else to offer you," he said.

"It doesn't matter. We brought a few things. Here's some coffee and sugar," said the grocer, smiling, and put the paper bags in his hand on the table.

He was very surprised. Why had they brought these things? At first he thought they had come to collect, but what were these gifts?

"Apparently you are moving away, if what we hear is true," said the fruit seller.

"Yes, I will be moving." Now he understood why they had come. They must have worried that he was going to move without paying what he owed them. "Yes, but where did you hear that I am going to move?"

"From reliable sources," said the coffee seller meaningfully.

"Don't worry. I won't move without paying my bills with you."

"Oh, you shouldn't have said that, brother. Who said anything about bills?" said the coffee seller. "It isn't even worth talking about, sir. How much is it, anyway?" asked the grocer. "I let you have it free. I don't want it at all, and if you were to give it to me I wouldn't take it," said the fruit seller.

"But why?"

"We know your value, sir. You have been very good to us."

"Don't mention it," he said with difficulty, feeling a knot in his throat. It meant that they knew who he was and that he had worked for these people. Why was he overwhelmed with hopelessness? Why had he become pessimistic and tried to withdraw from politics? How could he abandon them?

"We beg you to give up the idea of moving," said the coffee seller. "Yes, this is what we came to ask you," said the fruit seller.

"I need to move because I can't pay the rent."

"We know. We know everything. We, the merchants around here, thought it over and talked about it, and finally we decided to contribute your rent ourselves and pay it every month. Now you won't have to leave," said the fruit seller. "It's enough that you not leave us. Think nothing of the rent," said the grocer.

Soon he would have wept, his eyes welling with joy. At the end of his year-long struggle for the sake of the common people, he was valued primarily for himself. "It's impossible. I can't accept. It wouldn't be right. The rent—I'm out of work. It's hard to get by here. I'll move in with a friend of mine," he said.

"We tradesmen have been discussing this whole matter for days. We've thought about everything, and your livelihood, too. We'll come up with your living each month among ourselves and give it to you, no matter how much it is. Whatever happens, don't leave this place. Don't leave us dangling." They all begged at once.

Soon he would not have been able to hold back the tears. Say what you will, there was great progress in the country, and among men a great awakening, meaning that for all these years he hadn't worked uselessly. In the old days, these people wouldn't even have said hello to him. "Thank you very much," he said. "You have touched me deeply, but I can't accept your help."

They began to plead with him again. "This place is not good enough for you. It's no home to live in. If you don't like it here, there is a two-story house close by. The top floor is for rent, and it has its own bath, too. Let me take you there," said the grocer. "What we want is that you not go away from this neighborhood and leave us," said the coffee shop owner.

He became very curious. "All right, but why do you want me to stay here?"

"It's obvious, sir. All these tradesmen live thanks to you."

"I beg your pardon! I can't be doing that much business with you."

"Your shopping is nothing. The real trade is something else. You brought good luck to this place. Before you came, hardly three or four customers a day came into my shop. You made this place lively and cheered it up. Just look! New shops are opening one after the other. It's all on account of you," the grocer said.

"Have a little feeling for us. If you move away from here, we've had it. Ultimately, I'll be forced to close the coffee shop," said its owner.

"If you move away from this neighborhood, these parts will be again as lifeless as before, and all the shopkeepers will go their separate ways. We and our families will be hungry and miserable," the fruit seller said.

They kept up their entreaty. They had wives and children; he must have pity on them. Thanks to him everyone was managing to live, and so—they would have tied him up for a month if need be.

"Thank you, but my services are not so great. I must still work while I am strong and healthy. What have I done here that you should not want me to leave you?"

"Well, whatever you do, we cannot forget your kindness. When you moved to this shanty, the police came dressed as garbage collectors and house painters to watch you carefully and keep a close eye on you. Still more police came to keep those police under control. There was pandemonium here," said the fruit seller.

"At first they questioned us and learned what you were doing," said the grocer.

"They began to buy things from all of us. Then the old clothes man came, the shoe repairman, the candy seller, the pickle maker, the *simit* seller, and others came," said the fruit seller.

"I opened a coffee shop, too, and started to make a living, sir, thanks to you. They sit in my coffee shop until evening, play backgammon and cards, and they each drink at least three or four cups of coffee," said the coffee shop owner.

He looked bitterly at them. "They were all plainclothesmen?"

"Some were and some weren't. In one place ten people got together, and next to them fifty gathered. If you move away from here now, this place will return to the way it was before. All the police go in your wake. Then we're done for!" said the grocer.

"Have pity on the poor!" said the fruit seller.

"You can't leave before we've made some money," said the coffee shop owner.

He reflected. It would have happened in exactly the same way in any other place. "Very well," he said. "I won't move away from here, but you must bring me right away . . . " He gave the grocer four paper bags which were on the table.

"Shall I give the good news to the other fellows?" asked the fruit seller as they were leaving.

"Yes. I won't move away. There's nothing else I want from you."

"God bless you," said the coffee shop owner.

THE GREAT WRESTLING CAMEL
Samim Kocagöz
(*Translated by John Taylor*)

Hasan, the son of Mustafa Ali, the camel master, opened the huge stable doors in the morning darkness and pushed them all the way back against the wall. From inside the hot smell of dung spread through the air, and from outside the stable was filled with clean, cool air and the half-light of morning.

"Good morning, fellow! Good morning, İnjili Chavush! Good morning, my great wrestling camel!" Hasan cried joyfully.

İnjili Chavush was kneeling on the straw, chewing his cud. When he heard Hasan's voice, he stretched out his neck and moved his small ears. He murmured with joy and scattered the foam from his mouth. He pulled on his halter, which was tied to iron rings on both sides. Hasan came up to him and stroked his downy neck and head. He made İnjili Chavush a gift of a big piece of the dough he had brought in a copper bucket. The great wrestling camel opened his gigantic mouth and closed it on the dough.

Hasan turned and looked at Maya, kneeling in the other corner of the stable. "And how are you this morning, big girl?" he asked. He brought over a piece of the dough and gave it to her.

İnjili Chavush was very pleased at the interest being taken in his lady. Hasan was a good hearted young man, and İnjili Chavush liked him. Hasan turned and came back, picked up the cloth and combs and began to groom Chavush. At the same time he was giving İnjili Chavush advice.

"İnjili, tomorrow you'll wrestle for the championship. Stand fast. Let me see it. You'll be the champion. The champion!"

At this point three more young men came through the stable door in excitement. "Let's get İnjili Chavush ready!" they shouted.

Chavush was annoyed. He knew all of these young men and liked them. But he didn't like their making such an outcry, their getting all worked up over nothing, before every wrestling match. They were like children, not that he didn't enjoy the flattery and the attention he was getting from all sides. But where was Master Mustafa Ali? When he looked into İnjili Chavush's eyes, the camel understood everything immediately. The camel master had grown old, and his strength was not as great as it once was. At one time he would raise over thirty camels in this huge stable. But times had changed, and the transportation business had changed with them. The camel master conformed to the times, sold his camels and bought a truck for his oldest son. Little Hasan was helping his older brother in the trucking business. But he couldn't give up İnjili Chavush or Maya. Master Mustafa Ali could never abandon İnjili. İnjili Chavush thought, "It's good that my father was a champion. And it's good that I was born as a champion. Otherwise he would have sold me and my wife."

Now the young men were all around him. One was preparing Maya, and the others were grooming him. İnjili Chavush ate part of the dough they had given him and kept the rest in his mouth, chewing it as long as he could so as not to anger the young men. He drank buckets and buckets of the water they put before him.

Then Hasan cried, "Chavush's saddle!" İnjili Chavush's saddle was a saddle to be seen. His name in fact might have been taken in part from this saddle. It was decorated with small beads of every different color and with tiny mirrors. The blanket extended back as far as his tail, and its colored beads and mirrors dazzled all whom he passed. The bell at the top of the saddle could be heard ringing seven villages off. He wasn't ready yet, but they got him up from where he was kneeling. With his fully decorated halter and saddle and his bell, İnjili Chavush was truly awe-inspiring. They tied small bells to his knees. They tied large bells to the bottom of the saddle. Between the large bells they strung more small bells. They combed and fluffed the hair on his neck and wove it with ribbons.

Next to İnjili Chavush's decorations, Maya's seemed very ordinary. On her saddle were simply the medals İnjili Chavush had won and rich hanging carpets which covered her. Chavush never wanted to take the lady with him to the wrestling matches. But if he didn't, his mind stayed at home. When he took her, there would be a number of ill-bred wrestling camels annoying her and trying to attract her attention from a distance, and they would make İnjili Chavush very angry. He would soothe his anger by defeating whichever one came before him and with great pleasure would watch the defeated camels take to their heels. Then he would present his trophies to Maya and forget about the bad manners of those others.

When it was time to take İnjili Chavush out of the stable, he held back. Hasan knew his gentlemanliness.

"Mehmet! First bring out Maya, İnjili's lady," he said.

The young men laughed together. "Chavush is always a gentleman!"

They passed in front of the house. Master Mustafa Ali was sitting on a chair in front of the door of his house, drinking coffee. When she heard the ringing of İnjili Chavush's bell, which shook the whole village, the master's wife flew out of the house. She watched İnjili's approach, her aged face bright.

Mustafa Ali put his cup on the edge of the table and stood up. He stroked İnjili Chavush. He inspected the grooming and the decoration, and glanced at Maya. He stroked his own beard and put his hand in his inside pocket. He took out his wallet and gave each of the young men ten *liras*.

"Take this. In town you'll eat bread and *helva*, and you'll have some pocket money. First, take İnjili Chavush for a walk through the village. Then take him slowly on the road to town. Don't spend the night in an inn. Find a corner on the square where the match is to be held tomorrow. Keep your eyes open wide, and take turns standing watch. Don't allow any treachery. Hasan, you keep an eye on your friends. Don't get separated from each other. For goodness sake, be careful of İnjili. I'll jump in the truck with your brother and come tomorrow morning. He's returning tonight. If he finishes his work and gets here early, we'll follow you and catch up this evening. So long now. I'm depending on you, my sons. Show them what you're made of, İnjili Chavush!"

After this long piece of advice from the master, they set out for the village square. Hasan and Ali held the two sides of the wrestler's halter with a pair of ropes. Mehmet and Rejeb were leading Maya in front. Master Mustafa Ali wouldn't have had Maya, who was walking in front of the champion, pulled by a donkey. That would have been an insult to İnjili. While the village square was ringing with the sound of İnjili Chavush's bells, the sun reached the top of the Madran mountains and illuminated the place. From the square, the sound of the bells spread through the village. The village woke up. The children leaped out of their beds. The women left their work. The men hurried to put on their boots and sandals. İnjili Chavush seemed smaller with the crowd surrounding him on all sides, but they loved him. The whole village looked into the wrestler's eyes.

"Show them, İnjili Chavush!"

"Don't blacken our reputation, İnjili Chavush!"

"You're terrific, İnjili Chavush!" the villagers shouted. They accompanied him to the bridge and saw him off.

It was a cool, cloudless Saturday near the end of fall. İnjili Chavush took the road that went straight to the county seat, ten miles away. He would walk slowly until evening and reach the town without tiring. He would be rested and ready for tomorrow's wrestling match. İnjili Chavush didn't like to walk on the right side of the road. In fact, if they are careful, files of camels never use the right side of the road in Turkey. Like the English, they use the left. This English idea is a good one for camels, because walking slowly, it is easier to protect themselves from the motor vehicles coming from behind. It is good, too, for seeing the oncoming traffic and getting out of the way early, without upsetting the load. Due to this custom, İnjili Chavush had never met with misfortune on the road. The young men were walking with him on foot. İnjili Chavush was a little worried that they weren't on donkeys. But why should they mind walking if the great champion himself was walking?

İnjili Chavush was watching the fields they passed on both sides of the road, and he lost himself in thought. In times past, how did the camels of the great caravans walk? How did their bells beat? İnjili set his walk to the pompous pace of those old days. His bells beat the rhythm: "My master is rich! My master is rich! I am the lead camel! I am the lead camel!" Because of the sound of his own bells, he couldn't hear Maya's at all.

Sunday morning before the sun had risen, Master Mustafa Ali filled the back of his truck with as many villagers as wanted to go to the wrestling match. Both rich and poor filled the truck. To those who said, "Master, we don't have any money," he answered, "Who asked you for money, fellow? Come on, jump into the truck."

Later he said to Kasım, his oldest son, who was the driver, "For mercy's sake, drive slow. We can't go scattering our villagers on the road."

They arrived in the town early. The whole town was on its feet and excited. Before noon, everyone had gathered on the soccer field to see the wrestling match, which was being held for the benefit of the Red Crescent. A large number of famous wrestling camels had come from the surrounding villages and even from further counties to settle accounts. Immediately after noon, all the camels, with pipers and drummers in front and behind, paraded through the town's streets, market, and main avenue. As was the custom, each master walked in front of his camel. In front of İnjili Chavush, in new clothes and with a turban bound to his cap, Master Mustafa Ali was swaggering and pulling majestically on his grey beard. The streets were full of people running to the wrestling match and of those walking with the camels. Children were shouting to each other and clapping their hands with joy as they ran around all sides of the camels. Among the people were many who shouted, "Long live Master Mustafa Ali! Long live İnjili Chavush!" Both Mustafa Ali and İnjili Chavush took on more and more an air of importance, and Hasan and Mehmet restrained Chavush with difficulty. This Sunday had the atmosphere of a celebration.

One by one, the camels came and took their places on the field. The people had completely surrounded the square. The drums were more lively and beat louder. İnjili Chavush was standing grandly and haughtily, and he surveyed the people with pleasure. Hasan and Mehmet held his halter tight and viewed the villagers and their excited, gathered heroes. Now and then İnjili Chavush glanced at Maya, who with great quietude was looking through the crowd at him. It was when he was thinking, "It would be a real disgrace to be beaten in front of this crowd and in front of one's lady. I'll have to do this job well," that he saw a camel from another neighborhood pass by Maya, looking her over closely, and wink at her. His anger increased. It didn't matter that the camel's keepers pulled him quickly away from her. İnjili Chavush said to himself, "I'll finish you off in this wrestling match, you vagabond!"

İnjili couldn't stand still any longer. He wasn't watching the wrestling anymore. He understood that his turn would come near the end because they hadn't yet bound his mouth. He would fight two matches. If he won both of them, the first and the second, he would be a champion. He would win a trophy. When he walked out onto the square, there was a tumult of applause.

"İnjili Chavush, the lion!"

"Do your stuff, İnjili Chavush!"

The drums beat wildly, and the pipes encouraged him. Hasan took off the halter and let him go. When he faced the other wrestling camel, İnjili Chavush thought to himself, "Is this the scoundrel who was annoying my lady?" But he didn't think for long. Angrily, he locked his opponent's legs under his own. He brought his weight down on the enemy's back. The other camel was stunned. For a few minutes it resisted, but it was forced to flee. As soon as it could pull itself free, it took to its heels. It let out some confused noises. İnjili Chavush took a few steps forward, as though to give chase, and then stopped, saying, "Go to hell, you shameless thing."

Hasan and Mehmet ran up. Jumping up and down, they clung to his neck and stroked him. They passed the halter over his head and tied the bells back on his legs. They wiped the foam from his mouth and unbound it. İnjili Chavush took a victory tour around the perimeter of the field. He got great applause. While he was passing Maya he glanced in her direction, and she showed her approval. Now it was time to wait for the championship match. He looked disdainfully at the camels that came onto the field. They struggled with each other a great deal. Finally, İnjili turned and looked at Maya when the applause indicated that the match was over. He wondered who had won. But he thought, "You're a man, after all. What does it matter who? I'll win the final." So after letting the winner rest a bit, they got him ready, and in order to introduce him to the people together with İnjili, they took one more tour around the field. This time Maya joined the parade, too. This made İnjili Chavush very angry. What was going on that they should walk his Maya in front of that lout? His Maya was walking in front, but İnjili was a decent camel, and he didn't even look at her. He was very angry with his rival. "I'll fix you!" he said.

They removed his bells and his blanket decorated with beads and mirrors and bound his mouth. This time İnjili thought, "It's good they're using a muzzle, or I'd tear this lout to bits." He walked straight onto the field angrily and hurled himself on his rival. The beating of the drums excited the square, and the match began fiercely. First, İnjili struck his rival with all his weight. The camel was shaken, but he feigned indifference. Then İnjili tried another trick. He dived and reached for his opponent's legs with his head. The camel jumped back. The people applauded both İnjili and his rival. They struggled for a long time with each other. Finally, İnjili threw his neck across his rival's and tripped him with his front legs. His giant rival fell suddenly on his side. But the fall was so great that İnjili couldn't get his legs out from under the weight. They rolled over together on the ground. The rival jumped up and started to flee. İnjili Chavush felt a terrible pain in his legs. Then his stomach burned with such a hurt that he couldn't even think about chasing the camel, and he lost hold of himself. He started to cry painfully. His two front legs had broken together, and one of the broken bones had turned back and punctured his stomach. His eyes darkened, and he didn't see the people gathering around him. He was only crying from pain.

The people on the field were crying, too. "İnjili Chavush! İnjili!" they mourned. Master Mustafa Ali, Hasan, Mehmet, and the others knelt in front of his head. Tears were falling from Master Mustafa Ali's eyes into his beard. He stroked the wrestling camel's head and said, "You won, İnjili Chavush. You're the champion, the head camel. Look, the other one ran away." But İnjili couldn't stand the pain. Maya was coming close to him, and he looked at her hopelessly, with love in his eyes. He knew that he would die. To escape the pain, he was willing to die quickly. Master Mustafa Ali agreed. Everyone moved away from İnjili Chavush with tears in their eyes and turned their backs. A butcher with a huge, sharp knife came up to İnjili Chavush. First they took his finely beaded, mirrored saddle from his hump, and then they stopped the pain.

IN GOD'S PLAINS
Necati Cumalı
(Translated by Talat Sait Halman)

The truck forged ahead on a dirt road furrowed by wagons and riders, running through fields and pastureland. The slanted curves around the fields tilted it. Going in and out of ditches and crevices, it often shimmied and jerked. It was only on the short stretches of flat pastureland that it managed to find its balance and gain a little speed. At certain points, hedges of myrtle, Judas trees, and shrubbery narrowed the road. Branches of trees jutted out and swooped down to the dirt road, and the truck was forced every now and then to push its way through against all the hanging greenery that held it back.

In God's plains, a hunter had shot a woodsman to death. No one knew how the confrontation took place, what happened between them, how and why the hunter killed the woodsman. There were no witnesses. Now, the court officials, who were trying to solve the crime on the basis of presumptive evidence, were on their way back, following the on-the-spot investigation of the claims advanced by the defense.

The old judge and the DA sat in front, next to the driver. The court-appointed expert and the defense attorney sat in the back on precariously-placed chairs. Standing in the back were five woodcutters ranging in age from fifteen to eighteen. These youngsters, who had run into the murderer and his victim on the road on the day of the incident, had already given their testimony.

As the truck wobbled, jolted or bobbed up and down, the people in the back struggled to hold on to each other or to the side planks. They often had to duck or bend over to get away from the assault of the branches.

On both sides the road stretched desolately. Half a kilometer or a full kilometer apart, far removed from the roadside, they caught glimpses of squatty roofs with enclosures on all sides.

The heat of late May made the scent of the meadows lie heavy in the air. Only the birds shattered the silence of the plains. To their right and left, many species of birds kept flying, mates chasing one another. They were all so joyful, so intoxicated with the spring and with love that sometimes pairs of mates, dashing forward in their flirtatious pursuit, would fly past just a few inches above the heads of the people in the back of the truck.

The road now ran parallel to a stream. To their left stood a hill, with its groves of olive trees. To their right, long, narrow fields stretched up to the skirts of the hill.

They caught sight of a few horses and donkeys tied up at the borders of fields, and then a female dog which was being chased by three male dogs, making her run desperately.

Suddenly the truck came to a halt. The people in the back jumped to their feet, wondering what was going on. To the left of the truck, by the roadside, they saw a boy who looked about four years old. He was weeping.

When the truck stopped, the little boy cried even more loudly, rubbing his eyes.

The driver stepped down, and two of the young woodsmen jumped from the back. They walked up to the boy.

He was a chubby boy, barefoot, his head clean-shaven. He had a suntan. All he was wearing was a long shirt which came down to his knees. The shirt was open in the front. He had no underwear or pants on.

The driver squatted in front of the child and asked, "What's the matter, son? What happened? Did you get lost? Whose boy are you?"

Sobbing, the child muttered, "Rejeb's."

"Which Rejeb?"

The child failed to answer this time.

"What happened to you? Tell us."

The boy lifted his right hand and pointed to where the truck had just come from. His sobs grew louder.

"Is your home over there? Is that where you live?"

The boy thrust his head back, which meant no.

"Did they beat you? Where's your home? Where are your folks?"

The boy dropped his hand and pointed to his bottom. Then, clenching his fists, he rubbed his eyes again. Once more he broke into sobs.

The truck driver pulled the child close to his legs. No sooner than he tried to lift the shirt he let it go. His face was flustered, in anguish. A trickle of blood descended from the boy's anus to his buttocks.

The driver turned to the passengers. "God damn!" he exclaimed. "They have raped the poor boy."

They formed a circle around the child.

One of the woodcutters quietly said, "I had thought as much."

They stood stunned, speechless. Behind the boy they could see a thick grove in which brambles and myrtles were intertwined with the weeds and the trees. The child was a lone figure in the wilderness. To their right, across the stream, as far as a bullet's range, they noticed a white roof.

The driver called out, "Heeeyyy, neighbor!"

One of the woodcutters blew a long whistle. An old woman came out of the house. Putting her right hand over her eyebrows, she looked in the direction of the truck.

"Hey, granny, are you Rejeb's mother?"

The old woman raised her hand and waved back. She called something out, but no one was able to hear the answer.

"Rejeb? Who's Rejeb?"

Again, her answer could not be heard. Then, they noticed that her hand was pointing to the hill, to a little house whose roof tiles were barely visible through the branches of an olive tree.

The driver turned to the DA. "Goddamn," he said. "God knows where his parents are. Chopping wood? Doing the laundry? I wonder in whose hands they left this kid?"

The DA had nothing to say.

The driver held the child by his armpits, lifted him, and held him out to the woman.

"Take this child," he said. "Come and get him."

The old woman tugged away at her headscarf and made another sign with her hands.

The defense attorney asked, "What's she trying to say?"

One of the young woodcutters replied, "They'll come and get him."

"When?"

"She says let him stay there. I'll come and get him."

The truck driver turned to the judge. "Your command, sir? What shall we do, Mr. Justice?"

The judge, the DA, the attorney, and the expert looked at each other, wondering what to do. There was a felony, a crime. But they had no authority or power to do anything unless the boy's father filed a formal complaint with the DA's office and the pre-trial examination was completed. The attorney could not possibly speak for the boy's father unless and until he had his power of attorney.

The DA said, "There isn't much we can do, is there?" With a sad expression on his face, the old judge kept quiet.

The driver gently patted the boy on the head. "Just stay here," he said. "Wait for Granny." The lawyer added, "And tell your father all about what they did to you. Tell him to report it to the police."

They took their seats on the truck. As the truck took off, the boy, more frightened than before, started to cry again.

ÜSKÜDAR AND HAYRI BEY
Oktay Akbal
(*Translated by Janet Heineck*)

"Hayri Bey has received a three thousand-*lira* bonus," said my father. My mother was very pleased, and we were all happy. I saw Hayri Bey before me. He was stroking his sparse white beard or performing the prayer on his small silk prayer rug. I thought of Osman and Nesrin, who were so happy now. This was three thousand *liras*. Three thousand separate *liras*! You could never finish counting them. If you piled them one on top of the other they would reach the ceiling!

My mother reminded me of the dinner before me which was getting cold. "Hayri Bey came to see me yesterday. He asked what he was going to do now with all this money," my father said, smiling. "He should buy a house for himself," my mother exclaimed. "There are houses in Üsküdar for only a thousand *liras*! Then they would no longer have to pay rent. He has a daughter, and his son-in-law could live with them." My mother was always full of ideas. Here she had arranged house, Üsküdar, daughter, son-in-law, and rent all at once.

The house in which Hayri Bey lived belonged to one of his relatives. It had a single story, three rooms, and a stone cellar which went under the street. A little further on, one went down a slope to Salajak landing. In an empty lot on the hill the boys used to play soccer, and every time I came I would go and watch, and sometimes be the goalkeeper. When I didn't join the team I used to go off to watch the little steamers. I used to compete with Osman at throwing stones into the sea. Once a stone I threw did not make it to the water, and Osman said, "I wish we had a sling!"

He was a very pale little boy, a year older than I. As for Nesrin, she was two years older. She, with her deep black eyes, was at the threshhold of young womanhood. In one summer she had changed quickly. She no longer played tag and hide-and-seek, and did not go out into the street, but would read quietly in the corner of the sofa, collect twenty-five *kurush* novels, and ask me for books. She was never pleased with what I brought.

I was very glad about their three thousand *liras*. "Things will be easier for Zeliha," said my mother, Zeliha! Zeliha whose hair streamed while she was running, preparing the table, and cooking meals. Who knew how beautiful she might have been when she was young? Her daughter was dark-skinned; she herself was blond. Zeliha seemed to have been born to work, to cook, and to have children. Her first two children had died while they were small. Every time I went, she steered the conversation around to the subject of her dead children, and cried while she was talking about them. My mother too recalled her dead children, and they used to weep silently together. These tears shed for children who had died years before seemed out of place to me. That was ten or twenty years ago.

Now Zeliha was wild with delight. Three thousand *liras*! The best thing to do would be to buy a house with it. Perhaps her relatives would sell the house they lived in, and in this way they would be free of paying ten *liras* every month. My father used to give me a silverpiece on every festival day. I would buy things for three days, but I couldn't spend it all. Those big twenty-five *kurush* coins don't melt away no matter what you buy — hammocks, horses, donkeys, having your future told, candy, chocolate, magazines. How nice it was that Hayri Bey should get three thousand silver *liras*! He would look at them for hours, lining them up side by side, one on top of the other, and then in layers. Then he would pay half of that money and buy the house.

I had not been to Üsküdar for a long time. We were always curious about it, wondering what these people did there. One day Zeliha came to see us, and she and my mother sat in the garden. The talk was all about the house. Zeliha thought like my mother and wanted to buy the house where they lived, but Hayri Bey got the idea into his head of going into business, although he knew nothing about commercial affairs. "We'll lose all this money," Zeliha was weeping. A few days later my father went to have a talk with Hayri Bey, who kept on saying that he would open a grocery shop, a small neighborhood grocery store. "For years I was a civil servant in a white shirt, a starched collar, and a pressed suit, and what did I get?" Yet there was a Yorgi Efendi in the neighborhood, a grocer for years—the man had set up rows of of houses. "I'll bankrupt him," Hayri Bey was saying.

We all laughed, and it was my father who laughed the hardest. This project made no sense at all to my father. "It won't come to anything anyway," he would say. My father was so confident that at the last moment Hayri Bey would change his mind and abandon the project. But sometimes things which seem the least possible come true. Meanwhile, two or three weeks went by.

Zeliha came one day. She was overjoyed and laughing. My mother supposed that they had bought the house with those three thousand *liras*, but it wasn't so! Hayri Bey had opened a small grocery shop in the basement under the house. Zeliha had become more enthusiastic than her husband about it and kept on saying, "What would have been the good of buying the house? My husband was right. This is better. Look at Yorgi!" My mother did not have the heart to ruin her happiness. Let them believe themselves to be happy for a while, yet an apparent happiness instead of a home is an expensive thing.

I was lost in dreams. What would I not have given at that moment to see Hayri Bey's grocery shop! Days passed again. One day we were going to Üsküdar anyway, and Hayri Bey's grocery shop was waiting for us.

I came off the small steamer, and when I started up the hill I saw an isolated sign on the dilapidated wall at the street corner which read "Bereket Grocery is on this street." We were in Üsküdar, and I would finally see Hayri Bey's shop. I ran up to the house, and left my mother far behind.

It was four steps down to the shop, and there was nothing you could call a shop window. Two sacks of rice and a sack of sugar were set out in the street, and there was a signboard above the door. Who knows how many days Hayri Bey had worked on writing this "In the name of God, the Merciful, the Compassionate" in such elegant script? I lost myself in the Arabic characters, which seemed like small ships and sailboats.

A little girl came to buy vinegar. Hayri Bey, his black beret on his head, filled a jar with vinegar with a funnel. He weighed the bottle. It was too much, he poured some out, it was not enough, and he filled it again. "If it's too much, it's too bad for me, and if it's too little, it's too bad for you. It's neither a large crime nor a small one, my daughter. In the end it's all the same." He held out the bottle and took her five *kurush*. When the girl came out, I went in. "Some chocolate, uncle," I said. At first he did not understand and gave me a piece of melba chocolate, and then he recognized me. "Oh! You little rascal!" He filled my hand with the chocolate. "Put some in your pocket," he said. Osman had appeared, and I broke off half the chocolate and gave it to him. He gulped it down at once.

Just then a neighbor lady came into the store. "Five *kurush*-worth of *helva*," she said. Hayri Bey sat up straight for a moment and said, "Lady, I don't sell five *kurush*-worth of *helva* to people." The woman put down her money. Muttering "five *kurush*-worth of *helva*, a hundred *paras*-worth of quince, forty *paras*-worth of olives," he sliced off the *helva* and wrapped it in paper.

My mother had arrived, and we went into the house and sat on the sofa. Osman gave me a sign and I stood up. Hayri Bey had closed up the shop and had gone to talk with my mother, and Osman let me into the shop by the back door and led the way to the candy. "Take as much as you want," he said. Then we went out to the street, where I saw a big piece of chocolate in his hand. Nibbling on our chocolate, we ran to a spot overlooking the sea. "Why did you take these things?" I asked. "No one buys them," he said. "They all buy the little ones. These would become maggoty, so I eat them." "Does your father know?" He laughed. "Stay for dinner tonight. We're having a special dessert," he said.

The sea was below our feet. A small steamer was tying up, and a few people were about to climb the slope. It was as though we were watching a silent film, except that birds were singing and gulls were flying over our heads. "Is it good being a grocer? Do you work too?" I asked. "Of course. There's chickpeas to eat, candy to steal, and chocolate to swallow," he replied.

We stayed for dinner that night. There was that pastry dessert, and the pilaf was excellent. One dish after another. The dining tray was filled and emptied again, and Hayri Bey was all attentiveness. "It's a good thing that I opened this shop," he said, and talked about the advantages for people of having sugar, flour, and oil handy. I was watching his white beard while he was eating. It appeared happy. For the first time after his life as an official for thirty years, there was a light in his eye, and this happiness seemed to be reflected in his beard. At his fingertips were plenty of things to eat and sweet pastries. "Yesterday we had our cream dessert. We would have had it again if we had known you were coming." They were expecting us on Sunday, and my father ought to have come. We should have had that cream dessert.

After the meal, I went down to the shop along with Hayri Bey. My mother and Zeliha were on the sofa absorbed in conversation. An air force officer had asked for Nesrin's hand, and they were probably going to talk about that. I overheard that now she would have more suitors, and more men would be asking to marry her. After dinner, Nesrin took her novel and retreated to her corner. At dinner she had eaten very little, and her father had said, "Girl, eat as much as you can while you have it. Your future husband may not feed you so well."

An elderly woman was slowly coming down the three steps, resting for a minute or two at each one. Osman and I took her by the arm. The woman kept on talking, and what things she said! I looked at Hayri Bey. He was not pleased at all and had a long face. "The old woman worries us," said Osman. "She's as deaf as a post. Well, what does she want now?" The woman came up to the counter with difficulty. We were standing side by side and watching apprehensively, thinking she was going to fall. She held out a tiny bottle. "Put some olive oil in this." She took back the filled bottle and put down five *kurush*. We took her by the arm again, went out to the street and accompanied her to the corner. Just as we came back to the shop, a woman whose head was covered was wrapping up a hundred *paras*-worth of olive oil, seven and a half *paras*-worth of chocolate, and two hundred fifty grams of rice. The shop was running like clockwork. Osman and I were wrapping the packages and weighing them on the scales. Meanwhile we were gobbling the caramels that Hayri Bey would give us.

In the house at night my father burst out laughing when he heard my description. "One hundred *paras*-worth of vinegar, five *kurush*-worth of *helva*! Becoming a grocer — what an idea!" We were going to cross over to Üsküdar in a few days to eat cream dessert. They would soon be bankrupt anyway. "It would be good if they turned it over to someone and recovered the money," my mother was saying. Could it pay for a dinner table filled with fancy pastries and desserts every day? Of course he was going bankrupt, but at least he was spending it on himself.

We could not go to eat cream dessert. How quickly time was passing, and what things were happening in that passing time! The illnesses of my mother and the death of my father meant the collapse of our home and childhood's sudden end. It all seemed to happen in a moment.

Hayri Bey's grocery shop went under a long time ago. The *helva*, the candies, and the cheeses were all eaten. The ones that weren't eaten rotted, and rats chewed on the sacks. Hayri Bey went bankrupt. Nesrin got married, Osman joined the army, and the couple were alone now in that little rented house. Hayri Bey could not move from where he had been, and would while away the hours in his bed reading the old manuscripts inherited from his grandfather. My mother and I were in a distant neighborhood of the city, living alone. Our lives were like a lie, and Üsküdar was a long way off. Hayri Bey's grocery shop, the pastries and the chocolates were the made-up things you see in a dream.

Years flowed by like this. One day, it happened that I found myself in Üsküdar. I was grown up now, and everything seemed changed to me. Üsküdar was another Üsküdar. It was foreign, a place you wouldn't recognize. I went up the slope and turned off to the street where the little house had been. Yorgi's grocery shop had grown. There was a big refrigerator in the shop window, and Yorgi was at the cash register.

When I reached the home of the Hayri Beys, Zeliha was washing the front of the door. That golden hair of hers was pure white. She didn't recognize me, and we looked at each other for a moment. "I would have bought a hundred *paras*-worth of *helva* from the grocer, but I guess I was late," I said. Suddenly she smiled, and she seemed the Zeliha of much younger years who was gone for a moment and now back again. We went inside.

Hayri Bey was sleeping on the bed. He didn't recognize anyone, not even his wife and children, and had gone to another world. When he woke up I kissed his hand, and he looked at me and laughed. I spoke my name, but he did not understand. "Uncle, weigh out a hundred *paras*-worth of *helva*," I said. His laughter was cut off, and he looked up from the depths. A dark haze had clouded his vision. Did he remember anything? He seized my hand, squeezed it, and then turned his head away, back again to his own world. My conversation with Zeliha was exactly as before: the past, Hayri Bey, the girls, his son Osman. Then my father's death, my mother, me, school.

The evening was coming down on Üsküdar. The grocery shop was now a coal cellar. I stood for a while in front of the door and then left without looking back. There were no longer any pastry or sweets. I had to forget the aged couple getting by on the small pension. This life was hard, very hard, and Üsküdar was another Üsküdar. Hayri Bey's Üsküdar was lost, had died. In Uncle Hayri Bey's dead world, old Üsküdar was living with all its vitality. The grocery shops were still open, the customers were still coming, the food was still being cooked. Apartment houses went up and the cars multiplied around me. Jazz on the radio.

Another year passed. Zeliha came to see us one evening. Had I given her the address or had she found it out? She and my mother were in the visitors' room when I came home. I asked about Hayri Bey. She cried. Hayri Bey was dead. Three months ago he spoke once for the first time, breaking the silence which had gone on for years. "Bring me a dish of compote," he had said to his son Osman, home on leave from the army. Compote! He said nothing more. Osman brought the food. Hayri Bey was reliving those old days and that brilliant shopkeeper's life of his while eating the compote, and was happy. He laughed, kissed his son, and put his head on the pillow to fall asleep. In the morning he didn't wake up.

Üsküdar was now without Hayri Bey, a meaningless place. Streets, buildings, mosques, people come together and form a district called Üsküdar. For years I couldn't go to this Üsküdar which had become foreign to me, and then I began to hate cream desserts, candies, and compotes. How could people eat such rich sweets? What was it they liked about Üsküdar? I had lost my own Üsküdar, Hayri Bey's Üskudar, and I wanted everyone to lose it.

KIR İZZET'S GARDEN
Talip Apaydın
(*Translated by Janet Heineck*)

Halim Agha's hired man Kır İzzet, sitting on the threshold of his family's house had been waiting for the agha for half an hour. He was turning over in his mind the things he was going to say and was looking for words that would seem winning. "If I say that sort of thing he won't accept it. He'll become obstinate. If I say this, perhaps he'll be ready to say yes. Perhaps I can appeal to the good streaks in his nature." He had wanted to speak for a long time but couldn't find an opportunity. Today at noon had been his perfect chance. He would have spoken, but he couldn't because some other people came and interrupted. When he finished simply reporting about the field work, the agha said, "Well done, İzzet! You've pleased me. Take the day off. Tomorrow start to draw goods from the shop. Kerosene, salt, and other things. Winter is coming on. Pack the big mule and start work." "All right, sir," Kır İzzet had said. His face lit up, but the things he would have said were still right on the tip of his tongue.

He did not want others to hear. People are cunning. Someone could go and take possession of it. No one knew that water could flow from below Yassıkaya and that he would be able to plant a beautiful garden there. If they had been aware of it, they would have done something a long time ago. Kır İzzet had had his eye on that place since spring six months before. While driving the mule, he had seen wild plants which were signs of water. "Ah ha!" he said to himself. "There's water there, by God." If the lake area were dug out, he reckoned that a more than two-*dönüm* garden could be planted. He was one of the few people in this village who did not have a garden. While other children ate grapes in the summer and dried fruit in winter, his children had nothing. It was difficult to remain with nothing but dry bread in the countryside. If he were to become owner of this land under Yassıkaya, and if he were to dig a lake and strike water, his wife and daughter helping, it wouldn't be two or three years before they would make this land green and growing. Black grapes, white grapes, a couple of apricot and plum trees, even a little vegetable plot. Tomatoes, peppers, things too good to eat. Then he would leave the agha's service. After these seven years he was thoroughly fed up. He was working summer and winter. Was Koja Halim Agha's work ever done? While he was working on one thing, the agha would order something else. He had passed his fortieth year a long time ago and his hair and beard had turned white. His name in the village was "Grey İzzet" and he still was not a freeholder. He did not own an inch of land. Surely it would have been more pleasant for him to work on his own account, but he had never once experienced this. If the agha were to say yes once, neither peasant nor headman could touch it. Or wasn't the countryside around Koja Yapılı village big enough for a sheep and a cow? It wouldn't hurt anyone if İzzet, a pauper, should all of a sudden become the owner of two *dönüms*. After all, last year the aghas divided up Özlen hill among themselves. According to some, they bought it at fifty *liras* per *dönüm* and didn't even pay that much to the government.

"All I want is two *dönüms*," said Kır İzzet. "Two *dönüms*."

Then he got to his feet, thrust his hands into his sash and started to pace around in front of the door, saying over to himself, "Do it sir. Be a guardian for us. Show your generosity and say yes. By saying yes, you will have given Kır İzzet paradise."

When he heard coughing, he drew out his hands and let them drop. The skirts of his black overcoat were swinging back and forth. Kır İzzet softened his expression and moderated his voice.

"What's that, İzzet? What are you doing there?"

"Good day, sir."

"How are you?"

"I'm fine, sir. May you be well!"

"Did you feed the mule? Are you going tomorrow?"

"I fed him, sir. It's all set."

"Buy the salt first. Tell Fahri Efendi to make up forty or fifty sacks. You can start carrying it gradually."

"It will be done, sir. There's something—"

"Very well. Is there anything else?"

"One more thing, sir. I have something to say to you."

"What? Do you want more money?"

"No, sir. Er—"

He gulped and couldn't recall the speech he had prepared.

"Be a guardian for me, sir. It would be a great charity. Myself and the whole family beg you—"

"What is it? Say it."

"A small thing, sir. Er—there is a place below Yassıkaya. A grassy spot. I've looked it over. There's water there. To dig there, and make a two-*dönüm* garden—"

"Well?"

"In other words, this work can be done if you give your permission."

"You're quitting. Is that it?"

"No, sir. I didn't say that."

"When will you dig? What will become of our work?"

He really hadn't thought of this. He was confused.

"Not now, sir. It's enough that you say yes. I'll go and work even at night, by moonlight. That is, if the villagers don't object."

"Hmm."

The agha didn't know quite what to answer. He was thinking.

"Where is this place you mentioned?"

"A high promontory beneath Yassıkaya. Grassy."

"How do you know there's water there?"

"I know, sir. I saw the kind of plants that mean that water is close by."

Suddenly the agha laughed. "İzzet, you don't have any brains at all. How can you expect water there? It's a wasteland."

"Yes, there is, sir. I know. I looked it over. You give permission, and let the peasants not object, and it will be enough for me."

"Ha, ha, ha! If water were there, would people leave it until today, my poor son? Don't you know these people? Who knows how many people have felt out that place? Really!"

"You are right, sir. Alright, perhaps. I want to try my luck. I said nothing to the others in case one of them should go and take it over. Be a guardian for me. I implore you. Tonight I want to go and dig."

"What? Did you say tonight?"

"No. Er—another day."

"Look, man, tomorrow you're going to the city. How can you work there at night?"

"I won't stall around in my work, sir. At dawn I'll be starting down the same road."

"No, no, it can't be. You work both there and here? How can that be? Tell me frankly if you want to quit. I'll figure your wages and you can go."

The agha frowned. Who knew what he thought?

"No, sir. I said nothing of the kind. I am completely content in your service. God bless you. What I really want to say—if only I might become the owner of a two-*dönüm* place. You know my circumstances. I don't have a single green tree in the whole world. Poverty is evil, sir. I said, 'If the water just flows, I'll plant a few saplings below it. Three or four fruit trees.' "

The agha shook his head.

"Well, that's just great. But when will you do this work?"

"Just say yes, sir. If necessary, I'll put my wife and daughter to work. And I'll go at night. In the moonlight."

The agha didn't take him seriously.

"Alright, alright," he said. "Do it. The time will come. But now, get on with your work."

"Thank you, sir. God bless you. May God double your wealth. Let's not say anything to the others, sir, in case they go and take it over. The men of this village of ours are pretty shrewd."

"Alright, alright. That's enough. Start out early in the morning. Listen to me. Don't get the idea of riding the loaded mule. If I hear of it—"

"Mercy, sir! Does one ride a loaded mule? I swear it's a sin! There is a reckoning in the next world."

"I know, I know. Don't elaborate."

The agha had already gone in and shut the door. Kır İzzet walked away joyfully. He was muttering, "Bravo. He's a real man. He said alright. Once he's said alright, nobody can say anything. It's settled."

He came straight home.

From the door he called out, "Wife! Be quick! Bring out the pick and shovel. We're going."

"Where? What's the word?"

She was boiling soup, squatting by the earthen fireplace. The three daughters, the oldest of whom was twelve, were waiting for the soup in the pot to be ready.

"Get up, I say! Get the implements. You and the girl, we'll go together. Come on! Let the others drink the soup and go to bed. If anyone asks, say, 'They've gone out.' Do you understand?"

"Yes," said the middle daughter.

His wife and eldest daughter were bewildered. Where did one go and what did one do at this hour with a pick and shovel? They couldn't understand. But for the moment he was obstinate and would make them do just as he said.

"Are we going on an empty stomach, husband? Let's eat."

"Is it the time for food? Take some bread. We'll eat it on the way. Hurry up!"

A little later they were going toward Yassıkaya at a slow run, pick and shovel on their shoulders. They were gobbling dry bread as they ran. Kır İzzet still had not said where they were going.

It was almost dark. In a little while the moon would rise, yet it was rather light in that direction.

"You ask where we're going," said Kır İzzet.

"Where? You didn't say."

"Below Yassıkaya. We're going to dig a lake and strike water. We'll make a garden. Finally we'll have one too."

"Will we have our very own garden, daddy?" asked the daughter. "Really?"

"Really and truly."

Her mother was becoming interested. "From where will we draw the water?"

"I know the place. I looked it over. I spoke to the agha, and he said, 'Alright. You dig. No one will interfere.' "

"He must be kind."

"Naturally. Just keep going. God willing, we'll find water tonight."

They ran.

While the moon was rising they reached Yassıkaya. The valleys were in darkness. But the plains suddenly seemed to be growing light. It was a steeply sloping, broken land, with rocky places here and there.

When Kır İzzet approached the place where he would dig the lake, he speeded up and went ahead. He was very excited.

"Here it is," he said. "There's water right here. It's obvious because it's grassy. Surely you saw that. Here are the wild plants which show there is water. I found them while pasturing the mule. Let me dig one meter, that's all. Just let me dig down a little to expose the spring. Now then."

He walked toward the slope of the peak. He took off his jacket and threw it aside. He spat on his hands and began to swing the pickax rapidly.

"Quick! You clean up the area with the shovel. It's light, sandy earth. But it's hard and dry. It hasn't rained here for maybe six months. The surface of the ground has formed a stone-hard crust as though it's petrified. Unless you hit it several times with the pick, you won't break it up." Kır İzzet was flailing madly with the pickax. He probably hadn't reckoned that it would be this difficult. He quickly overcame his bewilderment and, after the second stratum, reflected that the digging was going easily.

"Come on! Hurry and clear up this stuff," he said to his wife. "Throw it far away. Otherwise it will be difficult to clear away the earth you shovel."

The woman was standing, looking all around. She wasn't convinced in the least that water would be extracted from this place. This man was mad. If he weren't crazy, would he have come at this hour of the night and become mixed up in such an impossible situation? If water were there, wouldn't the others have done something about it before this?

"Come on, girl. I'm tired. Dig a little bit! Take the shovel, too," he said to his daughter.

When he squatted down on his heels, his sweaty face shone in the moonlight. He was breathing heavily through his mouth, his chest working like a bellows as he panted.

"Give it some good ones, girl. Do you have any strength or not?"

No matter how much the girl struck, she couldn't get the pickax through.

"Give me that, you silly weakling!" he said.

He began to try again.

The moon was rising as this went on. It was round and flat like a plate, and seemed to be looking down and laughing. By the time the moon reached its zenith, they had dug out a place as long as six steps, about four pick-lengths long. Kır İzzet was stooping at every blow and feeling the earth, measuring its wetness.

"Look," he said. "It's gradually getting soft. And its moisture is increasing. Do you see?"

He was getting excited.

The woman looked but could find no such thing.

"And the color of the soil has changed. It's turning red. That means water is close."

He began to work with a new strength. He was very tired, but he didn't notice. His wife was still unable to say anything. This was not the time to speak. Her daughter had become sleepy and thought about stretching out on the ground.

"Daddy," she said. "Daddy, there is no water."

"It will come. It's near now. Just keep trying."

His wife lowered her tone in order not to show her anger. "Let's dig the rest of it tomorrow, husband. It will be morning before long. We're sleepy. Besides, you're going to the city tomorrow."

"I just won't go. Today I'll strike this water, do you understand?"

"What will the agha say?"

"What will he say? He allowed it."

"He gave his permission, but did he say don't go to the city?"

"He didn't, but what does it matter? Just let me strike water and the rest is easy."

"We'll find the water, man. What's your hurry? Is this the only day there is?"

"Didn't I say no? Don't keep this up! Get back to work!"

The woman threw the dirt out of the hollow with difficulty. Her arms ached. She was exhausted. "You go at least," she said, turning to her daughter. "Go and lie down somewhere. You'll collapse any minute."

"Where are you going?" asked her father. "I'm not making this garden all by myself! We'll dig it together. Don't make me angry. Do you want a beating?"

His voice was hoarse. He looked terrible in the middle of the night. The woman had to be very humble.

"Don't do it, man," she said. "At least let the girl lie down a little. She's sleepy. It's a shame."

"What's the shame? I'm making this garden for them. Tomorrow they'll eat grapes and fruit from it."

"Yes, but isn't today like every other day? I'm telling you, let's dig tomorrow."

"Impossible. We'll find water today. Afterwards someone could come and take it over. Don't you know the people of this village?"

The woman stopped talking. Kır İzzet started digging like someone insane, and the others wordlessly cleared the spoils. There was no other sound in the night than that of the pick and shovel.

In a little while it was daybreak. The moon was down, and the stars began to disappear.

The hole had become about as deep as a man is tall. Still no moisture had appeared. The red soil had ended, and a vein of whitish earth had begun, a muddy, gravelly, mixed soil.

Kır İzzet propped his hands on his hips. He was all sweat. His wizened body trembled. He shook his head and said, "Don't make it any harder on me. I'll bring water out of here. There is water here!"

His last words came out hoarsely. Suddenly his head was spinning. He collapsed where he was.

While the sun was rising, his wife and daughter were weeping at his side.

THE LOAN
Talip Apaydın
(Translated by Janet Heineck)

When morning prayer began, Kandil Omar stood at the door of the mosque and looked sideways and backward angrily. He had gray hair and his face was pale. He was in a thoughtful mood. He thrust his hands into his sash in order not to be cold, but it was no use. A trembling began which came from inside him.

The peasants were coming out of the mosque in ones and twos. Whoever had an overcoat wrapped himself up in it and hurried along. The weather was very cold. It made his shoulders tremble once or twice. He braced himself, relaxed and tried to warm himself. "Come on out now, you old rascal," he said to himself. "The prayer is over. What more are you waiting for?"

He turned around again. The door opened and closed but neither agha nor son-in-law appeared. "Nuts! I wish I had waited inside. I'll catch cold out here," he said to himself.

He walked slowly. He was dressed very lightly. There wasn't even a proper shirt inside his patched jacket, and his black rubber boots had split at the sides. He was shaking all over.

While he was going around Yakub's corner, he turned back again. Haji Selim Agha had come out and was coming this way, and his son-in-law Fahri was behind him. They were wrapped in their overcoats and neither of them were bothered by the cold, walking along in conversation. "If I wait, then they'll have a disagreement. Not while they are together. Now is the wrong time," he thought to himself. He went home.

On how many days had he found the right moment and been unable to speak? He needed a loan from the agha again. Two hundred *liras*. If he wouldn't give that much, a hundred *liras*. He would accept a hundred *liras*. Then he would buy a set of clothes for each child, two loads of wood, and half a can of kerosene. In the middle of winter, they were stark naked. Their situation was terrible.

Haji Selim Agha used to lend money a interest. He wouldn't give it to everyone but just to those who could pay it back. "I'd pay it back anyway but he doesn't think so. As if his money would be lost! How many times did I want it and he didn't give anything? I'll go and talk to his son-in-law Fahri. Perhaps he'll help. 'Give it, father,' he'll say. 'Your money won't be lost on Omar.' Perhaps it will coincide with a good time for him and he'll lend it."

He walked along thinking. His teeth were chattering in the morning cold, and he was cold as ice. He went into his house. His family had not yet risen. They were lying under horse blankets trying to keep warm.

"You're still not up? It's past noon! Why are you still in bed?"

"You're letting the cold in, man. Shut it quick!"

"Get up, old lady. I've gone to pray and come back, and you're still—get up!"

He pulled off the horse blanket and put it over himself. A woman twisted up like the number four staggered out with three children, two before her and one behind. The children awoke and huddled together to get warm.

The woman straightened up and covered them with the horse blanket again.

"Don't get up now. Stay in bed and don't catch cold," she said.

She turned to her husband. "My God, it's so cold again today," she said.

"It is cold. How could it be otherwise? It's the middle of winter."

"How did it turn out? Did you see Haji Agha?"

"No. I'm going now."

"Go, for goodness sake, man! If you can get a little out of him, we'll try to pay him back in the summer. If not, by God, we'll die."

Omar turned his head wearily.

"I know. Starting to nag again. Would he offer and I not take, for God's sake?"

He went to bed without getting undressed, lying down by his children. He pulled the blanket over himself and kept on shivering.

The woman looked toward the fireplace. She paced up and down and didn't know what to do. She put her hands in her bosom. Her thin body was trembling with cold.

"Shall I go?" she asked.

Omar raised his head and looked. "Where?"

"To Haji Selim Agha. I'll speak if you like. 'Give us a loan,' I'll say."

Omar looked angry. "Don't provoke me or I'll string you up," he said.

"Why, man? So what? We want a loan. We aren't stealing, are we?"

"Be quiet, I'm telling you!"

"He won't give it to you but he might give it to me. I'll describe our situation. 'My family will freeze, sir,' I'll say. Maybe he'll pity us."

"Be quiet, woman. Don't make me mad! Am I dead that you should go by yourself? Don't talk that way!"

"Alright."

She went to the fireplace, looking for something to burn, but found nothing. Absolutely nothing was left. She took the old haircloth from the sofa and covered her shoulders. "What should I do? Where should I go? This is no summer day when I could gather firewood from the countryside. You know, Lord," she said to herself. Poverty and helplessness had made her feel terrible anguish. She was at the end of her rope.

She put on her husband's rubber boots and went out. It was freezing cold. She looked toward the village. Houses, sheds, and smoking chimneys were all like enemies in the distance. No one turned and looked at them. It was as though everyone had turned his back. "God help me," she panted.

She went back in. Her poor body was frozen. Slowly she raised the end of the old blanket and got under it again. Her little daughter was crouched there sleeping, shivering a little. She did not embrace her, so that at least this once her daughter would not be cold. She lay there for some time.

"What happened? Did you go to bed again?"

"What could I do, man? I'm freezing. There's nothing to burn."

Omar didn't answer. He was breathing heavily, angry about something but he didn't know what. He cursed. Then he was quiet. No sound was heard from the house.

The elder boy was awake, but he didn't stir lest they give him something to do. He was hungry. If only they had a bowl of hot soup now. Then he would hurry to school. At least there would be a fire in the classroom stove, and he would get warm there. This is what he was thinking about.

He turned his head and looked at the small opening they called a window. Outside it was growing lighter.

"Is it time for school, father?" he asked fearfully.

"How should I know? Am I the principal?" said his father.

"It's time, Hasan. Go on, son. Get bread from the pan and eat it on the way. You'll be warm there, too," said his mother gently.

Hasan got up and went off. He was an undersized child. His black shirt had faded and taken on a gray color, and there was no jacket on his back. When he went outside his teeth started to chatter.

Omar turned over on his back which for some reason felt very cold. He tried to warm his shoulders and lower back.

"Oh! World!" he groaned. He couldn't find anything else to say.

His wife softened her voice.

"Come on, mister. Please go see the agha, will you? Perhaps if you approach him he'll lend you a little. So go on!"

"I said I'd go, so shut up. Just let me get warm first. Don't you know it's freezing outside?"

His wife didn't answer. She closed her eyes and slowly shook her head. She begged God for guidance and held back her tears.

A little later Omar sat up. He put on his boots and left without saying anything. When he turned the corner of the house, he pushed right into a strong, icy wind and was stunned in a moment by the cold. He clenched his teeth and swore to himself. "Enough to do a man in. My God! I never saw anything like it."

He reached Fahri's door and pounded on it. The door didn't open at once. He tucked his hands under his armpits. It was as if he were wearing nothing, it was so cold.

Fahri's wife looked through the window. She was a plump, well-fed young girl.

"What do you want?" she asked.

"Fahri Efendi isn't at home?"

"No. He went to the coffee shop a little while ago."

Omar felt sick. It was as though something inside him broke. He mumbled something, turned around and walked away. His shoulders drooped. He had to keep from falling down.

When he reached the coffee shop he slowed down. If he went in they would immediately offer him tea, which he couldn't afford. He bent toward the window and looked in. Fahri was leaning over a chair, playing cards with someone. If he called out, Fahri wouldn't come, but if he went in to him—"At least I'll get warm," he thought.

He opened the door slowly and went inside. He looked timid and downcast, hesitating because he thought someone was going to scold him. He drew near the table.

"Fahri Efendi," he asked imploringly. "Can I have a word with you?"

"Sure! Say here whatever you have to say."

"There's something—"

He stooped to his ear.

"If you were to mention it to Haji Agha to lend me some money at interest—"

"What? With interest? Ha, ha! Where will you get the interest, man?"

"We'll work during the summer and pay it back. My family at home is in rags, and we're out of firewood. Please, be so kind."

At the same time, he was watching the shopkeeper Nedim, hoping that he wouldn't bring any tea. It would be good to drink a hot cup of tea right now, but he had no money. A man could be disgraced over a cup of tea, and it would be better if he didn't bring any.

"Fahri Efendi, be kind enough, please. I am very poor. Do me this favor. I'll buy firewood and clothes for my children," he said, stooping down again.

"Ask him yourself, man. Why do you talk to me?"

"Haji Agha did not lend it to me."

"What did he say?"

" 'You have nothing, no field or anything else.' But we'll work during the summer and pay it back. If you mention it, he'll loan—"

"No, my good man, no. I don't want to get involved. Why should I? Go ask him yourself."

Omar accepted it. He remained standing, unable to say anything, confounded.

A little later he turned and walked out.

I'LL GIVE BIRTH IN THE MOUNTAINS!
Fakir Baykurt
(*Translated by Thomas F. Brosnahan*)

That slant-eyed nurse is always watching me. All made up, every day a different perfume, goes to the baths each day and rubs her hide down with soap and sponges. Cheeks and temples shine, even from a way off. "I'm married, but there won't be any kids. I don't want 'em. Why should I? Why be so dumb?" she says.

If a woman has the chance to have kids, doesn't she have 'em? Curse that woman! I don't like that slant-eyes. She looks like she's saying 'stupid woman' at me. I can see from her eyes, from the way they flutter, what's going on in her head. *She's* the stupid one! She's got the chance to have kids, doesn't take it, and goes around saying this is the smart thing to do. Puh! A dog should feast on that brain of hers.

That skin-headed what they call a doctor—I don't like that one either. He comes and goes, asks how I'm doing, and so on—feels my stomach, wants to make me laugh, changes my bandages. He asks me a million questions about all sorts of things just to get me to talk. He tries to make me laugh. I won't laugh, just for spite. Why should I laugh? What business do I have laughing? "Get up and walk around a little," he says. "I won't get up! I'll rot myself lying here!" I say. The hell with 'em all. I don't like any of 'em. If I caught 'em alone out on the plain or in some empty place, I'd bash their heads around! I'd set the dogs on 'em to rip out their throats. If they came to my door saying, "We're hungry; we're cold!" I wouldn't even look at 'em, wouldn't even budge for 'em.

Yesterday afternoon I got up and went to the toilet. I got there by myself, leaning against the wall. They've hung a full-length mirror in the lounge, and God! I saw myself in it. I hardly knew who I was looking at! Whatever I used to have inside me, they've taken it out—my stomach, my intestines, even the marrow from my bones! They've taken the fruit and left the peel. Oh, my God, my God! They took my baby. That's all I can say. Look at the skin on my face. It's all loose. I look like a bale of hay.

But oh, what I looked like when I was younger! Strong, good color in my face. I could wiggle what I had and knew how to have some fun. Vivacious, that's what I was. We went for a day's work on the plain. I always finished right away. Rıza Bey gave me a prize for the way I worked. I could pull weeds all day, and my shoulders never ached. When spring came and I was chopping dried manure—we call it chips—I could go at it in the glaring sun till it was all full of holes and never get tired. I could take all the laundry from the big house—underclothes, all the clothes—and get it spotless all by myself, and I'd never whine or complain about my arms or my back. I'd eat ten loaves of flat bread at a sitting, and ask if there were any more. My appetite was like a man's, and when I was really hungry there was no filling me up. It wasn't just bread and side dishes, or meat, or apples; I had to have seconds on everything. On feast days and fair days, everybody'd get up to dance, and all the women would get tired and drop out—all except me. I'd be dancing on all by myself. The sweat would pour from my armpits, and my face would turn crimson, like the flag. Everybody else envied me. Now I can't even budge and get out of this bed. I'm sick like I was gonna die, like a cat at the end of its ninth life.

Oh, I hope the people who did this to me get theirs. I hope the people who put me here roast in hell. Let 'em burn real good in the flames. I hope my mama, my papa, my mother-in-law, my father-in-law, and my husband go off to the undertaker. Only death is good enough for 'em. I hope they all end up in wooden boxes. The ones who gave me the evil eye or who have written charms against me. That skinhead doctor, that slant-eyed nurse. The people who hold me down and make me black out, who take out my insides. They all belong in the lowest level of hell! I curse them when I go to sleep and when I wake up. I curse them when I look up to heaven. When the young bride from Omarjıklı here in the bed next to me goes off to pee, I curse them. Someone asks me how I'm doing, and I say fine, and all the time I curse them. I won't let them get away with this. "Whatever happens, I'll get my revenge. I'll burn the villages you live in; I'll burn the marriage beds you sleep in! How could you take my baby?" I'll say. Oh, crooked world! Oh, hopelessness! Don't I have a right to cry? Empty—my womb's completely empty. I mean, why doesn't it move around in there any more? Why doesn't it kick? Why don't I feel that tickling inside? And why don't the little strings in my insides tingle so sweetly? I know why. 'Cause they took it. They made a fool out of me. They've disgraced me worse than a dog. How can I go back and face my village? How'll I knock on their doors and ask for anything? Don't I have nipples? Didn't I have milk in my breasts? Couldn't I take a baby in my arms and rock it? "Y-e-e-e-s, y-e-e-e-s." When it was six months old, wouldn't I take a spoonful of food and pretend to eat so it'd learn how? "Come on, little rosebud, swallow; come on, come on." Wouldn't I buy a piece of penny candy, tie it in a corner of my shawl, and give it to him to suck on?

Girls who were nothing compared to me, when we were kids, are buying cradles now. They fill up their houses and streets with kids. When the holidays come, you see them knitting booties or sewing maternity robes. Just to show off and get talked about, they dress up and walk around. I'm like a freak in the village. "She can't have kids," they say. "She shouldn't even try. She tries and she might die." How can they think it? How can they bring themselves to say it? What's wrong? What've I got missing? I could take these mountains on my shoulders and carry 'em all the way to the next village. I could break boulders and move 'em. Can't I give birth to a tiny seven-pound baby? What demon have I got against me? What's his grudge? Why is he laying these traps for me? Why, of all the things dear to my soul, does he have to take the most precious one?

Not last year but some year before that, at harvest time, they took me to a doctor. They took me around to midwives and sheikhs. The doctor put that accursed ear of his down and listened to my heart; he put his little cup thing under my breast. He took my wrist in his hand and felt my pulse. He felt my stomach. "Did you ever have a bad fall when you were a child?" he asked. He looked at my tongue. "When you were asleep at night, did you ever wake up in a fright?" No, I never fell, never woke up in a fright. I've never been afraid of anything, man or demon. "No, no; you must've fallen down. No, no; you must've had a scare." They put the blame on me and brought me back to the village. That doctor sends a message off to my unhappy husband-to-be. "I'm telling you, don't let her have children; if she tries to have them, she'll die." What does he know, that filthy-minded doctor? How could he know? Where in the holy books is that sort of thing written, for goodness sake? "I won't stand for it," I said. "I'll have twins, triplets, quadruplets. I'll show every doctor in the world." I kept it in my heart, in the deepest part of my heart. "I'll have children!"

And so they took me to Sakar Emin with a big dowry. (My papa was pretty well off.) They dressed me in all the best clothes and put on my chains of yellow gold coins. The doctor had said, "If she gives birth, she'll die." My brainy father-in-law, he took his son into a corner and said, "Whatever you do, don't get her pregnant! Don't put me in the fix of having to pay back her dowry. Keep track of what you do." And so Sakar Emin ended up a better midwife than the midwives. He knew all the tricks and methods to use. If he came to me on one day, there'd be a baby; if he came on some other day, there wouldn't. If we did it this way, it wouldn't take; if we did it that way, it would. Sometimes I'd know what it was to be a woman all night long. I lost my innocence just about every way there was. I dried up in my shell. They think in this world that the women are blind, that they don't know what's what. How could they not know? Just as I was about to taste the sweetest fruit of heaven, they snatched it out of my hands. They took all my joy right away. I started to get upset about everything, one day with my mother-in-law and the next with my father-in-law. I'd have arguments with four or five of the neighbors. If I saw a dog I'd kick it; if I saw a donkey I'd hit it. Nobody understood my problem or what I was talking about. "Ümmü used to be such a sensible girl. What's happened to her? Did somebody cast a spell on her, or bury soap and put a curse? Why has she gotten to be so bad-tempered and edgy?" they'd ask. "Somebody's put a curse on Ümmü. Somebody's buried soap and cast a spell on Ümmü, and now she's gone crazy because of it. She's possessed."

But I had a beautiful thought hidden away in my heart, in the most secret part of me. I'd do it without Sakar Emin's knowing or even suspecting. And if all the midwives in the world were to disappear, would I be helpless? Don't I have eyes? Don't I have a brain? Why shouldn't I be able to learn what they learned? While I was reaping grain in the harvest field, or milking sheep in the fold, or powdering dried curds on the house roofs, didn't I understand right away what those women were talking about? And this "don't do as I do, but do as I say"—that never works. If somebody wants to do it, they'll do it, for sure. I learned all the tricks of their trade. In fact, I learned them so well that I knew more than I needed to know for myself, and used what I learned to help others. And then I began to watch for the right day to come along. No matter what, one day, one night would be the right time, and I'd do it.

I'm a woman, praise be to God! And I'm like a rock, thanks and praise be to God. I have a right to have children. I have a right to bear them, to watch them run and play and celebrate the beauty of the world! Nobody can take that right away from me, not in this world, not in the next, not on land, not on sea. Woman and mother, they're the same. If you say "mother," that means there are children. Every woman has four or five children. Don't give me this putting curses on me, or casting spells, or any midwife or doctor saying, "She can't have kids. If she does, she'll die." Don't they even want to allow me one? In spite of all of them, I did it. I created my baby.

Sakar Emin was sharp. So smart, so careful. He never forgets a thing, even after fifty days. While other men let themselves go, with their arms around their women, nearly fainting with pleasure, that pig would keep track, just as though he were estimating a crop yield or his supplies. He'd say, "Okay, Ümmü, I'm gonna pull out!" and pull out. My father didn't give me to a man; he gave me to a torturer. "Emin, Emin, my he-man Emin. My tiger, sweet Emin," I'd beg and plead, but no number of kisses or caresses would change him.

But I changed his mind while he was asleep, deep asleep! While he's awake, forget it, but asleep he's the village's soundest sleeper. From daybreak to noon, he'd drive his team, plowing the fields, and then in the afternoon he'd set off with two donkeys to the mountains for firewood. For three days he had not been near me. When he got back from the mountain, he was good and tired. "The bit takes away the horse's tiredness, and I take away yours," I said.

He ate a big dinner and went to bed. Without raising a fuss, I went to sleep in my mother-in-law's room. But in the middle of the night I got up and went in to him. He was dead to the world. Sleep is like temporary death, they say. A man's half-dead. But the other half is very alive! I don't care about the dead part, but I took the live half and did what I wanted to. Now he couldn't say, "Okay, Ümmü, I'm gonna pull out!" I was on fire all through my body. I tingled to the tips of my toes. Had he said, "I'm gonna pull out," he couldn't have done it anyway; I was wrapped around him like steel bands. I wouldn't have let him even if he had been a ghost. We'd been married for seven years, and for the first time he was himself and I was myself. We understood for the first time what the world was, what was that cushion on which we put our heads, that quilt we lay under, and the washing afterwards, or at least I knew. I don't know about him."

That day, that week, that month there wasn't a sweeter woman in the whole village. When I smiled, roses bloomed in my face. When I laughed, it could be heard clear down to Devetashı. My complexion and voice became so beautiful that wherever I walked I made everyone happy. I'd come by and people asleep would wake up, people crying would smile. Sakar Emin started to take me right and forgot that "Okay, Ümmü . . . " I made him forget it. *I* did it. It was *my* success!

I was three months, four months pregnant. I didn't let on that my stomach was upset and that I got dizzy. If I felt sick, I'd keep from vomiting, and if I couldn't, I'd swallow it again. My mother didn't know, neither did my mother-in-law. Even Sakar Emin didn't know I was pregnant. I kept it hidden from the whole world, from the sharpest, the smartest, and the nosiest, from my enemies and from my friends. I said nothing to anyone and let no one see anything. I dressed and fixed up just like normal. If anyone asked about my stomach, I'd laugh and say, "No, no," and ask God to forgive the lie. The old women would say, "That's how Ümmü looked before she was married. She was always big in the stomach. Even if she were pregnant, why would she hide it?"

Then it was four, five months. Listen. People know what pregnancy is all about. It got harder and harder to hide it. All at once the world, so big and limitless, grew small in comparison. I wanted to crawl down a well, hide for four months, and then come up with a baby at my breast. I wanted to lift up a boulder and crawl underneath, or get lost in the branches of a walnut tree or an oak. I wanted to, but I couldn't. I was really into it now. Whenever I took a breath, my joy and happiness were smothered. My father-in-law would fix me with his eyes, look at me deeply, and then call his son and whisper something to him. My mother-in-law, my relatives, and my neighbors were all suspicious. Every day they'd get more so. If I went to the vineyard or to the orchard, everyone would sneak away, and I'd come home alone.

There's no stopping the months as they pass. I was at six months. God, how big I was! How hard it was to hide a little ball of flesh the size of a fist. I ended up being edgy and grumpy like before. If anyone said anything to me, I'd pout and go back home to my mama's. If my mama or papa said anything, I'd move on to my aunt's. Emin would come around looking for me all the time. I never had any peace anywhere. I'd fall in behind him and follow him home. But I wouldn't let him hold my hand. I always had a frown or an angry look on my face. If he said something nice, I'd snap at him. I'd pick fights, scratch like a cat, and bite like a dog. If it really got nasty, I'd make the rounds to my mama's and my aunt's again.

My belly was like a pig's and grew bigger every single day. When I lay down, I'd put my hands on my stomach and try to feel it. My stomach swelled up like earth a mole has burrowed through. I could feel it. Not only that, I could see it. I wanted to go away into the woods, get lost with the rabbits and foxes, have the baby, raise it, and then come back to this village of people and dogs. I thought over very carefully which mountains and forest I should go to and what clothes I should take for me and the baby.

One day, my mama, papa, mother-in-law, and father-in-law all came down on me. They turned me around and looked me over. "Ummu! Look, girl. We've been in this world a long time and seen a lot. We know about what goes on. You're part of our family, part of our blood, not somebody off the street. Don't hide it from us. Don't be obstinate. You're pregnant, and your life is in danger. Let's find a way out." So they put me first on a donkey and then in a truck and brought me to this damned city. "Just let the doctor take a look at you," they said. "Let him give you a shot or some pills, and then you'll deliver alright. Don't you think we want you to have a baby, too?"

"No, I'm not pregnant. I'm not gonna have a baby!" I said. I struggled and fought, but they held me down by both my arms. I swore and promised, but they wouldn't listen.

"If you're not pregnant, just let the doctor look, and he can tell us. Maybe there's something else wrong," they said. So they took me to the doctor. But they knew for sure that I was pregnant. I was already through the seventh month and into the eighth. Of course they knew.

When I'm well enough, I swear I'll take care of that skinhead doctor and everybody else responsible for this, one by one! I'll set that village and this whole city on fire and burn 'em. I'll bash in all their treacherous skulls. You don't think so? You don't think I won't? Wait and see. You just wait and see.

They laid me down on a bed with sheets, and held me by the wrists. They listened to my heart. Then they gabbed about this and that and all sorts of things, opened smelly bottles, and put me to sleep. My brain couldn't work at all! I mean, they *made* me black out. I don't know if I was out a month or a year. Then they took me to another room. When I came to, I saw that I was empty. They'd taken my most precious secret and left me an empty shell.

I started banging on the table and the walls, yelling. The slant-eyed nurse came and tied my arms down. They made me lay there for ten, twenty days. "You took my baby. You killed it!" "No, no! You weren't pregnant at all," they answered. They were just trying to mislead me, like I misled them.

For two weeks no one came from the village, from one market day to the next. But this week they're gonna come and get me out of here. They'll take me back home. How can I go back to the village empty and dried out like this? How'll I be able to walk down the street by the cemetery? How can I go to other people's houses and look them in the face? What'll I say when they ask? Hey, you skinhead doctor! Hey, you slant-eyed nurse! Hey mama, you whore; hey papa, you bastard! Hey, you snake of a mother-in-law, you lizard of a father-in-law! What good am I like this?

If I let myself go in grief, I'll crack up. I'll want to get up and throw myself out the window. But the slant-eyed nurse is always around, holding me down by the wrist. Right now, she's stronger than I am. I'm weak and don't have any energy. I think and think with my head in my hands, torturing myself.

No, no! I won't jump out the window! I'll let my wounds heal good. Then I'll run off to the village and from there to the forest I've picked. I'll hide away with the rabbits and the foxes, find some shepherd, some Joe-nobody, and get pregnant. I'll get to know all the mountain men and the people who live in the forest. And then I'll have my baby right there in the grass and the flowers, under the pine trees, with the birds singing all around me.

I don't care whether it's a girl or a boy. I'll still hold it to my breast. I'll dip it in a crystal-clear spring, wash it, and deck it out in multi-colored mountain flowers and in deep red mountain roses. Then one day, I'll get together all the mountain people, all my new friends, and take the baby down to the village in a procession. And I'll come into the city and show that skinhead doctor. I'll hold the baby out to him and say, "Look! I had a baby. Just thought you oughta know!"

No, I guess I won't burn down their houses. No. My revenge will be very fine and measured out. They'll burn themselves up when they see the baby I've had. They'll burn and end as a pile of ashes because of the fire I'll start in them.

YARAN DEDE'S STONES
Fakir Baykurt
(Translated by Thomas F. Brosnahan)

Some can do it, and some can't, I had said. And there's a lot who can't: the ones who never even get a chance, and the ones who get a start but can't follow through. Bald Fatma and İbrishah are the latter kind. Bald Fatma gets pregnant and even carries the baby here and there inside her for six or seven months, but before nine months comes she loses it and it's gone. As for İbrishah, she's given birth to four so far, and each one has lived eight months and then departed this earth.

And these two are now the village child-forlorns. You always see them together. Everybody feels so sorry for them. They've done all they could do: besides prayers and offerings, they even went to a doctor. Even so, nothing. No hope. Maybe there is hope, somewhere, but not in this village! If a woman could be proven sterile, then they could tell her and she'd give up hope. But their case is a puzzle.

Finally, Hoja Beytullah found a way! The hoja had a special craft. This was a business of casting horoscopes, contacting spirits, divining secrets by dropping open a book. And the news got around, and was spread so far, that not only our village, but all the surrounding villages had heard of the two local women named Bald Fatma and İbrishah who lived in the shadow of the fact the the children they conceived could not stay alive.

"I've cast your horoscopes, and this was the result. I've dropped open a book, and this was the result. I've interpreted a dream, and this was the result. I've consulted the spirits, and this was the result. Bald Fatma and İbrishah's husbands have stolen stones from Yaran Dede. Until they take 'em and put 'em back where they belong, they can marry twenty women and have twenty kids and they still won't have one that lives!"

The hoja spread the story, and everybody for miles around heard it, and everybody who heard it agreed that this must be the problem. The same day, all the neighbors got after the two husbands.

"Get going, stupid!"

"Get going, good-for-nothing!"

"Hurry up and get going, you two!"

"What are you waiting for? Wherever you took 'em from, wherever you put 'em, go find the Holy One's stones and put 'em back where they belong. Do what you gotta do quick, before something awful happens to the village!"

"Get going, stupid!"

"Get going, good-for-nothing!"

"Hurry up and get going, you two!"

The poor fellows hashed it over and hashed it over, and for the life of 'em couldn't remember anything about having done something stupid like this. But Hoja Beytullah had the answer to this, too.

"I'm eighty years old. I remember the day your father was born. Think hard enough and it'll come to you even if you're thick in the head. You must've forgotten about the stones Arif Bey had them take away the year the school was built. I see it clear as today. You two were schoolkids then, right?"

They heard what he said, and before you knew it they were out the door. The two of 'em grabbed Ibrahim, the schoolteacher, and ran to the school, bashed holes all through the wall and pulled out the two pure white stones and took 'em back to Yaran Dede. Whew! Were they glad *that* was over! They swore over and over they'd never get involved in that sort of mistake again. They begged for mercy, they repented, they made pledges. And now they wait, and as long as there're no other sins like this, the children'll be born, and they'll live.

While this news was still fresh, one afternoon at prayer time, Hoja Beytullah came to us to have his shoes mended. When he came, Ramazan was taking a nap. My mother was making stuffed vine leaves for dinner. I was sitting at the feet of my aunt, who was helping my mother, my poor aunt who had lost her mother, who had lost her father, whose husband left her a widow when she was still young. I sat there and I asked her, "Why did God treat you so bad? What kind of thing, what sort of justice is that?" Joking, of course. And just then he came through the door. I don't know how we moved so fast or how my mother got Ramazan up so quick, but before you knew it we had pushed a cushion under him and had him all comfortable, kissed his hand, told him "Welcome, welcome! You bring blessings to our house," and so on. And he didn't seem like any eighty-year-old man. He sure was hale and hearty! He knew what was going on all around him. When he talked about something, he knew what it was all about, and you couldn't catch him out on it. He'd read a passage from the Koran in Arabic and translate it right away without even thinking.

Ramazan went over and sat at his feet. We brought up the subject of Bald Fatma and İbrishah's problem. Everything the hoja said was against me. And my mother and my aunt joined in and said other things against me.

"Purpose, divine purpose, purpose everywhere."

My mother:

"Amen! Divine purpose! Amen!"

The hoja:

"Everything is full of divine purpose. Don't think anything that happens is meaningless. There's meaning in a tree! It's even in this sinner sitting here with us. One day Ali the Twin cut a branch off the bush in Beyönü. He was gonna make an axe handle out of it. That same day the guy learned his lesson, in a dream. They stripped him and stretched him out, and they brought that branch. Ali the Twin finally woke up, soaked in sweat. The branch was what started it all, but you gotta think it over: God created everything in heaven and earth, and would he create something worthless? There's a special meaning in every single thing. Every single square inch of earth has a master. God is the master! God is great! The Lord of the Worlds has given us four guardian angels. These four watch and protect us on all four sides. They're so powerful and so watchful that nothing in this world is anything like 'em. They're sort of like plainclothes policemen. You can't see 'em, but they go right around next to you and guard you."

My mother:

"Thanks and praise be to God!" She sighed deeply.

"We're under the watch of these four protectors all the time. Only, they leave us when we go to the outhouse. As soon as we're done there they pick us up and follow along with us again."

All of a sudden my aunt thought of something.

"They say you're not supposed to say, 'In the name of God' in the toilet. Is that true?"

"Four steps before you get there you say your *bismillah*, and then as soon as you get in and sit down right away you say, 'Pardon me!' The guardian angels will stop when they hear the *bismillah* and'll wait for you where you said it. But if you forget to say *bismillah* you may lose your angels, 'cause it's dangerous for 'em to go in and out of filthy places like that. You gotta be very careful. And then, if you forget to say, 'Pardon me!' when you sit down, the angels can't accept any responsibility for you. Keep this in mind. See, what'd I say? There's meaning in every single thing, a sacred meaning in everything. See that stone lyin' over there? Should you pick it up, or should you not pick it up? You gotta stop first and think it over."

"My friend," my mother said, "Arif Bey's committing more and more sins. Should one take any of Yaran Dede's stones?"

My aunt:

"Wait just a minute. Sometimes taking one of Yaran Dede's stones catches up with you, and sometimes it doesn't. Look at that crazy Kırali person. Kids like young colts! Yet, the stones he used to build that coffeehouse were all from Yaran Dede."

Just as Hoja Beytullah was about to pass on to yet another sacred meaning, my mother cut him off. "But God's gonna give him what he deserves, honey, don't worry about that. And it won't be long, either! What does it matter their kids are like young colts? His wife had those kids long before the coffeehouse was built. If he'd built it before the kids were born, then we'd have seen something."

My aunt:

"Women who have a lot of kids say to themselves, 'I'll miscarry and get it over with,' and so this is how they play around with the babies' souls. Let 'em send their husbands off, let 'em pull out two of Yaran Dede's stones, and that does the job."

The patches were finished on the hoja's shoes. He got up to go and wash before the evening prayers. We went with him down the steps and across the courtyard to the door. "Meaning, sacred meaning," he mumbled, and went off.

Mother:

"These things are important. You oughta know these things if you know anything at all."

I giggled. My mother got angry.

"Take that smirk off your face, you ninny!" she said. "Hoja Beytullah is special at this sort of thing. D'you know anybody who knows more divine secrets or who's got a deeper faith? What are you giggling for, right behind the guy?"

I saw an argument coming, so I stopped smiling.

RUINED MANSIONS
Sevim Burak
(*Translated by Thomas F. Brosnahan*)

THEY CAME IN THROUGH THE IRON GATES
  YESHILKÖY
    ROAD
      WOMAN
They passed down the corridors of the battle formation
  They marched one behind the other
Rooms
  Windows
They looked for and found one another
each with his particular characteristics.
  Doors
    Keys
      Locks
        attached where they should be
        and founded
          the work place.
  YESHILKÖY
    ROAD
      WOMAN
They entered via the room with the big safe
They left via the room with the small safe.
The conscientious recording secretaries
  Dressed well, keeping together
passed down the corridors hung with mirrors
Increasing in number as they marched.
  We are WEALTHY
    ARISTOCRATIC
      WELL-BRED, they said.

The general director, mounted on a bay, took his band of assistants
and led them to a place farther along.
   WOMAN
      YESHILKÖY
         TRAIN
They went into battle formation.
A steam bath in Chekirge
A row of shops in the bazaar of Eğridir
The Prophet Joshua's hill
THE WELL-BRED RELATIVES HAVE STARTED OUT AS WELL.
On their lips a snide remark
   a mole
      an overgrown
         hair
            They gazed in the mirrors.
A DAY IN MAY
WATER LILY
WALLFLOWER
TEVFIK BEY'S WIFE
LONG-EYELASHED CHERRY LADY
RING-SWALLOWING FAUCET
TEVFIK BEY
They approached Sirkeji
The ruined mansions
Long-branched candelabra
A coffee cup
IN SPRING THEY LIKE TAKING TRIPS
   YESHILKÖY
      ROAD
         WOMAN
They went into battle formation.
   LONG
   HEAVY
   ONE DAY
   MAY DAY
   NARCISSUSES
   WHAT WAS AUNT JONQUIL
   GOING TO DO?
   YESHILKÖY

ROAD
  WOMAN
    MAY
      DAY
In her bag the documents
Title deed
She sat down at the typewriter
and before starting to work
she thought about herself for a minute
  "DEAR SELF"
    she wrote
A bitter smile on her lips.
She looked at herself in the mirrors of the battle formation
It was she for sure.
  HERSELF.
Unchanged at all
A TYPIST FOR TWENTY YEARS
From a family of willful people
The face of a woman who stayed in the shadows
  Without any makeup
    Without any love
      Deathless.
      "I'M A CHILD," she thought to herself for a moment
    And she departed
      from everything
        from battle formation.
Her large tongue, making a huge arch, came out of her mouth
swam through the air
  trembled
Told THE OLD STORIES
The old noble families
Noble persons
THE TROUBLES OF THE EIGHTY-EIGHTH DAY
  Yeshilköy
    The pool
      the train.
In the evening, these entered the house with her:
  A hill
    A tower

A road
   A part of the sea.
What if the mansion catches fire one day at noon? With the fear of this thought, she was alarmed for a moment, and with a half-finished and forgotten glass of tea on her desk, she thought. She started with a joyous hop such as had furled the skirts of her child's dress many years ago: the garden; the names of the flowers; Aunt Jonquil; the balcony; the shadows trembling on the white front of the balcony; the titles written in gold in the remembrance book; the "Indomitable Turk" march of the General Kâzim Karabekir, and the day he came to the mansion in a black car with a red official flag on it and patted her cheek; a few of the great commander's words; the poem that Ali Yaver Pasha had written for his two daughters: "This is life / This is our goal/Sound basis for the fatherland"; the funeral services; the handkerchiefs of Japanese work pulled out after the funeral service; the tears; the crying with one another; the white balcony hanging straight down; shouts that the mansion was burning; the sound of water; the sound of flames; the cracking and crashing sounds and then no sound; a family all of whose members died in the fire; collapse of all that pomp and stateliness; one remaining alone; the day she began living under her own name, and the moment she put on the PITCH BLACK TYPIST'S SMOCK; the sad look on her face in the mirror; the bitter smile which revealed the MEMORIES buried deep within her; the MYSTERIOUS beauty granted her as a YOUNG VIRGINAL GIRL; the PRIDE; the MYSTERIOUS ADMIRATION which reposed with her and the others before their HONOR was lost; the MYSTERIOUS LIFE, she thought.
She went to the typewriter and sat down
   POOL
      FOUNTAIN
         TRAIN she wrote
Another long working day was about to begin.
   LONG
   HARD
   WORKING DAY
      MAY DAY
         THE NARCISSUSES
            THE HARD-WORKING OFFICE BOYS greeted one another
"WELCOME, O SPRING" is the song they were singing

The monster whistles of the battle formation sounded
The iron gates were closed
Everyone scurried as though it were the end of the world
   the typing girls
   the recording secretaries
   the office boys
The air was full of flying
   Title deed forms
   Carbon paper
The woman grabbed one out of the air and slipped it into her typewriter
   Titmouse
   Mercury-stone
   Beeswax
     she wrote.
In the far distance, the well-born businessmen began to come into view.
   Thirty-year-old businessmen
   Grown fairly old already
   Everywhere
     Beef intestines
       Tragacanth
         Lots
           Lots of it
              in these businessmen. The businessmen of her childhood.
Last of all, the oldest businessman
Turned in front of the mirror, gazing into it bitterly
He was **DEEP IN THOUGHT** as though he had not seen the woman
   As for the woman, as soon as she saw him her heart beat as though it would leap out of her breast
   Her hair stood on end
   "BARON SPRING" she thought
   This was an old cry.
   The battle formation's number one founder
   A millionaire
   Several times over
   A man among men
A VERITABLE UNCROWNED KING
she thought. She put paper for two copies in her typewriter and wrote

"THE UNCROWNED KING AND I"
Or, A TRUE LOVE STORY. That was just the right word order she thought
She found some insidious thoughts in her brain. She would hide them within herself:
 I LOVE YOU, BARON SPRING, she said, treacherously.
Baron Spring answered, *"This is an old song, Je vous aime beaucoup, mademoiselle."* and fell to the floor with a soft thud.
 The woman picked up the fallen Baron Spring.
 "WHAT DO YOU WANT TO SAY TO ME?"
Baron Spring:
 "There are several truths which I must tell you," he replied.
The woman put these into her typewriter to write
 Bill of lading
 Manifest
 Cement
 Iron spare parts
 The things Baron Spring told her
 Continued an entire lifetime.
 FLAT
 LONG
 THIN
The woman's arm, trembling with fatigue, all at once fell from its shoulder socket. The terrifying machinery noise of the battle formation stopped. Baron Spring, who had grown used to the terrifying noise of the battle formation, stood shocked in amazement at the sound of silence, and understood everything for the first time.
 It was
 QUIET
 FLAT
 LONG
 THIN
 Then:
 "This woman lives for her arm; as for me, I live for my overcoat. But can anyone live for NOTHING?" he thought.
With the expertise born of many years of practice, the woman put the arm back in place.
 SHE WAS GOOD AND LONELY
Baron Spring:

"What a gentille woman this woman is," he cried.

The woman, out of long habit, didn't cry.

She took out HER TROUBLES, the mansion, the title deed, the coffee cup and the photographs of her relatives, from her handbag.

THEY BECAME VERY GOOD FRIENDS.

Baron Spring, wiping from his eye the only teardrop to have appeared in years, bent over the photographs:

"They were certainly a good-looking group. This embroidered silk tablecloth is REALLY NICE. And this bridge is QUITE NICE. I recognize this cathedral, it's NICE,

he said. *"How many years has it been since I was there?* I haven't seen them for a long time," he thought.

The woman replied to what was going through his head:

"No, Baron Spring, THESE ARE THE YESHILKÖY MEMORIES
  MY MEMORIES
  I CREATED
  THESE MEMORIES
  WITH MY SPIRIT
  WITH MY BLOOD
  I KEPT THEM UP
  I OPPOSED THEIR COLLAPSE
  I HAVE BROUGHT THEM TO THIS MAGNITUDE
  EDUCATED THEM
  RAISED THEM
  UGLY
  BEAUTIFUL
  THEY ARE MY CHILD
  AND WHO ARE YOU
  ARE YOU TRYING TO RUIN
  MY HOUSE
  MY HOME
  WHAT HAVE I DONE TO YOU?
  I WORKED
  I STRUGGLED
  I GAVE
  WHAT I HAD
  IN MY HAND
  IN MY PALM
  I DIDN'T EAT

I DIDN'T DRINK
I DIDN'T LIVE
I DIDN'T MARRY
I WAS WIDOWED WHILE STILL YOUNG
I WAS BOILED IN MY OWN OIL
I WAS BURNT IN THE YESHILKÖY FIRE
I AM RELATED TO THE ARMENIAN COMMANDER ENTRENIK ON MY MOTHER'S SIDE AND ON MY FATHER'S SIDE TO İSMAİL HAKKİ BEY OF THE KHEDIVE'S FAMILY, she said
"MEMORIES LOVE PEOPLE
THEY RESPECT THEM
CHILDREN DO NOT FEAR MEMORIES
THESE ARE CHILDHOOD MEMORIES," she added.
Baron Spring:
"Now, I must struggle to work with children I have never known.
Well, we were all children at one time."
No doubt, we lived in a little world of our own, too.
We had favorite songs, too
We know what it's like
What if they stopped
he said.
The woman spread the photographs she was holding out on the table.   "The one in front with the thin eyebrows is my Aunt Jonquil; beside her is my Aunt Cotton; in front of my Aunt Cotton is my French aunt; the wife my uncle Majid Pasha brought from France; (in the other photo, again it's my French aunt you see, leaning against the famous Adapazarı mill; at that time she and Majid Pasha had been married twenty days; you can see, at the top they've written "A Twenty-year-old Istanbul girl on the Adapazarı mill"). This one shows how the French visitors were so enchanted by Turks, Turkish families, my uncle Majid Pasha, and Turkish cuisine. To the left of my French aunt is Monsieur Jacques, my Aunt Jonquil's French tutor, and the fat woman with the apron is my Armenian nurse Arusiak."
  ARUSIAK AND MONSIEUR JACQUES
  MONSIEUR JACQUES AND ARUSIAK
  As you no doubt can see,
IT IS A VERITABLE
NOBLE FAMILY GROUP
      she added.

"These are one's memories of ten years old, BUT NOTE THAT AT TWENTY ONE'S MEMORIES ARE VERY DIFFERENT. At that age a person struggles to DISCOVER HIS OWN THOUGHTS.

There's a bitter curve to my lips; I was hardly the loveable little girl in the crib anymore; I was thinking of the MAJESTY of the home I would set up in the future; I was holding a rose in my left hand; in my right hand I held the locket cut from around my neck; I had washed my hands for the eighth time; during the day I thought of the moment that night when I would get into my spotless bed and lay my head down on my carnation-scented pillow; at night in my blue-painted room, as soon as the orange lights were lit I would take out my toys, untouched before that, clean and bright, — *they* had no age yet; everything given to me was hidden in my drawers; the apples; two of the three oranges; bars of soap; my baby shoes; umbrella handles; coins with holes shot through at weddings; candies from weddings; and I'll put them all in boxes, packets and kerchiefs.

THE FAMILY IS A HOLY SECRET
I WASN'T GOING TO TALK TO YOU ABOUT THESE THINGS
SOME SECRETS INCREASE THE SANCTITY OF THE FAMILY,
but:

After awhile a child grows up. And when she grows up, she's a copy of her family; and this brings the family closer together. I memorize every word said to me, and do my duties as I'm supposed to. If my Aunt Jonquil doesn't come out of her room, I wonder if something's wrong; but should I begin to be afraid something terrible's happened? I think to myself, standing in front of her door. Trembling, I whisper through the keyhole,

"Aunt Jonquil, Aunt Jonquil, do you remember me?
  I say.

A voice from inside:

"You came my way when you were still in swaddling clothes," she replied. *Your mother and father were drowned. You were in a priceless chest covered with emeralds and rubies. Don't be afraid, you won't be put out to live in the streets. In fact, I'm very pleased with you; but you must continue to be good in my sight, and keep working for my love.*

WHEN I DIE
THIS MANSION
THE MEMORIES
AND THE COFFEE CUP

WILL ALL BY YOURS
"At that time, I didn't know what life had in store for me."
Some people, at this age, lead lives full of jealousy.
MY LIFE
WAS
COMPLETELY
HAPPY
AND JOYFUL.
"Young girls like that bring happiness to all the people in the household." My bedroom; the tiled basin I washed my hands in; I lived a fortunate life with my drawers full of toys. Who knows how many unfortunate young girls would love to have been in my place? At night, stretched out on my clean bed, Aunt Jonquil's wooden house was an inseparable part of my body. I was like a part of the decor. My life began in that house. When Aunt Jonquil looked into my eyes, she'd cry, "A FAIRY-TALE, A REAL BEDTIME STORY!" She must've been listening to *LaTraviata*.
At her feet slept a dog with a Parisian pedigree; on the table were fruit and flowers; she'd cross herself continually.
AS FOR ME, IT'S A MYSTERY WHY I DIDN'T CRY
WHAT EXTRAORDINARY PHILOSOPHY IS THIS?
WHO'S TO BLAME THAT I'VE NEVER REGRETTED MY LIFE?
"I think some of it's because, on my mother's side, my family was drowned while crossing a river with the great commander ENTRENIK, because they were bound to one another by heavy chains around their ankles; and part of it's because, some of them had been saved, and brought ME in their arms to Aunt Jonquil, and having left me with her, went back to the river and drowned."
WHERE DID I READ THIS?
HOW DID I BEGIN MY LIFE?
WHERE DID I COME FROM?
IT'S A SECRET TO ME,
WHO SHOT HIM?
YOU, *Baron Spring, you don't think at all about the terror of life:*
YOU HAVE EVERYTHING
YOUR CAR
YOUR YACHT
YOUR HOUSE WITH THE SEVEN DWARFS
YOUR STOCKS

YOUR CHILDREN
AS FOR ME, I'M SO ALONE I'M NOT
EVEN AFRAID OF DEATH.

Baron Spring fell completely in love with the woman. *"This is a very good typist here. I'm very pleased with her. This typist is very good."* he thought.

The woman, as though she read Baron Spring's thoughts, said: *"Thank* you;

     LIFE IS LIFE
     LIFE'S PROBLEMS
     OUR PROBLEMS
     WHAT CHANGES IS US
     BUT IN FACT PROBLEMS
     AREN'T ABOUT TO
     DRY UP AND BLOW AWAY
     NOTHING REALLY CHANGES
            she added.

Baron Spring: YOU KNOW EVERYTHING
YOU'RE REALLY SOMETHING
YOU'RE LIKE A SIP OF COOL WATER
YOU'RE SOMETHING he said, and he rested his head on the woman's knees:
WE HAVE PROBLEMS TOO
WE'VE HAD TO STRUGGLE TO OVERCOME THEM
BUT WITHOUT THEM THERE'S NO ZEST IN LIFE
WE CRITICIZED, he said, and he lightly squeezed the woman's arm. The woman, without pausing in her narrative, put two carbons in her typewriter and continued. *My Aunt Jonquil* sat on the balcony of the mansion, holding a coffee cup in one hand, and shook a red-nailed finger at Monsieur Jacques, scolding: Why have you chosen these words to teach me? *LAISSEZ moi vous baiser.*

oh, you naughty boy, you!
ME
I EARNED THIS LIFE
BY FIGHTING
TOOTH AND NAIL
I WASN'T FOUND ON THE DOORSTEP
I STRUGGLED FOR A HUNDRED DAYS
YOU ARE A MAN

REALLY A MAN
YOU CAN SLEEP WHEREVER YOU LIKE
AS FOR ME
I'M
NOT A BEAST
I'M A WOMAN she said.
IT WAS A SUMMER DAY, BUT DARKNESS WAS EVERYWHERE. My Aunt Jonquil sat on the balcony. There was a bond between the cup in her hand and me. I couldn't take my eyes off that cup. I saw my Aunt Jonquil's red-painted nails tapping, tapping lightly on the cup. Ting, ting, ting, the sound came from the cup. I wanted to rescue the cup from the red-tipped claws. Ting, ting, ting, ting. Aunt Jonquil's nails began to make nicks and chips in the delicate surface of the cup. Ting, ting, ting. Pretty soon the sound could be heard all through the garden. The cup was calling, crying out to me, but I couldn't take it away from Aunt Jonquil.

It's a living being
It's a magical toy
It's the voice of my childhood days
The worst illness of my childhood.

Give me the cup – the cup – the cup – I screamed.
Aunt Jonquil didn't hear.
For days, I spoke in a language my Aunt Jonquil couldn't understand.
    FA UPON FA
    FIN UPON FIN
    JAN UPON JAN
    TOP UPON TOP
Forty days I talked; with the furniture; with the roof tiles; with the stones; with the birds. It was bitter, the way the little birds flew through the air; the cup was still in my Aunt Jonquil's fingers; I waited for my Aunt Jonquil to die, so I could get the cup.
BUT GOOD BREEDING IS UPPERMOST, AFTER ALL. YOU
BARON SPRING
    YOU ARE OF GOOD FAMILY
    YOU ARE ABOVE ALL NATIONS OF THE WORLD
    YOU HAVE MONEY IN THE BANK
    YOU LEND MONEY AT INTEREST
    I CONGRATULATE YOU she said.
Baron Spring, *"This woman's sights are on higher things, while mine*

can hardly see. I HAVE BUSINESS TO DO in GERMANY, he thought.

The woman put a double carbon into her typewriter. Typing, she continued her narrative.

MY DEAR TOYS
MY AUNT COTTON
MY THREE ORANGES
MY DEAR NURSE
MY BOXES
MY BABY SHOES
MY HAT SHAPED LIKE A QUEEN'S CROWN
MY KEYS
MY WINDOWS
WHEN I SAY GOOD-BYE TO MY ROOM, YOU BE GOOD TILL I COME BACK
JUST DON'T YOU GET INTO TROUBLE
YOUR MASTER HAS A LITTLE ERRAND–*DEATH.*
I'VE BEEN GETTING READY FOR IT FOR DAYS
I STARTED WALKING
IT WAS A BEAUTIFUL DAY
SUCH A BEAUTIFUL DAY
IT WAS AS THOUGH I HAD JUST ENTERED A FOREIGN COUNTRY. I WALKED ALONG BOTH STRAIGHT AND CROOKED ROADS. AS I APPROACHED THE MANSION THE ROAD BEGAN TO BECOME WHITE. I WAS WALKING ON A LONG CHALK LINE WHICH LED STRAIGHT TO MY AUNT JONQUIL'S BALCONY. NOISES AND RINGING FLOODED IN ON ME FROM ALL SIDES. AUNT JONQUIL'S HAND WAS ON TOP OF THE CUP. THE TING, TING, TING NOISE COMING FROM THE CUP BEGAN TO MAKE THE MANSION SWAY BACK AND FORTH AND BREAK UP, TING, TING, TING, AND THE SOUND MADE THE YESHILKÖY
STREETS
AND
ME
SWAY
SLOWLY
SLOWLY
TOGETHER
I PASSED BY RUINED WALLS AND GAPING HOLES. ENVELOPED IN FLAMES, THE BALCONY BEGAN TO FALL FORWARD AMIDST

A CHORUS OF SCREAMS. I FELL TO THE GROUND AND BEGAN SCREAMING WITH ALL MY MIGHT
AUNT JONQUIL AUNT JONQUIL
I SHOUTED
CAN PEOPLE BE KILLED FOR NO REASON AT ALL?
THERE WAS ONE CUP
AND ONE PERSON

Baron Spring: *WHAT'S THIS ABOUT A DISASTER IN MY COUNTRY? BUT WHAT CITY AM I IN NOW?*
Rome
Paris
Zürich?

Baron Spring turned onto *Fifth Avenue*; before him was a street he had never seen before in his life; from that he turned onto another street he didn't know at all; before him was yet another street; "I'm slowly disappearing" he thought, and began to run toward another unknown street.

THE LAST BIRD
Bekir Yıldız
(Translated by John Taylor)

Since morning, the sun had shone on the roofs of Diyarbakir. It melted the iron-colored mountains and turned the people, afraid to touch each other, to sweat.

The sun kept at this torture for hours. Then night followed.

Zulkuf got into his bed in the garden. When he was in bed, he turned his face to the sky. The sky was bright, and the stars were passing close to the earth and winking from God's garden of light. For the people lying on the roofs and in the gardens, to escape from the heat was a gift from heaven.

Zulkuf had come here to study. This house in which he was staying was his uncle's.

Zulkuf was crying. But no noise was mixed with his tears, because his uncle and his uncle's wife and children were lying nearby. Not only did he want to leave this house and his studies, he wanted to go back to his village. But when he thought of what his uncle had done for him . . .

A few hours later he was able to forget himself. He put his cheek on his wet pillow and slept.

Before the cocks crowed, the sun was up.

The people rose even before five o'clock because everyone slept under the sky, and the first light of the sun stirred their bodies.

Zulkuf got up, too.

In one corner of the courtyard there was a single bird, an extremely rare and beautiful bird.

Uncle Hashim came up to the bird, which had a crown of white feathers on its head and bracelets on its feet. He stretched out his hand to it. Just as it was Uncle Hashim's rarest bird, it was the rarest bird of Diyarbakir. It had a name—Sultan.

THE LAST BIRD

Before he lost his job, Uncle Hashim was the happiest person in the world. In the evenings, when he returned home, he would immediately feed the birds. They moved back and forth like sails, their feet moving so quickly they were almost invisible. Sometimes they would fly a little into the air and so let Uncle Hashim, their sweetheart, taste one of the most beautiful and generous of their pleasures.

A few months earlier, he had received a letter from one of his brothers in the village. "My brother Hashim," the letter began. "I would like to send you your nephew Zulkuf. He's very bright. I don't want him to be wasted like the others. What do you say? Shall I send him to you?"

Uncle Hashim had been without work for six months. His family were cheating their stomachs and putting them off with flour and cracked wheat. Nevertheless, he couldn't say no. "Let him come. It's my pleasure," he wrote.

A few weeks after Zulkuf arrived, the traffic into the pantry stopped. The tops of the sacks had reached the bottoms.

When Zulkuf was out of bed, he went to wash his face. Then he sat in a corner and opened a book. He wanted to study and learn but was bothered by his uncle's situation. When he first came, his uncle had nearly fifty birds of every kind and color.

"I don't mind losing them for you," his uncle had said, and slaughtered one for each meal. He killed and fed to Zulkuf the birds he had loved and couldn't bring himself to touch otherwise. He didn't want to lower himself in the eyes of his brother.

Uncle Hashim caressed Sultan's feathered crown and the bracelets that encircled his thin legs. He looked at the sky. There were multitudes of birds in view. The face of the sky was covered with countless wrinkles. His own cheeks were completely sunken.

"How many years older than my father are you, Uncle?" Zulkuf asked.

Uncle Hashim turned his face from the sky. "Eight or ten years, nephew."

Before Zulkuf was able to turn the conversation in the direction he wanted, Hashim asked, "Are you hungry?"

Zulkuf blushed. It was Sultan's turn for the knife. Zulkuf's head fell to his book.

"No, uncle. I'm not hungry at all. And I won't—"

Uncle Hashim didn't believe these words. He raised his face again to the sky. The birds were still flying.

Uncle Hashim was about to take the biggest gamble of his life.

Up to that day he had captured a great number of birds. First, he would choose the cleverest of his own birds and, holding the feet together, would leave the wings free. The bird would struggle to fly but couldn't, with its feet in its master's fist.

Meanwhile, birds which belonged to others were circling in the sky above. But Uncle Hashim wouldn't immediately release the bird in his hand. As he raised and lowered the bird, it would beat its wings more and more fiercely. Finally, when it might have pulled Uncle Hashim into the sky too, he set it free.

In one breath, the bird would explode into the sky and join its friends. First, it would circle them and then would fly in among them.

He had done it many times. Either the bird would mix with the others, alight at another house as a guest and be captured, or it would seduce another bird and present it to Uncle Hashim. To this day, Sultan had always come back with a guest. He had never been duped into going somewhere else.

But for some reason, today Uncle Hashim didn't have the heart to send Sultan off. What if he didn't come back? Sultan fluttered his wings. He wanted to teach a lesson to those birds challenging him from above. But his master's mind was fixed on the nephew's empty stomach.

Zulkuf understood all this from where he sat. He did not at all want to witness this battle that his uncle and the last, so valuable bird were entering. He got up and went over to his uncle. He was just beginning to get a beard, and there was something of the brave young man in his attitude.

"Don't do it, uncle," he said. "Don't kill another one. You've done everything for me. This would be too much. Please don't send Sultan off. Please don't kill him."

Uncle Hashim was miserable. His voice was weak.

"What are you saying, my young lion? Every one of the birds can be killed for you. What a terrible fate that you come to me at my most helpless moment. Whatever he has to do, your Uncle Hashim isn't stingy. But this time I've had some bad luck, curse it!"

Zulkuf released his uncle's hand. He was embarrassed but in spite of everything wanted to put an end to the problem.

"Listen, uncle. My dear uncle. You must know that every bird you slaughter makes me more unhappy. Every time you have me eat a bird, it's as though I'm eating my own soul. Give me your hand. Let me kiss it, and let me go. Let me leave here now. I'll promise that I won't say a word to my father about you and your poverty. I'll take all the blame myself. I'll say I did something wrong, that I was dishonorable. Let's agree on it."

Uncle Hashim's face was ashen. He let Sultan go.

Sultan pulled himself into the air, but they did not look up to follow his flight. They looked at one another. Uncle Hashim shook his head.

"Oh, little one. Oh, I wish you'd put a bullet in my head, instead of making a bargain like that," he lamented in a trembling voice.

A short way off, Hashim's wife was trying to light the dung fire, and the children moved in their beds.

Meanwhile, Sultan was returning home with two birds at his side. Uncle Hashim's ashen face was lit with joy.

After a few turns around the house, Sultan and the two birds alighted at Uncle Hashim's feet. A huge success shone in the bird's small eyes.

For Uncle Hashim, this victory opened the door to new hope. He turned to Zulkuf.

"Well, my nephew, stay with us a few more days," he said.

> The man of the East dies for
> his love, and kills to live.

RESHO AGHA
Bekir Yıldız
(Translated by Thomas F. Brosnahan)

Beating the tops of his high boots with a riding crop, he strode from the courtyard into the house: Resho Agha, a notable of Urfa. Resho Agha had three wives. He was of a noble bloodline, of an irreproachably honorable family. Some could count ten, others twenty generations of tradition to support Resho Agha's position as agha. As he came into the room from the courtyard his three wives got down on their knees, ready to remove his boots. And it was her, the small-waisted, large-hipped one with green eyes and black hair called Güllü, to whom he extended his boots for removal. Güllü pulled at Resho Agha's boots with joy. Whoever pulled his boots off, she was the one who slept with Resho Agha. Tonight Resho Agha would take Güllü in his arms.

At one end of the courtyard was the stable with eight or ten donkeys, six horses and six camels, along with a groom. The groom slept in the stable together with the animals. Late that night he was awakened by a noise. An unruly donkey had begun to sniff another one and had started a fight.

"What's this business in the middle of the night, you stupid ass!" the groom muttered, and got up to stop it in a fit of anger.

But then he couldn't get back to sleep, so he went out into the courtyard. Resho Agha's daughter couldn't sleep either. From the window of her room the weak light shone blindingly in the pitch dark of the night.

The groom didn't want to look into the room. "It's my agha's daughter," he said to himself. Even so, the light from the room drew his eye, and the groom saw Resho Agha's daughter. She was undressing.

"Oh, for all the saints!" the groom whispered, and turned back quickly to the stable. Just then the two donkeys in the stable went at one another. The groom's lust overcame him in a flood, and in a breath he was by the room where the light burned, staring in. Had he opened his mouth to take a breath, he'd have collapsed and died of passion. With one hand, Resho Agha's daughter was fondling her breasts. Then she closed her eyes, and putting her index and middle fingers of the other hand together, she pressed them to the lips of her tender, feverishly burning body. She was trying to imagine a man—beyond the mountains—up in the clouds—a man powerful as a giant, but cunning as the devil himself, a man who would sneer at her father's noble family, a man who would tower over her father's thick-walled house. Seeing this, the groom leapt through the window and landed with a thud.

Resho Agha's daughter, with her naked breasts and two fingers on her lips, was so startled to see not her lover from beyond the mountains and up in the clouds but the groom that she couldn't even make a sound. Her eyes grew wider than a calf's with fear. The groom used the moment of fear to his own advantage. He tied his belt across her mouth, took her across his shoulders and ran off to the stable as quiet as the wind. There he lifted her onto a horse and climbed on behind. In the darkness of the night he headed the horse out through the courtyard and away to the horizon.

Soon, the sun was up about a spear's length. Resho Agha was dead to the world in Güllü's arms. Zeyno, Resho Agha's first wife, thundered at his door.

"Agha, get up! The girl's gone! Run away! We've been humiliated!"

"What's that, you fool? Don't give me heart failure!"

"They've kidnapped your daughter! Come and look!"

In one breath Resho Agha was up and running to his daughter's room. The bed was empty. The clothes she had been wearing were beside the bed.

"This is impossible! Where's the girl?"

"The groom's missing, too, and one of the horses."

Resho Agha's face went ashen.

"This is the work of some enemy," he said. "That little girl—the groom wouldn't even dare touch the shit from one of Resho Agha's children. Puh! Woman, get out of my sight! I'll bet the girl's whoring is partly your doing. Your milk was foul."

Zeyno cowered in a corner. "What'd I do, Agha? I don't know a thing about it. Go get your horse. Go after her and bring her back," she mumbled.

Resho Agha kicked Zeyno violently in his rage, then found his Mauser and slung it across his back. He mounted his horse, and as he left the courtyard he shouted, "Lock all the doors until I come back, and don't let even the birds flying overhead hear anything about this." He rode out through the big street gate and headed his horse at a gallop for the steppe. All the doors of the house were bolted behind him.

Resho Agha came into the nearby village harboring a thousand suspicions, a thousand hates. Before he got to the village square, all at once he stopped his horse. Foam dribbled to the ground from the animal's mouth. Resho Agha had seen a pair of women's underpants hanging in front of a house to his right. As far as he was concerned, this was the most disgraceful thing in the world. Throwing himself down from his horse in a fury, he banged on the house door with the toe of his boot. A woman's voice came from inside.

"Who's that?"

In his anger, Resho Agha could hardly stand in one place.

"Open up, damn you, woman. It's Resho, your agha!"

The door opened.

"Welcome, Agha."

"So you put out your whore's flag, eh?"

"Why, Agha! How could you say such a thing?"

"Alright, then, what whore's pants are these? Who hangs women's underclothes outside in my village?"

Shaking with fear, the woman ran to where the underpants were hanging and took them down. At this Resho Agha took his Mauser, aimed at the woman and fired. After the first bullet she was still standing. After the second she rolled to the floor, the underpants still in her hands. Without turning to look at the woman, Resho Agha mounted his horse and headed for another house.

All the village came to its feet at the sound of the shots. "What's that?" sounded from each mouth. The village square filled with people.

Resho Agha reined in before a certain house and began to bellow, "Hey, Dagger Shigo, Dagger Shigo!"

Soon a man wearing a rough woolen cloak came out; his long, curved moustaches stretched past the width of his face.

"Welcome, Agha."
"Get the men together quick and meet me at the Bloody Cave."
"Right away, Agha!"
"The Bloody Cave, quick."
"The Bloody Cave."

Resho Agha beat his horse in the direction of the Bloody Cave. Shigo the Dagger had already rushed off to get the men together.

The Bloody Cave was at the top of a narrow pass. Resho Agha couldn't stay in one place and kept pacing in and out of the cave. Dagger Shigo came into the cave with eight men.

"Salaam aleikum."

Without answering the greeting, Resho Agha said, "Dagger Shigo, listen to me. This is the toughest day of my life. You're gonna send the men out in all directions to search the mountains, quick! They're gonna find my daughter and my groom, even if they have to look down in the seventh level of hell. And as soon as you've found them, shoot the groom, but bring me the girl alive. I'm going back to the city. Now get this into your head: the world is a prison to me until I've got that girl by the hand again, so go to it. And listen—I've let you in on a secret here in the Bloody Cave. Let it out and lead'll be poured in your ears, and your tongue'll be cut out, and your eyes'll be smashed so bad you'll think it was lightning!"

Dagger Shigo came close to Resho Agha, who seemed ready to go to pieces from his grief and anger.

"I'm your man, Agha. You don't have to worry. Your honor is our honor. Even if they're hiding in an ants' nest, even if they're at the bottom of the ocean, we'll find them. So long!"

"Good luck. Find the blood you're after," said Resho Agha. The words rolled from his mouth like molten lava.

• • •

Then a day, a week, more than a month passed. They found neither the groom nor the girl, not dead, not alive.

Resho Agha and all his relatives were sunk in deep shame. None of the men were allowed to leave the house, not to go to the coffeehouse, not to go anywhere. Their beards grew to a span in length. They went around with their heads bowed, chins on their chests. The women weren't allowed out to the neighbors' or to the baths. Meanwhile, the city passed the time muttering:

"Resho Agha's daughter's run away."

"Resho Agha's daughter went bad."

"Resho Agha's daughter has stained the family honor."

"Resho Agha's daughter's turned into a prostitute, become a whore, lets her pants down."

"Resho Agha is not fit to be agha after all; he couldn't even keep control over one girl."

Resho Agha didn't go anywhere, didn't talk to anyone. But he had a good idea of what was being said outside, because there was no worse calamity than having your daughter run away, whether it was in this town, or in Urfa, or in Siverek, or anywhere else. All there was for the girl's family to do was wait, wait till she was found. Any other course was pointless. If you take a walk, everybody'll stare at you, but no one will say hello. If you sit down in the coffeehouse, pretty soon you'll be the only one there. It's as though you were diseased; a girl from among the children of your family has run away.

That's how the great Resho Agha felt. The man whose legend could strike terror in so many hearts was turned into a kitten that had spilled its milk.

• • •

There were a few more days to go before two months would be up. It was long past noon—you could even look straight at the sun and not be blinded. Resho Agha was sitting cross-legged on a mat in the courtyard. Zeyno, the girl's mother, was sitting on the doorstep, staring vacantly into space. A knock came at the big street gate. One of the servants opened it, and Shigo the Dagger came in. He went up to Resho Agha and whispered, "The girl's outside."

Resho Agha leapt from his place. "Ha! And the groom?"

"We shot him."

Resho Agha turned his face to the wall. "Bring her in," he said. "Put her in the back room."

The girl, wrapped in a shawl, came into the courtyard. She stopped and looked for a minute. Her father's back was to her. Her mother sat on the doorstep, and made no move to get up or cry "daughter!" and run to her. What had she done wrong? The groom had let the devil possess him and had kidnapped her. While they were still on the road, his fear of Resho Agha had come back to him, and so he never even touched the girl. Zeyno came over to the girl standing alone in the courtyard and took her by the hand to lead her away—to the back room.

For the first time in weeks she would sleep under her father's roof again, but all love and affection for her was gone.

As soon as it was morning the house was nervous with activity. Messengers came and went. Everyone was edgy and tense again.

Zeyno came in to the girl. Her eyes were scarlet from crying. Had Zeyno been permitted to cry out loud she wouldn't have been in such bad condition. She was torn between custom and her mother's love for the girl, still burning within her. Zeyno looked into the girl's face. She was not even fifteen. Zeyno saw that youthful hope and fear were battling in her face, and that fear had won.

"I have nothing to say to you. You're a victim of fate. Your papa's gonna take you to the vineyard!" Zeyno said.

The girl threw herself on her mother.

"Don't let him, mama! Don't let him! I haven't committed any sin. I didn't run away. He took me by force. And afterwards we were like brother and sister, and we suffered through a lot. Save me!"

Zeyno wanted to unwrap the girl's arms from her neck, but they were locked there by the fear of death. Zeyno was quivering inside with love for her child; she put her hands out to caress the girl. Overcoming her fear, she grasped the girl. For the first time in months she wept out loud, and the wailing coming from the room filled the neighborhood.

• • •

For the first time in months, Resho Agha could go out of the house, because he was no longer alone there: his daughter was there as well. He sat ramrod straight in the saddle like a victorious commander home from the war. As for the girl, who sat in front of him and leaned against his chest, she hung her head in deep shame. The girl's shame would assure Resho Agha's immortality. It would be his decoration, his fame.

They rode out of the city and headed along a road deserted by everyone else. After passing a few vineyards and orchards they finally came to his vineyards, to where as a small child his daughter had run and played, where she had lain under the vines and picked grapes from the bunchs with her lips.

Seven or eight men stood to one side of the vineyard: the other notables of the family. They had prepared a grave.

Resho Agha stopped his horse. One of the men from the group helped the girl down. Resho Agha dismounted slowly.

Everyone's head was bowed. Before they could lift them up and face the world again, they would have to offer a sacrifice to honor.

Resho Agha took the girl by the arm and dragged her toward the freshly-dug grave. The girl had long before realized that there was no way of escape, nothing she could do in the midst of all these men. But she was so terrified of the grave she did all she could to stay away from it. But it was no good.

As a pistol shot exploded in her ears, the girl collapsed where she stood. The blood pouring out was beneath her scarf and couldn't be seen. Even as the fresh earth was being thrown down on the girl, already the best rider among them was racing toward the town.

The rider stopped in front of Resho Agha's house. He was the son of the dead girl's uncle. The door opened, and he went into the courtyard to give the good news.

"Aunt, aunt! It's over," he said. "May she rest in peace."

In a second, the tears were running like water in Resho Agha's house, and the wailing split the air.

• • •

Zeyno, the girl's mother, prepared for what must be done next. She would go to the baths and henna her hair. Now their honor was clean and pure once again.

THE RIVER
Füruzan
(Translated by Louis Mitler)

Long ago, they had called her older sister to work as a cook.

It was spring. The clean, orange blossom fragrance of the south was growing. The lady of the house lived in Adana. The climate of this city, rattling with horse-drawn cabs, had not improved the health of this lady with short hair and thick legs. She was the daughter of a former governor and was older than her husband. They said that inside she was more passionate than a fifteen-year-old girl. (Until the lady said, "I can't live in a place with no sea.") They had built a marble bath in her village house and later even bought her songbirds.

Had the lady been a virgin? In that district, the hidden shame of virginity was the most valuable of possessions, particularly in those years. No one could criticize her lineage. Her father was no ordinary fellow. He was a Europeanized man, knew two languages: Persian and French, and played the lute. Throughout his life he had been so prodigal that when he was appointed to this southern city all he had was his salary. His inheritance from his father and the years of plenty that his wife had assured him all lay in the past.

His wife had aged, too. Her frozen white flesh grew still fatter. She contented herself with listening to household gossip on her reception days and not going out of the house, whereas the governor still had the passions of his youth. The handsome blond Sıtkı of bygone days was reduced to his shadowy green eyes. They didn't call wispy men handsome then. In fact, the only son of the chief sealkeeper's magnolia-surrounded mansion used to powder his face. Later, they called him Powdered Tevfik. (What a pale and sensitive male beauty he was!)

Nowadays the girls in the office all looked to him like houries from paradise. How hard it used to be for women to please him! His youth had departed, and now his every gesture reflected the crisis he was experiencing. He dreamed of the legs, discolored from the cold, of his house girl. He had been sleeping apart from his wife for nine years now. His wife had learned to wash in cold water and look virtuous from the French nuns at school. Later, she started to gaze about with an innocence bordering on idiocy. He couldn't say just when she had started to grow frigid. He kept his philanderings scrupulously from her, not wanting her hurt in the least.

With the years his indifference had become so concrete that, in the winters turned to frost in that west Anatolian town, he would ask his wife, still lying silent, still in self-abandonment in bed,

"Do you think that I don't love you?"

"No," his wife said. "Of course you love me. I'm your wife."

How did his wife use her French? He never saw her read anything, not even once. The traditions of her family had made the knowledge of a foreign language compulsory. When they married, full-bodied, lustrous-eyed, and wealthy, she had come to him with everything that the daughter of a sophisticated family ought to have. "The governor's wife knows French as though it were her mother tongue," said acqaintances. Her Turkish might have borne inspection, however. But that virtuous silence achieved a superiority for her in the circle in which she moved. One needed not to belong to that clique to understand her silence for the placidity of stupidity that it was. On the first night how exciting the soft tension of her legs and her silence, above all that silence, had been. But years passed. Years. She was the living proof, a necessary condition of being a leading government official. That is to say, she was no longer a woman.

"How can you do this to me, daddy? In that country town for the rest of my life with people that I cannot possibly accept! Perhaps you will say that *you* existed with my mother in the same situation. But it's not the same. Her family was your equal. You took a girl from a well-known, wealthy, cultured, Istanbul family. Can the daughter of a governor possibly be the wife of an agha?"

In fact, the daughter didn't resemble her mother at all. There was none of his wife's impenetrable silence about her. She had been twenty-eight in those days and was living with her father's sister. Twenty-eight in those days was a fearful and hopeless age. At twenty-one, she had been engaged to a first lieutenant in the navy. The fellow was the apple of the eye of the young girls in Moda, and was like a sea gull in his resplendent white navy ducks. They stayed engaged for two years. Backs covered with pine needles on Heybeli Island, the embarrassment of boarding the ferry with rumpled skirts. The facile emotions of the first tangos.

When she read that her daughter had broken her engagement, his wife collapsed into an armchair in the sitting room.

"That older sister of yours. They say my daughter has taken after her. Just think, to break off after two years' engagement. I trust that nothing has happened. Ah, that girl is nothing like me."

For the first time, then, he thought of his daughter naked. This nakedness that he would never see irritated him. In the engagement pictures they had sent them, the man was holding his daughter so tightly.

"As a father," his wife was saying, "you should call her here."

She didn't return to them for another three years. She insisted on staying in the many-halled, pine and magnolia-surrounded house of her aunt, who was formerly on the palace staff. "All men are the same," her aunt used to say. In the evenings, she used to drink her tea and eat her pastries at some obscure table at Le Bon's. She was dazzling when she sat in the first class section of the Kadıköy ferryboat in her silk stockings. Half the time she complained about her cruel destiny, and half the time she spent awaiting a lucky match. When that match turned up in the shape of an elderly, rich, former diplomat, she said no. Then she reached twenty-eight, twenty-eight in those days.

"The agha's connections are impeccable," her father would say. They called them the Topakoğulları in the area, which meant that they were none other than the old Topak family.

When the first fat started to accumulate between her shoulder blades, it only took her a little over three months to give in to the acres of land called Topukköy, a village that yielded its produce in all four seasons.

A sumptuous wedding was held at the Taksim Municipal Music Hall. People talked about the buffet for months. A French singer by the name of Avril sang weepy love songs. She was overcome with emotion, like her mother at the same moment, but for different reasons. Women, flushed with drink, were gazing at themselves dreamily in the huge wall mirrors. She didn't look at the people whose hands she pressed as the party broke up.

"The governor's daughter is past her prime but still beautiful." "I wonder whether she was a virgin?" "Ah, if those pine trees on Heybeli

Island could talk." "And at Le Bon?" "What else could she do? In the end, she married a farmer."

The governor began to play his games at the club more freely now. They referred to his woman-chasing activities by innuendo. (He's a real gentlemen.) They attributed his babblings about pure love, uttered in his most inebriated moments, to some romantic disappointment suffered in his past. However, such a thing had never occurred in his whole life.

One night he entered his wife's room. The woman asked, "Sıtkı, is something the matter?"

It was a hot summer night, heavy with the smell of orange blossoms. The river was very low. The room smelled of lemon-flower eau d'cologne. It was a place that had known no love, cold and orderly. This was enough to disperse the heat.

"Do you love me?" he asked.

"Of course," his wife said. "I'm your wife. I'm the mother of your daughter."

● ● ●

Once, her older sister had brought her here from her poor neighborhood on her return from a day off. "Come," she had said. "The Istanbul folks are gone—the old lady, the mistress, and the two maids. They won't be back now. Yusuf Agha will go to Istanbul."

The kitchen was on the second floor of the house. It was very big. They stood with their dark color against the river, a row of four-story houses left over from the Armenians, decorated with pretty wood carvings under the eaves. The doors had bells but the brass knockers were still in place. A whitewashed smoke hood was over the kitchen. The tin pots stood arranged by size on the shelf to one side. A tile stove with images of birds on its burner covers greatly heated the kitchen. Her older sister was always cooking food.

"Let your hair down, girl," her sister said. "Don't plait it so tightly. Plait two braids and let them down your back. Don't cover your head. Who's in the house besides you and me? Don't mind the servant. You mind what's taken to and from the table."

"And the master?" she asked.

"The master?" said her sister. "Just fancy. You're thirteen. He's old enough to be your grandfather."

Suddenly, from her past in the poor neighborhood, she remembered the taste of bulgur pilaf, the smell of damp wood, and her two aunts, paid mourners. Her aunts were renowned for wailing the best dirges and for their self-flagellations. They were even invited to those wealthy homes still attached to tradition. When they came back exhausted in their long black dresses, their eyes swollen, how they had cried for dead they didn't even know.

"Come on," they would say, looking at her. "The house we went to was fine. The funeral feast was plentiful, too. We wrapped some up for you. We're not hungry. Fix our beds."

The furnishings in their two-room house consisted of cushions filled with pieces of old cloth, a bed, and a meal stand. That was all. A picture of the Kaaba was on the wall—a sacred place wrapped in black veils. The inhabitants of the house, her big sister, the two aunts, and she herself lived moving about noiselessly on the floor matting. Their days and their pains amounted to a pocketful of small change which they would put in her hand.

"Go to the grocer and get them changed for bills," they would say.

The grocery was dark. A blind cat with agate eyes was wandering around. The inside stank of rotten vegetables. She stopped and stood silent in front of the scales with the small change in her hand.

"Your people have really shaken down the folks at Castle Gate again," he would say.

Later, she learned that this talk about "shaking down" meant begging. The older aunt would say, "What can we do? There aren't as many people dying as there used to be. And if there are, nobody calls in mourners. Should we die of hunger? They give alms for the welfare of others. They prevent calamities by almsgiving."

When she said she wouldn't go to the grocer to get the bills, they beat her.

"Do you trust in your older sister? She wormed her way into a plushy job. What good has it done us?"

The night her big sister said, "I'll take her tomorrow," the older aunt had taken out the Koran and read at the top of her voice for hours.

"You got your buried treasure," her older sister said. "We're going. We'll take a couple of clothes for her. The rest is yours."

"No."

"But if the ones from Istanbul come back?"

"They won't come. If they do come, the lady won't want this girl."

"They won't come. I told you, what's left is yours."

"Just look at that. Two old bags, two old rags they leave, cruel wretches."

"You must have treasures yourself."

They were on the road before day. The houses seemed to have emerged from the mud. Inside, she felt a panic. Her sister had said they were going to a palace larger than anything she had ever seen. (What was a palace?) Here it always rained in winter. The ground became all mud. There the streets were paved with stones. In the house they were going to, you couldn't count the kinds of food.

"Do they have dates?"

"What's a date? Ah, my stupid child. You'll eat and drink and put on a little weight."

The houses were so beautiful. Those she saw from the bridge amazed her still more with their beauty. What was a bridge? Everybody walked over it. But those houses. Not one or two, all of them. They were huge and they all belonged to Yusuf Agha. When that door was shut, that was it. No one could enter.

"She was beautiful. White like cotton. She was a lady. She understood ladyship well. She couldn't bring herself to like these places."

"Is Istanbul more beautiful than here?"

"There couldn't be any place any more beautiful than here, but when you can't get on with your man every place is hell. A man is everything. What's a woman? The most wretched of creatures. She was rich and a lady, too. Her fingers were hung with diamonds. She had cut her hair short. Hair is a woman's dower."

Seated in the kitchen some distance back from the window overlooking the river, they watched the flow of the water all day. Her sister wouldn't allow her to do any work.

"Let me crochet," she said.

"No, no. Your face is the color of pus. You're skin and bones. Eat and drink; put a little meat on your bones. Anyone who saw you would think you were ten years old. You're of marrying age now."

Work in the kitchen increased on the days that Yusuf Agha returned from his estate. They roasted lamb livers just so. All sorts of greenery, sliced red peppers, all kinds of food.

She ate all the time. A hunger that she didn't know was in her bones showed itself. Her older sister drank syrup in the mornings.

"Drink it, girl. It'll make blood."

Afterwards, one day, she took her to the steam bath and washed her from head to foot. She rubbed violet perfume on her hair and took the hair off her legs with depilatory. "You are dark-skinned. You've got too much hair, but we'll take it off from now on. For women, being hairless is the thing. Anyway, it's a sin in Islam to go around hairy."

One evening, she said, "Go upstairs. Heat the water for the master's feet."

Silently, she did as she was told. She emptied water into a wrought copper basin, folded the gold-embroidered hand towel over her arm, and began to wait. She knew that when he entered a room, Yusuf Agha sat down in a certain place. The embarrassment she felt prevented her from looking in that direction.

"Come here then, my girl."

She set the basin before him and took the dark-colored stockings off his feet. Her hands were tiny beside these big feet. She worked up a lather and started to wash them.

"You've grown up since last I saw you," the master said.

A plait of hair hung down from one shoulder. His feet in the basin were bony and huge. She hadn't asked her sister how long she should wash them. The agha watched the washing without saying a word. When he said "Enough," a fine sweat bathed her back.

As she was going out, he said, "Tell your sister. Tonight I'll drink alone. She should chill the *raki* well."

"He asked for *raki*, then? That means he's in a good mood. Just look at this house, this great big house. The Istanbul lady had charge of it for years on end. She couldn't even make a baby. And why? She didn't like the master. She was the daughter of a governor. It was her father's womanizing and gambling that brought her here. Whatever comes from the soil, most of it goes to them. That's why a barren woman is no woman. That you should know. Her loins are cold. She became frigid and shriveled up like an orange. She wasted his youngest and most youthful days. They say you can tell a real man by the back of his neck. Ömür Agha had a strong-looking way of standing, seen from the back. If a woman doesn't know how to be a woman, a man will find another one who does."

She went to the tile stove and started pouring the thick olive oil into the shiny tin frying pan.

On the other side of the river, pale, twinkling lights shone. Were her aunts still begging in their black garments under the heavy, warm downpour? Whenever she thought of them, she heard afresh in her mind the dirge that she had heard one day when passing through Castle Gate.

What a beautiful kitchen they had here! It smelt of butter and cumin. It was warm, full of fresh vegetables and row upon row of sausages. How pretty was the bright color of the banana stalks and particularly the walnut paste that she ate sitting in the window alcove facing the river.

"You wash the radishes," her older sister said, "and line them up properly beside the salad stuff. Don't cut the green part off the onions at the root. It's enough if you take a little off the ends. Don't pile the Circassian chicken high up on the plate. The table should be filled with lots of things to eat in little servings. That's the way an hors d'oeuvre table should be. Pull the tulle curtains all the way back and open the windows so that he can hear the sound of the water. That's the way the Istanbul lady used to do and Yusuf Agha wants it just that way. Rub your hands with coffee. It'll take away the smell of onions."

The weight of Yusuf Agha's shriveled, pendulous belly seemed to hang to one side. She held her hands firmly at her sides and thought of how the rooms filled with carpets and gilded furnishings used to look. She was perplexed and stealthily touched things with the tips of her fingers.

"The lady furnished the house, girl," her older sister had said. "You'd have thought that it was the house of a fairy-tale king."

Bunches of grapes were depicted on the ceilings. How was it in this room? She closed her eyes tighter still. Yellow grapes were sprinkled among purple. Well, why did they make the leaves purple? They grew smaller and smaller.

The river rose high that year from the rains. The swollen corpses of drowned animals caught on the corners of buildings with the retreat of the water. They were large cattle. Far, far away the clouds were passing, carrying the cold to the north, to the masses of mountains.

THE HOMECOMING
Vüs'at O. Bener
(*Translated by William C. Hickman*)

The station lay behind us: massive, compact, stone. Its misty lights diffused. Bitter cold. The horses' shoes broke the ice. Street lamps lackluster in the dull light of predawn. My toes ached, knees numb. The naked trees hard and frozen. The city lay contracted and shriveled up, chimneys cold and silent. Even the tiny coals in braziers would be nearly out, covered by ash long since cooled. Rooms would smell of stale breath, heavy and acrid. Yellow white matter would have formed around eyes closed in sleep. My teeth chattered. The backs of the horses steamed, the vapor rising with the breath of the driver. My fingers felt strangely detached when I touched them to my warm, moist mouth. The city was meeting me as a stranger. We passed in front of the lycée. It was scarcely a year since I had left. I had returned with my father over this same road, drenched with sweat. We had seen my mother off from the station now left behind. Mother sighed constantly. She seemed to cry all the time. "Boys don't cry," father had said. And I hadn't cried. Mother didn't want me to go. I was too weak, she said. I couldn't do it. Maybe I could be a schoolteacher. I had felt frightened, but proud, as if I were going off to war. I had tried to cheer her up. My father had sent her away for a while. She cried a lot, and for no reason at all. The tears streamed down her cheeks. She didn't hide them. But she hadn't called out, either. The car of her train had slipped past us slowly. Before we realized that it had speeded up, the train was gone. Later, on foot, we had returned, the sun overhead, the blazing sun. Father had taken my arm. My father! And now here I was, coming back again after months which once had seemed endless. I would kiss his tobacco-stained hands. My father's hands were hot. Where his thumb joined the palm it was red as a pomegranate. Whenever my stomach ached as a small child, I got chills and cramps and cried a lot.

But as soon as he touched his huge hands to my stomach I would stop and become quiet. Or so they tell me. My father's hands were piping hot like oven-heated bricks. He used to beat me, too. I had hated him silently then. I consoled myself with the thought that someday I would be able to give him a beating in return. The carriage turned off. Sharp pointed icicles of all sizes hung down from the eaves of the houses. I bit my fingers slightly. They were numb and unfeeling. The horses coughed. The minaret of the market mosque pierced the cold. The carriage lamps streamed rays of light. The angry light of the street lamps made my eyes water. The wires gleamed. Above them I made out small, dark shapes. They must have been sparrows clinging by their feet, like stains or spots against the sky. The horses stopped abruptly. The driver bent down under the carriage top. "We're here." His face was crusted in layers. The light had reflected in the pupils of his eyes, the insides lined as though cracked, the glassy outer surface glistening. The hairs of his spiky mustache bristled.

I stood there in the empty street, bag in hand. The carriage receded in the distance, the wheels and horses leaving behind the sounds of earth and rock sliding, tumbling. Soon they were out of sight as though swallowed up in a muffled softness. Sounds made no echo. The houses and walls were hard. Zinc gutters ringed the roofs with their crystal glitter. There was not a dog to be seen. The streets were deserted. I squatted down. Was the knocker of the house like this, in the shape of a hand? A bronze hand. Was that dark stone right here? They must have filled in the ruts where we shot marbles. I felt along the wall. They had cracked my brother's skull right here on this street. Not a trace of the blood remained. No trace of our hoops, either. The door to our house was rough. Painted, ash-colored or green. Cold. There were knots in the wood. I had pushed one of them out. From behind the door I used to squirt water at passersby on the street. My father had forbidden me to play knucklebones. Henna- and wine-colored, blue, green, and speckled knucklebones with their bulging ends leaddipped. The deep, full sound which the bones made. All that I had, a whole basketful, he had burned. The house had smelled foul, the smell of burnt bone. I wondered what the son of the chief of the military gendarmerie was doing now. We had tried to steal batteries for our flashlights and got caught. I pressed my ear to the door. There was no sound of splashing fountain. It must have frozen. It was frozen. The windows were dark. They didn't know I was coming. In the beginning, I had wanted to run away from the school where we slept in dormitories and went to classes by the sharp, high-pitched sound of a bell. But now I had grown up. How surprised my mother would be when she saw me grown so big in my formerly ill-fitting, too-long-sleeved clothes. The windows of the neighbor's house across the street reflected a glow of light from an uncertain source. I raised the hand-shaped knocker. The bronze stuck to my fingers. The coldness of it chilled me from deep within. I let it strike and pulled my fingers away. It produced a full, dry sound. There was not a dog on the street. Not even a moan was heard. I waited. It was as if the knocker had been struck on the doors of the entire city. I stood poised as if waiting for the light of a single candle to appear behind the frosted panes of every house, waiting for the light to flicker and grow. The noise would arouse the whole city from the drowsiness which had penetrated to its core. A light moved about behind the windows of our house. A shadow parted the curtain and looked anxiously out at the street. I hadn't been able to make out the face, but I knew it was my mother. It seemed that I could pick out the strands of her straight hair, the straight heavy strands of her chestnut hair. Now she had reached the head of the stairs. She was waiting, frightened, listening to the silence. The silence was unbroken. The street crossings, the empty spaces of the rooms, earth and sky, all had become hard and brittle. They had kidnapped her child. Now they had brought his corpse and dumped it in front of the door, his small child's body flecked with snow, his warm body with the blood still oozing from the mouth. Broad feet, white and naked, had slipped away stealthily without living prints. Her child's body in front of the door. Her child come home. She had wanted to call out, but her voice refused. Her insides were growing cool, her strength slipping away, her knees giving way beneath her. She was shivering. It felt as if her skin was being flayed. It really was he. The one at the door. Her son. From head to toe. "Son!"

I had heard her. "It's me," I called back. "Open the door, mother. Don't be afraid!" She lunged down the stairs as if her heart had suddenly stopped, the blood vessels drained. She couldn't cry. She was suffocating. The lamp had tipped to one side, soot blackening the glass chimney. She hadn't set it down. Instinctively, with all the strength of one hand, she was pressing my head to her flat, weak chest. I felt I was suffocating. She was drawing her rough hands blindly over my cheeks. All at once I was seized by a feeling of distance from my mother. She was still the same woman whose anxious eyes I feared. Still the woman who pierced me with strange, lingering looks so full of affection I could not bear them. "Come on, mother," I had said. "We're freezing. It's me, alright. Look!" She was still talking to herself. I must have scared the life out of her.

My father and brother had awakened. The door was open. I stood there, rooted to the threshold. Bolt upright in the dark blue uniform which hung off me loosely. Bag in my right hand. My visor cap tilted slightly to the left.

My father had sat up in bed. The other one, the child, looked on with dazzled eyes. His head was big and fair. And bald, with no eyelashes. It seemed as though he could scarely hold his head up on his slender neck. He had honey-colored eyes open wide and round as saucers. As if he were grinning, his mouth was half-open. His few darkened teeth showed small and pointed. My throat went dry. I felt like crying. He stood there with the miserable hurt look of a child alone on the street.

My father's hair had thinned out. There was more gray now. That child had emerged from the small storeroom next to the bedroom. Once I had shared that room with him. The stale smell of sleep which permeated the room, mixed with the odor of burnt lemon rind and charcoal, suddenly took my breath away. The furniture in the room had started to swim before my eyes. "Look who's here," my mother had said with pride. Uncomfortable, I looked at my father's face. His nose had become a little redder. His cheeks were pale. He didn't have his gold tooth anymore. His upper molars shone with the glitter of yellow and tin. He must have had them newly done. "Let's have a look at you, young man," he had said. I had moved closer, haltingly. The gaping, dark hollow of that child's mouth hovered over me. I was going to cry. The buttons of my father's pajama tops were undone. The ones on his flannel undershirt, too. I could see his naked, white body. He drew himself up repeatedly. His huge hand hung in space. Bending forward, I had kissed it. A cold, limp hand. It didn't smell of tobacco. Yellow matter had collected around the corners of his dark, sunken, lashless eyes. His cheeks seemed translucent. They hung down heavily. "Mind you, kiss your big brother's hand," mother had said to the child. With a disingenuous admiration, he had grasped both my hands and pressed them to his forehead. Then he had moved away. He stood looking at my clothes, looking at my shoulders, at my wide pants cuffs, my big shoes, the polished cast-iron insignia. My cap was still on my head. He pulled it off with a sudden motion and began to rub the shiny visor. I felt uncomfortable. "Well, now, let's hear all about it," my father had asked, and I began to explain. Mother was throwing wood on the stove. Now and then she joined the conversation. I wanted to ask about Nejla, the girl we used to shut up in a closet in our games of hide and seek. I was about to, but I couldn't. It wouldn't sound right. They'd misunderstand. Abruptly, I grabbed my bag, opened it and pulled out a box of candy. "You always liked *lokum*," I said to my father. Pleased, his face brightened. "Have you given up smoking?" I had asked. "No." I was surprised. When I left, I had kissed his hands almost as if I were smelling them. I had breathed in deeply the odor of nicotine, the heat of his hands. The next day was a holiday. I would have to kiss his hands again. This time,I'd be careful to catch the smell. Maybe I had missed it now in my confusion and awkwardness. Then, turning to my brother, I had said, "Look what I've got for you." Suspicious, he had moved closer. It was a ball. A large, colored, rubber ball.

The stove was crackling. I had loosened up. The teakettle sputtered. Strips of window molding were sticking out, apparently warped from moisture. They must recently have bought the mat on the floor. "What happened to the chiming clock?" I had asked. It was sold. It used to make old, broken sounds. Then I realized I hadn't hugged *him*. I used to sit him on the crossbar of a bike–I rented the bike with money scraped together–and go off on long rides. I couldn't stand his crying. I had put up with it. Then quickly I remembered that I hadn't. I had hit him until his mouth and nose were bloody. I was hurt that he didn't like the ball. Before, I would have beaten him. I would have yelled at him. I didn't think he'd told anyone how I knocked him off the trapeze, the trapeze I set up with a stick hung by ropes from the ceiling beams. The blood had gushed from his nose. No one had been at home. The blood had made a puddle on the floor. I had held his head under the fountain. He was with me,too,the day I tried to steal batteries with the son of the police chief. The owner of the store had let us go, mostly out of respect for his father, asking whose kids we were and scaring us half to death. *He* had understood everything, but he hadn't told my father. "I'll kill you if you tell," I'd said. Ashamed, I remembered one by one the tortures I'd practiced on him. Nights our parents went out and left us home alone,I had scared him half to death making terrible, contorted faces and letting out hideous sounds. I remembered how he fled from the room into the hall and from there to the stairs. Now I called him "little." Miserable little boy. Sometimes I had used the word *petit* instead. Whenever I called him *petit*, I felt less guilty, more comfortable, correct, more distant. The tea was well steeped. Steam filled the room from the kettle on the stove, turning the windowpanes white. The glasses gleamed coldly. My father had climbed out of bed and sat down on the sofa. The wick of the lamp was burning red.

I still saw my mother as she looked then, less than life-size, from behind that train window with her large, white handkerchief. My mother had grown old! And how quickly I was growing up! How was it that I once played with *him*? Later, we were setting out again, father and I, in a phaeton. He was going to leave me at the school, in my thick, close uniform of coarse cloth. His mustache had pricked me in the eye when he said good-bye. From behind the iron grillwork surrounding the courtyard of the school, I watched him as he left, waving his hand. I had wanted to shout, "Don't leave me here, father!" At his every step I felt like calling out, "Father!" He receded into the distance, the full lower part of his dark coat swirling around him. His tall figure gradually became small. "My right eye is twitching," he had said that day. "Good luck, I hope."

"He's turned into a real man, this young fellow of ours. Hasn't he, woman?" He laughs. When he'd had a lot to drink and was in a good humor, he used to sing the melody from Tatyos Efendi's composition. I'd keep time with a spoon. His voice was deep, robust, and pleasant. Now he coughs badly. He used to give *him raki*. "Let him drink it, the big-headed blond," he'd say. Then, indicating my brother, "He's going to be a big man someday. But you take after me. You're a scatterbrain like me. You'll get your share of knocks in life." That hurt my feelings, and I would shut myself up in the bathroom and cry my heart out. Once he'd caught me using his razor on my chest, trying to get the hairs to grow. He had given me a real thrashing that time.

I looked at the hairs on his chest showing behind his flannel undershirt, stray, wispy hairs. The skin of his neck was wrinkled. His body was as white as a woman's. The day he took me to the public bath, I had seen the traces of pimples on his back, dried-up red marks. I had recalled what my mother used to say: "Smooth men turn out to be pitiless." And then their fights. For days they wouldn't talk to each other. I tried to help out. My father would mutter out of the hollows of his cheeks. He talked to himself. On days when they weren't speaking, I caught sight of him through an open door. He was mumbling questions and answers, raising his eyebrows and making his eyes move. He was resentful and laughed with hurt and anger. His face was contorted with loathing. He laughed a twisted, crooked laugh.

The day before he left me at school his manner was even more strange, as though he were secretly rejoicing. The day before that, we had gone to Temenyeri. We had sat on the grassy meadow. He had smoked his cigarettes. His face was drawn. He wore the expression he always had when he was going to talk about something important. I waited for his shy, hesitant words. This time he didn't start right away. He seemed to be thinking a long time. "I have to talk to you about some things. Maybe you know about them already," he had said finally. At first he spoke as though he were telling a secret. Then he became more expansive. "They call this—," he was saying openly. "It happens like this." I was listening with my head down. Now and again, I looked at him with sidelong glances. He appeared serious but then quickly would start to laugh. His eyes were soft, bluish, pale, and shining. The gleam in his eye was strange; his lips were moist. "So that you won't hear these things from other people and get bad advice," he was saying. I couldn't take my eyes off his large Adam's apple.

Mother filled our glasses once more. The tea was a rich, dark red. And hot. The glass burned my hands. I gulped down the scalding tea. Again I felt slightly sick to my stomach. The blond child picked up the ball next to him and turned it in his hands indifferently. He appeared uninterested, but his eyes kept wandering in my direction. I tried not to look him in the eye. I knew that he had not called me "big brother," nor had I used his own name in speaking to him. "Look," he had said later. "I wrote this myself." The writing was crooked and irregular. I looked into his face, wondering how he managed to hold up his head. His legs were skinny, the knees brown and sharply pointed. *Petit*, I said again to myself. I tried to grab his arm. He pretended to run away. A photograph of my grandfather hung on the wall. It hadn't been there before. I stared at it. Once when he was angry, the child had spit in my face. Inconspicuously, he moved closer to me, the ball in his hand. "Grandfather died," he said. His eyes filled with tears. I stroked his large head. He said nothing. I was waiting for the cock's crowing. An iron-wheeled cart passed by on the street outside. Pale, weak rays of the sun filtered diagonally into the room. "Your uncle is very ill, too," my mother said. "We didn't write you."

LIBRARY OF DAVIDSON COLLEGE

Books on regular loan may be checked... two weeks. B